AN IMPOSSIBLE ESCAPE

An Impossible Escape

First published in the UK in 2017 by Dr iSeb Ltd

Cover image by Rightly Designed

First edition

Print book 978-0-9931585-3-7

ebook 978-0-9931585-2-0

Printed and bound in Great Britain by Clays Ltd, St-Ives plc

For more information visit

www.sebastiankalwij.com

AN IMPOSSIBLE ESCAPE

By Sebastian Kalwij

For

Dorothea, Josephine & Felix

1

São Paulo, Brazil

'The next round's on me,' Claudia Valenti said as she slammed her empty collins glass on the bar. The sharp hollow clink on the marble surface echoed her thirst. She and her friends had been standing at the bar for the last two hours, loud and exuberant, having to compete with the ambient noise which got cranked up several notches as the evening drifted into the early hours of the morning. Right now, more than anything else, they needed another drink.

Claudia tried to get her boyfriend Mario's attention, but even for her, during a busy evening like this, getting served was a challenge. Mario and his colleagues had turned cocktail making into an art and a spectacle. Most regular customers came for the entertainment and so the queues were long. Mario's bar was Claudia's second home, the site of all-night drinking fests. When it got busy like this, the tension would rise, customers would get agitated, they'd start pushing and shoving, often resulting in a fight. But Mario seemed oblivious to it all; he'd never cut corners on a custom-made drink. He was a master at creating the most colourful and original potions. Claudia couldn't care less. She was more interested in getting another drink and getting it quickly; she and her friends were slowly getting drunk on the world's best mojitos. If there was one perk to being a popular bartender's girlfriend, it was getting a drink quickly. She had ultimate bargaining power.

It was Claudia's last night in town before moving to the UK for six months and she had every intention of making it a good one. Her favourite drink was Mario's Sublime Mojito, prepared with fresh mint leaves of the Yerba Buena variety, specially imported from Cuba and crushed to extract the best flavour with a quick but firm flick of the wrist.

Claudia turned around and stood on tiptoe, leaning forward against the bar as far as she could, raising her arm and rotating her index finger. Mario noticed her from the side and knew right away that she and her friends were ready for another round.

Mario rushed over to Claudia, smiled and gave her a kiss on the lips. He ignored the hisses and shouts from other customers who had been waiting much longer than his charming girlfriend.

'Another round, carinha?'

Without waiting for an answer, he filled four glasses with ice to cool them down before emptying them again a minute later. After spinning around to grab the bottle of rum, he crushed some mint leaves, filled the glasses with a generous layer of rum, tossed in the mint, and mixed it all with lime juice. When the mint leaves had sunk to the bottom of the glasses, he poured some freshly crushed ice on top of his potent concoction and topped them to the brim with sparkling water. Before serving the cocktails, he gave each drink a quick stir with a long spoon.

'Only the best for you, my darling!' he said. 'You won't get them as good as this in London.'

Claudia smiled and threw a kiss at Mario, who was already attending to an attractive brunette. Claudia watched as the brunette put her hand around Mario's neck and the two started laughing.

The bar in Vila Madalena, a hip and bohemian section of São Paulo, was packed like a Monday morning rush-hour metro train; any more customers had to be shoehorned in. Claudia and her friends raised their glasses and made another toast. 'Viva Londres!'

The ceiling fan swivelled above their heads; more decorative than functional, it barely stirred the sultry air.

Claudia smiled. 'Well,' she said to her friends, 'I've got a surprise for you. I've got something in the works!'

'Come on, tell us!' Rafaela teased Claudia, sure that she was bluffing.

'Not yet,' she said. 'You'll need to be patient. Listen to the news on Saturday and all will be revealed. Expect some fireworks. I can guarantee you that it'll be all over the news and the Internet.'

Mario overheard these last words while gathering empty glasses.

'Ai florzinha! Can I expect some fireworks tonight?'

Claudia smiled. 'Depends on when you finish your shift.'

Mario leaned forward and placed his right hand around Claudia's neck and whispered in her ear, 'Just stay right here. Any moment the band will play its first set and it'll be a lot quieter for me behind the bar. My colleague will hold the fort. I just talked to him. He owes me a favour anyway. I can sneak out into the office for a twenty-minute break.'

Claudia pinched his cheek; she knew what Mario had in mind.

'I need to make sure that when you're in England under the weight of that heavy grey London sky, you'll miss your Brazilian lover.'

'That's for sure, querido!' Then Claudia put her hand around his neck and pulled him towards her, ruffling his black curls.

'Join me in the upstairs office in a few minutes,' he whispered in that seductive voice. 'I'll come and get you.'

Mario kissed her fleetingly and then went back to work. She saw him pouring shots with bottles in both hands. Without spilling a drop, he created a four-layered drink with blue curaçao and cream-coloured coconut rum. The customer emptied the drink in one gulp and ordered a dozen more for his friends. Mario was going to be busy for a long time. Claudia turned around to join her friends. She raised her glass.

'We'll miss you, Claudia,' Leticia said while clinking her friends' glasses. 'Don't stay away forever!'

'Just a couple months to brush up on my English and get some work experience. I'll be back before you know it.'

'That's what they all say,' Rafaela sulked.

'Come on! Just a change of scenery, it'll be fun!'

'You'll meet a nice man, settle in London, have a new life with kids and all,' Julia added.

'Anything's possible,' Claudia said. 'But sitting at home

and just letting life slip through my fingers isn't exactly what I have in mind.'

'Mario will be pining for you!'

'I doubt it. Look at him now, surrounded by the most beautiful young women in São Paulo... But, who knows? He says he might start a new cocktail bar somewhere in London. It's a city full of opportunities. We've talked about it plenty of times.'

'Just wild dreams,' Rafaela said, slurring her words.

'I guess they need all those bars to keep out of the rain,' Leticia said, trying to cheer Rafaela up. 'They spend their days going from one bar to the next.'

'That sounds like fun to me. Life is for living. Let's drink to that! Let's have another round.'

Claudia had heard this all before. From the moment she'd announced her plan to go abroad, her friends had tried to persuade her to stay. It irritated her at times. She'd planned her trip to Europe almost a year ago and there was no way she was backing out now. She'd taken on an extra cleaning job to pay for her ticket.

'And... What about your fight to save the Amazon rainforest? You're going to abandon your mission just like that?'

'You were all about saving the planet and the last remaining jungle, but now it's like you've forgotten that,' Julia said accusingly.

'We need you here,' Rafaela added. 'Brazil needs you.'

'Don't you worry; Brazil is in me! It's in my heart and in my genes, that'll never go away. And as for saving the rainforest, I'm keeping my promise. I've been working behind the scenes these last few months.'

'You mean you've been cleaning the offices of one of the biggest logging and road construction companies in São Paulo.'

'You've sold your soul to the devil!' Julia teased.

'It's all part of a plan,' Claudia defended herself.

'What? Violating your principles at the first chance of earning some money?'

'Be patient. Stay tuned to the news on Saturday.'

'You're just trying to shut us up. It better be something good, because I'm sure you'll forget us as soon as you're gone.'

'Don't be so dramatic! I've known you all since nursery school. I'll be back before you know it.'

'You better Facebook every day.'

'I can't promise you that, I may take a break from social media for a while.'

'That's a shame, think of all the gossip you'll miss out on!'

'I prefer to hear it in person over a drink, rather than reading it on my phone.'

'Leave her alone, she's brave to go away for six months and making a new life for herself. If you find some handsome guys, please let us know.'

'You'll be the first on my mind!'

'Let's have another round, the night is young!' Rafaela slurred. 'Claudia, do your magic trick!'

Claudia knew what she had to do. She stepped on the plinth underneath the bar, leaned forward as far as she could and whistled loudly with two fingers in her mouth. Mario laughed.

'Well done, amiga,' said Rafaela in a mocking voice, and

clapped Claudia on the back. 'You know how to get a man's attention.'

'Shut up. Next time, you can get us a round.'

'Then you won't get your drink before sunrise.'

Mario served the four ladies another round of mojitos. The alcohol was going to Claudia's head, and before long it would inflame her temperament. She was getting tired of her friends' critical remarks, as well as their ingratitude for the free drinks that night – every night, really.

'While you're wasting your time with useless online petitions, I've been doing some hardcore work.'

'Sounds promising, tell us more.'

'All I can say is that very soon, you'll realise why I had to leave.'

'You keep saying that. Why don't you tell us now? Your secret is safe with us, honestly,' Rafaela said, trying to coax it out of her. 'Our lips are sealed!'

'Hope you're not involved in something stupid,' Leticia said.

'Please tell me you're not doing anything illegal,' Rafaela scolded. 'You can't get away with anything risky. It's impossible these days with the Internet and CCTV. All our moves and whereabouts are stored somewhere, in some giant computer.'

'Ah, shut up! Don't steal her thunder!' Julia said in Claudia's defence.

'Just keep reading the news!' Claudia shouted, as the music was getting louder.

Carnival in São Paulo was only three weeks away. Preparations were in full swing. Every evening, local samba schools rehearsed new repertoire and dance routines in the nearby Dolores Ibarruri Park. To fund their new costumes and instruments, some band members played in popular bars all over São Paulo. The rhythm of samba was everywhere. Bars were bursting at the seams, overflowing onto the pavement and adjacent squares as even at night, the temperature never dropped below a sweltering twenty-nine degrees Celsius.

A band started playing. It was anyone's guess how those musicians managed to squeeze onto the tiny raised podium in the back of the bar. With the first few bars of a quick melody, people started dancing. Claudia and her friends moved to the rhythm without giving up their precious spot at the bar. Rafaela grabbed Julia by the waist. Dozens of other revellers pressed against them. The bar became a pulsating, gyrating mass of bodies. Claudia was soon drenched in sweat. Suddenly she felt herself being lifted and turned around. She wrapped her legs around Mario's waist for a few beats, then he lifted her higher. She pulled free and landed on her feet before getting back into the rhythm on the crowded dance floor. Mario held her body close while they danced.

Twenty pairs of hands played tambourines, timbas, surdos, repiniques and cuicas. Thirty-odd fingers played saxophones and trumpets. A lead singer, two backing singers and one teenage girl in a silver-coloured catsuit and a pink wig blew the apito at each transition, transforming the bar into a mini samba-drome. The rhythm held steady at ninety-six beats per minute; it sounded like an endless round of ammunition fired from a dozen AK-47s. It was loud, a hundred-and-thirty decibels loud, with the stage a mere four metres away.

Claudia could feel Mario pressing against her, chest against chest, hips against hips, Mario's hand placed firmly on her lower back, touching the thin hem of her slip. Her wet dress was stuck to her breasts. She thought she'd faint in the heat. She pulled Mario's head closer to her. 'I need to get some fresh air,' she shouted in his ear.

Mario took her by the arm, led her behind the bar and then upstairs to the office which doubled up as a storage space for crates of beer and soft drinks. In the corner, near the window, was an old wooden desk, covered in papers, receipts and order forms. The ancient computer was covered in a layer of dust. The keyboard looked greasy, the letters on the keys almost impossible to make out. The air in the office was just as dense as it was on the dance floor. In January, there was hardly any relief from the relentless heat, even during the early hours of the morning.

Mario opened the French windows to the balcony, letting in a much-needed faint breeze. He unbuttoned his shirt whilst making a few dance moves. Claudia had to smile. He was such a flirt. It was impossible to have a conversation; the music was just as loud in the office as it was downstairs. Stage lights were shining through the gaps in between the floorboards creating an eerie effect.

The entire ramshackle building vibrated with the samba beat. There were cracks in the ceiling and plaster had fallen off during previous concerts. A loose bit of plaster vibrated ominously right above Claudia's head; she stepped out of its trajectory, strutting over to the mattress on the floor behind the beer crates.

As Mario removed her dress she lifted her arms

mechanically in an alcohol-induced haze. It was soaked in sweat. Mario draped it over one of the crates. He held her close – her skin smelt sweet – it brought back memories of previous encounters in the same room. Claudia removed her yellow Chuck Taylors and her striped slip. She sat on the old mattress, folding her knees beneath her. The sheets looked like they hadn't been washed since the last time she and Mario made love in the same sweltering room, with the same passion. She was pretty sure those sheets never got washed. She was also sure that she wasn't the only woman ending up with Mario on this very mattress. The thin linen sheet smelled of sex. Cream-coloured semen stains mottled the mattress cover, strewn about with pubic hairs of different colours and shades. At least a dozen bartenders worked at the bar, all good-looking and charming, so it was entirely likely that not all those stains belonged to Mario.

Anyway, this wasn't the time to make a fuss about it; tomorrow she'd be on a plane headed for Madrid. She shook her matted blonde hair and slowly reclined on the mattress. Mario caressed her breasts, her slender waist and kissed her left nipple. He then slowly moved his right hand towards her trim sliver of pubic hair. Claudia parted her legs in anticipation. As she arched her back, she felt Mario sliding inside her, any concern about the sheets was now an irrelevance. She hooked her legs around Mario's waist and squeezed his buttocks. The floor vibrated, the mattress vibrated, her body vibrated. A saxophone screamed. The beat of the drums was like a machine gun firing joy instead of bullets at the crowd, elevating people into a state of ecstasy.

'If only all the Kalashnikovs in the world could be turned

into trumpets and saxophones,' Claudia giggled, 'the world would be a better place.'

Mario laughed and held her even closer – he loved that about Claudia; she could be such a dreamer. He wouldn't let the noise distract him. His pelvic movements became firmer as he slowed down, trying to disengage from the manic, thumping rhythm of the samba. He tried to prolong their union, tried to postpone the moment of climax. Claudia dug her nails deep into Mario's back. He flinched. She felt her pelvic muscles contracting and a warm glow engulfing her body. Claudia came with a deep sigh. She rotated her hips a few more times until she felt Mario becoming limp. She closed her eyes. Her body relaxed and she soon fell asleep, exhausted.

When she opened her eyes, Mario was gone, the band had stopped playing and her body was covered with a thin sheet. She felt cold. She looked at the time on her phone – 2:14 a.m. Turning around, she closed her eyes again and thought she'd better get some rest before starting her final early morning shift in a few hours.

It was three months since she'd taken on a cleaning job in a medium-sized office. When she was told that she would be cleaning the head office of one of the largest logging and construction companies in the city, whose owner was the State Governor's cousin, she'd jumped at the opportunity. She realised that she'd be given totally unsupervised access to places even the owner of the company didn't know existed. Four months was ample time to gain her colleagues' trust and to sort out her plan in fine detail.

2

London, UK

Just after six p.m., Peter Miller opened the door of his 1930s semi-detached house in Crystal Palace, a comfortable residential neighbourhood in south-east London. It was a short walk from the station. Peter was a creature of habit. He worked as an accountant for a life insurance company on the fourteenth floor of a nondescript office block in the heart of the City, doing the same work for fifteen years, from the same desk in the same corner of the office. His desk was conveniently located close to the elevator and the water-cooler, the main social hub. At half past four in the afternoon, Peter would wind down his work with a final toilet break at four-forty, log off his computer at two minutes to five and make a beeline for the exit. He pressed the button at five o'clock exactly, not a minute sooner or later – he'd learned the hard way. The one thing about this routine that he was uncertain about was the time it took to wait for the lift. If he'd leave a few minutes after five, he'd have to take a jam-packed lift, which would make even a sardine feel claustrophobic. Taking the stairs was an alternative, but Peter felt that being on the fourteenth floor exempted him from doing his bit for the planet.

If all went well, he'd stride across the lobby a minute later with a polite nod to the security officer, never slowing down. Peter was punctual. He got paid to do his job as a senior accountant from nine until five, and he made sure that he worked those hours. He wouldn't slack. In all the years he'd worked for the insurance company, he'd always presented the weekly figures on time; most years, he was able to save the company far more money than he earned. In Peter's opinion, he didn't owe them any more loyalty or overtime.

The only departure from his routine was on Wednesdays when Peter arrived to an empty home and had to put dinner on the table. Joanne, his wife of eighteen years, would take their children, Tom and Lilly, to their piano lessons. Joanne was able to work from home several days per week editing articles for a fashion magazine so she could be around when the kids came home from school.

Peter took his cooking seriously and tried to come up with a new recipe most weeks. Some recipes were more popular with his children than others. Last week's attempt to be creative with Brussels sprouts hadn't been a great success; even the added pomegranate seeds and maple syrup to offset the bitter taste hadn't changed his kids' minds. He also had to impress his wife. She wouldn't be pleased with leftovers or a microwaved pizza. Rule one for Joanne was that all meals had to be cooked from scratch with in-season ingredients. This meant no to jet-lagged broccoli from Thailand.

Peter looked at the oven clock; he had just over an hour to come up with something new. He opened the fridge and rummaged through the bottom drawer hoping to find some essential ingredients. Somewhere there must be a small pack of pancetta tucked behind the various Tupperware containers.

At twenty past six the phone rang. Peter was startled and felt a lump coming up in his throat. He closed the fridge and walked over to the phone with a feeling of apprehension. It could be anyone – a nurse phoning from King's College Hospital Accident and Emergency department to tell him, in a solemn voice, that there had been an accident on the South Circular and that his wife and children were under observation in the resuscitation unit. Or it could be his aunt in Suffolk reminding him to carry out some essential repairs at her farm the next time he'd come up. On a more reassuring level, it could be a desperate parent trying to arrange a last-minute play-date with Tom or Lilly. Or it could be an Indian call centre trying to sell him a pension scheme. It was hard to tell. In any case, Peter rushed to the phone and picked up the receiver. He paused for a minute, caught his breath and said warmly, 'Mr Miller speaking.'

A jovial young woman with a northern accent introduced herself as Angela Johnson. 'Hello, I'm calling on behalf of a marketing research company and I wonder if you could spare a few minutes to answer some questions?'

How could he refuse? She had a disarmingly charming voice, a voice you couldn't say no to, a voice that could sell anything – a new fridge, a pension plan, a Caribbean cruise. She was dangerous.

Peter looked over his shoulder at the oven clock: 18:21. Less than fifty minutes to prepare the evening meal.

'Yes, of course. I've got some time.' You're such a sucker! Peter said to himself. Hang up now!

'Thank you very much, Mr Miller. I won't take up much of your time. We're conducting a study into the domestic use of alternative forms of energy.'

Peter tried to extend the telephone cord to the kitchen island. The coil cord had been overstretched too many times; it looked worn and twisted. Soon he realised that trying to make dinner and holding the receiver between his shoulder and his ear distorted his voice and made it impossible to chop the onions at the same time. It was better to give up on food preparation and hope that he could end the conversation quickly and politely.

'I can see from our data that your electricity company sources its energy from a range of suppliers. None of these come from a sustainable source.'

'I didn't know that.'

'And are you aware that emissions from fossil-fuelled power stations are a major contributor to climate change?'

Peter swallowed. He had no idea where this conversation was going, but he knew how Joanne would feel about it.

'I can offer you a special deal. It's your chance to play a role in the fight against global warming.'

'I didn't know there was a united front against global warming.'

'No, there isn't, you're right. But it's about gaining the right momentum. And right now some innovative alternative energy suppliers are switching to wind energy. Did you know that one of the largest off-shore wind farms is under construction in the Thames Estuary?'

'Yes, I've read about it. It looks awful.'

'I'm sorry, Mr Miller,' Angela interjected, growing agitated. 'Have you any idea what a field of oil drilling platforms looks like? Customers want all the benefits but none of the disadvantages. That's a luxury. When's the last time, Mr Miller, you stared at the horizon of the North Sea and your precious view got spoilt by wind turbines? It's time that people take some bloody responsibility for their carbon footprint. There's a lot more at stake here! Aren't you worried about climate change, melting arctic ice, starving polar bears and rising sea levels?' Angela was more passionate than one could expect of a call centre agent.

'I'll certainly talk to my wife about this tonight. Just for the record, the area where I live, Crystal Palace, is on a big hill, more than a hundred metres above sea level, so it would take centuries for the water to reach my doorstep.'

'We know where you live. But that's not the point; that's just a selfish I'm-all-right-Jack kind of attitude. You might be safe on your hill, but the rest of London won't be, and by then, they'll all be camping out in your front garden!'

Peter was sure this wasn't part of her script.

'You'll get riots, famine… it'll be the end of civilisation as we know it,' she continued passionately.

Peter was looking at the oven clock. 18:27. Time was marching on. In forty-five minutes his kids would come running through the door, kicking off their shoes and demanding to be fed.

'Well… I'll certainly discuss this with my wife tonight.'

'Thank you, Mr Miller. We also have a special offer on double glazing. Do you know that you can save up to thirty per cent on your heating bill?'

Peter was anxious to end the conversation as the clock was ticking and time was running out. His answers were getting shorter.

'We already have double glazing.'

'Very good! And can I perhaps interest you in a deal on loft insulation. Most of your heat, as you might know, escapes through the roof.'

'I am aware of that. I insulated our roof and loft myself ten years ago.'

'Excellent. If you don't mind, I'd like to follow up this conversation in two months' time. Would that be OK with you?'

'OK,' Peter replied without really having listened to the question.

'In that case, I won't hold you up any longer. Thank you very much for your time, Mr Miller.'

'My pleasure.'

Peter put down the receiver and checked the time again on the oven clock. Thirty-six minutes left to come up with a meal for four. He scratched his head. When time is of the essence, a quiche is the best solution. Once it was in the oven, he would prepare a healthy salad and set the table. It was a race against time.

It started drizzling outside. This change in the weather would slow down traffic and buy him another ten minutes. He lined a ceramic oven dish with ready-made shortcrust pastry and poured the filling on top; it didn't take long to make. Then he sprinkled a few walnuts on top of the quiche mix before placing it in the preheated oven.

Whilst the quiche was cooking, Peter reflected on the phone conversation. He considered himself environmentally conscious but he'd never thought about changing energy providers, or about the wider implications of climate change. Some warmer summers would be welcome, of course, but the true impact of climate change would a different and unpredictable story. People dream of growing sunflowers and sipping white wine in a warm afternoon sun; they don't imagine a new reality bringing increased rainfall, regular floods, eroding coastlines and an eternal autumn. Perhaps the woman from the call centre was right and mankind was sleepwalking towards the end of civilisation.

3

São Paulo

'Had a long night, Claudia?' asked the night porter as Claudia swiped her work pass over the ID reader. The speed gate would open with a three second delay. During those three seconds a computer algorithm determined if she had a legitimate reason to gain access to the office building at 4:30 in the morning.

'How can you tell?'

With a gentle swoosh, the gate opened and Claudia walked through the entrance. She turned to face the porter as she always did when she walked across the lobby. He often helped her move heavy items or empty bins.

'Your hair, minha linda. Your radiant smile, your dress, the way you walk, your energy. Not to mention the smell of stale beer and cigarette smoke; telltale signs of a fun night out.'

'It was a great night for sure, Rodeo! But after this four-hour shift, I'll be more than ready to head home for a siesta.'

Rodeo didn't reply. He respected her privacy and, as

long as she arrived on time and finished the job, he didn't care what the employees did in their spare time. He glanced away to look at some of the screens on his desk. There was no movement. The pavement in front of the building was deserted. The car park at the rear of the office block was empty and it would be more than another hour before sunrise.

'Well, I'm nodding off now,' Rodeo said, as if he'd already begun his siesta. 'You're the last cleaner to come in. Your colleagues are having coffee in the kitchen on the first floor. Three and a half hours before my shift ends, so I'd better make the most of it.'

The chubby porter put his walkie-talkie in front of him and reclined his chair. He put his feet on the desk and tilted his cap over his eyes. Claudia had witnessed this ritual many times. Rodeo would be fast asleep within a couple of minutes, snoring after five and unconscious to the world for the next three hours. The double-glazing in the main entrance hall reduced all street noise to a minimum, and nothing would wake him up. Like most night porters, Rodeo had a day job too, working as a car mechanic. Whatever sleep he could get now meant more energy for the rest of the day. He'd get another chance to catch up with sleep after dinner and before the start of his shift at 11 p.m. It was a hectic schedule, but with sky-high rent to pay and two young kids, he had no choice but to work hard.

'It's my last shift today,' Claudia said cheerfully.

'Good for you,' Rodeo mumbled from the comfort of his seat. 'I didn't think you would last this long anyway. I've seen so many young women like you come and go.' Claudia didn't hear this part of Rodeo's mutterings as she'd already made her way to the lift at the far end of the entrance hall.

Claudia's cleaning crew was small, comprising just two other women, who were middle-aged and spent most of their time gossiping and complaining about their husbands, their teenage children and not winning the Mega-Sena, Brazil's largest biweekly lottery. Claudia knew their routines. They'd mop the three office floors and tidy most of the desks for an hour. Then they took an hour-long break, slumbering in a quiet corner before a last-minute frantic cleaning spree. Rodeo would then unlock the front door and the first shift workers would arrive.

Claudia had volunteered a while ago to clean the toilets and bathrooms. Her colleagues had laughed at this. In their eyes, it was the worst job of all. There were six bathrooms spread out over three floors and each bathroom had four toilet cubicles and two sinks. The bathroom on the ground floor in the reception area took the longest to clean, since it was used by employees, visitors, passers-by and the odd homeless person managing to sneak in. The ones in the accounts department were the cleanest, only needing a flush with bleach and a quick sweep around the toilet bowl rim with a cloth. The bathrooms were strategically placed throughout the building. To clean them all thoroughly took her colleagues two hours, though Claudia managed to do it in an hour and a half. That would leave her with enough spare time to bring the office waste to the basement and make sure the boiler room was tidy before going to the top of the building, out on the roof, and checking the air-conditioning filters. Claudia had unrestricted access to the entire building and its innards. She knew exactly where gas pipes entered the building and which air-conditioning unit belonged to which floor. Claudia was one of the select few who had access to the owner's private bathroom in his office.

His office suite was panelled with dark, tropical hardwood. There was a large, tasteful silk rug on the floor and two expressionist oil paintings on the walls. On each windowsill was an expensive china pot containing a rare Amazonian orchid. Near the entrance to the bathroom was an abstract sculpture in the style of the famous Brazilian artist Bruno Giorgi. The sculpture resembled two half-moons in white marble. Claudia liked it, but she was sure it was a copy.

Roberto Sousa's personal bathroom was an equally opulent affair. The taps were gold-plated, matching the door handles. The lava stone worktop was polished to resemble a dark lake and the black slate walls added to the illusion that this was his private cave in a turbulent world. It was a tasteful design, Claudia admitted regretfully. She often used his bathroom. But at the same time she despised herself for enjoying it, for sharing a toilet with a man she detested so much. And yet, knowing that she'd get sacked if he found out that his inner sanctum had been violated, she enjoyed it even more.

Claudia often played with the idea of leaving her underwear behind as a sign that she'd been there, just to drive him mad. Since today was her last day, it was also her last chance to play a trick. She took off her underwear as she sat on the toilet, stretching the material over her yellow canvas shoes. Her tiny slip was still moist with sweat from dancing with Mario. She dried herself with some toilet paper.

As soon as she got up from the seat, the toilet flushed automatically. She walked over to the sink to wash her hands. She stroked her hair to make it look less ruffled. She folded her slip threefold and placed it in the small basket with neatly rolled white fluffy hand towels, another token of luxury, which meant so much to the pampered class. Her striped, folded up underwear formed a nice contrast with the white flannels. She then placed the basket next to the washbasin on the small side table in between the small stack of soap bars and a flask of Dior Eau Sauvage aftershave. Claudia looked at the clock above the door: one more hour to go. All her cleaning work was done; she had an hour left for the finishing touches. She was very pleased with herself.

When Claudia checked on her colleagues in the kitchen on the first floor, she found them fast asleep, lying in a corner with a rolled up kitchen towel for a pillow, as she had anticipated. The morning sun, the already sweltering heat and the exhaustion of the work they'd done so far guaranteed that nothing would wake them for another thirty minutes. Gabriella, the corpulent middle-aged cleaner, had her hands tucked into her apron and gave a deep sigh when Claudia opened the door, then turned onto her side continuing her slumber.

Claudia had prepared for this moment for over two months. She had installed a well-concealed network of cables to connect several explosive devices around the building. The main one was near the gas boiler in the basement. Claudia had hidden several sticks of dynamite in the ceiling above each cubicle. Her plan was foolproof.

There was no shortage of explosives. The warehouse in

the basement was full of detonators, Cordtex and dynamite left over from various road construction projects in the Amazon rainforest. What would blast through a massive granite mountain would certainly blast through a cheaply constructed office building from the '70s. Claudia had been smart enough not to buy any explosives or materials herself; her record was clean. She was sure that the amount of Dynamax Pro she had distributed throughout the building was enough to reduce it to fine rubble within seconds. She had been surprised when she'd found a cache of disordered, hastily disposed explosives in the basement of an office building in the middle of São Paulo. They were stored in boxes and crates haphazardly, none of them numbered or sealed. Most were stained with mud from previous jobs. Some of the fuse cables were just thrown onto a big pile. Nobody would notice if a couple of kilos of dynamite were taken away. Seeing this cache of explosives week in, week out at the end of her shift while filling up the refuse containers with bags of rubbish, she came up with an infallible plan. It seemed wild at first, but having thought about it long and hard and having read various Internet guides on how to detonate explosives, it was too good an opportunity to dismiss. Soon she'd be a Joan of Arc of the rainforest, an improvement from being a petitioning chat-room activist. Destroying the office of the destructor would send a loud and clear message into the world. It would rattle the cages of the establishment.

All that was left to do today was to set the timer. Claudia went upstairs to the top floor where she had installed the digital clock behind one of the smaller air-conditioning units. It was well hidden and quiet. She knew that various security officers made their rounds throughout the building several times a day. The timer had been in place since last month, and if it hadn't been detected by now, the chance that anybody would find it in the next few hours was slim. Her flight to Madrid would leave in less than four hours. She'd arrive eleven hours later in Spain, then after a short rest, make her way to Paris by night train and travel onwards to London via Eurostar. With her blonde hair, blue eyes and back-packer gap-year appearance, she'd whiz through customs. Nobody would blink an eye. By the time the police cordoned off all airports, bus and train stations in Brazil, she'd be long gone. And once detectives started trying to string the pieces together and solve the puzzle, she'd have found a room in London and perhaps even a job. Between now and then, hundreds of planes carrying hundreds of passengers would take off from a dozen airports in Brazil. It would take months to track down each passenger on the passenger-list from each airport. With so many Brazilians working under the radar in the States, Australia and in Europe, it would take thousands of man-hours to track down every single passenger. In a week's time, something else in Brazil would crop up and there'd be new priorities. Within a couple of weeks, the whole affair would blow over, and it would only be a matter of lying low and following events from a safe distance without leaving a trail. Claudia had read a dozen books on forensic science. The common theme was that people make mistakes when they rush or when they panic. She'd prepared for this day with immaculate precision.

4

As soon as Peter walked from the lift at nine o'clock on the dot, he made a beeline for his desk, brought his computer back to life after logging in and hung up his coat just behind his desk. He had adjusted his tie in the lift on his way up and straightened his short and neat light brown hair by patting it on all sides, maintaining a left-sided parting to hide his thinning crown. He looked dapper.

'Good morning, Peter,' said Duncan, his colleague in the neighbouring cubicle. 'Let's go to the cooler.'

Peter had just opened his company email account and counted at least fifteen emails marked as urgent. His heart sank. Often on Thursday the office floor manager would get nervous about the lunchtime deadline. He was new on the job and wanted to impress his seniors. The manager had already invested a good part of his monthly income in a new suit, shirts, ties and matching shoes, and he didn't want to come across as unprepared when it came to the latest sales figures.

'Why not? Cedric can wait.' Peter exclaimed ironically,

referring to their manager. 'He drives me bonkers, stalking me all week like a hungry jungle cat.'

'Let him stew a bit longer,' Duncan said.

'I've got all the figures he needs, stored up here,' Peter said, pointing to his head. 'I can recite them by memory at the team meeting. A glass of water is just what I need.' He said it with the right cynical intonation, and they both laughed.

The manager had his whole team on a chilled water regime. He saw this as a major victory, since the accounts staff's productivity had improved significantly.

To Peter and his colleagues, the daily gatherings near the cooler were as close as one could get to planning a revolution. The daggers were out. While some employees had simply resigned and taken up jobs elsewhere in the City, Peter and Duncan decided to wait in the wings and watch the cocky Cedric fall from grace in real time, close up. That day couldn't come quickly enough.

During Cedric's short career as the floor manager, he had made many enemies and left many casualties. The first to go was Ann, the tea and coffee lady, a true gem – a relic from older, better times. Everyone had loved Ann. She was the office mum; a kind woman in her late fifties who, twice a day, would stroll out of the lift with her tea trolley. It was as if a giant light switch was flicked on and the entire office changed colour. Her tea was weak and the coffee had a bitter aftertaste, but she handed out complimentary biscuits and always had something nice to say. She offered career advice and listened to people's relationship problems. As the tea and coffee lady, she was also the most informed person in the building. Even the porters in the downstairs lobby couldn't compete with her insider's knowledge. She always had the latest gossip, and that made her indispensable.

Behind closed doors head office had agreed to cut more costs. One day Ann was bringing tea and coffee, the next day somebody saw her sobbing at the reception desk. One of the porters – who usually only talked about football – had his arm around her and was overheard saying, 'They're all bastards, love. It'll be us next; soon the robots'll take over!'

Ann was dearly missed. The share price on the company stock dipped in sympathy, albeit temporarily.

The tea and coffee lady was replaced the same day by a fancy but temperamental coffee machine with countless options. Unfortunately, the quality of the coffee was equally dubious. Soon one of the temps came up with an elaborate plan of running to the nearest Starbucks and returning with a tray full of steaming caffè lattes, espressos and cappuccinos. Cedric was quick to calculate the cost of lost productivity and disruption caused by these runs. All office workers were sent an urgent email advising them in no subtle terms to use the new machine instead; it was widely ignored. After several weeks of gathering dust in the corner, the coffee dispenser got taken away.

One of the longer serving secretaries, Emily, found a study published on an agency website, claiming to have found a link between office productivity and a steady supply of cold fresh water. Cedric didn't need any further encouragement. In fact, he stole the idea and used it to his own advantage to score points with the senior management. Emily was miffed at first, but since the cooler had become a source of new enthusiasm in the office, she focused her energy on more important matters. She organized a weekly office pool. The floor would bet on whether Cedric would last another week or not. So far, against all predictions, he had lasted for more than three months since the water cooler had arrived. Emily was profiting handsomely from it. This week the odds were again 12:3 in favour of leaving.

Peter followed Duncan on his trail through the office, taking every opportunity to banter with colleagues. The cooler had been placed near a large window overlooking a building site. It provided much needed distraction and entertainment. Peter was looking out of the window waiting for Duncan to return from the bathroom. The building team was making steady progress. The high-rise had reached the same level as Peter's office only a few days ago and was getting taller and taller each week. The view of St Paul's cathedral was now completely obscured. There were dozens of cranes scattered around the City.

'I read in the Evening Outlook that at least another hundred-and-fifty high-rises in London were approved last year alone,' Duncan said upon returning from the toilet.

'I love it,' Peter said. 'The future's here. We have to stop this endless suburban sprawl. I can barely tolerate my commute from Crystal Palace. I feel sorry for those who commute more than an hour each way. We need to build more flats close to where people work.'

'But it'll be like living in Manhattan!'

'That'd be great. Wouldn't you love that? I remember it so well from twenty years ago. It's my favourite place, so quirky – all those basement bars, jazz cafes and diners. Of course it's a bit rough around the edges; you know what I mean...The homeless sharing the same space as the rich and famous.'

'Peter, you surprise me. That's not what these developers have in mind. London will become more like a bland version of Singapore or Dubai. You'll get ghettos for the rich, no-go areas for the likes of us. Soon nobody will be able to live in London apart from investment bankers; and what then?'

'Don't be so gloomy. It goes in cycles! House prices won't go up forever. Soon people will start selling at what appears to be the height of this bubble; others will follow and before you know it, the market will correct itself.'

'I guess we were lucky to have bought something all those years ago.'

'And the younger generation may be lucky to be part of something else, something even bigger.'

'Like what?'

'Sustainable development and getting less dependent on oil; that will truly liberate us, and of course reversing climate change.'

'Adapting to climate change you mean, global warming is a fact, we already passed the 400 parts per million carbon dioxide threshold, the point of no return, we won't be reversing any of the damage done already, we have to learn to adapt in order to survive!'

'Exactly! Funny you should mention that. We're thinking about changing our energy provider. Joanne agrees with me that it'll be better for our future. I spoke to a woman from a call centre about it last night.'

'Will it be cheaper?'

'I didn't get that impression.'

'Well, that's the problem, mate. We're all hooked on cheap oil and gas and it's getting cheaper by the day. No windmill can compete with that.'

'I disagree. Sometimes these things are about principles and values.'

'Principles don't pay the mortgage. We'd better get back to work and answer those emails.'

'No, I'm serious. That woman last night opened my eyes. We can't go on like this. The Greenland ice sheet is melting at an alarming rate, temperatures in Spitsbergen are significantly higher than the same time last year and the arctic sea ice cover is at an all-time low. In ten years' time you'll need to row to work. In fact, if the forecasts are true, we'll soon be able to moor right outside these windows.'

'Sounds convenient enough to me!'

'Joking aside, we're in deep shit.'

'Don't tell me you're having some kind of existential crisis. There's no use for that. One day you'll just have to come to terms with the fact that what we're doing is insignificant. Look around you – our lives revolve around meaningless office jobs.'

'So why are you still here?' Peter teased Duncan.

'For the same reason as you I guess, I've got bills to pay, kids to get through school.'

'We are stuck, stuck in a rut.'

'Now you sound like you're having a mid-life crisis.'

'It doesn't hurt to reflect on your life from time to time.'

'Come on, mate. You're not reflecting; you're being gloomy!'

'Guys, Cedric's headed towards the cooler,' said Emily,

warning Peter and Duncan. 'You'd better roll up your sleeves and do some work, your heads are on the block!'

'Here, another quid for this week's pool!' Peter threw a coin onto Emily's desk.

'Stay or go?' she asked.

'He has to go. Or I'll go!' Peter said.

Emily took the pound and inserted it into a small box in her top drawer. She marked Peter's weekly contribution on a spreadsheet she had created for the occasion. She stared out of the window. It was impossible to tell what the weather was like. The new building obscured her view of the sky and it had stolen the sun.

5

São Paulo

'It's quicker to walk! This bloody bus isn't going anywhere. Let's get off at the next stop,' Juan Conseillo complained.

'Traffic is getting worse all the time,' Enrico Delgado added.

'It's gridlocked, the whole city is permanently gridlocked from dawn till dusk.'

'And this on a Saturday, I hate to think what the traffic will be like on Monday,' Enrico added.

Juan and Enrico were summoned to attend a meeting at the head office of Amazorico, a medium-size road construction company which had been awarded a ten-year contract to upgrade a dirt road into a four-lane motorway in a remote part of the Amazon rainforest.

'I can't wait to get back into the field to continue our construction project. I can't this traffic. It drives me mad.'

'If it wasn't for this emergency meeting, I wouldn't have bothered coming all the way. I could have worked from home. It took me an hour and a half this morning. It's a joke! My kids were fast asleep when I left. This is supposed to be a day off, for my family.'

'Same here. Let's get this meeting over with and get our proposals finalised. Hopefully by the end of next week, we'll be back in the jungle.'

'Still... I prefer being stuck in this bus than being out in the bush, getting bitten alive,' Enrico said.

'I hope we'll convince the others at the meeting that we need to crack on with the second stage before the rainy season starts and those vicious mosquitoes are back with a vengeance. And just one day of rain can wash away three months of work and then it's back to square one.'

'Yep, and that means that our nice bonus gets washed away too.'

'It all depends on how quickly the paperwork gets done.'

'It's up to the boss really – he's the one who has to suck up to his cousin, the state governor.'

'I suggest we carry on with the work and ask questions later. Nobody's going to ask us to tear up the work we've done. Once we've blasted our way through the rocks, it's a matter of getting enough bulldozers to the site, bringing in truckloads of ballast and sand, and rolling out the tarmac. We won't need more than two months for that. As soon as the first cars start using the roads and bringing business to those remote villages, nobody's going to ask questions about permits.'

'We'll see what his mood will be today.'

The doors of the bus were locked so there was no way of getting off before reaching the next stop. Other passengers were getting anxious too. A fat man in a suit standing in the aisle was huffing and puffing and using his newspaper as a fan. Sweat dripped from his forehead. He looked as if he was about to faint. He loosened his tie and hollered at the bus driver to let him off, but his shouts fizzled out in the ambient noise of passengers talking, music blasting from the tinny overhead speakers, and the revving bus engine. The bus gained some speed before the driver slammed on the brakes after less than a minute.

Finally, the doors of the bus opened. Juan got out of the bus first. The man in the centre took his seat as soon as he had stood up. Juan had to get used to the heat for a minute. It was even worse than in the bus. A heavy blanket descended on him – a combination of diesel fumes and the thick air, already heated up unbearably in the early morning, which made it difficult to breathe. He felt dizzy and had to hold on to Enrico.

'I'll buy a drink first before we walk the rest of the way,' Juan said.

'Drinking only makes you more thirsty. You have to conserve your water intake. Basic survival technique number one.'

'Nah! Some freshly squeezed fruit juice'll perk me up in no time.'

There was no shortage of fruit juice bars in São Paulo. Juan chose an orange and maracujá smoothie.

'Make it two,' Juan said. 'One for my friend.'

'Cheers, buddy! You're right, it's murder out here.'

They drank through a thick straw while walking down the street, slurping all the way to the office; a short fifteen-minute walk was enough to get drenched in sweat.

Roberto Sousa wasn't in a good mood. He had arrived early and spoken to his cousin, the governor. His cousin had explained in tedious detail why a permit for his construction work would have to be postponed till after the committee meeting next month. He knew what this meant. He couldn't wait another month.

'Of course, there are ways to speed things up a little,' his cousin replied curtly.

Roberto Sousa was used to doling out bribes to his cousin like sweets. Over the years he came to see this as an unavoidable business expense. But it irritated him that it would bite into his own profits.

'What's the point of having family in high places and still having to pay bribes?' he'd confided in Ariana Evora, his personal assistant.

'The only difference is that at least you know who to bribe and it stays in the family,' she'd replied.

It made him sick. But what else could he do?

Roberto walked over to his private toilet and sat down. He could no longer trust his aim; his urine flow had become erratic and unpredictable with advancing years. He left the door of the cubicle open so he could hear his phone ring. He stared at the wall.

What did his cousin mean when he said, 'We've got ways to make you pay'? Was he part of the mafia? Was this how business had to be conducted in Brazil now? Roberto Sousa was a proud man. He had worked hard over the last twenty years to expand his construction company. He had built thousands of kilometres of roads throughout the Amazon rainforest. He was proud of the work. All he wanted now was for a bigger company to take over and pay him no less than ten million dollars so that he and his family could retire comfortably. His latest project would give him the publicity and high profile he desperately needed to get his competitors interested in his new road.

He reached for the soap and noticed some striped material in his towel basket. 'What the fuck is this?' Roberto blurted whilst inspecting the garment in further detail. It was a woman's tiny slip, a woman no more than a size eight. What the hell was this doing in his toilet? Was this a set-up? He was sure that it hadn't been there before. Someone must have planted it recently. This was no accident. Was this a warning? A sign? Did it mean that somebody had been in his office, in his bathroom? He hated the idea of someone using his one and only private toilet seat. Not even his secretary had the privilege of using it.

Roberto sniffed the slip tentatively and recoiled. It smelled of sweat, beer and cigarettes, and was slightly soiled in the front. It reeked of sex and booze. Right here in his office! He felt furious, offended and threatened at the same time. He had enough of his scheming cousin. There was no doubt he was behind it all. He zipped his trousers, washed his hands and rushed to the phone. He called his secretary and barked through the phone, 'Get me security at once!'

Juan and Enrico were relieved when they entered the air-conditioned head office, close as they were to suffocation and heat stroke.

'Look at you, guys,' Rodeo said as he put the receiver down. 'What have you done to yourselves?'

'It's like a sauna out there!'

'We got off the bus a few stops earlier,' Juan replied, wiping sweat from his forehead.

'We walked the rest,' Enrico added.

'Only a madman would walk on a day like this.'

'You haven't seen the traffic out there.'

'That, my friends, is why I ride a motorbike. I just zoom along those traffic jams. But anyway… I'll come up with you in the lift.'

'Sure, you think we will all fit in?' Juan teased the security guard.

Juan patted Rodeo's fat belly.

'All those doughnuts you eat.'

'Well, they keep me going through the night!'

'Hasn't your shift ended?'

'The boss wants me to go up to his office. It seems urgent; he was beside himself with anger.'

'Is nobody taking over from you? I am sure the boss can wait.'

'No chance buddy. There is no on-site security staff over the weekend so it's down to me. I just hope it won't take too much time. I've got to go to my next job. But I tell you what; he found a suspicious item in his private bathroom and that's too good to miss.'

'Now we're interested!' Juan probed the security officer.

The doors of the lift opened. Rodeo pressed number four, top floor. Juan leaned across Rodeo's stomach and pressed number three.

'So what's about this suspicious item?'

The security officer chuckled. 'He found some racy

underwear in his office.'

'Did you get him on camera?'

'I wish; his office isn't on CCTV. You know him, he's quite paranoid when it comes to his privacy.'

'That's a real shame. Who was it then? His secretary?'

'That's where I come in. This warrants a full investigation. The slip was rather petite, so that rules out Ariana.'

'An escort perhaps? Are there any security cameras in the lifts? You didn't see anyone going up?'

'Are you mad? These lifts are the only safe places in the building apart from the toilets, for obvious reasons. You think I'd be spilling the beans when I can be recorded? Anyway, this is your floor, guys. And mind you, not a word about this to the boss at the meeting.'

'It's these small things, Juan, which keep me going. Who would have thought, our boss caught in the action!' Enrico chuckled.

Rodeo straightened his shirt and adjusted his tie when he knocked on the door. He went straight in without waiting for a reply.

'It's still in the bathroom, Rodeo!' Roberto Sousa barked with a certain disdain for this peculiar situation.

'Did you touch it?'

'Yes, of course I did. I had to know what it was. The bloody cheek of it!'

'I'll have a courier send it for DNA analysis straight away. It'll be in the lab before noon and we'll have an answer by the end of next week,' Rodeo said trying to calm down his boss, who seemed beyond himself with fury.

'Next week? I can't wait that long. I have to sign an important contract today.'

'Sorry, boss, that's the way it is.'

'I see... well, I guess you better get on with it.'

'I'll seal this sample first and send it off immediately. My shift has already ended and there won't be any security on site till Monday. I'll coordinate the rest of the investigation next week.'

'One thing, Rodeo. We have to be extremely discreet about this. If my wife finds out, all hell will break lose.'

'I'm sure she's got nothing to worry about.'

Rodeo put on latex gloves, and with some tweezers put the evidence in a plastic bag and sealed it in front of his boss.

'You're a good man. If you don't mind I'll leave you to it, I've got a meeting to prepare.'

'Of course.'

Rodeo closed the door behind him. He returned to the small security office at the entrance and rummaged through some drawers. He found several pre-labelled envelopes for a private forensics lab. The courier arrived within a few minutes. Rodeo smiled. This came as close to CSI as he could have hoped for.

6

Suffolk, UK

Another routine Peter regarded as the bedrock of a secure and happy life was the trip to his aunt Doreen's house in Suffolk once a month. She lived on an old and somewhat dilapidated farm, charming in many ways, but utterly devoid of modern luxuries and comforts. However, the wood fire in the living room, the Aga cooker in the kitchen and the farm animals were enough to keep the family entertained. Aunt Doreen was a widow without any grandchildren of her own and she doted on Tom and Lilly. Her apple crumble had long been the gold standard in the family against which all other cakes and puddings were measured. For Peter it was a necessary escape to satisfy his alter ego. Dressed in faded jeans and a charcoal hoody, sporting a rampant Saturday-morning stubble and his hair unkempt he would have been unrecognisable to his colleagues in the office.

As children often live for the moment, Peter and Joanne faced the same difficulties getting Tom and Lilly in the car every second Saturday of the month, especially having to leave early in the morning when it was still dark and cold outside; that was particularly hard.

'Do we have to go to see Aunt Doreen again?' Tom whined.

'You'll love it, you always do. Nothing beats escaping the city from time to time,' Joanne said.

'It's cold and it's still the middle of winter. Why don't we go for Easter?' Tom pleaded. 'Besides, I don't want to miss football training! The coach'll kill me.'

'It's too long in the car and too boring,' Lilly chimed in.

'Yeah, it's really boring, why can't we have a car with a DVD player, just like all my friends?' Tom sulked.

'When I was your age, we just looked out the window and we never got bored,' Peter replied curtly.

'When I was your age, life was so much better!' Tom mimicked his dad sarcastically. Lilly started giggling as her brother was making a funny face behind his dad's back. Peter pretended he didn't hear his comment.

'Just ignore them,' Joanne said. 'They're always like that. Once they're on the farm, they'll love it and won't want to go back.'

'I'll double lock the doors, check the alarm and then we're off.'

'Thermos with coffee?'

'Check!'

'Petrol?'

'We'll get some on the way.'

Peter started the engine of his cherry red Volvo 940. It had been in the family since the kids were born, replacing his battered Fiat Punto when they needed space for a pram, nappies and other baby paraphernalia. He had bought it second-hand and it had soon become a well-loved member of the family. Peter was determined to keep it going until the bitter end. He'd read somewhere in a newspaper that a sales rep in America had done almost a million miles in a Volvo, so there was plenty more life and plenty more countryside trips in his car. It still looked good on the outside, in a vintage cool kind of way.

By the time Peter stopped at the first service station outside the M25, both Tom and Lilly were asleep, slumped against the windows, covered in several layers of sleeping bags and pillows propped up between their heads and the windows. Peter chuckled. There was no need for airbags the way his kids travelled.

The way up to Suffolk was a smooth journey. The sunrise over the sleepy region, blanketed in a fine layer of frosty mist, was picturesque, like in an old photo, a stark contrast to the gloomy city. The shoulder of the motorway was covered with a thin layer of snow and the bare branches of distant trees were powdered white. It wouldn't last long; the pale and weak sun would push the temperature to a few degrees above zero Celsius.

The road ahead was empty; nevertheless, Peter obeyed the speed limit. He was a stickler for traffic rules. He'd bore them all to death by reciting the Highway Code whenever Joanne tried to spur him on to drive a bit faster. Keeping to the limit of seventy miles per hour, they usually made it in time for mid-morning coffee and cake.

Aunt Doreen was pleased to see Peter and his family; she regarded his children as her own grandchildren, having had no children herself. She considered herself the last of a generation, having inherited a large farm from her parents, which she and her husband had tried hard to maintain. They'd toiled on the land every season without a break, never enjoying a single holiday in their lives. When her husband died, Aunt Doreen didn't have enough energy to keep it up herself, so she sublet most of the fields to local farmers. She was determined to keep the farm going, though she realised that when she was gone, the land would be sold and the farmhouse would be upgraded and converted into a luxury home. And that meant another family business biting the dust. She'd hoped that Peter would take over one day, but she knew that that was highly unlikely. He lived a pampered life in London and his kids would never adapt to living in a remote place like Suffolk; they had long stopped asking for a Wi-Fi password.

Surprisingly enough, Tom and Lilly always managed to occupy themselves on the farm. The barns were full of old equipment to play with, and they never got bored gazing at the cows in the fields or feeding the chickens and collecting their eggs early in the morning or chasing lost sheep and herding them back to the meadow.

For Peter, visiting his aunt once a month was a perfect excuse to show off his DIY skills. Looking after a dilapidated farm like hers needed full-time attention, and his skills had been stretched to the limit. There was always a light bulb in need of replacing or a fence to repair. This weekend, he'd promised to fix the roof. Some of the old roof tiles had blown off in an autumn storm and Doreen was tired of emptying buckets of rainwater after each downpour. His aunt had eight buckets spread out over the first floor of her farmhouse.

When Peter walked over to the furthest barn to fetch a ladder, he found Tom sitting high up in the cabin of a giant combine harvester.

'Don't press any buttons or pull any levers,' he shouted at him.

Tom acted like he hadn't heard him.

Peter smiled; he remembered how he used to climb that same old harvester himself with his best friend. The highlight of his holiday was being allowed to steer the harvester himself. He'd felt like a king.

High up on the roof, Peter was replacing more than thirty roof tiles. He could see his daughter Lilly running after a few sheep in a meadow close to the farm. Joanne was leaning over the fence with a mug of coffee in her hand. Peter waved at them.

'Can we come back again soon?' Lilly shouted to her dad. 'Some of the sheep are pregnant and I want to see the lambs when they're born. They're so cute!' Her words faded in the wind, but Peter got the gist of it. They were all happy.

Lunch was a traditional affair. Roast belly of pork for the adults, sausages and mash for the children accompanied with some overcooked carrots and peas. For dessert there was homemade blackberry and apple crumble with custard.

'I wish we could come all the time,' Tom said.

Peter started laughing out loud. He reached for his iPhone. 'Can you repeat that?' he said. 'I'd like to film it.'

Tom sat up straight and deepened his voice for a more serious effect. 'I wish we could come here all the time.'

'Me too, it's awesome,' Lilly butted in. 'Soon there will be newborn lambs.'

'Now compare this to a short video I made of you guys earlier this morning.' Peter showed Doreen and his wife the video of two whining children, complaining about going to the country again. 'It's so boring.'

'You were the same, Peter,' Aunt Doreen said. 'Your parents had to drag you here each holiday. And when you finally got out of the car, you'd hide in one of the upstairs rooms and read a book for an hour or so, until you could smell my apple crumble. Then slowly you'd start talking, and it wasn't long before your friend would storm in. Remember Barry? You were the closest of friends during the holidays; inseparable. The two of you would disappear for hours on end. When the weather was warm enough, you'd go swimming or fishing. In the autumn you'd help your uncle on the combine harvester. Other times you'd go shooting birds or scaring them away. Really,' she chuckled, 'I don't think either of you ever caught anything.'

'Yep, I certainly remember that. Those were happy days.'

'They were indeed. The summer holidays seemed endless.'

'Speaking of Barry, whatever happened to him?'

'Barry? I'm surprised that you lost touch with him. You were such good friends. As it happens, I ran into him only a couple of days ago. He's doing well, very well indeed. Mind you, he's still single. It's such a shame really. He needs someone to look after him. He's a bit chubbier these days. He was such a skinny lad. I always gave him an extra piece of cake whenever he came by.'

'Interesting… how is he? I haven't seen him in ages, thirty-odd years or more.'

'Funny, he said the same thing.'

'Does he still live at the same place near the old military airport?'

'It's no longer a military airport, more of an airport for local enthusiasts. He runs some kind of salvage operation there. It's an amazing site. In the middle of nowhere, you suddenly see this big beat-up airplane from a defunct airline. It's next to the scrapyard.'

'Can we go there? Please, Daddy?' Tom asked.

'I suppose we could have a drive through the country after lunch.'

'That's boring, I'd much rather stay here and help feed the sheep,' Lilly said.

'Why don't you go with Tom? Scrapyards are not really my thing either,' Joanne said.

'Or we can go next time? I don't think he'd appreciate seeing a ghost from his past without any warning. I need a good excuse.'

'Dad, do you promise?'

'Of course, son. But first I need to fix the roof before it rains again. Have you seen the weather forecast?'

'Dad, there's no Wi-Fi out here. Don't ask me about the weather forecast. None of my apps work.'

'Well, look at the horizon... you see those dark clouds? You see the cows huddling together? Mind my words. We'll be in the middle of a downpour very soon. I'd better get those tiles fixed.'

'And what do we do then?'

'Sit next to the fire and read a book.'

'Come on, Dad! That's boring!'

7

São Paulo

The mid-morning sun heated the meeting room on the top floor to an unbearable pitch. The air-conditioning system was old and couldn't keep up. Ariana Evora opened all the windows hoping it would create a breeze. It helped cool down the meeting room, but also invited street noise and pollution. Knowing her boss, she knew he'd keep the meeting short, having seen him in a bad mood earlier in the morning. She knew that he hated coming in on a Saturday to chair a meeting. He would cut off any lengthy discussion and make the meeting even shorter. She was sure that he'd leave the building immediately afterwards to join his friends at his club. She often joked that her boss could run the company from Club Estrela da Noite as he left most of the groundwork and daily decision making to her. He called it effective delegation; she called it something else. Ariane often considered leaving. Having worked for Roberto Sousa since she was eighteen years old she felt stuck. Over the years her monochrome life had become intertwined with her boss'. It made her feel like an essential part of the extended family albeit on low pay. Not that she'd earn much more elsewhere. In other words, she was trapped. Her boss knew it and all her friends knew it. Somehow she'd made peace with her situation as in the short term there was no escape.

Roberto Sousa depended on his cousin for lucrative contracts, upcoming invitations to tender and insider information when land was up for sale. It was a beneficial relationship, but it came at a price. He often confided in her that he wanted to work for himself, start a new company, get out of the jungle and work in residential construction, high-rise luxury apartments and condominiums. The margin was much higher on these contracts. Flats often changed hands during construction. A lot of money could be made in speculation, much more than in constructing roads. Once you started building a road it took years before it was finished and the maintenance contracts were another poisoned chalice. It was a long-term commitment and a lot of hard work for meagre returns. His cousin loved these contracts because they guaranteed long-term income and support for his political ambitions.

Ariana knew it all. She remembered the countless emails she had to write pleading for new contracts and having to edit cryptic and ambiguous contracts, over and over again. She was stuck to this company like her boss was stuck to his contracts and his cousin. All in all, it was impossible to escape. So she focused on the small things in life: her husband, her kids and their school friends, school evenings, homework and school theme days, the office gossip and the affair of the striped underwear in her boss's bathroom. That certainly made her day.

Juan and Enrico were the first to come in.

'Good morning, Ariana,' Enrico said cheerfully.

'Thanks guys for coming in on your day off.'

'It's too damn hot in here,' Juan said. 'I feel like taking off my shirt, but I don't want to leave a trail of clothes behind. Is it always this hot on the fourth floor?'

'Guess what I found in the bathroom on the second floor?' Enrico said smiling.

'Striped underwear?' Juan replied.

'I wish!'

'It's obvious there are no secrets in this building,' Ariana observed. She didn't like her boss being mocked by his employees. It would undermine his position and hers too. She knew that some employees had been insinuating that the skimpy piece of underwear belonged to her.

'Not when you involve Secret Agent Rodeo, aka Blabbermouth!'

'Shh! This isn't common knowledge and there may be a police investigation.'

The door to the boss's office opened. Roberto Sousa took a seat and started the meeting without further ado.

'Ariana, could you start taking notes? We'd better start this meeting. Let's move straight to the first item on the agenda. It's almost eleven o'clock. I want to be done by noon. Over to you, Enrico.'

Enrico got up and walked over to the screen, turning it on with a remote control. It was difficult to see the slides with so much sunlight. Ariana had noticed this too and flicked a switch behind her to lower the blinds on all sides. Twelve electric motors started whizzing as the blinds descended in slow synchrony. Enrico paused and took a sip of water. It was like watching a solar eclipse. Light kept streaming in until the last centimetres had been covered and then it was suddenly pitch dark.

'We all know about our road construction project in West-Pará. We've already started widening the road in the first section, and I'd like to give you an update.' He showed a slide of the new section road; an endless strip of pristine tarmac, a black belt stretching all the way to the horizon, cutting through the dense jungle. 'The problem we're facing now, you can see in the next slide.'

The next slide showed a mud road with potholes and puddles. A truck was immobilized on the roadside by a broken axel. 'Imagine driving on a road like this… two hundred and thirty kilometres long, through dense jungle, driving at less than twenty kilometres per hour, pothole after pothole. And all it took was one night of torrential rain to wash away all the enabling works. If we can complete the next phase of the project in the next two months, we can avoid a similar scenario this year.'

'What's slowing us down?' Roberto Sousa asked.

'This!'

Enrico showed some slides of an enormous rock, at least twenty metres high.

'If we could blast our way through this, we could create a nice shortcut. It'll come at a price, but it'll pay itself back over time.'

'Can we afford it?'

'In my opinion, we can. We've got the expertise and a basement full of explosives near expiry date. We bought them for a previous contract. They come at no additional cost to the company.'

'But we can still charge for them!' Juan added.

'You got it!' Roberto Sousa beamed. He loosened his silk tie a little and opened the top button of his shirt. His mood had improved.

'And why haven't we started already?' asked Romero Oliveira, the chief engineer on the project.

'The proposed road will go through a protected area. Some local tribes use this rock as a religious site.'

'Bullshit, bullshit, bullshit!' Roberto Sousa banged his fists on the table to emphasise his frustration. 'We don't have to put up with the superstitious nonsense of some tribes in loincloths stuck in a time warp.'

'They may be dressed in loincloths, but they have a Twitter account and are very active on social media.'

Enrico got the next slides up.

'Here you can see various quotes from Twitter: #savethelastjungle. Ancient burial site under threat.'

'I can't bloody believe this.' Roberto Sousa hit his forehead with the palm of his hand in utter disbelief. 'I say stuff these idiots and let's get on with it.'

'You're the boss!' Enrico said.

'You better be quick. Before you know it, they'll mobilise celebrities and activists who'll tie themselves to those trees. Then the whole project gets stalled,' Juan said.

'Start as soon as you can. We can always erect a little shrine somewhere else later as a token of goodwill.'

'And if there's resistance?'

'Then we resort to our usual methods,' Romero Oliveira

said.

There was an awkward silence. Amazorico had been in the news during an extensive investigation two years ago, which concluded that a local tribe in Maranhão had been obliterated during a road and dam construction in a remote part of the Amazon. Locals found a mass grave, but a cause of death was never established. This led to wild speculations from mass suicide to poisoning, epidemic and cold-blooded murder.

'Of course we don't have to let it get that far,' Roberto Sousa hastily remarked.

'Offer them some money, some toys, some game consoles – that's what I meant,' the chief engineer continued.

'We'll do that anyway; starting with T-shirts and mugs and then we can crank it up a bit if there's still any resistance,' Juan explained.

'Exactly. We can always build a little school along the road or a health centre to please the local politicians,' Romero added.

The mood livened up again and the discussion quickly got side-tracked.

'Silence, please!' Roberto Sousa called out. 'Let's continue with agenda item two.'

Suddenly there was a loud bang above their heads. Plaster rained down on the table and the projector. Within seconds, the room was covered in dust and people started coughing. It was impossible to breathe or to see anything as more debris came down.

'Open those damn blinds, I can't see a thing!' Enrico shouted.

Ariana tried to get up and reach for the switch to open the blinds, but she was stuck underneath a pile of rubble. She could smell blood. She looked to her right and saw Juan's body lying underneath the table, his head crushed by a piece of ceiling, blood splattered everywhere. Ariana screamed at the sight of Juan's brains stuck to her tights. Her legs resembled a bloody mash of pulped muscles and squashed bones. That same instant she realised she couldn't move her arms or legs, and she felt no pain.

It was a surreal experience. The projector had fallen down and its light beam was directed at a far corner of the room. Then there was another explosion, a deep rumble; it felt like a tank division rolling down the street. Was this a rescue team? Ariana drifted in and out of consciousness. She cried out to her colleagues, but no one heard her feeble voice. Neither were there any other voices. She knew they were dead. Most of them she'd known for over ten years, all good, reliable lads. Ariana groaned in despair.

Within a split second her life as she knew it had changed. How would she cope? Then the floor gave way. It lasted a mere three seconds. There was no panic – she felt calm. She was surprised to realise that her sense of smell had lasted this long, detecting now the pungent odour of death, concrete, blood, sweat and coffee.

It soon grew dark; no more flashing lights from the projector and no more sunlight streaming in through the windows. It became cold, black and then silent – the sense of hearing went last. No more traffic noise, no more screams. It was a welcome silence: no end credits, no final theme song – just silence. The weight of the top floor collapsed onto the floor below and the floor below that, accelerating the destruction, leaving no time to think or raise an alarm, let alone escape or seek cover. The four-storey building had collapsed like a house of cards. The head office of Amazorico Construction was now a four-storey hole in a row of office buildings. It had been a perfectly controlled demolition.

8

London

The weekend in the country had been a welcome break for Peter. He felt recharged, embracing the new week with optimism and hope. He was more jovial than usual when greeting the porter at the front desk. On his way up to the fourteenth floor, he hummed a tune that got stuck in his head, an uplifting earworm: 'Starfish And Coffee' one of his favourite Prince songs, a distant memory from his student days.

As soon as Peter strode out of the lift he almost walked into Anita, the floor manager's personal assistant.

'Just as I expected, nine o'clock sharp!'

'Yep, that's me, no exception to the rule.'

'Well…' Anita paused, her facial muscles contorted a little, her smile alternating between a frown and a neutral expression that feigned ignorance. 'The manager would like to see you,' she said.

Peter turned around, looking pale.

'Did he say why?' Peter tried to penetrate Anita's well-maintained facade. Her light-beige coloured business suit was immaculate, her blonde bob trimmed neatly, not a single stray hair. Two gold ear-studs with a small pearl inset enhanced her look. She wore a light blue, freshly ironed shirt – only the top button was undone. Anita was dressed for success, poised to move upward. Being the CEO's personal assistant could be next. She didn't reveal any emotion, though her voice was warm and pleasant.

'No, he didn't.'

'Shit,' Peter mumbled, dropping his shoulders and trying to control a sudden urge to go to the toilet. His nerves worked in sync with his digestive system, his bowels unable to disguise his unease. He clenched his buttocks and walked towards the manager's cubicle displaying an unusual level of trepidation.

Everyone knew that Cedric Mason didn't get on with Peter. Whenever they met by chance in the lift or near the water cooler, there'd be an awkward silence. Cedric would scroll through the messages on his iPhone to avoid eye contact. Peter never cared much for the manager either or for managers in general. He was used to seeing them come and go, the revolving door of the office management was always in motion. He was just another middle-manager, poured out of a freshly opened tin of newly qualified business school graduates, more focused on tables and graphs than human relationships. During the weekly meeting, Cedric Mason was often the first to make a sneering remark to Peter when he presented the weekly accounts. There was no love between them.

Peter reflected on recent events as he slowly made his way to the lion's den. The company was going through yet another restructuring following an aggressive acquisition by the billionaire investor, Mikhail Zoblovski. Peter had survived four restructurings. When he'd started out, the London-based insurance company had an illustrious reputation, with a three-hundred year legacy. Its first accounts dated back to the 1700s, the golden age of the West Indian spice trade. A model galleon in the lobby reminded employees of the company's rich history.

The century old company was taken over by an American conglomerate specialising in asset stripping before being passed on to a Hong Kong-based investment firm like an unwanted child from an orphanage and now Zoblovski owned it. To his credit the revitalised company had grown bigger and bolder over the last five years with new offices in New York, Hong Kong, Shanghai and Turks and Caicos. Zoblovski was a private man and was rarely seen. He ran the company via an intricate net of people he trusted. Peter got more information from the gossip columns in the Evening Outlook than from office briefings. According to the news, Mikhail Zoblovski collected airlines, metal works, oil refineries and sports clubs around the world, like a boy would collect Premier League football stickers. Peter had also seen photographs of Zoblovski in the paper, often seen in the company of a much younger woman in her early thirties, a ballerina at the Bolshoi. She looked like the Sugar Plum Fairy stepping out of the Nutcracker with her elegant pose and head slightly tilted upwards like a Degas statue, a pretty dancer working her way up from a 1970s St Petersburg apartment block. Thousands of hours of painful practice, rehearsals, competitions, auditions and a gruelling performance schedule had finally paid off. She'd won the jackpot. The gossip pages loved this modern day fairy tale and there was a lot of speculation about an upcoming wedding. Mikhail didn't like this kind of media exposure; he preferred to see his name mentioned favourably in the economy section of papers and magazines. Of course, what was missing in his collection was an insurance company in London to offset his taxes against his other companies.

Duncan saw Peter's worried look as he passed his desk. He stood behind him and clapped Peter on his back, a jovial touch. 'You may get fired and that would be the start of a new beginning. I'll give you some advice: just say thank you and take the golden goodbye. Don't make a fuss and above all, don't grovel. Hold your head high! Think of Kevin Spacey in the film American Beauty.'

'Thanks, mate, but it didn't end well for that guy.'

'True, but he had the guts to stand up against his boss, and that's how he'll be remembered. You have to be the master of your destiny. Don't let these bastards get you down.'

'It's easy for you to say that, I hate to be put on the spot. You know that Cedric hates my guts.'

'Come on, mate, you're exaggerating. Cedric is just immature. He's risen too quickly, flying too close to the sun. One day he'll come crashing down.'

'Sure, but I won't be there to witness that.'

'Perhaps none of us will, but it's his destiny. What goes up must come down, rule number one in the world of finance!'

Peter walked to the end of the long corridor crossing paths with Emily. She felt sorry for Peter. His hunched look made him look like a condemned prisoner walking to the gallows.

'Hold your head high, Peter,' Emily called to him before she opened the toilet door.

Peter tried to focus on his breathing and wiped his sweaty palms on his trousers before knocking on Cedric's door. He didn't wait for an answer and opened the door with some hesitation, at first just a couple of inches in anticipation of some abuse. As he didn't hear Cedric barking 'Close the bloody door!' or throw a stapler or a mug at him, he opened the door a bit further. He heard Emily's voice in the back of his head and straightened up, stepped forward and said in a more cheerful tone than he intended, 'Hi, Cedric! You wanted to see me?'

'Just take a seat,' Cedric said curtly as he continued to stare at his computer screen. His body language said it all. He wasn't happy. He looked extremely annoyed. It was a familiar face. Something hadn't gone the way he planned. Peter looked around him; there was an awkward silence. Cedric's office was quite stark. No artwork, no plants, not even any knick-knacks on a shelf or family pictures. There wasn't a single personal touch; it looked as spartan as a cheap hotel room. The only splash of colour came from a couple of printouts of the latest sales figures pinned onto the wall directly behind Cedric's desk.

'They don't look bad,' Peter remarked, trying to break the ice as he pointed at the graphs. Peter was the one who produced these graphs and all preceding fifteen years' worth of weekly growth charts.

'Are we waiting for somebody?' Peter asked after two minutes of uncomfortable silence that followed.

'Someone will come down to collect you.' Cedric didn't

look up. He just kept looking at his computer screen like it was a crystal ball.

Peter feared the worst; he should have made more of an effort with Cedric.

Then there was a knock on the door. Peter tried to guess who it could be. It was a determined but polite knock.

Peter looked at Cedric, who sat behind his desk motionless, almost frozen and didn't react at all. Then after five seconds came a louder knock, followed by a couple of shorter, lighter knocks, a rap more than a knock. Cedric lifted his head. He slowly engaged with the rest of the world again. Then the door opened wide.

'Why didn't you say anything, Cedric?' a woman said.

Peter turned around and was pleasantly surprised to see a familiar face.

'Sylvia!'

'Hi, Peter, I've come to get you.' Sylvia stretched her arm and shook his hand.

Peter smiled. His prospects were looking up. Sylvia was the new owner's personal assistant. Owners changed but Sylvia remained a constant, the captain navigating the ship. She looked attractive in her white shirt, curly auburn hair and a matching tartan red skirt, which was somewhat shorter than office policies allowed.

'You don't mind if we borrow Peter?' Sylvia said to Cedric.

'Be my guest,' Cedric growled.

'Oh, you're such a grump,' Sylvia remarked. 'People like him just sap staff morale,' she added on the way towards the lift. 'Peter, we've got a little problem and we'd like you to meet somebody upstairs.'

'Sure.' Peter felt apprehensive. Bad news often gets wrapped up nicely and delivered like a sandwich. He imagined the news: 'We really like your work, Mr Miller, but we have to let you go – company reshuffle, I'm sure you understand. But... with a résumé like yours, you'll find another job in no time. I'm sure you don't want to be stuck in a dead-end job forever. Good luck, Mr Miller.' Peter had it all rehearsed in his head.

'I'm glad that you agreed to come with me.'

Peter didn't reply.

Sylvia pressed the button. While waiting for the lift, she put her hand through her hair and straightened her skirt.

The lift was empty. Sylvia pressed the button for the top floor, a secret domain to which Peter had never been granted access.

'We're going to have a chat with Human Resources,' Sylvia said casually.

Peter let out a sigh. He tried to relax his buttocks but was worried about the unwelcome consequence of doing so.

'Couldn't Cedric have just fired me? Do we have to go through all these formalities? I don't need any counsellors on standby when you deal the blow.'

'Have you got any idea how many lawyers work for our company? We do everything by the book. We don't want any relatives to sue us,' Sylvia said to tease Peter.

'Relatives?'

'Relatives, you know. Some people can't take bad news, so they jump off a building or in front of a train, and then we get blamed. We've got to follow procedures and guidelines to the letter,' Sylvia replied deadpan. Her eyes twinkled at the same time but Peter was too nervous to notice.

Peter swallowed. He remembered Duncan's advice. Take it on the chin!

The lift doors opened and Sylvia walked across a long corridor in a steady and purposeful gait.

'Here we are!' She opened the door.

'May I present you Carla Griffin, head of Human Resources, and Mr Prudzinsky, head of Fraud Investigation.'

Peter's face drained of all remaining blood. His palms became sweaty and his upper lip beaded with sweat. He nervously wiped these drops away with his sleeve.

'Thanks, Sylvia, that'll be all,' Carla said.

'Peter, how many years have you been working for us?'

'Just over fifteen.' Peter composed himself and gave short and unemotional answers. There was a slight tremble in his voice.

'That's correct. Never a day of sick leave?' Mr Prudzinsky continued.

'No, sir.'

Mr Prudzinsky scribbled this on a sheet of paper leaving a palpable pause before asking the next question.

'Always leaving on time, never any overtime?'

'I'm afraid not.'

Carla smiled; she noticed Peter's weary look and short answers. 'Don't look so scared, we like your self-discipline. You're efficient, good at prioritising, and quite rightly so! Every evening you make a beeline for the Tube station at five o'clock on the dot. I really admire that in a man, a man brave enough to commit to his family.'

Peter cleared his throat and smiled. His worries started

to melt away. He shuffled to the seat, sat down, and straightened his back.

'And your reports are excellent. Every week on time: neat and very detailed,' Mr Prudzinsky said.

Peter nodded, taking in his compliment silently.

'You're reliable and committed! That's a rare trait these days. Staff turnover in the City is just too high. You never know who you can trust.'

'And that's the reason we want to talk to you,' Carla interrupted.

'Our owner, Mr Mikhail Zoblovski, is a stickler for details and he happened to spot some, let's call them anomalies, especially in the Hong Kong and New York branches.'

Peter looked at the pile of papers neatly stacked between Mr Prudzinsky and Carla Griffin. The front sheet was covered with scribbled question marks and yellow stripes from a highlighter.

'We'd like you to help us with the investigation.'

'Why me? I don't fancy flying to Hong Kong,' Peter said sounding alarmed.

'Don't worry about the details. You don't have to fly anywhere. We've got all the files here for you. All you have to do is to confirm our suspicion.'

'Sylvia will bring your files one by one each day.'

'Can't you just email them?'

Carla started to laugh. 'We might as well post them on Facebook. We're no WikiLeaks. This is a strictly confidential internal investigation. Mikhail Zoblovski has his own way of dealing with the outcome of your report.'

'As I said, Sylvia will bring you the files every morning.

Some files are large and it may take several days to work your way through them. You can use pencils and highlighters, all very low tech.'

'And what about my own work, my weekly reports?'

'Don't worry about that, it's time that someone else was doing that for you. We've just outsourced your entire department to Bangalore. Cedric is going to oversee this project himself; he'll be leaving by the end of next month.'

'Is that why he looks more glum than usual?' Peter quipped.

Nobody replied.

'When do I start?'

'As soon as you've signed these papers. Just a formality.'

Peter looked at a daunting pile of papers.

Carla opened the documents at a tabbed page; all Peter had to do was sign. She pointed her finger at the bottom of the page.

'And how about a pay raise?'

'You should have asked for that before you signed,' Carla replied sternly.

'I haven't signed yet.' Peter was hovering his pen above the dotted line.

'Your payment depends on the outcome. It's a percentage of the money we can recoup,' Mr Prudzinsky explained.

'It'll be in the order of a hundred and twenty K, at least,' Carla reassured him. 'Perhaps even double.'

'Not bad. I can finally pay off my mortgage and retire.'

'Who said anything about retiring? Once you've solved this, there are many more investigations. Fraud is a global phenomenon. You can make a name for yourself,' Carla said.

'Besides, you'll get bored staying at home; you're way too young to retire. Or have you made any plans already, any interesting hobbies perhaps?' Mr Prudzinsky added.

'Not particularly.'

Mr Prudzinsky leaned forward to shake Peter's hand.

'It's great to have you on board,' Carla said enthusiastically. She walked to the door and signalled to Sylvia to come and get Peter.

'I'll escort you back to your floor. Tomorrow I'll come and find you at your desk, sometime after nine; it depends on when the accounts department releases all the files. I don't want to put a damper on your promotion, but please keep it quiet, it may cause some unneeded envy amongst some of your colleagues, if you know what I mean?'

Peter nodded, beaming. On the way to the lift, he even skipped. It had taken fifteen years but finally his hard work and dedication was being recognized. Standing in the lift on the way down, he looked in the mirror, straightened his back and adjusted his tie.

9

'Well, if you don't mind sleeping on a foam mattress, you can stay for a couple of days, but I want you out before the weekend when my boyfriend comes over,' Virginia said over the phone.

Claudia felt relieved; she was tired from her long journey from Brazil. She put her small backpack down outside the Eurostar arrivals hall. Someone was playing piano; the station looked welcoming. She tilted her head. The roof of the building was spectacular, a fitting tribute to the Industrial Revolution. She was sure it would all work out.

'That'd be great. I promise you I won't be staying more than two or three nights. I'll find my own place real soon.'

'Meet me at Café Gloria in Islington, opposite Angel station, and I'll give you my keys.'

'I will, I definitely will, I'll meet you in thirty minutes.'

'You know how to get to Angel station?' Virginia sounded a bit more helpful now.

'Yep, I'm sure I can work it out.'

Virginia hung up. Claudia looked around her and saw

an empty bench, not far from the upright piano. An older gentleman with a black velvet hat and a grey dishevelled raincoat played the piano beautifully. A group of young backpackers were sitting around the pianist; one of them asked him to play 'Yesterday'. He ignored the request, and played an arrangement of 'Let It Be' instead. Claudia felt relaxed. She sat down and studied the Underground map she'd picked up from a stand near the exit. It looked complex; none of the routes seemed straight. It was a mishmash of brightly coloured lines. Angel station, however, was only one stop away on the black line. She had plenty of time.

She was pleased that her Brazilian expatriate network had helped her land on her feet. Virginia was the older sister of a school friend. They'd met briefly at a party before she left for London. Virginia offered an open invitation to all friends, acquaintances and random people she met at parties in the safe bet that none of them would ever come and visit.

Café Gloria was directly across a busy road, not far from Angel Underground station. The journey from the Eurostar terminal was easy enough. The escalator up to street level seemed endless. The area around the station looked a bit run-down, though in an old-fashioned and charming way, she thought, quite unlike some downtown areas in São Paulo. The area in the vicinity of Angel station would have perfectly suited an English period drama; it seemed stuck in time, unchanged since the eighteenth or nineteenth century, an artefact of history. She could imagine Sherlock Holmes combing the streets of this neighbourhood looking for clues, Harry Potter flying on a broomstick high above the Victorian houses with their beautiful gables and quaint chimneys. It all seemed to belong to a different era. Though London was one of the biggest cities in Europe, according to her guidebook there were surprisingly few high-rise flats. It looked more like an enormous village. In the area where Claudia had grown up, there were only large apartment blocks as far as the eye could see, often more than thirty storeys high. Apart from the iconic curved Copan Building, most buildings looked uniform, clones of the same 1960s and '70s blocks, a relentless concrete jungle.

Virginia looked up when the door opened and walked over to Claudia as soon as she entered. Claudia recognised her right away and smiled. Virginia hugged her and introduced her to Ignas, the barista, as her school friend from back home. He looked hip with bleach-blonde short hair and a Breton shirt.

'Another fortune seeker,' Ignas remarked.

'Indeed, but only for a few months to learn some English.'

'That's what they all say,' he replied. 'London is the party capital of Europe. You'll never leave. Once you've lived in London for a few months, the rest of the world looks provincial, a dull backwater – you'll never go back. Look at me; I came from Lithuania three years ago. I'm still here making espressos and lattes.'

'Ignore him. He just got sucked into the gay scene, that's why he doesn't want to leave.'

'I heard that!' Ignas replied, pretending to be offended.

'Why don't you make my friend a nice cappuccino? I bet she needs some caffeine after such a long journey.'

The barista turned around and filled the portafilter basket

with freshly ground coffee from the doser, clicked it back into the group head and opened the steam valve with a delay of a few seconds. It hissed violently. Ignas dipped the steam wand into a jug of milk to froth it up and minute later he placed a skilfully decorated cappuccino in front of Claudia.

'It's on me. Welcome to London.'

'Thank you very much!'

Claudia stirred her cappuccino, waiting for Virginia to ask her some questions. She liked the cafe – it was so different from Mario's cocktail bar. It was quiet and dark, with soft music playing in the background. A customer was reading a newspaper at a long table. He looked serene, cocooned off from the modern world.

'Not many of my friends make it all the way to London,' Virginia said to break the ice.

'It's a long way to go and the ticket was expensive.'

'Indeed, that's what they all say.'

'It is a major obstacle. I am sure that many of your friends were planning to come over but were brought back to reality when they checked the airfare,' Claudia said.

Virginia waved her arm in front of her, dismissing Claudia's comment. 'Ah... they soon forget about us. Life goes on, I suppose. We're the ones who left. Anyway, I'm looking forward to catching up with you on some gossip tonight.'

'I've got loads to tell you! You missed out on some juicy stories.'

'Great.' Virginia hesitated before continuing. 'I hope I wasn't too hard on you. Finding a room in London isn't easy and finding a cheap place is impossible. You can take your time. I'm sure we'll get along.'

'I'll be out of your way when your boyfriend comes over.'

'I can always go to his place.'

'What do people do over here? How do they manage?'

'No idea. Many of my friends still share a flat and a fridge with strangers, even after the age of thirty. Some friends even share rooms.'

'That can't be true. Doesn't anybody complain? Isn't there enough social housing?'

'The last thing they'll do is complain; they just grin and bear it, they take it lying down. Londoners know how to turn suffering into an art form. Don't expect any revolution soon.'

Claudia nodded, though she didn't know what Virginia meant. 'But there must be another way?'

'Dream on! Most social housing has been sold off years ago, and those flats are now changing hands for an insane amount of money. Honestly, owning property is way out of our league. Don't even think about it. Live cheap, save some money, send it home and when you go back in a couple of years, you'll have a nice sum waiting for you in the bank.'

'Nobody told me about that before I left.' Claudia dropped her shoulders and stared at her empty cup.

'Don't worry about it; you've only just arrived. Some of us get lucky. You may find an elderly lady who needs a live-in caretaker. Those are much sought after jobs. Some pensioners live in these enormous mansions in Hampstead or Belsize Park but haven't got the money to heat the place. Instead of selling up, cashing in and living a life of comfort, they huddle underneath a blanket with their arthritis and aching joints, next to the only gas stove – and that's in flats and houses worth millions. All they need is some company and help cooking a meal.'

'I wouldn't mind doing that at all, it beats sleeping on a mattress on the floor.'

'Don't be ungrateful, I'm doing you a massive favour.'

Claudia blushed. 'Of course, I'm very grateful.'

Virginia got up and took some keys from her jeans and put them on the table.

'Don't lose them; these are the only set I've got. The landlord charges a fortune for a duplicate.'

'Don't worry, I never lose keys.'

Virginia wrote down her address on a piece of paper and showed her the best way to get to Brockley.

'On a good day, it takes forty minutes.'

'And on a bad day?'

'An hour!'

'One more question. Where should I start looking for a job?'

Virginia smiled; she liked to see how Claudia took initiative. No doubt she'd go far.

'Check on Gumtree. You can always find a job handing out flyers. That's what I did for the first few weeks, handing out flyers for shops or for shows, musicals, and concerts, that kind of stuff. It doesn't pay that well, but you'll meet lots of people. You never know. Mind you, lots of weirdos and loonies will try to talk to you too.'

'They're harmless. It can't be worse than São Paulo.'

'Sure, honey, nothing's worse than São Paulo. One thing you can say about us Paulistanas, we're streetwise and we don't take any crap.'

'I better get my arse into gear.'

'For someone who arrived only an hour ago, you're doing pretty well.'

A few more customers came in; it was a cue for Virginia to walk back to the counter and get to work.

'We can have a drink when I come home,' Virginia said when Claudia walked out.

'I'll buy a bottle!' Claudia said just before closing the door.

Virginia looked our through the window of the cafe and smiled when she saw Claudia walking toward the Underground station. She reminded her of herself. She'd also relied on some vague contacts she had.

Claudia checked her watch; it was almost rush hour. She wondered if it was too late to start looking for a job. Near the station entrance she almost bumped into a guy in the middle of the pavement handing out a free paper. She hadn't seen him.

'Evening Outlook, love?' he said with a big smile.

'Sure, thanks.'

Claudia looked at the front page; there was a picture of a bland looking man in a dark suit whom she didn't recognise. Then she stopped in her tracks and walked back to the guy handing out the papers. The metal rack behind him was almost empty.

'Excuse me. Do you know how I can find a job handing out newspapers?'

'Why do you want to do that?'

'I'm new in London, I don't speak much English and I have no idea what's going on in this city, so handing out newspapers and reading them may get me somewhere.'

'Keep dreaming, love; I've been doing this for months. The money's OK but you have to get used to thousands of people every day grabbing your paper and ignoring you, like you were a newspaper-dispensing robot.'

'I can live with that!'

'Well, in that case, stay here, Jimmy'll drive by any moment to bring some papers. He'll know exactly where they need someone.'

'Well, I'd be happy to try it.'

'Just wait for Jimmy, he'll be here any minute. He's already fifteen minutes late.'

Half a minute later, a white van with green livery came to a screeching halt. The front wheels crashed onto the pavement; there wasn't enough space on the street to park. A man jumped out, yanked open a big sliding door and rolled out a large pile of papers, fresh from the press.

'These are the latest ones with new headlines. Have you got any copies left?'

'Nope, all gone.'

'Good job. I'll be back in another hour or so, just finishing my round. Keep it going, try to get rid of all of 'em.'

'Mate, you don't happen to know if they're looking for another distributor?'

'You're kidding me? Every day I'm looking for distributors, half the bloody time they don't even have the effing decency to tell the agency they're not coming any more. Take today, there's nobody at Oxford Circus. I've got a service gap at Aldgate East and Liverpool Street station, and that's just my round. I just drop off a pile of papers and people help themselves. It doesn't look good but what can I do?'

'I can help you,' Claudia said.

Jimmy started to laugh. 'Are you kidding, love?'

'I'm serious. I just arrived today and I'm looking for a job.'

'Well, I'm not going to turn down an offer. Hop on! You know what, why don't you do the Liverpool Street station spot. Mind you, you can't trust bankers with your money, but they never give our distributers any trouble. I wouldn't put you anywhere near Whitechapel.'

'I've never even heard of those places.'

'Trust me, you'll hear about 'em soon enough. Keep reading that paper.'

The traffic was just as bad as in São Paulo, though there was less noise; nobody honking their horns like a herd of wild elephants. People seemed to endure the traffic with a calm patience unfamiliar to Claudia. Though Jimmy was cursing at anyone who crossed his path, he suppressed his anger. He didn't roll down his window to shout at anyone, and he certainly kept his distance from the car in front with the serenity of a Tibetan monk. And with the grace of a true gentleman he even let the odd taxi get in front. But this civility had a thin veneer.

'Those bloody cyclists. Do you have them in Brazil? They're maniacs, obeying their own laws, have no respect at all! Look over there – jumping red lights, paying no attention to zebra crossings. They just pop out from all directions. Never realise that if I can't see 'em in my mirror, I can't see 'em. The other day I was pulling up near the station to deliver some papers and a guy in bright yellow Lycra cycled straight into me as I was opening the sliding door, like a deranged jack-in-the box.'

Claudia just looked out the window; she had no idea where she was. She didn't pay much attention to Jimmy's rants.

'Look for yourself!' Jimmy lifted his shirt and showed her a large bruise next to an equally large tattoo. 'I was lucky I wasn't knocked over. They're pests.'

'Well, at least they help the environment.'

'What good is it to help the environment and crisscross through the city like bloody devils? They'll be extinct before the sea levels rise if they continue to drive like kamikazes. They may want to save the planet, but they're not doing themselves any favours. They're a bloody menace!'

Claudia had to laugh; she only understood half the things he said but he talked in the same animated way and with the same intonation as taxi drivers in São Paulo.

10

Peter was walking on air. He hadn't told his wife about his promotion yet. He would surprise her tonight, Wednesday night, with a homemade gourmet meal and some nice wine to celebrate his new position as Financial Fraud Investigator. He must have walked faster than usual as he emerged from the lift at six minutes to nine.

'Hi, Peter, are we early today?' Anita asked. 'Trying to impress the manager? Did he give you a hard time yesterday?'

Peter stopped and smiled. He walked over to Anita's desk instead of making his usual beeline to his own. He'd been sworn to secrecy and played along. 'I guess I have to roll up my sleeves like everybody else.'

'Glad to hear the penny's finally dropped. It's taken a while, you slacker.'

Duncan joined the banter. 'I was worried they'd sacked you without giving you a proper send-off. Glad to see you, mate. It wouldn't have been the same without your sparkling personality.'

Peter took it on the chin and brushed off Duncan's

sarcasm.

'Back to the same routine, I guess. The new sales figures from Hong Kong came in last night, so there's plenty of work to do.'

'There's always plenty of work to do, Peter. The conveyor belt never stops.'

The morning passed by quickly, and around midday Peter was getting anxious about the new job. So far he hadn't heard from Sylvia. Cedric, the floor manager, had kept to himself in his own cubicle, the blinds drawn. He was glad he hadn't told Joanne about his promotion, which as the hours dragged on looked like an empty promise. At twenty minutes past one, Peter couldn't contain his nerves any longer. He started pacing up and down the small corridor near his cubicle.

'Are you getting nervous about something, Peter? You're not your usual self.'

Peter didn't reply.

'Cedric must have given you a right clip around the ear.'

Peter looked at the clock. 1:25. By now he was bursting to use the toilet. His nerves had a profound effect on his bladder. He was shaking and all out of sorts. He wasn't sure why this promotion meant so much to him. Was it a sign of finally being recognized? Was it time to get out of his shell and take whatever life threw at him with open arms? Or was it merely a tantalizing carrot held out in front of him only to be withdrawn?

When Peter returned to his desk, he saw Sylvia chatting with Duncan.

'We thought you'd done a runner,' Duncan teased Peter.

'I just went to the toilet.'

Sylvia had a large pile of A4 folders in her arms. She carefully placed them in front of Peter's keyboard. 'These are the files we were talking about. It took me all morning to get the right order. This is just the beginning. We've got a warehouse full of them for you to work through.'

'That'll keep me busy for weeks!'

'Nope. I'll collect these folders again at five today. I have to make sure they're locked up overnight. I expect you to have finished these by then. I'll come back with more tomorrow morning.'

Peter looked at the pile of work in front of him. He had four hours to get through them. 'This is a Herculean task.'

'Poor Peter, I hope we didn't overestimate you. This is the time to prioritise. Our Bangalore branch will produce your reports from now on. Cedric is coordinating it as we speak. See you before five! You'd better get cracking.'

'I'll leave you alone with your mountain of work, Peter. I'm glad I'm not in your shoes. I'd finish those files first if I were you and prepare your financial report at home,' Duncan said.

'That would be a first, taking work home. I've never crossed the border between work and non-work!'

'Welcome to the real world. It amazes me that you've lasted this long without going the extra mile. I work from home all the time, sometimes till after midnight.'

'That brings new meaning to the word "slave labour".'

'There's no escape, mate. Keep your eye on the money, pay off your mortgage and get the hell out of here, that's my advice.'

'Cheers. That's exactly what I've got in mind. Thanks for the tip!'

Sylvia had ordered the files chronologically, and that made his work a lot easier. It was obvious that the Singapore and Hong Kong branches had used the same tax loopholes and that large sums of money had disappeared into a Turks and Caicos bank account. More worrying was the amount of money used to invest in unauthorized share dealings. Peter estimated the loss of this particular transaction to be $16 million. It wasn't clear who the main beneficiary was.

At four-forty, Peter turned over the last page of the last file. His work was done. He folded his arms and rested his head on the pile of papers. He must have dozed off as suddenly he felt a tap on his shoulder. Sylvia stood behind him.

'All finished?'

'Indeed. In the nick of time!'

'Well, I'm glad that you're not disappointing us. I'll bring you another set of files tomorrow morning. Enjoy your evening!'

Sylvia disappeared as quickly as she had arrived. She walked to the lift resolutely. Peter was proud of his achievement. He could either break his routine and finish his regular work before going home, or take his work home and jeopardise a nice dinner with Joanne. He could also try winging it tomorrow during the weekly accounts meeting. Peter felt uncomfortable about having his own work outsourced. He decided to have a look at the figures himself. He hated the idea of not being prepared for tomorrow's meeting. He reckoned that he could finish some of this work on the train home. It was just a matter of cross-checking all the accounts. He printed an anonymised version of the latest sales figures. If he left it behind on the Tube, nobody would be able to trace it back to the company. At five p.m. he stepped out of the lift and turned onto busy Bishopsgate. He was elated. The day had been an emotional rollercoaster, but it definitely called for a celebration.

Peter went into a wine shop near Liverpool Street station and bought a nice bottle of Châteauneuf-du-Pape, one of Joanne's favourites. It reminded her of their first holiday together in Avignon while backpacking through Europe.

Waiting by the till to pay for his bottle, Peter stared out of the window. He saw a steady stream of people passing by. What at first was a trickle of office workers had swelled into a dense mass of commuters desperate to get home quickly, like a lava stream gaining momentum before solidifying at a pedestrian crossing. As soon as Peter stepped outside, he couldn't help getting dragged along in the mass; going upstream would have been impossible. He looked over his shoulder, and all he could see was a sea of people, though more of a North Sea, Skegness kind than the Mediterranean-Juan-les-Pins variety.

After a few minutes, Peter bumped into a young woman with an outstretched arm handing out the Evening Outlook.

A trolley with a stack of newspapers protruded into the stream like a rocky outcrop, forcing commuters to slow down. It was an effective way to hand out more papers. Peter wasn't quick enough to dodge the trolley; he got stuck between the woman's trolley and the constant stream of people. He tried to catch his breath and jump in again at the right moment. He was puzzled. Usually his walk from the office to the station was less busy, less hectic. His ten-minute delay in the wine shop had cost him dearly. None of these people, he thought, left on the dot like he did. He hoped that with his new project he would still be able to leave on time.

'How about a paper while you're stuck?' the woman said. She had a radiant smile. A blonde tuft of hair stuck out from the side of her woolly striped hat.

'No thanks, I've got some papers to read.' Peter held up the folder with his printouts.

'I don't blame you, even that looks better than the news today.'

Peter didn't reply as he was anxious to move on. After a few minutes, he was still stuck behind the trolley. He spotted a gap in the flow of commuters and waited for his chance. He took the opportunity to glance at the graphs.

The young woman laughed as she saw Peter resigned to his awkward position.

'It looks like you're stuck forever.'

'Tell me about it!' Peter sighed with some frustration.

'Are you a banker?' the woman asked, keen to strike up a conversation, as handing out papers proved thankless and lonely.

'Me a banker? No, not at all! I'm a financial fraud investigator,' Peter said with pride. It was the first time he'd mentioned his new job title.

'That sounds interesting. I could have used someone like you a couple of weeks ago.'

'Where are you from?' Peter asked, knowing he'd be stuck for at least another few minutes as the pedestrian crossing lights changed signals.

'I'm from São Paulo.'

'You don't look Brazilian.'

'That's not very original. I get that a lot. Around two per cent of Brazilians are blond! Some of us have Scandinavian or German ancestry. By the way, I'm Claudia. I arrived last week, Claudia Valenti.'

'I'm impressed. And you've already found a job? I'm Peter, Peter Miller. I work in the big office block across the road.'

'That side's much quieter, a lot less people. That's why I chose to work on this side. I get through my papers a lot quicker. There you go, almost finished.'

Peter nodded and kept on reading his papers.

Claudia looked at him, hesitated for a moment and then asked, 'Would you mind having a coffee with me? I'd like to hear more about your fraud investigation.'

Peter was taken aback and looked at his watch to hide his embarrassment. 'Thanks, but I'm running late. I just bought a bottle of wine to celebrate some good news with my wife.'

An instant later he regretted saying it. He was flattered. In all those years of marriage, not a single woman had ever asked him out. His wedding ring had been an effective deterrent. With his youthful looks fading quickly, he knew that chances like this wouldn't come along forever. Perhaps his new job title had made him more confident, and women like a confident man. Peter rotated the bottle of wine in his hand. He looked at the label. Joanne would surely get suspicious if he came home later than usual.

'No problem, private investigator,' she said coyly. 'I

understand.'

'Financial fraud investigator.'

'Sounds equally thrilling to me!'

Peter felt uneasy. Perhaps it was best to say no and stay on his side of the street forever – or say yes and see what might happen. Did he ever allow chance to play a part in his perfectly calculated life? No, never. Perhaps this was another decisive moment. It would go down in Peter's history as the day he reinvented himself.

'I can't meet you after work, but I could meet you in the afternoon, for instance before you start your shift. Perhaps I can help you with your fraud investigation.'

Claudia had her back turned to Peter. He wasn't sure if she'd heard him. The young woman struck him like someone who moves on quickly. When she turned around to pick up a handful of papers from the trolley, she said, 'Oh, you still here? Yes, that'd be great. Meet me at Starbucks; there's one around the corner from here.' Claudia pointed in the direction of the coffeehouse.

Peter smiled from ear to ear. He felt a sudden rush of blood to his cheeks.

'I'm looking forward to that.'

'There you go, last few papers gone.'

A green and white newspaper delivery van stopped alongside the pavement. A young man jumped out, letting the engine run. He jerked the sliding door open and pulled out a large pile of papers.

'Claudia, well done. Here's the next edition, just off the press.'

'I was hoping you were stuck in traffic and wouldn't

come by for a second run tonight.'

'Sorry, love, we've got more papers to shift. It pays our wages!'

The van had blocked part of the pavement. This was an opportune moment for Peter to get going. He looked over his shoulder. He wasn't sure if Claudia meant what she said. She saw him look and shouted after him:

'See you tomorrow at half past one!'

'I'll be there,' he replied.

Claudia gave him a thumbs-up and carried on handing out newspapers. Peter looked over his shoulder once more. All he could see was her blue and white striped hat with a white pompom bopping up and down as she leaned towards the pile of papers and then stood up again to press them into people's hands.

Peter changed his strategy. The Evening Outlook van reversed, stopping traffic on both sides – nobody wanted their car damaged by a briskly reversing delivery van. Peter took advantage of the moment and dashed across the road before the driver shifted into first gear. He was glad to be back on the other side of the street. When Peter arrived at Shoreditch High Street station and looked at the departure screens, he realised he was late, very late. Twenty minutes later than usual. If he was lucky, he'd just catch the forty-three to Crystal Palace. He'd be home just before six-thirty.

Platform number two was teeming with people, many of whom stood dangerously close to the edge of the yellow platform. It was difficult. A train for Clapham Junction arrived and around half the people on the platform boarded.

He was pleased. It meant more space on the next train, and with some luck, even a seat – though there was no guarantee, at least not until New Cross Gate or Brockley, where most people got off. Soon the track would dive into a tunnel and Peter texted Joanne before he would lose his signal. 'Sorry for running late. I've got a nice bottle of wine and something to celebrate.' He pressed send. Just before the train arrived at Whitechapel, Joanne had answered back. 'Can't wait to hear the news. Jxxx.'

He never understood why she always had to add those xxx's at the end of each message. It seemed so unnecessary.

11

Virginia poured coffee she'd made in her Bialetti coffee maker and added a few nuts and a sliced pear to a small bowl of yoghurt. Claudia was awake but still lying on the mattress on the floor. It irritated her.

'The shower's free; why don't you go now before my boyfriend gets up. I've got to leave in twenty minutes.'

'I didn't even hear you getting up. I must have been fast asleep.'

'You were awake most of the night. You are so restless when you sleep. You must be over your jet-lag by now.'

'I don't know. So much has happened over the last month, I can hardly digest it. I'm so happy that I found a job, literally less than thirty minutes after I spoke to you.'

'I told you. London's full of opportunities for anyone who wants to work.'

Virginia put her mug of coffee down and tucked into her breakfast. Claudia stretched once more before going to the bathroom. She was wearing an over-sized T-shirt.

'There's a freshly washed towel on the shelf next to the

sink,' Virginia hollered.

At first Claudia had been surprised by the rickety state of the shower with its rusty old sprout, chipped tiles and fragile telescopic curtain rail. By now she had gotten used to it. The rim of the bath was covered in a thick grey-black layer of mould and the toilet was equally neglected, limescale had tainted the inside dark brown. Even with her experience of bathrooms she couldn't improve their appearance. Claudia had realised after flushing the toilet twice that these old Victorian houses didn't seem equipped for modern living. Claudia preferred the high-rise apartment block she had left behind. It was a solid structure where everything worked well. She twisted her body into odd angles to capture enough water to rinse the foam from her body. After ten minutes she felt refreshed. She wrapped her wet hair in a towel and walked back to the kitchen.

'Did you check the Brazilian news website recently?' Virginia asked.

'Nope, why?'

'I'll show you on my iPad. Apparently there was a big explosion in an office block in São Paulo a couple of weeks ago, not far from where we grew up. I hardly check the news myself. Brazil seems a world away!'

'Tell me about it. I completely lost touch myself, time flies,' Claudia feigned. She deliberately hadn't done any on-line searches to avoid leaving a digital footprint, an electronic tag shouting: I am in London now, come and find me.

'My mum sent a link to this page a few weeks ago. I never had the time to read it until now. Let me read some paragraphs out to you: The Amazorico head office was reduced to rubble in just seconds.'

'Amazorico? Well, that serves them right.'

Virginia looked up. 'Isn't that a bit crass? Why do you say that?'

'For decades they've been destroying the Amazon rainforest. They razed not just thousands of acres of jungle but they also wiped out the habitat of many animal species and obliterated the livelihood and homes of indigenous tribes. Don't they mention anything about that?' Claudia tried to justify.

Virginia read the next paragraph in silence. 'No, they don't mention that. In fact they praise Amazorico for having brought prosperity to hard to reach places in the jungle.'

'They've got it all wrong…'

'What do you mean?' Virginia asked.

'Don't know. Perhaps the attack was meant to raise awareness about the destruction of the rainforest,' Claudia was quick to reply.

'You mean an eco-terrorist attack?'

'An eye for an eye is a pretty strong message, don't you think?'

'That sounds a bit drastic. Can't anyone just take them to court instead?' Virginia scanned the rest of the article.

Claudia looked disappointed. The fireworks she had hoped for turned out to be a damp squib.

'Hang on, read this. The governor's cousin is said to have been killed along with four employees. They're trying to keep it low profile to avoid political embarrassment. But there's been a lot of speculation. They say the governor staged the attack to gain more control of the construction industry. It's sick, really. How can you murder your own cousin and all those employees and get away with it? It's truly sick!'

'What?' Claudia's face drained of all colour. She covered her mouth with her hand. Her eyes wide open, her heart racing, a rapid adrenaline response.

'Are you all right? You look like you've seen a ghost.'

Claudia swallowed, she looked shell-shocked. She didn't know what to say. What had gone wrong? The building was supposed to be empty. Rodeo had assured her that on Saturdays and Sundays the security cameras were being monitored off-site. Weekends in the office were eerily quiet. My God, all those people who had died. All those lives lost. She'd seen pictures on their desks of their families and loved ones. Damn, what had she done? She had been the one who planned it all, rigged the explosives and set the timer. In the eyes of the law she was nothing more than a dangerous terrorist, a mass murderer. Sooner or later it would be linked to her. All she had wanted was to make a statement. The collapse of the Amazorico office would send a strong warning. But now with so many people dead, everything had changed. She was in deep shit. Would she be safe here, across the Atlantic, nine and a half thousand kilometres away? Would she be able to live with such a heinous crime on her conscience? Would confessing to that crime and taking the consequences be the best option? Claudia ran several scenarios through her mind. She started perspiring profusely. She felt sick.

'Listen, check this. "It was an accident waiting to happen",' Virginia continued.

'Who says that?' Claudia stammered.

'That's the governor's official response. The basement was full of nearly expired explosives.' Virginia looked up. 'Are you feeling OK? You're sweating and trembling like a leaf.'

Claudia started to weep. What had she done? How could she ever get away with this? Her activism had led her to violence and murder. In the end, it was really no different from the destruction of the rainforest, in fact it was far worse, a million times worse.

Virginia got concerned and walked over to Claudia. She realised that her friend was very upset about this awful news in their home city; she put her arms around her.

Claudia's mind scrambled to make sense of what she had done. Perhaps this was a dichotomy that society had to come to terms with. Perhaps there was no growth and development without destruction. But what about those casualties? They were just hard-working people trying to provide for their families. She had crossed the thin line between eco-activism and terrorism.

She shook her head in dismay. She'd gone too far, way too far. She was in deep shit. Sabotaging Amazorico had always been her focus. Initially she had only planned to take Roberto Sousa hostage, force him to apologize on film, and make him donate his entire fortune to the Save the Last Jungle Foundation. All she had to do was wait for the right moment. But finding those explosives in the basement had seemed, at the time, too good to be true: it was a sign to take her fight to the next level. Had she really considered the consequences of her actions then? She shivered at the thought of being an internationally wanted terrorist. She had to keep quiet and surely not tell Virginia anything about this. The chances of the Brazilian police searching for her in south London were pretty slim. Looking out the kitchen window, she noticed the large tree obscuring her view. A grey squirrel jumped from branch to branch. London was so quaint, so peaceful and secure...

'My God, you are miles away.'

'Sorry, I feel awful about all those people!' Claudia answered hastily. She took another sip of coffee.

Virginia let her friend cry for a while whilst hugging her. When Claudia wiped away the tears she tried to cheer her up by changing the topic of conversation. 'How's the job? Don't you think it's time to move on? It seems such a waste of your talent.'

'Well, I figured out that my savings wouldn't last very long in Europe, so I just asked the first person I met and took the job they offered. I am grateful for the chance I have been given. Of course I'd love to do something else. I am looking.'

'Sorry I was a bit hard on you when you called from the station that first day. I don't want to come across as inhospitable. It's just that I didn't know you all that well. Last year, Julia came to stay with me – you remember Julia? She's a few years younger than us. Her mum and mine are good friends. Between them they'd arranged that Julia would stay with me and that I'd look after her like an older sister.'

'Yeah, I do remember her. Didn't she go out with Ernesto? He was great at basketball.'

'And so was Julia. She was the captain of our school team, wasn't she? I think that's how they met.'

'Anyway, that's the one – tall, willowy, big dark eyes.

Well, it turned out she didn't speak a word of English. I had to help her with everything! She was a total drain on my time and energy. She complained about everything: the weather, the food, how expensive everything was. She was homesick, missed her friends, her family, the local shopping mall and her boyfriend. They'd never been apart since they'd met. They were Skyping all the time, several hours a day. It drove me absolutely mad. I introduced her to my friends and all she could do was moan about London, moan about not finding a job – actually, she thought every job was beneath her. I told her these jobs were springboards to other things.'

'Is she still here?'

'I threatened to kick her out after six weeks. I barely saw my own boyfriend in that time. She was like a creepy shadow following me around everywhere. Her dad bought her a plane ticket back home. I haven't heard from her since.'

'I'm not like that. I like to find my own way. I settled into my job already, I have explored new parts of London and I am sure I'll find a better-paid job soon. But first I need to find my own place, not a flat share. Mario may be coming over next month.'

Virginia stood up, rinsed her mug under the tap and turned it upside down on the kitchen worktop to dry.

'I am glad we had this conversation, I don't want this to cause friction between us,' Claudia said.

Virginia smiled, looking relieved and kissed Claudia goodbye.

Claudia had a few hours to kill before the start of her evening shift; she couldn't bear staying in the flat on her own. Most mornings she'd attend her language course but with the first part of the course completed she had some time for herself. A walk around the quiet neighbourhood would clear her mind. The weather was grey and grim but refreshing at the same time. São Paulo also had some grey depressing days when the amount of air pollution obscured the sun for days on end. It was unbearable in a different way.

Claudia browsed through a few charity shops, looking for another pair of boots and a warm coat. She couldn't believe what a bargain these shops were. Some of the items seemed brand new or hardly ever worn. After a while, she got tired of shopping and entered an inviting-looking cafe at Brockley Cross. The rich chocolate brownies were to die for, the coffee was strong and the music was uplifting; living in London was growing on her.

The cafe had withstood the criticism of a Paulistana, who had grown up on great artisan food. When it came to food, London hadn't been as bad as her friends had warned her. Nevertheless she couldn't escape an intense feeling of guilt and remorse. What was she to do now?

A waitress clearing her table interrupted Claudia's train of thought and asked her if she needed anything else.

Claudia looked up. 'Well, I've been in London for just over a month and I'm looking for a small flat. Do you happen to know anywhere I could rent?'

'You should have asked me two days ago!' the waitress replied. 'My flatmate moved out, but that room's gone already. Sorry.' She wiped the tabletop, collected Claudia's plate and left again.

'Thanks all the same.' Claudia looked disappointed. She shrugged. Perhaps she should just keep on asking random strangers when handing out the evening paper. Taking advantage of the free Wi-Fi she sent a short message to Mario: 'Love being in London. I'm sure you'll love it too. You could set up a nice cocktail bar in the neighbourhood where I'm staying! Miss you xxxC.'

Claudia waited for a reply. It was more than three weeks since she had heard from Mario. She had kept his last message, he had sounded like he was planning to come and visit. After a few minutes there was still no reply. She got up and wrapped her scarf around her neck. Claudia enjoyed dressing up for winter. A bobble hat, a striped scarf, black leather boots and a warm coat, there was so much choice. It was much easier to express your personality in winter clothes than in summer dresses. Now all she needed was some money and a place for herself and Mario, if he would ever come.

A cool breeze entered the cafe when Claudia opened the door. Her scarf came undone, she stepped back into the cold drizzle – the cold weather in February didn't matter to her. It'd be spring soon enough but the permanent dark cloud inside her head was here to stay for a long time. How could she ever learn to live with herself? Should she turn herself in? Present herself at the nearest police station? Perhaps she should confess to a priest, see a counsellor or bury the whole affair deep into her brain and hope it would never resurface again.

12

Tom was the first to see an old Air Solinca jumbo jet across the field behind a row of trees. It looked surreal, out of place like a ballerina at a barn dance or an elephant on stilts in a Salvador Dalí painting. The remains of the Queen of the Skies was towering over the flat Suffolk countryside. Its paint was flaking, its engines removed and some of the windows too. It looked sad and macabre. Peter had read in a Sunday paper that Boeing was scaling down production of the 747, which for him epitomized the end of a great era of glamorous international travel – not that he ever took part in it. Peter had known the small airport for years. As a child, it was easy to climb over the fence and sneak up to the runway and watch airplanes taking off. He and Barry had been chased away more than once by Royal Air Force personnel. With Norwich International Airport expanding, this small airstrip had fallen into decline until Barry tapped into the lucrative trade of airplane recycling at the back of his car scrapyard.

Peter had the perfect excuse for visiting Barry. He had spotted an old VW camper which Barry was selling online.

He'd promised his family that he'd take them on a tour around the UK in a camper. With his promotion, a substantial pay rise and a bonus at the end of the project, he was sure he'd be able to afford a second-hand VW, even though he was surprised by the asking price of £11,000. Peter did some more research and found that it was the going rate for campers like this one – they were in high demand. A newer Brazilian Kombi import would be around £20,000. Other makes were a lot cheaper, but they lacked a certain bohemian appeal. Then again, as a financial fraud investigator, Peter was not exactly a bohemian.

The entrance to Barry's recycling yard was difficult to find. Peter had to reverse several times as he kept missing small tracks leading to the airport from the main road. At last he saw a small shed at the end of the main track. A light was on. A dog started barking as soon as Peter's car got closer. He turned the car around, parked at a safe distance, switched off the engine and waited for a minute.

'Tom, stay in the car, I'd better check this out first.'

A black and brown Rottweiler jumped up and down, jerking his lead. It was bearing its teeth and looked menacing.

The door of the shed opened and a big gruff man in a brown parka stood in the doorway.

'Quiet, old boy, quiet! Sit!' The dog responded to his owner.

The big man waddled over to the Volvo and inspected it from all sides.

'I've got plenty of stuff for this type. It's the last of its kind. So is the old, solid and reliable Volvo driver, the family man – a dying breed these days.' He sounded worn down.

'Thanks. I'm really here to have a look at this VW camper I found on your website.'

Barry squinted his eyes, cleared his nose and spat on the floor sideways.

'Well, have I ever… Peter, it's you, isn't it?' Barry's face perked up, and he beamed from ear to ear. 'Well, well, you lost your mop! You didn't get an ounce fatter, but what happened to your face? All those wrinkles!' Barry slapped him on the shoulder.

'Thirty years!'

'More than that – thirty-five at least! Where have you been?'

'You know, studied in London, worked for a bit, got hitched, kids, mortgage, job, and before you know it, I'm middle-aged.'

'Join the club. I did the same, minus the missus and the kids. Don't tell me I'm looking as old as you?'

'You must feel younger, being active and outdoors all day.'

'Dream on, my back's killing me, whisky's giving me gout and my doctor keeps on nagging me about my cholesterol. It's hard work, and youngsters these days haven't got the stamina. They all bugger off to Norwich, the big city lights. It's a shame really. There's good money to be made in this business. You need a new mirror for your car? It'll cost you two-fifty at least for a Volvo like yours. Come to Barry and I'll get you one for forty quid. I'll also spray paint it in any colour you like. You need a new wing after that small collision you had in the supermarket car park? Barry'll fix it. You name it; I've got it! But face it, without eBay I'd have packed up a long time ago. It's a new way of doing business.'

A car door slammed. Now that the dog had been quiet for a while, Tom was keen to join his dad and hear what they were talking about.

'Look at you! You look just like your dad back in the day. Spitting image.'

Peter smiled. He remembered the great times he and Barry had spent together during the holidays at his aunt's. Carefree fun.

'Are you guys staying in the area?'

'Yep, at Aunt Doreen's farm.'

'I remember your aunt. I ran into her the other day. She was a great cook. Always making cakes and pies.'

'Well, she still makes the best apple crumble.'

'Come over to my office, I'll make you a nice cuppa.'

Tim looked bemused at all the car parts and junk everywhere. It was a man's paradise. They followed Barry into his shed. It was dark and littered with piles of papers, MOT certificates, empty grease tins and spray cans in any possible colour. A pile of car tyres with a plank of wood over them served as a bench.

'Sit down, my friends.'

Peter wanted to ask about the camper, but it was hard to get a word in. Barry talked non-stop as if Peter was the first human contact he'd had in weeks.

'Look at this parcel, for example. A guy in Wales is after a new roof antenna, a shark fin for his BMW. Brand new, it would have cost him a fair bit of money. Come to Barry and he'll get it for a tenner. I charge a little extra for postage and packaging. I get a dozen of these requests every month. It's keeping me above water.'

'Can I have a look at the airplanes now?' Tom asked.

'Hey, steady, boy, you're just like your dad. We'll come with you. It can be dangerous roaming around on your own. Before you know it you'll fall through the fuselage and that's a fifteen-foot drop. I'm not one for health and safety, so you have to watch out yourself.'

'What about the camper you're trying to sell?'

'Are you sure? Have you ever driven one of those? They're old, over forty years old, also slow and noisy. They use a lot of petrol and they're bloody uncomfortable. You're better off sticking a mattress in the back of your Volvo. What do you need it for anyway?'

'An old promise I made to my wife, a touch of nostalgia. I'm also slowly getting fed up with my dull and boring life in the City.'

'Well then, join me,' Barry laughed. 'I can kick a mid-life crisis in the arse. Anyway, I could do with an extra pair of hands, and there's never a dull moment with Barry.'

'I'd love to! But just to set the record straight, I am not having a crisis.'

Barry ignored Peter's comment. He scratched his head, cleared his throat and spat on the dusty ground.

'Tell you what, I've been tinkering with an idea. There'll be an air show at the airport in April, the weekend after Easter. No doubt it'll get me some attention.'

'So what are you thinking of?'

'Something to impress the punters. Something lasting – a model spaceship.'

Peter started laughing. 'I love that idea.'

'Seriously, I think it'll be great and when the show's over, I'll rent it out on Airbnb.'

'Are you serious?'

'It'll put my scrapyard on the map, and it'll become a destination in its own right. A couple of pictures on the Internet and it may go viral.'

'Keep dreaming, pal.'

'Hey, it gets kind of lonely out here at times. I have to be creative.'

'And where are you going to build it?'

'Your aunt has a few empty barns, they're massive. Maybe she can rent one out to us. It's easier to work indoors.'

'When's this air show again?'

'In just over two months.'

'Whoa, you're leaving it a bit late. I'll speak to Aunt Doreen… I like the idea of building a model spaceship, but what's stopping us from building one for real?'

'Money and common sense?' Barry chuckled. 'Now you do sound like you're going through a mid-life crisis.'

'Christ, maybe you're right!'

'You know what, Peter? Why don't you just borrow it for a weekend, see it as an experiment.' Barry chuckled.

Tom was getting restless. 'Can I have a look at the planes now?'

'Let's first have a look at the camper,' Peter suggested.

Barry opened a drawer and rummaged through its contents for a while looking for the keys. He looked flustered when he finally retrieved the set he was looking for.

'Follow me,'

Tom rushed ahead of his dad and Barry. The dog was

running next to him, barking with excitement.

The camper Peter had set his eyes on was dark-red with white. It was an old-fashioned T2. He loved those. 'I can imagine Joanne's reaction.'

'Women love those vans for some reason. Call it nostalgia. Mind you, this old camper needed a lot of restoration. I did it myself last summer. It's a good runner. But as I said, not as fast or as comfortable as your Volvo. It's hard work. The clutch cable and the brake pads are new. You need to be realistic. A tour around the UK will take you weeks in a van like that.'

'I hope to retire soon. Time won't be an issue then.'

'I've heard that before – bored of the job, bored of life, early retirement! Retiring is for wimps! You should start doing something you're passionate about. Then you'll never think of retiring. They can cart me off in a box when I die. As long as I've got my hands and common sense, I'll keep on working.'

'Barry, I'll take you up on your offer. I'll borrow it for the weekend, and if we like it, I'll buy it.'

'High five, buddy! For old time's sake!'

'I am going to see the airplane now,' Tom said and shot off. The dog ran alongside.

Peter looked chuffed. He liked the idea of spending a weekend in the camper with his family. It would break up the monotony of the winter. He could imagine the family playing games together inside the camper whilst it was cold and raining outside, Joanne would love it.

'Come on, dreamer, let's catch up with your lad.'

Peter and Barry walked towards the airstrip.

'Barry, I said to myself some years ago, what can we do with this airport? I liked the guys who fly these small airplanes. Real enthusiasts – without them, this place would be dead. It gets really busy, especially during the weekends when the weather's nice. Don't get me wrong, I like my own company, but I'm no recluse. And more women are flying small planes these days, if you know what I mean.'

'Keen to get your leg over?'

A twinkle appeared in Barry's eyes.

'Some women like to talk fashion and celebrities, some women like to talk about cockpit gauges, flaps and landing gears with real men, like me. And sometimes things go wrong, especially after a rough landing, so they'll knock on my door to get some spare parts. I'll make them a cup of tea and just listen to them. You see, I've got all the time in the world. I'm not rushing about like you guys. Quality time. I'm the antidote for people who rush. And some women like that.'

'Glad to hear that romance isn't dead in this part of the world.'

Barry chuckled. He paused, then padded his parka and took out a pack of Golden Virginia tobacco and some Rizla rolling paper and with one hand made a perfectly shaped cigarette. He turned to Tom.

'You see that old 747?'

'Cool!'

'Yep, it was an Air Solinca jumbo jet. They went bankrupt in 2010. They didn't know what to do with their ancient fleet. It was too expensive to maintain, nobody was interested. I heard about it and offered to take it off their hands for free!'

'For free? You got a jumbo jet for free? How much do they cost new?'

'Over $300 million.'

'And you got that for free?'

'Well, this is a 1974 model and would have cost probably $25 million at the time. It's paid back its investment over the years, several times over. It was the airline's workhorse. They've used them to the max. Almost forty years of service, around forty thousand cycles of taking off and landing, and now it isn't economically viable. From a commercial perspective, it's not worth anything. Newer planes are more fuel efficient, lighter and simply better. Most airports charge thousands per week to park an airplane on their grounds. You have to look at this from the bank's point of view. The company went bankrupt. They're are trying to minimize any further costs, so giving it away will save them some serious money. And that suits Barry very well. Come on over to the hangar, I'll show you.'

Tom was really excited to get this close to the airplanes. He even spotted an old military jet.

'It's a specialized trade. I spend most of my time categorising spare parts, bolts, lightbulbs… you name it.'

'Who do you sell all this stuff to?'

'You'd be surprised. Some airlines, mainly non-European, rely on good quality, second-hand gear. Some of this early 747 material is high quality. But you'll be surprised to hear that I sell most things to private buyers. Plane nutters buy all sorts of aviation stuff. A pilot's seat sells on eBay for more than a thousand quid, a normal bog-standard economy class seat will start at two-fifty. They look cool in clubs and bars. Airplane wings could be turned into coffee tables or a kitchen worktop. A jet engine will sell for anything upwards of twenty-five grand, but nobody's bought that yet. So it's just boxed up to keep the dust out. One day a very sophisticated looking lady, probably in her fifties, drove up in a smart little Mercedes, an SLK, really sleek, pearl white. She said she used to be a flight attendant and wanted to buy an airplane trolley from me. Obviously she must have married well since she offered £400 for it. You should have seen the smile on her face. She rolled it towards her car in front of me, strutting like a business class purser. She must have thought she looked thirty years younger. I asked her what she was going to do with it.'

'What did she say?'

'She said she was going to use it to serve her husband his daily gin and tonic.'

Peter laughed. 'You haven't changed a bit, always wheeling and dealing.'

'That's what keeps me ticking. I'm master of my own destiny. I admire you, going to the same desk in the same office every single day. I couldn't do it.'

'Someone has to; makes the world go round.'

'Are you kidding me? Who's fooling who? It serves no purpose in life whatsoever; you're wasting your life!'

'What can you do with that jet engine?' Tom asked out of the blue.

'I don't know. I suppose you can strap it onto the back of that VW bus and fly to Mars.' Barry laughed, a deep roaring laughter; his chest was crackling and wheezing. He bent double and slapped his knee.

'Or park it outside your entrance. That'll certainly put your business on the map.'

'Great seeing you again buddy, I'll catch you next time you come over. I can't wait to start building that spaceship.'

'Mars, here we come!' Tom yelled before getting back into the car.

13

Halfway through the morning Peter felt the need to stretch his legs and walked over to the water cooler. He took a sip of water and stared out of the window.

'A penny for your thoughts,' said Anita, the admin support officer.

'Just thinking about last weekend.'

'I know what you mean. I'm already planning my next weekend – keeps me going through the week.'

Several more colleagues walked over to join Peter and Anita.

'So how was Suffolk?' Duncan asked.

'It was very good, actually. I met up with a long lost friend.'

'That's nice. Single?' Anita enquired. It was a question she asked all the time. Anita was in her mid-thirties and looking for a way out of temping. She no longer trusted her own judgment in finding eligible young men.

'Well, he's in his late-forties and balding. He's got an enormous potbelly and he keeps a dog for company. In other words, yes, he's single.'

'I can always get him to work out with me. What does he do?' Anita asked, hopeful.

'He owns a scrapyard in Suffolk.'

'Oh, that's a bummer.'

'He also owns a jumbo jet.'

'You're kidding. Don't tell me he's like one of those billionaires who owns a bunch of steel plants around the world you keep reading about.'

'That sounds exciting. Did you get to fly it?' Duncan asked with a hint of jealousy.

Peter started laughing. 'Yeah, we did a few laps with the old jumbo jet, but it got a bit hairy when my mate Barry insisted on doing handstands on the left wing mid-air. I was just trying to do an inside loop.'

Duncan slapped Peter on the back. 'You've become funny since last week!'

Anita wiped away tears of laughter.

'Guys, you won't believe this. Barry started with a small scrapyard. He was known all around Suffolk – you know, small country lanes, people driving too fast, braking too late. There're lot of accidents on those small roads. Lots of small scrapes: a dent in your front wing, a clipped-off mirror, or a crack in your fog-lights. You name it, there's a dozen reasons for young guys to go and visit the scrapyard on a Saturday.'

'So where does this jumbo jet fit in?'

'Well, Barry's an enterprising guy and he realised there's a growing market in second-hand airplane parts. His scrapyard's next to an ex-military airport, so he started this plane recycling business. It started with small Cessnas and an old decommissioned fighter jet; now he's got a jumbo jet and a hangar. My son really loves it there. It's a paradise for boys!'

'I bet it is,' Duncan said.

'Well, that doesn't sound like my future husband. I'd better finish last week's minutes.' Anita walked back to her desk.

'My son Tom has his eyes set on a jet engine, and now all he talks about is making a rocket to fly to Mars.'

'That sounds like one amazing weekend project. It would certainly help me through the week,' Duncan said.

'Peter, I'm on your team!' Anita called out while waiting for her document to open. 'I'll do the background research for you!'

'Seriously?'

'Look! I just searched the Internet "how to build a spaceship". There you go! Hundreds of thousands of pages. Let's look at this one: Twelve NASA blueprints for building your own spaceship.'

'When NASA publishes its manuals on the Internet, we know the end is nigh,' Duncan added sarcastically.

Peter looked bewildered. 'Come on, guys. It was a joke.'

'It doesn't need to be. Look around – we're all working on an escape plan. Joan's taking acting classes after work,' Anita added excitedly.

Joan heard her name mentioned 'I'm working nine to five for service and devotion,' she sang in a theatrical manner, mimicking Dolly Parton. 'But at the weekend I am Lady Macbeth,' her voice having dropped an octave. 'Fringe theatre. We tour the country, nothing glamorous. Bangor last weekend and Chichester next. It's great fun.'

'Bob the IT support guru plays drums in a 1980s revival band.'

'Yep, sold-out gigs every weekend. I saw him last month and the bass guitarist is just gorgeous.'

'And he's twenty-three,' Joan teased Anita.

'I write novels, love stories, and I self-publish on Amazon,' Emily confided to her colleagues. 'Just hoping that one day Hollywood comes calling with a screenwriting contract. And then I'm out of here!'

'Writing from experience, an autobiography?' Duncan asked.

'No, it's pure fiction,' Emily replied dryly.

'What about you, Duncan? Don't tell me you just go home and read the evening paper?'

'Me? My true passion's collecting mushrooms.'

'The magical ones?'

'Yes, those too,' Duncan laughed. 'I organise mushroom collecting trips every autumn. It's all part of the sustainable living society that I belong to.'

'How long have I known you guys for? Eight years?'

'Twelve years in my case,' Duncan said.

'How come I never knew?'

'Because you keep to yourself. You dash off at five on the dot. We always thought you were having an affair, un cinq à sept, as the French say it.'

'Ooh la la,' Anita butted in. 'You're a man of mystery – the unassuming accountant, flying his young mistresses to Mars. That's so romantic.'

'No, I'm not having an affair at all. Why do you think that?'

'Just the usual. You're a middle-aged guy, not too bad looking, not over the hill yet; but you're taken hostage by your mortgage and a needy wife, stuck in a dead-end job with no sign of promotion. You look to us like someone who needs some excitement in his life. So an affair with Roslyn, the divorcee in her mid-thirties from the marketing department, seemed the logical explanation. You always seem to leave the building just after each other.'

'We have our sources!' Duncan joked.

'You're having me on! I leave at five and I'm home at five-forty, every day. You can ask my wife.'

'Peter, what happens on the road, stays on the road. We're leaving your wife out of this. Your secret is safe with us. Just come out with us once in a while. We love some good gossip.'

'And what about that young blonde we've seen you with at the Starbucks near Liverpool Street station?' Emily said. 'That was a scream. Anita was completely baffled when she saw you staring into her big blue eyes.'

'It was too good to be true; it made my lunch break,' Anita added.

Peter shook his head. 'It's not what you think. She's Brazilian, just arrived in London a couple of weeks ago and asked me to help her with some fraud investigation project.'

'That seems an elaborate excuse to get you into the sack.'

'It's not like that at all. I'm just helping her find her feet in London.'

'My lips are sealed.'

'Give the guy a break. She may be his secret daughter from a relationship twenty years ago. Anyway, in the meantime, I discovered a rather interesting fact. It's legal to build a spaceship, but not to fly one, according to Reddit.'

'Well, there you go. No more obstacles in your way, Peter!' Duncan said.

'Hang on, guys. You'll need a permit and that's difficult to get,' Emily added.

'I won't be breaking any rules soon. Right now, it's just an idea in my son's head.'

'How old is your son?'

'Nine and a bit.'

'Well at that age, kids are determined. You can be the cool daddy you always wanted to be. Don't disappoint him now. Don't make him realise that life sucks and you have to forget your youthful ambitions and dreams. Make him believe that everything's possible.'

'Think about it. Your son's iPhone has more computing power than the computer running the Apollo space programme back in 1969,' Anita said.

'Well, in that case I'll just download the spaceship launch app.'

'Ask the IT guys to develop it for you. They're fiddling their thumbs most of the time, bored senseless in that windowless basement office. They'd love a challenge like this,' Duncan said.

'I already messaged them,' Emily said.

'Oh no, I don't want to be the laughing stock of the company.'

'Too late. Bob already replied.'

'What does he say?' Duncan asked.

'"No sweat, mate. Give me a few days and I'll have the app ready".'

'It seems you've got your crew selected,' Emily said.

'If you need a young lady to come along for the Intergalactic Space Breeding Programme, count me in. I'm a size eight, in case your spacesuit designer needs to know,' Anita chuckled.

'I'll certainly keep you all in mind. First of all, I need to strap a jet engine to a camper.'

'It gets more bizarre by the minute,' Anita said.

'Barry's selling an old VW camper. That's how I found him in the first place.'

'And with that time machine, you're planning to go to space?'

'It needs some tweaking here and there,' Peter said.

'All you need is escape velocity, and the Milky Way'll guide your way through the Galaxy,' Anita added sarcastically.

'Oops, deadline time,' said Peter, looking at his iPhone.

'Aha... That other secret rendezvous with Sylvia from upstairs. We've seen you! What is it with you, Peter? You look so... average. But you've got all these young women swooning over you.'

'Knowledge and determination is power, and that equals sex appeal. The nerds rule the world.'

'Now we know that the end is nigh. There really is no escape from this mad world!' Duncan said.

14

Foggy Bottom, Washington DC
New Dawn Counter Intelligence Organisation

'That's odd,' Detective Dave Johnson said, rocking his swivel chair on its back wheels, a habit of his when he was onto something. The worn-out office chair was too small for his large frame. He looked like an adult sitting in a child-seat in a classroom during parents' evening.

'One day, that chair's gonna snap,' said Mike, his partner, annoyed that he was being distracted. 'You'll end up banging your head against the radiator. There's gonna be blood everywhere.'

'Have a look at my files, I just sent it over to you. I think we finally found her – Claudia Valenti.'

Dave pushed himself away from his cluttered desk and wheeled his chair over to the opposite desk. One of the wheels was stuck and made the chair screech. Dave was a doughnut-eating office junkie, who at nineteen stone believed that a stroll to the lift right outside their office and from the lift to his Chevy Trailblazer in the underground car park or wheeling his chair around his desk counted as strenuous exercise. His excess calorie intake alone would add another two inches to his waist and another fifteen kilos in extra weight every year. His cars grew in size and proportion to his weight gain. Soon he'd be driving a truck instead of an SUV.

'Are you sure?' Mike Dimito sneered.

'I'm ninety-eight per cent sure I've got her,' Dave said. 'I emailed you the file. Open it. Our associates in Brazil gathered all the evidence they could get their hands on and translated it into English.'

'And the remaining two per cent?' Mike asked whilst opening the attachment. It was a map of London and several screenshots from CCTV footage.

'That'll come down to clever and intelligent investigation.'

'You mean, it'll come down to me.'

'Exactly. Have a look first.'

'Who am I looking at?'

'Facial recognition software ID'd the woman we're interested in. She was waiting for a train at Brockley station in London. There are cameras all over the London Underground system. You must love that; they make it so easy for us. The best thing is, you can link it to the Oyster card travel data. All Londoners use an Oyster card. It's the ideal tracker. We have an Oyster card registered under the name Claudia Valenti, which was first used at this station on Tuesday January 19th and without fail she makes the same journey every day, leaving home around two p.m. and returning around eight. Same routine, every day apart from the weekend.'

'What does she do on the weekend?'

'Weekend stuff.'

'And how can you be sure this is the woman we're looking

for?'

'I just know. Look at the following images from CCTV Bishopsgate near Liverpool Street station. She's been standing there every evening for the last month or so, handing out newspapers.'

Dave produced more images of a tall slim blonde young woman, radiant blue eyes, a slightly pointy nose and her hair in a single plait. She wore jeans, boots, a fleece jacket, a striped scarf and matching blue and white bobble hat. She looked like she wasn't trying hard to look pretty.

'That's her. You see the young woman with a striped bobble hat? That's our Claudia Valenti.'

'Does she fit our profile?'

'The profile of a mad and dangerous eco-terrorist? That's the difficult part. If we could only predict who turns into a terrorist and who doesn't, the world would be a safer place. Most terrorists are perfectly decent people, well respected by neighbours and colleagues, until they snap. Something changes, and suddenly they're wearing a suicide vest, or firing a semi-automatic in the lobby of a suburban movie theatre, or blowing up an office block. These people are different from fanatics and sociopaths.'

'I still find it hard to believe.'

'She's well-educated. She snuck into Amazorico's office as a cleaner three months before the attack, lasting longer than most young cleaners. That was suspicious in its own right,' Dave chuckled. 'She gained her colleagues' trust, working five mornings a week for those three months. She had plenty of time to prepare a well-orchestrated attack. She had access to all the areas. For a terrorist, this was a perfect opportunity.'

'Anything else we've got on her?'

'She went to a couple of demonstrations, the usual stuff: climate change, rainforest destruction. She once tied herself to a tree for a couple hours in front of some bulldozers to block a dam construction.'

'And that didn't help?'

'Of course not, what do you think? She also posted a few blogs on the university website.'

'Facebook profile?'

'She had over six hundred friends or followers. She ranted about various ecological issues. Hardly anything personal. But she did write this a couple of days before she left: "Dear friends of the Amazon: countdown to revenge has started. Three days and counting".'

'So what links her to the attack?'

'Keep on reading.'

Mike looked at the screen.

'"The only way to stand up for our planet is to fight back. Expect an explosion soon",' Dave read out loud.

'Are you sure this is enough evidence?'

'She spent some time with her boyfriend the evening before the attack. He had no inkling at all. He's being interrogated as we speak. She was having drinks with her friends and after work she headed to the airport and flew to Spain.'

'So at the time of the explosion she wasn't even in São Paulo.'

'That's right.'

'She wasn't at the crime scene? Nobody saw her pressing a button?'

'Right.'

'Conveniently, the building's been reduced to a pile of rubble, all evidence destroyed.'

'Hang on, there's more. Open the next file.'

Mike's face froze. 'A striped slip? Damn, you can get fired for sending those images using your work-account.'

'Don't worry, it's all encrypted.'

'Is this supposed to turn me on?'

'Whatever rocks your boat, buddy. What you are looking at is the only piece of hard evidence we've got linking this case to Claudia. Those tiny and cheerful, yellow and white panties once belonged to Miss Valenti. Her DNA's all over them.'

'That's been confirmed?'

'It's a long story, but a security officer named Rodeo sent the underwear to a private forensic laboratory. It was found on the top floor, in the owner's office. He went ballistic and demanded an investigation. Rodeo sent it off with a courier just after he finished his shift and before leaving the building.'

'Is he a suspect?'

'Rodeo? Don't think so. He seems to have a solid alibi. He works in a car shop and was there at the time of the explosion.'

'It sounds all a bit circumstantial to me. Can't she just have had an affair with the boss?'

'Well, so far it's the only clue we've got from the crime scene. We need to solve this. Boss says it's a high profile case. They want to keep the media out of it. That's why we've got it.'

'So this Claudia woman, a student from São Paulo, blows up a building, then flies under her own name to Spain? And she takes a night train to Paris. She's never been to Europe before, but doesn't spend any time sightseeing and moves on to London by Eurostar. Then within a day of arriving she somehow finds a job handing out newspapers in London.'

'That's her, yes.'

'And this is your terrorist?'

'Absolutely, she fits the bill like nobody else.'

'And the boss wants us to eliminate her.'

'Affirmative, without a trace, after we film her confession.'

'And you want me to be part of this sinister fairy tale?'

'We're partners in crime.'

'I think it's getting late,' Mike said, 'and we need a beer.' He looked at the clock – it was close to seven pm and time to get home.

'Buddy, why don't you just print out these documents and we'll take it to the bar and talk about it over a cold one.'

Mike closed the files he was working on and packed his briefcase. 'Sorry to be blunt, but you're wasting your time. I'm happy to explain why over a Bud. I'll wait for you by the elevator.'

Dave got up and gave his chair a firm push. It crashed against the side of

his desk. Ignoring it, he stuffed the rest of his doughnuts into his satchel.

Dave opened the doors of the Trailblazer and got behind the wheel. It was a snug fit. 'All I'm trying to say is, I started following Claudia Valenti, just like I was asked to. Took me a few weeks to trace her to London. And there's another twist: she's been meeting an older man on a regular basis. They always choose the same Starbucks. I don't know who he is yet, but he may play a crucial part in all of this.'

'Now it's getting interesting. Go on.'

'You're asking for my personal opinion?'

Mike nodded.

'She's either expanding her network in Europe, setting up another cell, or trying to get another sponsor for something even bigger.'

'And all big fires start small.'

'Exactly, and we're today's fire-fighters.'

'You're such an idiot. The reality can't be more sobering – we're just sitting in a concrete bunker four floors down, scrolling through hours of CCTV footage.'

'Come on, it's a cushy job. Spying on people by remote control. I love it. It's like playing video games with human targets.'

'Get real. Our job is so much more than that. This target of yours is responsible for five deaths. Five people didn't come home to their loved ones. Five people got crushed or burnt to death in São Paulo when she triggered the demolition of that company's head office. It was one big explosion, mid-morning. If what you showed me is true, she couldn't have picked a worse time. That wasn't just about making a point. This is serious stuff.'

'Right on, I am glad you see it too.' Dave looked smug. 'It gets more complicated. The owner of the company is related to some kind of governor and they want justice. If that fails, they want revenge. This is a high profile case, heads will roll.'

'And that's where we come in.'

'Exactly.'

Mike sighed. He stared out of the window. The droplets

on the car window dispersed the hundreds of car and street lights into a kaleidoscope of colours before the wipers would erase them every few seconds. He was not looking forward to the next few weeks. A new investigation at this level only meant a lot more overtime and less time with his family.

The Trailblazer trundled along Pennsylvania Avenue. The giant obelisk at the horizon was brightly lit up, a beacon of hope and power. The streets were quiet.

'I'm pulling over, buddy. There's a great parking spot, right in front of my favourite burger joint. Those doughnuts whet my appetite,' Dave said to break the silence.

For a quiet Tuesday evening in March, the restaurant was pretty full. A waitress showed them to the last remaining table. She smiled at Dave. 'Your usual killer burger with large fries, mister?'

'And two Buds,' Dave added.

'A cheeseburger for me please, but no fries.'

'He's on a diet.' Dave chuckled.

'It's two for one today, you can always take the second home for later tonight,' the waitress was quick to add.

'Come on, buddy, go for it. You can always give the second one to your kids.'

'Awesome.' The waitress took this as a yes.

'You see. That's what I call value for money. I love this place,' Dave beamed.

Mike rolled his eyes.

'All right, let me tell you how this all fits together. My theory is that somehow this older guy arranged for Claudia to come to London and he's helping her get established, or he's having an affair with her,' Dave continued.

'Possible, but just as unlikely as the waitress having a crush on you.'

'Wow, that's pretty low, but I take it on the chin. Didn't you see the twinkle in her eyes when we came in? She rushed towards us as soon as she saw me.'

'Really? I didn't notice. Anyway, perhaps it's that generous tip you give her each time, and she remembers,' Mike sneered. 'Over the years it must have added up to a substantial sum.'

Dave didn't react.

'Suppose you are right and there is a link between London and São Paulo, then this connection is the only thing we can go on for now, anyway. And, if we can somehow find a financial connection between the guy in London and that state governor in Brazil or the owner of Amazorico, we can figure out who was behind all this,' Mike speculated.

The waitress returned to their table and put two bottles of ice-cold Budweiser down. She didn't linger for a second longer than necessary. Dave took a swig straight from the bottle. He stared at the waitress, who was now at the other side of the aisle helping another customer; he took another swig. He was silent for a while. His mind was rattling.

'You aren't paying any attention to anything I just told you,' Mike said.

'Eight hundred and sixty four dollars,' Dave replied.

'What the fuck are you talking about?'

'Suppose I visit this place twice a week, and I tip on average six dollars, and I started coming here since they opened eighteen months ago. That makes it just under nine hundred dollars. That's how much in tips I've given her.'

'That's amazing. You know what you could get for nine hundred dollars in a strip-club?'

'Shut up, that's no way to talk about a lady. She's classy. One day my generosity's gonna get noticed. You're just frustrated. When was the last time you had a decent fuck with your wife?'

'Stop right there. Life's been difficult lately – ups and downs, kids and all that. But that doesn't mean I'm lusting after any woman who walks by. Besides, we've got an interesting case to worry about now.'

'The only good thing that could come out of this is that they'll send us on a field trip to London,' Dave said.

'You don't get it, do you? We have the world at our fingertips. Our computer screens are like crystal balls. We don't have to leave our office. We can hit any target with the click of a mouse.'

'Send in the drones.'

'Once you've been given permission from the boss, and the only way to convince him is to put in some legwork first, get a feel for the scene and report back. Then he can discuss it with the executive board, and someone'll tell you when to click your mouse.'

'I'm sure we can get the boss to arrange a car for us. A change of scenery will be good for both of us. Since you started having kids, you became such a bore. When was the last time we left the office to go on a fieldtrip? Remember what we were told during our job interview: This is your chance to see the world. Well, so far it's been one amazing opportunity to stare at a computer screen ten hours a day.'

'We went to Paris last year.'

'Eight hundred and twenty-eight dollars.'

'What?'

'I forgot. Last year we went to Paris, for three weeks. That means I came here only one hundred and thirty-eight times since they opened, giving our waitress only eight hundred and twenty-eight dollars in tips.'

'You should have taken her to Paris instead.'

'Instead of you, that would have been great. You were a pain in the ass, moaning all the time.'

'OK, OK. You and me in a small Renault Clio on patrol in Paris for three weeks wasn't my idea of sightseeing.'

'Just because you missed your wife and kids you took it out on me.'

'No! It was because your fat ass was occupying two thirds of the car. I couldn't shift gears because your massive thighs were hugging the gear stick like a horny hippo.'

'I lost weight in Paris. The food was awful.'

'The food in Paris had taste, that's what you didn't like about it. Even the kebabs tasted a hundred times better than here. Your taste buds have only three settings: burgers, chips and beer. Parisian food could've reanimated the rest of your tongue and palate.'

'Everything tastes of garlic over there. Never again for me. And for your information, my tongue has four settings; add doughnuts.'

'Nope, that's still the same setting; sugar and fat, the same stuff you get in in burgers and chips.'

'Sugar in chips? I've never heard such crap in my life.

'Then how do you explain the golden colour of your chips?'

Dave shrugged. He was immune to Mike's constant lifestyle advice.

'And now you want to go to London.'

'They've got some of the best burger bars in the world in London. I read that this place has opened several franchises in London. Look, it says so at the bottom of our menu: Soho, Vauxhall, Dalston and Deptford, wherever that is.'

'All the hip places. And your waitress is coming with us?'

'Maybe she could do a waitress exchange programme. I'll ask her manager.'

'Top secret, buddy. Our missions are top secret.'

'She could go undercover.'

'That's pure fantasy, pal. Let's forget about work,' Mike suggested. 'I know a bar next door with some great live music. I just texted Alice that I have to do some overtime.'

'As long as you don't expect me to back you up.'

'Of course you'll back me up.'

'I won't lie to cover your ass.'

'What's up, guys?' the waitress said when she returned with two plates.

'My colleague would like to ask for your phone number, but he hasn't got the guts to do it,' Mike said to tease Dave.

'Now I get it. That's why you come in twice a week. Silly me. I never get guys.' The waitress smiled coyly and quickly walked away.

Dave's face went bright red and he tried to kick his friend's shin, but he hit the table leg instead and winced. 'What did you do that for?'

Mike smiled. 'Just to make sure that you'll back me up.'

As soon as they'd finished eating, the waitress stuck the

bill underneath the ketchup bottle.

'See you around, guys,' she giggled.

Mike snatched the bill before Dave could take it. Then Mike saw that the waitress had scribbled what looked like a cell phone number on the back of the bill.

'Give it to me,' Dave hissed.

'You back me up? You buy me a drink at the next bar and whenever Alice asks where I'm at, you tell her I was on patrol with you.'

'Fine.'

Dave looked over his shoulder. He could see the waitress in the distance talking to one of the chefs. They were laughing. He hoped she wasn't playing some kind of game with him. He'd been the butt of similar jokes in the past.

'I'm sure she just wants to increase her tip.'

'She took the first step. Now be a man and give the woman a call. Ask her out, and not to a burger joint. Take her somewhere classy. Women like suave men who take them to fancy places. The ball's in your corner, buddy.'

15

It was early in the morning. Virginia was holding a mug of coffee at the breakfast table. She was waiting for the right moment. Claudia had established a routine of taking a shower as soon as her friend was in the kitchen, making sure that the bathroom would be free in time before Virginia had to go to work. Virginia tapped her feet against the table chair. Finally, Claudia emerged from the shower wearing a comfortable, inoffensive charcoal grey indoor tracksuit. Virginia looked nervous as she waited for the right moment.

Claudia sat down at the table and looked at Virginia. She poured the rest of the coffee in a mug.

'As a friend, I find it hard to say this to you,' Virginia started.

Claudia stirred her coffee and added some more milk. She gave her a puzzled look. She had no inkling what was coming next. She raised her eyebrows to encourage her flatmate to continue. What had she done wrong? She'd cleaned the fridge last week and kept it fully stocked, replacing whatever she had used.

'I agreed for you to stay for a couple weeks. It has been almost two months now and it's pushing my hospitality to the limit. I like you very much, but I need some space for myself when I come home. That restaurant's driving me mad. I have to deal with demanding customers, a needy boss and a snappy co-worker all evening. I just want to come home, smoke a cigarette, chill out and go to bed.'

Claudia looked away; she had seen this coming for a while. She had made some lacklustre attempts to look for another room but never saw it through.

'I understand, but I never realised that finding a place in London would be so difficult.'

'It's not difficult, it's expensive. Those are two different things. You have to prioritise. You either have to find a job with longer hours which pays more or you have to look in places outside London which are cheaper.'

Claudia took a sip of her coffee.

'I understand that I'm overstaying my welcome. I'm really, really trying!'

'I don't want to ruin our friendship, but by the end of this week I'd like you to be gone. I want to spend some time with my boyfriend without having to worry about you sneaking in on us.'

Claudia didn't say anything, she just stared at the coffee in the bottom of her mug.

'Are you alright? When I first met you, you were full of energy. You found a job within minutes. I expected you to have a place and a new life by now. And you seem to be losing weight. Have you lost your appetite? I've never seen you eating anything more than a slice of toast. Perhaps you are homesick, just like Julia. Tossing and turning every night. You must be exhausted.'

Claudia tried to put on a brave face. She'd been tormented by feelings of guilt for weeks. Of course she was homesick. She missed Mario more than she could have imagined. She had nightmares of being arrested at the airport in São Paulo, soon after arriving, spending the rest of her life in jail. A girl like her would struggle to survive the rough prison environment. She only had herself to blame. She had to get Virginia off her back before she started prying into her private life even further and once the truth had come out, she'd be arrested in no time. In the current political climate she'd be extradited without a second thought.

'I get it.' It sounded more miffed than she had intended. Claudia got up, rinsed her cup under the tap and placed it upside down on the worktop. She grabbed her small backpack and closed the door behind her. Next, she texted Peter. 'Meet me for a coffee. Am being kicked out of my flat. I need your help.'

Peter replied quickly. 'At 13:30, usual place.'

'xxx.' Claudia replied less than two seconds later.

Peter looked at the message several times and smiled. Over the last few weeks he had grown fond of Claudia, and he cherished the moments he met her for coffee. He fantasised about meeting her after work, on a weekend or on a business trip. Perhaps he should insist on going to Zurich and speak to his colleagues in the Swiss branch, pretending it was part of an extensive financial fraud investigation exercise. He scratched the back of his neck. Was this a trap that so many middle-aged men fall into? Was this history repeating itself over and over again? He could foresee how it would all end. If Joanne found out, she'd be furious and leave him on the spot. His daughter would hate him for the rest of her life and become cynical about men and relationships in general, and might even get addicted to drugs and after having serial boyfriends out of revenge, catch chlamydia, at the very least, along the way. And what about Tom? How would Tom react? He had no idea and he had no desire to test out his theory. He had one more look at Claudia's text message before deleting it. After all, both his kids knew his iPhone passcode and they might read all his messages. Was that perhaps why Joanne had been a bit more distant lately? He had to make it up to her and put all doubts to rest. He had a plan.

Work had been busy for Peter. He had established a routine with Sylvia. She'd bring him a new large file each day. On the whole, it was very easy to find fraudulent transactions. Peter managed to trace the fraud to two traders. They had worked together in Hong Kong two years previously before being transferred to Zurich and New York. Their methods weren't very original. In fact, they were quite predictable. Within a few weeks, Peter could skim a large file in under an hour. The rest of the time he spent researching space travel. It fuelled his imagination and his son loved it. He planned another trip to Suffolk next weekend and tinkered with a novel experiment. He smiled. He had taken up Barry's offer to try out his VW camper. It would radically change the family dynamic, make it simpler in a back-to-basics kind of way.

'Still dreaming about Mars?' Sylvia asked. She'd been

standing behind his chair for a while. Peter had been absorbed in his Internet search.

He turned around and made a clumsy attempt to close down the web page he was looking at.

'Who told you?'

'We all know about your space mission. It was one hell of a surprise. It's quite mad.'

Peter felt awkward. He didn't reply, instead opening up a spreadsheet he'd been working on earlier that day.

'Don't worry, Peter. Your secret's safe with me. I don't care how you spend your time. As long as this project's completed by the end of the month, everybody's happy, and we're well on track. And who knows? After that, something else may crop up.'

'What do you mean?'

'Nothing in particular, just some rumours. Really, anything's possible.'

Sylvia tried to sound vague but realised that Peter wasn't easily satisfied with a half-baked answer.

'OK, it's just a rumour, really, nothing more than that. This building's from the early eighties. Mikhail's got high ambitions. The sky's the limit.'

Sylvia looked at him with an air of conspiracy. She leaned forwards. 'Last week Mikhail Zoblovski was here. He usually stays in the top floor apartment for a couple of nights. Had a meeting with several architects. His only brief was to build something bigger and more impressive than the Shard, something as tall as planning regulations would allow.'

'I hope Zoblovski realises that public opinion's against these skyscrapers, especially after the last glut of ugly buildings. People feel they no longer own the city. They worry that big money's destroying it.'

'He's a persuasive man. He already threatened the planning committee that he might construct the tower somewhere else in the city. He mentioned Catford, in south-east London. It would regenerate the whole area. Trust me, he knows how to get things done.'

'Well, it would suit me. What about you? A nice apartment in Mikhail's tower block?'

'I've set my eyes on a small cottage in the country when I'm out of here.'

'You should come with us one day; we often go to Suffolk.'

'I love Bury St Edmunds, lovely pubs, nice bookshops, a small theatre. For me, that'd be the perfect place to escape.'

Peter felt his phone vibrate. He had forgotten the date he had with Claudia. 'I'm on my way', he texted.

'Sorry, have to meet a friend.'

'Interesting. Is she pretty?'

'It's not what you think.'

'I wouldn't be so worried about what I think. I'd be more worried about what she's thinking…'

'You don't happen to know anyone with a spare bedroom?'

'A convenient place to meet your lover?'

'I told you, it's not like that. Why don't you come and meet Claudia? She's Brazilian and her friend just kicked her out.'

'I'd rather stay out of that messy business.'

'She's just a friend and she's desperate to meet new people.'

'How old is she again?'

'Twenty-one. I'm sure you two would get along.'

'I'm way too old to be her friend. There's a whole generation gap.'

'What? Nine years, you call that a generation gap?'

'Oh yes, it's a whole new world out there. You have no idea what you got yourself into.'

'She's a really nice person.'

'I'm sure she is... And what's your connection with her again?'

'No connection. I just met her on the street.'

'As you do. You weren't introduced by a mutual friend?'

'No!'

'Men are so naïve sometimes. Has she got big brown eyes?'

'No. In fact, she's a blonde with blue eyes. You'd like her. She read environmental studies.'

'And what's she doing in the most polluted part of London? At times it's so bad, you can hardly breathe.'

'Handing out the Evening Outlook. It's just a temporary job. I'm looking into something for her, fraud investigation in the construction industry in Brazil.'

Sylvia started laughing. 'That sounds like a job for life; fraud investigation in the construction industry. She's having you on. I'm curious now. Maybe you can introduce me to her.'

'Come along then!'

'Not now, there's work to do – another time perhaps.'

Peter shrugged. Sylvia tapped him on his shoulder just before she disappeared into the lift. 'Be careful, Peter. You've got a lot to lose. You've got such a lovely family.'

Peter hated being the centre of office gossip, although it had made him a lot more popular. The office atmosphere had become livelier since he had got his promotion, or was it because he had opened up and shared some aspects of his life with them?

The lift arrived. It was 13:41, according to the clock above. He had to rush. The lift stopped on every floor, so he had no other choice but to accept that he was running late. He hoped that Claudia would still be waiting for him. He felt anxious, like going on a date with the intensity of a teenage romance. He looked in the mirror of the lift and adjusted his tie, ruffled his hair to look a bit less conventional, a bit less middle-aged – more of a financial fraud investigator than an accountant. Peter almost forgot to get out of the lift at the lobby. Only when someone got in and pressed the button to the eleventh floor did he jump out, just in time.

'Sorry for being late. I got held up at work.'

Claudia got up from her stool near the window and gave Peter a kiss on the cheek.

'Don't worry, I'm glad you're here. I didn't know who else to turn to.'

Peter felt chuffed. 'Let me get some more coffees. Latte for you?'

'A caffè latte, yes please.'

'Of course,' Peter replied.

The barista overheard the conversation. 'Can I take your name?'

'It's Peter,' he tried to stay as casually as possible.

The barista scribbled his name on his cup to add a personal touch.

While hovering near the enormous coffee machine, Claudia explained how she'd overstayed her welcome.

'Can you help? Do you know anywhere I could stay?'

Peter scratched his head.

'Perhaps you could stay with us for a while. I have to talk to my wife first. Is that OK? That's the best I can do.'

'Maravilhoso!' Claudia clapped her hands in excitement. 'Of course, I understand, talk to your wife first. I don't want to cause any trouble.'

'Don't worry, it's no trouble at all really.'

Peter had several scenarios running through his mind. He had no idea how Joanne would react to him inviting a young attractive woman to live with his family.

'I could be a live-in-nanny!'

'My kids are quite independent. I don't think they'd be too excited having a nanny.'

Claudia looked disappointed. 'I don't want to take advantage of your hospitality.'

'You know what – we'll be going away for a weekend, perhaps you could do some house-sitting for us.'

'Thanks, that would be great.'

Claudia was overjoyed. She leaned forward and aimed for Peter's lips. Peter was unprepared, and at the wrong moment he averted his head and Claudia's kiss landed on his shirt. He flushed. 'I'm sorry.'

'No, I'm sorry,' Claudia laughed. She tried to wipe her lipstick from his collar but only caused it to smudge more.

'I really have to go back to work now.'

'I understand.'

'I'll text you my address and the code for the alarm. I'll

leave the keys to the front door with the neighbours. They're an elderly couple and they're always at home.'

'Wonderful! I really appreciate your help.'

Back in the office, Sylvia was waiting for him with another large folder in her hand; Anita stood nearby.

'Lipstick on your collar? You better remove it before your wife sees it!'

'It's not what you think. Claudia just got kicked out of her flat.'

'And you offered her a bedroom?'

'Wouldn't you? I'm just helping a friend.'

'Your wife'll be delighted with you bringing a young woman home. You've only just met her on a street corner a few weeks ago. You must have one hell of an open relationship,' Sylvia remarked sarcastically.

Anita laughed. 'You just helped transform the public opinion of accountants. I always saw you as risk adverse, but now you're planning to fly to Mars, inviting young women into your married life… I can't wait to hear your next plan!'

16

Foggy Bottom, Washington DC

'The more I look at all the evidence we've got so far, the more I'm convinced that our Brazilian eco-terrorist is building up some kind of European network,' Dave Johnson said.

'That's quite a bold statement. Have you considered all other possible explanations? Why can't she just be a student working a couple of hours each day as a cleaner in an office block and travelling to London studying English for a few months to get a better job when she goes home? Combined with a degree, she'll have a good job at an international company in no time. Millions of kids do that. It's a rite of passage. That explains why she booked her tickets three months in advance and why she signed up for a language course in London.'

'Yeah, but on the other hand, we've got emails and Facebook posts proving that she was cooking up something. She had the right kind of access to a building full of explosives.'

'You've been watching too many movies. Your imagination's far out there.'

Dave moved his chair closer to the wall and tilted it back. He picked up his pen and started spinning it between his fingers to add some gravitas to his argument.

'Occam's razor explains it all. When things look complicated, all you need to do is to find the single most plausible explanation to link everything.

'No matter how ridiculous it sounds?'

'It's not ridiculous at all. A young ambitious woman is, quite rightly, upset about the destruction of the Amazon rainforest. She's absolutely right on that one. What happens with the rainforest the world over, be it in Brazil, Indonesia or Africa, is tragic, beyond tragic, and one day we'll all be paying a big price for it. But she's passionate and stumbles upon this once-in-a-lifetime opportunity. She can make a name for herself, she can set an example. A strong message that enough is enough and that those who are directly responsible for destroying the rainforest should get punished.'

'And now she's in London, doing exactly what?'

'How do I know? Maybe she's planning on sinking some fishing boats on England's west coast to stop the depletion of the Atlantic Ocean.'

'OK, OK, OK… suppose she is teaming up with others.'

'Or maybe she's planning an attack on a nuclear power station! Who knows? We can't let her slip through our fingers.'

'How on earth would she be able to attack a nuclear power station? Those are like fortresses; nobody can get access without thorough security clearance.'

'Listen, buddy. Someone's paying a few million bucks to our organisation. They want results and they want it yesterday. All we have to do is finish our research, file a report and hope for no more attacks. Everybody's a winner. Terrence'll be happy for a change.'

'You presented him the facts?'

'I did, and he's impressed. We don't have any jurisdiction to carry out an in-depth investigation in São Paulo, but we asked a local team to assist us. So far there are no results. All our leads hit a brick wall. My gut feeling is that someone's protecting someone else. And that's usually a politician.'

'That's when it gets dirty.'

'And nasty. They know no scruples when it comes to protecting their own interests. That's why my theory's so convenient. We can swing a deal with the Brits. You know how they keep harping on and on about our so-called special relationship. We bailed them out so many times, this is a small favour.'

'Why don't we discuss it with Terrence? We're meeting him later tonight. I told him to meet us in a bar just off Pennsylvania Avenue,' Mike suggested.

'Can't we go to the same place as last time? The waitress always gets me a bigger portion.'

'You know what Terrence is like. He never meets in the same bar or restaurant twice. That way you avoid predictability.'

'I know, always on the move, always paranoid.'

'There are too many crazies who take things into their own hands.'

'That's for sure.'

'Well then, we've got an hour or so to polish up our proposal.'

With a big thud, Dave's chair fell back on all four wheels. He opened his top drawer and got out a white chocolate and raspberry doughnut, took two bites and started another Google search. 'So what do you make of Claudia meeting this guy?'

'My opinion? She's his secret lover,' Mike replied.

'Why? He's way too old for her.'

'Wake up, buddy. That kind of shit happens all the time. History's littered with the same old story. She's an attractive woman trying to make a living in a big city. Life's expensive, jobs are hard to get. She's ambitious and he helps her along. In return… You get the gist.'

'In return she meets him in a coffee shop. This doesn't look like a desperate middle-aged man spending his life savings on a young chick.'

'As long as we don't know where she goes, where she lives, we don't know anything. She may invite him back to her apartment.'

'That sounds a bit far-fetched.'

'How did I deserve to work with a dimwit like you? She is having a bloody affair with him!' Mike shouted in frustration.

'I bet you twenty bucks that she's not.'

'Deal! You better give me the money right now because once I report on the rest of my investigation, you'll see you've been wrong all along. Let me open your eyes, brother!'

Dave opened his drawer again to eat the rest of his doughnut and took a swig of the coffee'd he bought earlier in the afternoon. It was stone cold by now but Dave preferred to drink his coffee that way. He was determined to prove Mike wrong.

A silence of more than thirty minutes followed. A clock ticking above the door was hypnotic, setting a mood of complete concentration. The computer fans made the only noise. Dave's chair squeaked, signalling the end of another intense Internet search.

'Got it!'

Mike stopped typing.

'Go on, I'm listening.'

'I ID'd her mysterious lover. It took me all of thirty minutes. Here we go: his name's Peter Miller; forty-four years old, married with two kids and lives in Crystal Palace, not far from Brockley, conveniently. He's a fraud investigator in London.'

'Must be one hell of a busy job,' Mike sneered.

'Don't write him off just yet. I said fraud investigator. He's been busy, but not with what you think.' Dave scrolled down the list of companies he was searching.

'How'd you get into his desktop? How'd you get through the firewall?'

'This, my friend!'

Dave rolled his chair to the end of his desk and heaved himself from the seat. He leaned forward to grab something from underneath his desk. It was a two-inch thick book and while still on his knees, he held it high above his head for Mike to see. 'This is essential for any private investigator of the twenty-first century! Computer Hacking for Dummies!'

'Duh!'

'Well, look at this: Bingo! Amazorico. Hope that rings a bell!' Dave pointed at a spreadsheet on his screen.

'The company your bio-terrorist was working for which

disappeared in an explosion. I think we're on to something, something bigger than we expected,' Mike added.

'The plot's thickening!'

Mike got his wallet out and put it on the table in front of him just in case he needed to hand over a twenty-dollar bill.

'Listen to this. The company Peter Miller works for recently changed hands when it was bought by a Russian billionaire named Mikhail Zoblovski.

'Doesn't ring a bell.'

'He's in his mid-sixties, made his money in steel, refineries, food production; and he recently branched out into football clubs, theatres and other more glamorous and high-profile ventures. Look, here he is with his girlfriend.'

'She looks like a model.'

'She's a dancer, ex-Bolshoi, by the name of Yana.'

'Dancers get arthritis. I would have gone for a model.'

'Where did you get that one from?'

'My nieces, they all want to do ballet. It's murder on your feet, blisters, corns, stress fractures, infected ulcers and nail deformations. You can look it up. And they all suffer from anorexia.'

'And models don't?'

'We're getting distracted.'

'What's even more glamorous than owning a football club, a two-hundred foot yacht and a private jet?'

'A private island in the Caribbean?'

'He's already got one in the Bahamas.'

'Can't we discuss this over a beer?'

'That's too risky; too many people can overhear us. Anyway, look at this. He's involved in the Russian Space

Programme.'

'I already like him.'

'And guess how Peter Miller spends the rest of his working day?'

'I guess what most middle aged men do.'

'No, no... he's researching space travel, space colonies and survival in space.'

'Sounds bizarre. How do you link this all together?'

'It's not just him. Several others in the same firm are doing extensive Internet research about spacecraft design and rocket building.'

'Sounds suspicious, I have to admit.'

'Claudia's trying to escape. She's on the run. Zoblovski's trying to make history, so he's paying for a space programme. Miller helps him and is planning to take Claudia along with him.'

'Isn't he married? Why doesn't he take his wife?' Mike said.

'To start a new life in space, you need a young woman.'

Mike started laughing. 'I love the way you make this up. It's pure science fiction. Ridiculous! Don't tell Terrence, he'll have you investigated for insanity. And once the shrinks start working on you, you'll end up institutionalised for the rest of your life. Escaping from these governmental mental institutions is impossible.'

Twenty minutes later, Mike and Dave were sitting in a restaurant awaiting Terrence. Dave wasn't pleased with the venue.

'The menu's pretty measly!'

'Personally, I find restaurants with more than fifteen

varieties of hamburger bewildering. I'll just go for the house cheeseburger and a large Bud.'

'The quadruple burger with guacamole and large fries for me, please,' Dave told the waitress. She smiled at him.

Mike rolled his eyes.

'That'll keep me full till midnight.'

'More like it'll keep you full till lunchtime next week. It's a guaranteed heart attack on a plate!'

'Nothing can come between me and my midnight snack!'

'I find the amount of food you eat obscene.'

'I'm not listening. Whatever comes out of that critical mouth goes in one ear, out the other. If you're like this with your kids, they'd love it if you went away for a couple of weeks.'

'I hope you haven't ordered already,' Terrence said, taking a place next to Dave. He looked out of place in the burger bar. Terrence was tall and slim and dressed immaculately in a three-piece charcoal suit, a crisp white shirt and a burgundy paisley tie. He spoke with a deep voice.

'The service is slow so I'm sure you can still order yours now,' Dave suggested.

'If there's anything left to order – Dave just ordered!'

'I'm glad to see you're getting on so well. I've got some news for you. I've been studying the evidence and there's only one way to get to the bottom of it all,' Terrence said.

'You see, Mike. Terrence agrees with me.'

'I'm sending you both to England.'

Mike and Dave looked at each other but didn't protest.

'I'm jealous. Would have loved to come along. Spring-time there is just wonderful,' Terence mused. 'Rolling hills and daffodils. Country pubs with wood fires and artisan ale.'

'You're watching the wrong TV shows,' Mike said. 'We're talking about eco-terrorism, exposing a network of global fraud and money laundering. The Russians may be involved too. This is dangerous stuff.'

Terrence nodded. His decision was made.

'What about this link to the Russian space programme?' Dave asked.

'I've discussed it with my counterparts at the Pentagon. That's an extremely worrying situation. More and more wealthy entrepreneurs are trying to develop their own space programme. Since NASA's no longer a major player, Internet rich kids have been filling the void. Technology's come a long way. The software behind a successful launch can be run from any mobile phone. The hardware, the rockets, the fuel – it's all expensive, very expensive, but not out of reach for those billionaires.'

'Sure, but it's not a crime to develop a spaceship,' Dave said.

'The main concern is that when the rich start to leave our planet others may follow. Many are convinced we're headed for a major ecological disaster. The pace of climate change is set to accelerate, and these guys are planning to set up camp elsewhere in our solar system. The Earth may survive; the ecosystem may reboot itself over a period of millions of years. But humans won't be part of it.'

'Who cares? A few rich people escape to greener pastures,' Mike said.

'More like a red desert than a green meadow,' Dave said.

'Many of today's wars, especially in the Middle East and

parts of Africa, are a direct result of global warming. Think about it: as access to drinking water becomes even scarcer and harvests fail year after year people begin migrating to places with a more favourable climate. They're panicking. Can you imagine what'll happen in a decade or so when Mexico becomes even more unbearably hot than it is now? When California will finally run out of water it will incite mass migration to Canada. Soon millions of people will start crossing international borders just like migratory birds, their travel unhindered by artificial borders. Even the highest wall won't deter the truly desperate. The future will be more bleak than Blade Runner.'

'And some of us prefer to leave Earth before it gets to that stage,' Dave said.

'And we can't allow that to happen,' Mike added.

'Of course not. It'll send the wrong message. It'll symbolize the failure of our political system and this, gentlemen, is what we've vowed to protect,' Terrence said.

'Besides, there's nowhere to go,' Mike said.

'Exactly! It'll be a suicide mission for amateur astronauts,' Dave added.

'Enjoy your beers,' said Terence. 'You'll be on the move tomorrow. Sorry about the short notice. Time is crucial here.'

'What? Tomorrow? That's insane,' Mike protested.

'Look at the job description you signed. Clause fourteen: you agreed to be dispatched anywhere in need of in-depth investigation within twenty-four hours' notice. Your flight leaves in eighteen hours.

'But here comes the clincher,' Terence continued. 'I phoned around, pulled a few strings and managed to get you onto an unclassified flight to an RAF base a hundred miles or so north-east of London. There'll be a car waiting for you. It's a 2013 Buick Lacrosse with UK number plates so you'll blend in nicely. Remember our motto: we have to keep a low profile.'

17

'I'm home!' Peter hollered as he opened the front door. Usually his kids came running to the door as soon as they heard his keys in the lock. The corridor was dark; the lights hadn't been switched on yet. It was eerily quiet. There was never a moment's rest with the kids around, but when they weren't, the silence was unbearable.

Peter kicked off his shoes and rushed up the stairs to get changed into black tracksuit bottoms and a fleece hoody. There was still no sound in the house. Peter washed his hands and splashed his face with cold water. He was glad to be home again, but something didn't seem right.

Peter opened the door to his son's room directly opposite the bathroom. He expected to see him sitting in a corner, near the radiator, headphones on, playing Minecraft on his iPad. He scanned the room. Tom's bed was made up neatly and the heating was switched off. No sign of him. He walked into Lilly's room; her door was always wide open as she was scared of the dark. Her room was equally tidy. Peter was puzzled.

But then it all made sense. It was Wednesday evening. The days were just flying by lately. His life was sweeping him up like a tidal wave. What was once a dull existence had been transformed by his new role as a fraud investigator and his friendship with Claudia.

He still hadn't told Joanne about her staying at their house over the weekend. Several scenarios ran through his head on how to bring this up. He had never even mentioned her name to her, so how on earth could he just introduce her without raising a lot of uncomfortable questions? Dropping her name casually a few times during conversation, just to let Joanne get used to it? How would he feel if Joanne suddenly invited a handsome young bloke handing out The Hot Topic at Crystal Palace station? He knew exactly how he'd feel! He'd ask her to make him leave immediately. He clapped his forehead feeling stupid for making a promise to Claudia without thinking about the consequences. What had he been thinking?

The phone rang. How inconvenient. He rushed down the stairs skipping several steps, almost breaking his neck over his own shoes at the bottom of the stairs. Slightly out of breath he picked up the receiver.

'Good evening, Mr Miller, it's Angela again. I hope you remember me. I agreed to call you back this evening.

Peter sighed and rolled his eyes. How could he have forgotten Angela with her silky and seductive voice who'd taken him by the hand and made him change his electricity provider. He had hoped that she'd forgotten about him. It was most annoying, how could he get rid of her in a polite but firm manner? His problem was that he was too friendly to strangers, so they kept pestering him. The same had happened with Claudia. He'd already done enough to help by listening to her. He shouldn't have given her any false hope. She was resourceful; she'd find somewhere else to stay for a couple nights. He'd text her tonight saying the deal was off. One less headache!

We spoke two months ago.' She sounded even more upbeat and positive than before. 'I hope you're still free to talk tonight.'

Peter lowered his voice an octave. 'Of course.'

'Excellent. I notice that you've set up a direct debit payment with your new energy provider. That's awesome.'

'Thanks. It was really my wife who encouraged me to change.'

'Understood. Well, Mr Miller, I've got more good news for you. We've noticed a significant increase in your monthly salary and that means you could either pay off your mortgage a year earlier, or you could increase your purchasing power. Have you thought about how you'd like to spend the extra money?'

'I haven't thought about that.'

'You've got two children, so how about sending them to a good private school?'

'My wife and I don't agree about sending our kids to a private school – that's akin to social cleansing. Kids coming out of private schools end up with this assumption that they're somehow more special than their peers. Their social skills dwindle through years of elitist indoctrination and they'll end up as deluded snobs living an unjustified privileged life. I don't wish our kids to be part of that kind of social structure. Our kids go to a loving, socially inclusive and nurturing school not far from where we live, and we'd like to keep it that way. Private schools and their policy of social exclusion just don't sit well with our values.'

'Thank you, Mr Miller, I understand. How about spending some extra money on holidays? A trip to Disney World Florida, perhaps?'

'A trip to see Mickey Mouse? That sounds like my worst nightmare. No thanks! We take regular trips to the Suffolk countryside where our kids roam free and their minds and creativity run wild. They'll certainly have fond memories of these times, just like I still do. Thank you very much.'

'I understand. One final question; is there anything else our financial services can help you with? A loan offset by the value of your house has never been easier, thanks to our tailored products aimed at our most valued customers, like yourself, Mr Miller.'

Peter was tired of this conversation and was keen to start preparing dinner. He looked at the oven clock. It was already 18:42. There was only enough time to make a quick pasta dish. Tom and Lilly would love that. Perhaps a side salad for him and Joanne, accompanied by a nice glass of wine?

'Mr Miller, are you still there?'

'Eh, yes, I am.'

'For a valued customer like yourself, is there anything else we can do for you?'

'Come to think of it, I'm planning to build a spaceship. Some extra money may come in handy.'

The line went silent for a few seconds.

'Is that a joke, Mr Miller?'

'Nope. I'm dead serious.'

'I see. I'm not sure we can accommodate such a request.'

'You have to look at it as an investment in the future. One day your financial company may offer travel insurance for trips to Mars.'

'I don't think so, Mr Miller.' Angela sounded worried. She messaged her supervisor, who shook his head and signalled to cut off the conversation. Angela nodded, understanding that she had a madman on the line. Besides, there were more valuable clients to call during this golden hour when most people have returned home from work. Nobody wants to get a phone call after 7:30 p.m.

'One day,' Peter continued, 'we'll have a launch app on our iPhones for our own personal spaceship. While it's true we still haven't created flying cars or hover-boards, perhaps it'll be easier to design a spaceship. For my interplanetary project to get off the ground, I'll need a lot of money – hundreds of millions, I'm talking about.'

'I hear what you're saying, Mr Miller. But I'm sure your bank won't be able to extend your mortgage that far.'

'Oh, now you disappoint me.'

'It's all about a return on investment. A good education for your children can set them up for life and they'll end up getting better paid jobs.'

'In fifteen years' time.'

'Exactly. You have to plan ahead.'

'I hope to have left this planet with my family before then.'

Angela tried not to laugh.

'I'm sorry, Mr Miller. You'll have to speak to our customer relations department. I'm sure I can arrange a telephone call at some point.'

'I look forward to that.'

'Good night, Mr Miller.'

Peter was sure this would end another round of telemarketing; that was one less worry. But now he had to chop the onions and slice three cloves of garlic finely, fry them in a bit of olive oil until golden brown, and add two tins of tomatoes. Once they'd been infused with the flavour of caramelised onions and garlic, he added a tin tuna for some extra protein. Topped with some grated cheese, everybody would be happy.

Peter started singing a David Bowie tune 'Space Oddity'. His son loved it when he called him Major Tom.

At ten past seven, Peter opened a bottle of Italian wine, an Abruzzo from the supermarket, nothing special but perfect for a mid-week dinner. He poured the wine into two glasses and took a sip. He texted Claudia: 'I'm sorry, I don't think it's possible for you to stay here this weekend. Really sorry. Hope you'll find somewhere more suitable. Peter.' He read the message several times. Should he add an x or xxx at the end of the message? He scratched his head and decided to send the message just as it was.

Peter waited a few minutes staring at his phone, hoping for a quick reply. His phone was silent. He wasn't sure how to interpret this.

Eighteen minutes past seven, Tom rang the bell several times impatiently. Lilly stormed in and Joanne followed after locking the car. 'We're absolutely starving!' Tom said.

'All right, Major Tom. I've got some protein pills and a tube with lukewarm potato mash before we blast off into space.'

'Thanks, Dad, but I'd rather have some of that delicious tomato sauce.'

18

After they devoured their dinner, Peter made an announcement. He stood in the middle of the kitchen with a tea towel slung over his left shoulder and a box of dishwasher tablets in his right hand.

'I've got a surprise! Next weekend, we're going to practise how to survive a space journey. It'll be a great experiment. Tom and Lilly, you can write about it and present it at school. Your friends and teachers will love it!'

'Wicked! Are we going to go to space for real?'

'No, of course not. It's just pretend. I just want us to better understand what space-travel really entails and how people behave when stuck together in a small space.'

'It sounds like a social experiment,' Joanna said.

'I see it more as a family bonding experience.'

'Can I bring along some toys?' Lilly asked. She was very excited.

'Of course! We can all take something to keep us busy for a couple of days.'

Joanne saw the kids bursting with enthusiasm. She

walked over to Peter and gave him a big hug. Tom and Lilly recoiled in horror. 'Yuck,' Tom said.

'Peter, I love you! Since your promotion, you're a changed man. But what is this all about?'

'Remember, Tom? The camper we saw at Barry's scrapyard?'

'Yeah, it had an awning and a bench you can lie on.'

'Well, I decided to borrow it for the weekend. In return, Barry wants us to help him build a model spaceship for his scrapyard.'

'That sounds exciting. What does he want to use it for?' Joanne asked.

'Not sure. He said he wants to use it as a beacon, near the main junction, because too many people miss that particular road. He is planning to turn it into a B & B, a bijou destination in its own right.'

'Interesting,' Joanne said. 'Not sure who would want to go and stay there, though. And why exactly do we have to go camping?'

'Ha... just to illustrate what space-travel feels like, to make it a bit more real. At work we talk about it a lot. Don't worry, the kids'll love it.'

'That's what Barry said,' Tom butted in. 'Strap an engine on the back of that VW and fly to Mars.'

'Well, it's not that easy. But it's a start in talking about adapting to climate change. Once people realise that setting up a space colony will remain a fantasy for a long time, people may take better care of our planet.'

'It seems a bit far-fetched,' Joanne said, 'but I'm up for it. It'll be fun. Playing Monopoly all weekend.'

'I prefer playing Minecraft on my iPad,' Tom said.

Joanne laughed. 'Of course, darling, I was hoping to bring along my Kindle, so I can finally catch up on all those books I downloaded ages ago.'

'Sounds like the perfect hibernation plan,' Peter said.

'So we can't leave the camper for two days. You're not serious, are you?' Tom asked.

'Correct, two nights and two days.'

'But how do we go to the toilet?'

'I hope there's going to be a chemical loo?' Joanne asked.

'Yep, that's all part of it. Barry's camper comes with a state-of-the-art portable flush toilet.'

'That'll smell terrible, yuck!' Lilly said.

'That's all part of the social experiment.'

'It may end up in our divorce!'

'We can all take some sleeping pills. I've read that the best way to travel through space is while asleep. The metabolism slows down and you minimize your hunger. During a real space voyage, our bodies will have to be cooled down to lower our metabolism even further.'

'That would be a step too far!'

'We can leave the windows open to keep us cool. That'll help with those smells from your thunderbox too!'

'A trip to Mars will be six months or so. How can you cool down a body that long?'

'Oh, that's nothing. Medical science can deliver on that one.'

'Then we may need to bring along a medic.'

'Not this weekend, but on a future real trip, for sure!'

'Well, there are enough young doctors utterly disillusioned with the state of the NHS, so I'm sure it'll be easy to find one willing to come along. Look at it as an extended gap year.'

'But there won't be any coming back.'

'Not right now, but perhaps in a couple of years' time you'll have regular shuttles between Earth and Mars, especially since they found traces of water.'

'I'm serious. Ask Shereen, the one who lives down the road. She's just finished her A & E rotation, and according to her mum she's thinking of going to Australia for a couple of years. I bet it would be more interesting to come along with us!'

'Let's not get ahead of ourselves. All we've got is a forty-year-old van. It's not going anywhere near a launch pad.'

'That's a relief. I've got some things planned for Monday, and the kids'll have to be back at school.'

'In any case, it beats being bored at home,' Peter said.

Joanne took her task seriously. Peter had brought the van home the night before, leaving his Volvo at Barry's scrapyard and parking the VW outside their house. It smelled rather musty inside, and the mattresses were well worn. Joanne was pleasantly surprised to see how big the van was once the awning was extended. She could easily stand up, and there were two additional sleeping places. Tom and Lilly could sleep in the awning beds. Joanne cleaned the van and emptied all the cupboards of random stuff left by the previous renters. After two hours of cleaning furiously, the van had a lemony smell and was packed to the brim. Joanne stocked up on sleeping bags, pyjamas, towels, a Monopoly game and some playing cards, seeing that the weather forecast predicted rain. Plenty of snacks were needed to keep morale high.

She also prepared a few meals, which were easy to heat up on the small propane burner in the rear of the van. The kids couldn't wait to leave.

On the way to the A2, they discussed nicknames for their van. The Robin Williams movie RV was an all-time family favourite. The camper in the movie was named 'The Big Rolling Turd'.

'No, our van is too cute to call it a turd,' Lilly said.

'Then you better come up with a better name,' Tom challenged his sister.

'Let's call it the fart!'

'That's funny. Just because it makes fart noises when it tries to go faster,' Tom said. 'Nah, we need something better. How about The Space Explorer?'

'Mum, which one do you prefer?'

'I like them both. The Fart is funny and The Space Explorer sounds pretty grand,' Joanne said diplomatically.

'Dad?'

'I like fart! Small and innocent.'

'Not in your case, Dad,' Tom sulked.

Peter looked over his shoulder as he struggled to speed up. The engine sounded like it might collapse.

'If we can't get across the Dartford Tunnel, what hope is there of reaching escape velocity in this tin can?' Joanne remarked.

'That's where Barry's jet engine comes in,' Peter joked. 'We take this engine out. Create more space for storage and strap the engine on top.'

'But then the awning won't open.'

'Well then, we strap the engine to the side. Or even better, have an engine on either side. Twice the speed.'

By the time they arrived at the campsite in Suffolk, it was cold and late. They were the only campers in the field and there was no sign of life. The office had long been closed and boarded up. The toilet block was dimly lit. Peter drove to the furthest end of the field. The grass was long and trailed along the bottom of the camper.

Peter switched off the engine and the headlights. It was silent and pitch black. It took a few minutes before his eyes adapted to the night. Slowly more and more stars appeared in between the clouds. In the distance, he could make out the silhouette of the village church.

Tom switched on his light and helped extend the awning. Joanne made the beds quickly.

'Come on, brush your teeth before you go to bed, just like at home,' she told the kids.

'Do we have to? Aren't we supposed to conserve water for real emergencies?'

'Waking up with foul breath counts as an emergency. It's a violation of basic human rights. In space, there are no dentists.'

'Space sounds cool – no school or dentists!'

'Yep, and it's pitch black all the time,' Lilly threw in to dampen her brother's enthusiasm for the absurd.

'It's not. Look at all those bright stars up in the sky. We'll be racing towards them, with the speed of light.'

'I'm afraid your sister's right, Tom,' said Peter. 'It's called the Olbers' paradox. There are trillions of stars out there and many of them brighter than the sun, but because the universe is expanding at the speed of light, darkness expands at an accelerating rate too. I'm sure you've heard of the Voyager space probe. It launched in 1977. I remember it very well even though I was only five years old back then. I was allowed to stay up. Our whole family watched it on TV. It's been travelling through space at around seventeen kilometres per second for the past forty years. And even at that speed, it's only just left our solar system. It won't reach the next solar system for another thirty-thousand years. That's how enormous space is, and that's why it's pitch dark.

Lilly yawned. 'I think I'm going to sleep.'

'Me too,' Tom said.

'That leaves you and me and a bottle of wine!' Peter said to Joanne.

'So far, space travel doesn't seem too bad.

The next morning Tom and Lilly woke up to the sound of rain pounding the awning. It was waterproof. It would have been more difficult to persuade the kids to go outside than to stay inside all day. Only Peter was happy with the miserable weather. Sun and a clear blue sky would have jeopardised his experiment. Making kids do things you want them to do is next to impossible, but to Peter's surprise they adapted very well to their new environment. Joanne seemed very content too, lying in bed reading a novel on her Kindle. Peter realised that as a family, they had never been so close. He was thrilled. Once in a while, Tom passed round a family-sized bag of Doritos.

Peter had no idea what to do with all this free time. He

didn't want to switch on the radio, in order to save the battery. Everything in the camper was old and dated. He didn't want to risk getting stranded in the middle of nowhere on a remote campsite with a dead battery, unable to get back to London on Sunday. He was counting down the hours.

Tim and Lilly entertained themselves with drawings and puzzles. Halfway through the afternoon, Joanne read them a story. She and Peter were amused by the kids' lack of appetite. She was only concerned that they'd have to take most of the food home.

'I'm not sure how much longer this can stay fresh,' she said. 'The fridge stopped working the minute we got off the M25.'

'I wonder if it's the lack of fresh air or the fact that they're not moving around a lot that they're not hungry.'

'Or the three giant packs of Doritos we went through in the space of a day. If we ever pull off this experiment for real, we need to bring along an extra space shuttle full of nacho crisps.'

'And that's never going to happen. That's why these protein pills come in handy; they take up less space.'

'I think I hear something,' Joanne said. 'Quiet, kids!'

It took a while for Lilly and Tom to stop giggling.

'I'll have a look.'

The windows were damp, and it was difficult to look outside. Tim drew some faces on the window with his finger, but within a few minutes they would disappear again.

'What do you see?'

'Nothing really, false alarm.'

Lulled by his own comfort, Peter didn't notice two men

standing ten metres next to their van. They were both holding an umbrella. If he'd watched more carefully, he might have seen them standing next to a black Buick Lacrosse. The taller of the two men finished smoking his cigarette and threw the butt on the grass, which extinguished with a hiss on the wet ground. The other man unwrapped a chocolate bar.

'Guess there's nothing much to report, then,' Mike said.

Dave shook his head. He was disappointed.

'Let's go back to that nice country inn and get something to eat on the way. I think this guy's a red herring,' Mike said.

'Let's wait in the car for a while and see what happens.'

'I can tell you exactly what's going to happen: nothing!'

'Observation is the only tool we've got, buddy.'

'They're one weird family, I tell you. Who in their right mind would go camping in this weather in such a desolate place? What a glamorous career we've got,' Mike said. 'I better go and take a leak. When I get back, I suggest we leave. Wait for me in the car.' He walked to the outhouse. He tried several doors, but they were all locked. He was slightly annoyed. He hated having to urinate behind a tree and get wet at the same time.

Not long after Peter and Joanne discussed their lack of appetite, Tom started to get restless; he was hungry.

'It's almost eight, Mum.'

'Let me warm up some pasta for all of us. I prepared the sauce back home and all I have to do is heat it up. It's your favourite: tomato sauce with meatballs.'

'I love that! I could eat a whole plate!'

Peter had this niggling sensation that they weren't alone

on the campsite. With the four of them in the camper, the windows fogged up easily. He wiped them again. Much to his surprise, he saw the rear lights of a car disappearing in the distance.

He wiped the window again for a clearer look. He couldn't identify the make of the car, but it reminded him of something he'd seen in American movies. He couldn't quite place it. Perhaps they were tourists who'd gotten lost. But at this time of year, it seemed highly unlikely.

Peter wasn't sure if he should tell Joanne what he'd seen. He could anticipate her reaction. She'd tell him to stop worrying and set the table.

By the time Joanne had finished preparing dinner, it was almost the kids' bedtime. Lilly announced with great fanfare that she had used the chemical toilet again. She showed no inhibition or modesty when it came to bodily functions.

Peter had been suppressing a strong urge to go for most of the day. He couldn't cheat on his experiment by making a quick run for the campsite's lavatories. To avoid embarrassment, Peter changed seats and went to the front of the van. He managed to swivel the front seat around so that nobody could see what he was doing. As soon as he started to relax and felt himself about to go, Lilly shouted, 'Daddy, you're so smelly. Open the window!'

'Mayday, mayday! Abandon space ship! Women and children first,' Tom chimed in.

Joanne laughed out loud.

In all those years, Peter had never felt so uncomfortable and embarrassed. He resented this the most. For him, this was the end of the experiment. He had no interest in leaving a civilisation where private toilets were an essential aspect of life. He had no wish to go through this again, ever.

Lilly was yawning and Tom's eyes were getting smaller by the minute.

'We can have an early night,' Peter suggested. 'How many hours have we clocked up inside?'

'Just over twenty-six hours,' Joanne said.

'Five more months and twenty-nine days to go,' Peter joked.

Joanne sighed. 'I'm not so sure about the whole thing. It seems such a pointless struggle.'

'I'll sell the Volvo when I get home and cycle to work for the sake of bringing global warming to a halt. Then nobody has to leave the planet, at least not in our lifetime.'

'Ah well, it has all been a bit of a laugh. It's been a good bonding activity. You should write about our adventure and get it published in one of the weekend papers to raise awareness, it will certainly encourage more people to join you on your bike. Then you have a real impact.'

'Now you've planted a seed in my head!'

Joanne looked at Peter; he had changed, she thought. He was a lot more confident and much more environmentally aware. He seemed more focused. Was it his promotion at work, or was it something else?

'The kids are fast asleep. I think you should join me, an early night will do us good.'

Peter leaned over Joanne to open one of the windows.

'That's cheating!'

'We wouldn't be able to survive the night. I wonder how

they cope with stale air in a space ship.'

'I don't want to think about it. It sounds too rank.'

'I'd better research that next week.'

'Don't they keep you busy at work?'

'Right now I don't want to think about work.' Peter switched off the bedside light and moved closer to Joanne. She put her head on his shoulder and her hand on his chest. He could hear a barn owl in the distance and a church bell chiming. A welcome breeze cleared the air.

Lilly was the first to wake up. The weather had improved. The sky was blue with scattered clouds, and though it was still cold outside, it was a lot better than yesterday.

'Can we go to the beach now?' Lilly asked. 'I'm so bored!'

'We'll have to wait till Daddy wakes up,' said Joanne.

Lilly did not wait a minute longer, and turned over to Peter and tried to open his eyes. When that didn't work, she tried squeezing his nose. This only made him snore louder. Lilly resorted to sitting on his chest; with her full weight, she bounced up and down till Peter woke up. He looked at the alarm clock and saw it was almost eight a.m. Thirty-seven hours; he sighed. He wasn't quite sure how much longer his experiment could last. The kids were desperate to run around. He could do with a stretch. But he didn't have to think about it for long when he heard a dog barking.

'Funny, I thought I saw another car yesterday!'

'Why didn't you say anything?'

'I didn't want to make a fuss.'

'What could possibly happen here? It's the middle of nowhere. If there's one place safe in this country, it's here!'

Then there was a knock on the side of the van.

'Open up, Mr Miller!'

Peter opened the passenger front door and leaned out, seeing a middle-aged man with an extremely displeased look on his face.

'Mr Miller?' he asked.

'That's correct.'

'You booked this site two days ago.'

'Yes, that's correct, and I paid on-line. You must be Marvin, the owner.'

Marvin nodded.

'And you ticked the terms of agreement box?'

'Yes, indeed.'

'Then you must know that litter on the grass is against camp regulations. I'm obliged to fine you.'

'What do you mean?' Peter asked.

'This!'

Marvin showed him a cigarette butt and a wrapper from a Snickers bar.

'It's a filthy habit, anyway,' said Marvin. 'Smoking is for the weak and the stupid. You come all this way from the city and instead of inhaling our clean and fresh air, you keep on sucking on those bloody fags. What would happen if a child picked this up, put it in its mouth and choked on it? I'd be the one in court. You wouldn't like it if that happened to your child, would you? I tell you, I've had enough. I want you, your family and your camper to leave immediately!'

Peter stepped outside for the first time in more than thirty-seven hours; it felt good, the air crisp and fresh. His anger was stripped away. He stretched his arms before turning towards the owner of the campsite.

'Sorry, Marvin. Neither I nor my wife smoke. You can have a good look around our van. You won't find any cigarettes. I don't even own a lighter.'

'Well, you've been the first guests on our site since New Year's Eve.' 'Again, it's not us. It must be from that New Year's Eve party.'

'You can't fool me, Mr Miller. That fag was put out recently. You can see the burn mark in the grass over there.'

The man pointed at a spot ten metres away.

'You must get more visitors, I'm sure of it.'

'It's those damn cheap flights,' Marvin ranted on. 'Years ago, lots of city folks would come here to escape for the weekend, just like you. A bit of fresh air, a nice stroll on the beach and a barbecue lunch. Now they take a train to Stansted airport, and for a tenner, they fly to Turkey or Spain. Just for the weekend. How can I compete with that? Last year, I had a new toilet block installed. Six grand it cost me. How am I going to earn that back?'

'Now let's calm down, aren't you overreacting a bit?'

Marvin looked miffed.

'Actually,' Peter remembered, 'there was another car here last night.'

'Nobody told me that,' Marvin growled. 'There's a sign on the gate to report at reception.'

'I guess they drove up to the gate, had a look around and decided that they didn't like the place.'

'Nonsense. This is a beautiful spot. It's been on the list of top twenty small campsites in Britain since 1998. Why would you drive all the way from the main road to turn around again? There's something fishy about your story,' he said. 'I hope you're not making this up, Mr Miller.'

The dog had run off and Marvin walked away towards the entrance. He realised that he might have been a bit rude to Peter, but who cares? City people were rude and arrogant to him all the time. He was sure he'd caused no harm.

'Nice character,' Joanne said.

'Tell me about it,' Peter agreed. He saw Marvin looking at the tracks in the grass and erasing them with his feet. The car tracks were a lot wider than the camper's.

'I'm sure I saw another car last night,' Peter said. 'I didn't hear it arrive because the kids were chatting. But I remember how it moved away silently in the night. The church tower chimed eight times, the moon shone through the clouds and I could even see a few stars. The question is: who else could have been here last night?'

'We'll never know. Let's have lunch on the beach. I brought some blankets. We have to hurry and then head home before the Sunday afternoon traffic starts building up.'

Joanne kissed Peter. She was enjoying this weekend together.

The kids ran out in front of them towards an endless and empty expanse of sand dunes. It was cold and dreary; wind was lashing their faces; the rain had stopped but the dark grey sky in the distance looked ominous.

The blanket flew away as soon as Joanne had spread it out. The kids ran after it and held on to it together, then ran off with it again as though it were a sail. With their backs against the wind, Peter and Joanne ate their sandwiches.

'Tastes good!' Joanne said.

'A short walk and some fresh air changes all perceptions,' Peter noted.

'It would be a shame if mankind had to leave all of this behind in search of other planets.'

'But how do we make people understand that we're on a path of self-destruction?'

'By leaving this place in a better shape than we inherited it.'

'Let's start by planting a tree in the garden.'

'A cherry tree. I love its blossom!'

Peter and Joanne embraced, a stolen moment before Tom and Lilly galloped back with a handful of shells they'd collected to take home.

19

Shoreditch, London

Nina Simmons was sitting on a giant beanbag waiting to meet the features editor of the news website Yellow Sparkle. She was playing nervously with her hair. A nose ring and a purple streak highlighted her independence, though knowing her editor she should have chosen a more conventional style instead of a hipster look – skater skirt, red tights and a crop top, emblazoned with a giant Damian Hirst diamond encrusted skull. A lot depended on today's meeting with Alistair Mohair.

He arrived fashionably late; she hardly noticed him as he appeared from behind a large palm tree. Alistair walked without making any sound. She looked at his feet; he was wearing soft leather Moroccan slippers. He walked over to her with an outstretched arm.

'Please don't get up. We have to cover a lot and I am a bit strapped for time. Busy, busy, busy…' Alistair shook her hand and plonked himself next to her on the beanbag. They gravitated towards each other. Nina felt uncomfortable at first but the situation had something endearing at the same time. The beanbag had certainly the capacity to bring people closer together.

'I read your email and I do feel strongly that we should do a feature on the impact of global warming on our day to day life,' Alistair said.

'It could run for weeks, I could interview some influential scientists in the field. Looking at it from a different angle each week.'

'I am not so sure about that, Nina. People distrust so-called experts, we have to reach their hearts.'

'Perhaps I could travel to Canada or Greenland and write about the impact of the melting ice on local fishing communities.'

Alistair Mohair stroked his well-trimmed beard while staring pensively at his iPad.

'I like your idea, I really do. But what I'm really looking for is a personal interest story, something closer to home. All those abstract stories about the sea level rising in a hundred years' time won't swing our readers into action. It's old news. People are immune to these alarmist messages; they're passé. I'm looking for more edgy, gritty stuff, a story that'll hook our readers for more than a millisecond. If they don't get sucked in after the first sentence, they click to the next site.'

'Can I help it,' Nina said, 'that our readers have the attention span of a goldfish?'

'You have to learn to live with that, that's the new reality. You need to dazzle them right away.'

'I know.'

'I'm just outlining an interesting series of articles. I don't want to be didactic.'

'So, you've got no idea either?' Nina teased Alastair.

'No, no, no, of course not,' he said. 'I've got loads of ideas. My mind is literally overflowing with creativity.' Alistair made a wild gesture illustrating his overflowing mind. 'We have to focus on one or two ideas. We need to get down to the essence of global warming in a way that connects with our audience.'

'I wrote to you some time ago about champagne production in south-east England. With global temperatures rising, more champagne is being made there. Just say the word and I'll arrange an interview with some of the local producers.'

'No, no. That's good news. Nobody can complain about more champagne.'

'Exactly.'

'That's not what I had in mind,' Alastair said. 'The article has to reflect the values of our organisation. Cutting-edge news is our lifeblood. That kind of article would only interest the middle-aged, Sunday paper-reading crowd.'

'It's still expensive. Prices won't come down as demand outstrips production.'

'Still… champagne, fizz, bubbles, parties. No threat, no sensation there. Nobody's going to jump on their bike in the name of preventing more champagne production in West Sussex.'

'Start with the good news first.'

'Rule number one in journalism: bad news sells.'

'Sex sells, you mean. Look at how well my first blog Supercharged was doing.'

'But that story had everything: a potential epidemic, a

deadly new supercharged microbe and an attractive villain having sex with her potential victims. People were scared; they just lapped it up. It was brilliant.'

'Champagne and sex is a good combination.'

'Somehow I don't see how an interview with a bunch of eco-farmers in West Sussex harvesting grapes in green wellies can capture the imagination of millions of young people. You need to shove a rocket up their arses.'

'Well, it's not just wine growing on the south coast; there are even vineyards in East Anglia.'

Alistair checked the time on his iPad. He was running late.

'You're kidding me?'

'No, definitely not.'

'Now you've got me, you see. I didn't know that. Well done. Champagne in East Anglia… It has a nice ring to it.'

'You're saying this to get rid of me?'

Alistair didn't reply.

'You'll have to excuse me, Nina. I've got a Skype conference call with the San Francisco office.'

Nina looked disappointed. She was desperate to start writing again. Her star had fallen as quickly as it had risen in the Internet stratosphere, back when she was blogging in London about a chlamydia outbreak. Although she was earning some lucrative commissions, they were more about product placement and turning readers into consumers – a shallow pursuit. She yearned for something meatier, something provocative, stories that would challenge vested interests, rock the boat of the establishment, expose scandal and restore justice. That's why she had become a journalist in the first place. She sighed as she reminisced about her early ideals, and the lack of opportunities to realize them any more. At least she had a job, she thought. It paid the rent; that was one less worry. She was grateful to Alistair for giving her a chance. But was her heart was in it? Not a chance. Maybe it was just a matter of keeping her eyes and ears open and seizing the next opportunity. What if it never came? She could always consider starting a food blog.

Alistair tried to get up elegantly from his beanbag, but instead he nearly lost his balance, gripping Nina's shoulder. She laughed out loud. He straightened his pullover, picked up the iPad from the floor, turned around and looked at Nina.

'Since you're so determined, why don't you travel around Suffolk and East Anglia for a couple of days? Let's see what you come up with. Mind you, if it's not good, we won't post it on the site. You'd better make sure it sizzles.'

'Awesome!'

'Talk to Amy. It would be good to arrange some wine tastings. We could generate ad revenue by linking your blog to a few wine merchants. Leave it to Amy, she'll sort it out.

'Thanks.'

'You've got a car? Public transport in those backwaters is completely unreliable. A journalist without a car out in the sticks is like a…'

'Roving journalist without a Wi-Fi connection,' Nina was quick to add.

Alistair smiled. 'Yeah, something like that. Again, talk to Amy. The company has an old Mini in the basement car park. It hardly gets used. Just fill her up with some petrol when you get back.'

'Nice one!'

Alistair made his way to the polished metal slide and was about to whizz down to the second floor. It was a popular gimmick and promised to cut down on the company's energy bill significantly; in the long run, it would save the planet.

'And don't forget to add some pictures to your blog – hills and daffodils, that kind of stuff.'

'Would bluebells do?'

'Whatever. As long as it makes people feel nostalgic and lights a fire under their arses. Frighten them, make them realise what they are about to lose very soon. Get them hooked, get them to crave more and more!'

'I've already done my research. Bluebells are affected by global warming too. The earliest flowering date recorded was the 4th of April 2012, twelve days earlier than in the 1980s.'

'So there you go – champagne and bluebells it is.'

'Give me a few days to make some contacts. I'll call you once I've settled down somewhere, a nice country inn or pub. All expenses paid?'

'Not quite, Nina. First show me a good story. When you work for me, you have to sing for your supper. Remember our motto: our stories have to sparkle! Too-da-loo.'

Finally, Alistair sat down on a jute mat and pushed himself down the slide.

20

Peter's routine as a financial fraud investigator had been well established after several weeks. He was quick to spot the loopholes some of the senior accountants had used. Sylvia had written a detailed report and together with Mikhail Zoblovski she worked on a case against these accountants. At first, Mikhail wanted to use his own in-house security team to deal with the culprits, using unorthodox methods to end their shady practices. Sylvia convinced him to use more conventional methods of bringing them to justice.

'It's not about revenge or getting your money back,' she said. 'It's about setting an example for the world.'

'You don't understand, Sylvia. It's very much about getting my money back and sending a strong message not to mess with me.'

'That often ends in bloodshed.'

'It'll be done discreetly. Did I ever mention that I own some mines and a small steel and metal works in Magnitogorsk? A most convenient place for organizing meetings.'

'I don't follow you.'

'I won't expand on the topic, but the average temperature of a smelting furnace is around 1500 degrees Celsius.'

'I'd rather see these thieves in jail.'

'What you call a jail is called a Hilton in my country. It's a joke. Inmates here have Internet access and the choice of a three-course meal.'

'True, the Gulag it is not. But sentencing is about giving people a second chance at life, giving them time to reflect on their crimes and rebuild their lives.'

'I don't get that at all, but all right, I'll go with the flow. I'm a guest in your country – a well-paying guest – but a guest nevertheless. This is your project.'

'I think we owe Peter Miller a lot of credit. He got to the bottom of it all.'

'Make sure he gets a bonus. I like to reward people that are good to me. Perhaps I can meet him one day.'

Sylvia looked at her watch. 'There's no time for that today. Your car is waiting outside. Remember, lunchtime concert at the Wigmore Hall.'

'That's right: a piano recital, scherzos and mazurkas. Chopin. Natalya Ivratinova, a most promising young Russian pianist, is playing. She's amazing. I'll have a late lunch with her afterwards.'

'That's correct. I've booked you a table at the Purple Cherry Club.'

'Excellent, Sylvia… What would I do without you?'

'In the meantime, we'll deal with the international court orders,' Sylvia continued unfazed.

'Brilliant. I'll look through them on my way back to Moscow. I promised Yana that I'd spend some time with her.'

Zoblovski disappeared into the lift humming the beginning of 'Scherzo No. 2'.

Peter hadn't heard from Claudia for a while, despite sending her several messages. He'd almost given up on hearing from her when he received a short message ending with a series of smiley face emojis. Something must have been going well for her. He agreed to meet her at one.

She was so excited to see him, she kissed him.

'This time I'll get the coffees,' Claudia said.

'Time for a celebration?'

'Yes, it is. I found a new job and I start on Monday.'

'Well done, congratulations! How did you find it?'

'Just like how I met you. I was handing out a paper; someone said something in Portuguese, a joke. I started talking, and guess what? He turned out to be from Rio de Janeiro. One thing led to another and now I'm going to do the marketing for a Brazilian company in London. Isn't that marvellous?'

'What kind of company?'

'Clothing, mainly beach wear. But they sell well on the Internet and in high-end stores. They've got some great designs.'

'I'm really happy for you, but doesn't this also mean that you won't have time to meet up again?'

'Oh, silly man. Of course we can.'

'Nah, I am sure once you start working with your new friend, you'll forget all about me.'

'Who knows?' she said with a shrug. 'He is an attractive man, early thirties, tall and single.'

Another short awkward silence followed. Peter checked his watch. He wanted to go back to the office. It felt like a rug had been pulled from under his feet and he was now lying on his back and feeling bruised.

'What about your boyfriend in Brazil? What's his name again?'

'Mario,' Claudia said calmly.

'Yes, of course, Mario. Wasn't he supposed to come and visit you?'

'Mario was full of plans, ideas and promises, and then one day he just stopped answering my messages. It's obvious; he's met someone else and forgotten about me. If he moves on, perhaps I have to move on too. It's no fun being on your own in a big city like London.'

'Well, you always had me,' Peter sounded hopeful.

'Of course, I love talking to you and I admire how you try to protect the environment by switching your energy provider and build your own spaceship.'

Peter raised his eyebrows.

'And you're a wonderful friend to me, almost like a father figure. But then I never had a father, so I'm not quite sure how that feels. My dad left my mum when she got pregnant. He had dark blond hair according to my mum – just like you, I suppose.'

'A father figure?' Peter looked disappointed.

Claudia gave him a quizzical look.

'What else could it be?'

A silence followed.

'Oh come on,' she said. 'You didn't think… Oh, Peter. You're so funny. You're a real dreamer, my dear astronaut.

I think you're wonderful, generous and helpful, but you're not the kind of lover I'm looking for. I'm less than half your age,' Claudia laughed.

'Almost half my age!'

'I'm twenty-one and you're forty-four. You're the senior accountant here. Forty-four divided by twenty-one equals two and a bit.

'I guess I forget my age when I'm with you!'

Claudia smiled and shook her head. Her plait flicked from side to side.

'Ah, and speaking of accounts, did you ever get information about that company I mentioned, Amazorico?'

'As a matter of fact, I did.' Peter looked through his briefcase nervously. It was full of reports, sales figures and graphs. He rummaged through the same papers several times.

'Damn, I should have brought those papers with me. There's some good news, some bad news and some terrifying news.'

'Let's start with the good news first.'

'The good news is that there's a financial connection between the owner of Amazorico, Roberto Sousa, and the governor of the State of São Paulo. I can confirm that he made several large transactions to the governor at regular intervals.'

'Could that be blackmail?'

'Who knows? That's not for me to decide. I'm merely stating the facts.'

'And the bad news?'

'The bad news is that you won't have much of a case

against Amazorico.'

'But you just said you've got all the facts.'

'Yes, but the problem is that Roberto Sousa and the company itself, including the building, no longer exist.'

Claudia's face turned pale and she felt dizzy. She added some more sugar to her caffè latte and finished it in one gulp.

'What do you mean?'

'That's the terrifying news. The owner of the company, along with four employees, was killed in a huge explosion.'

'When?' Claudia tried to feign ignorance.

'Around the time you arrived in London. It was on a Saturday, end of January. I can get you the exact date once I find my papers again.'

The colour drained from Claudia's face. She looked away, avoiding Peter's intense gaze. 'That is awful.'

'Now listen to this. I did some further research, and I'm breaching confidentiality here. You understand?'

Claudia nodded.

'This may be a long shot but I discovered a link between your state governor and some influential US congressmen. Large sums of money have been transferred to an off-shore account over a period of more than ten years. We are talking about a lot of money. But you can't mention this to anyone yet. This can potentially be very damaging and we must tread with caution.'

'Wow, that's a lot of information!'

'So tell me, Claudia. Why are you so interested in this company and the accounts?'

'I used to work for them before I left.'

'Oh my God. I had no idea.'

Claudia held her empty cup and didn't respond. The net around her was closing. She had escaped her friend Virginia's barrage of questions and probing just in time and now Peter would be linking her directly to the crime any time soon. She might as well turn herself in right now. What was the point of running away? The day of reckoning would come sooner or later. The happiness of finding another job and a new boyfriend had evaporated instantly like a drop of water on a hot cooking plate. Claudia's face showed it all.

'I can tell you must feel devastated hearing about what happened to your colleagues. What a nightmare.'

Claudia nodded.

'You are one lucky woman. A narrow escape if you ask me.'

'You can say that again, Peter.' What else could she do? She had to keep up the pretence.

Peter rummaged through his briefcase, allowing for a silence. He felt sorry for Claudia and was worried that he'd opened a can of worms. With the information in his hands and considering the magnitude of the explosion in Brazil and the potential political fall-out, he couldn't brush this under the carpet. He had to report this to the financial regulator. Right now he had enough on his plate. He'd discuss it with a legal advisor in his company later in the week when he had more evidence.

'So how is your rocket shaping up?' Claudia was keen to change the subject.

Peter realised that Claudia was teasing him, which he took as a good sign. He decided to play along as a future space explorer.

'It's going well. We've made a lot of progress. Our camping trip last month was a useful experiment in space survival technique.'

'So when's the launch?'

Peter paused for a second. He thought it was best to dampen her enthusiasm. Now that Claudia would start working elsewhere, he had given up any hope.

'There are some practical issues to be addressed first... in fact, quite a few. It's like the more you start to read up about things, the more you realise how little you know. There are teams out there who have been working on space survival for the last fifty years, and here's Peter Miller from Crystal Palace trying to build a spaceship in a barn and set off towards the Andromeda Galaxy in a modified Volkswagen camper. People end up getting sectioned under the Mental Health Act for less bizarre obsessions.'

'But think about it, it'll start making people realise that there's a real problem, that we're all fucking up this planet.' Claudia seemed to have found her spark again.

'Well, there's time, for me at least. I live on a hill in Crystal Palace; it's one of the highest points in London, well over a hundred metres above sea level. It'll be centuries before I can start a beach bar outside my front door.'

'You don't get it, do you?' Claudia exclaimed. 'Think about the millions of people in Bangladesh, Vanuatu, New Orleans, Florida, or elsewhere in the world. In the next twenty years, the sea level will rise high enough to force a mass migration to higher and drier places. And at some point, those immigrants our leaders try so hard to keep out will come knocking on your door in Crystal Palace.'

'Funny, I've heard that before.'

'It's not so funny if you live in Bangladesh and your livelihood gets washed away in a storm. Wouldn't you pack up and leave?'

'Sure, but flying off into outer space isn't the solution to global warming.'

'It may be the only option left,' Claudia said solemnly.

'Anyway, Barry wants to finish our project soon and put it near the entrance of his scrapyard to attract more visitors.'

'Well, I'm glad to hear that you're not giving up on that. It's not a bad idea at all. At least it'll get the locals talking about it. I'd love to come along one day to see it for myself.'

'Of course you can. We'll be there practically every weekend. You can join and help us anytime.'

'Why not, that'd be great.' It sounded noncommittal.

Peter got up and kissed Claudia goodbye. 'I'd better get back to work and read up on how to get beyond escape velocity with a recycled fighter jet engine.'

'Maybe a Formula One tuning kit will do the trick!' Claudia chuckled.

'I guess I need a lot more than a tuning kit.'

Claudia shook her head. He was quite endearing. Twenty years too old, but charming nevertheless. She leaned forwards with her head in her hands, elbows resting on the table. Perhaps Peter would be the one who could help her out of her situation. He was a bit too old to consider a long-term relationship, but he was not bad looking, a short fling could be on the cards. He had solid values; he was perfect father material. A journey to Mars sounded like science fiction but it didn't have to be like that. A European probe had crash-landed not so long ago. The Chinese had set their eyes on going to Mars and every so often computer rendered images of colonies on the Red Planet appear in the papers. Perhaps she could volunteer. She could kick-start a human reproduction programme; after all, she was the perfect age. Then she had to laugh. She imagined seducing Peter one day; that would be the least painful part of her escape plan. She smiled, fantasising about flying to Mars at more than fifty thousand kilometres per hour, leaving her earthly troubles behind. Peter's rocket could solve all her problems, if it would only exist.

Sylvia was in a good mood when she met Peter. She loved it when Zoblovski supported her decisions and let her get on with running his business without too much interference. He was a tough but fair boss who ultimately put his own pleasure before profit. Peter liked Sylvia's effervescent personality and how it rubbed off on him and the rest of the team, in sharp contrast to Duncan's managing style.

'Shall we get back to business?' Peter enquired. 'I'm planning to leave a bit early tonight.'

'Any interesting plans?'

'Just the usual weekend in the country.'

'Ah, building your space rocket.'

'Spaceship!'

'That's what I meant. I'd love to see it one day.'

'Sure, why not… Claudia's coming too.'

'It's going to get crowded in that spaceship of yours.'

'All in the name of genetic diversity.'

'In case you're going to build a new extraterrestrial colony?'

'Exactly,' Peter said with a smile.

21

'The soil is just perfect! Look for yourself.'

Nina turned around and prodded the soft soil with the tip of her welly. It was dark and crumbly, soft and smooth, unlike the heavy London clay she was used to. Nina lifted her head and let the faint midday sun warm her face. She took a deep breath, the cold air filling her lungs and reviving her spirits. Just being here for a few minutes made the long car journey worth it. A few more days in the country would revitalise and inspire her.

Jonathan Appleton, a London investment banker-turned-wine grower after the financial collapse in 2008, was unstoppable. In the first five years, he'd ploughed all his savings into converting this part of rural England into champagne country, rivalling Reims. He leaned forward and took a handful of soil. He let it run through his fingers.

'It's perfect; sandy clay and organic matter mixture,' he said. 'The best soil conditions for our Pinot Noir and Chardonnay grapes. I'll let you taste some in a minute.'

'Do you think that English champagne will dominate

clubs and fine restaurants around the world one day?' Nina asked, holding her notebook in her hand.

'Mind you, Nina, I'd prefer that you call it sparkling wine. The name champagne is protected, and only grapes produced in a certain area around Reims and Épernay can be used to make champagne. Perhaps we should just call it "Suffolk".'

'Mmm... It hasn't got the same ring to it.'

'I agree, but with time, it may rival the prestige of Cristal champagne.'

'Perhaps we could arrange a joint venture with some rappers.'

'I'm not so sure, Miss Simmons. That may send the wrong message.'

'Our website is popular with young people,' Nina said. 'And they need to be able to relate to someone endorsing your product. Leave it to our marketing team; we can be quite creative when it comes to product placement. I can help you with that.'

Jonathan didn't reply. He paced steadily past rows of neatly planted vines. Once in a while he stopped to trim back some branches with a pair of clippers he kept in his back pocket.

'You have to train these vines. It takes years of investment, care and protection. One hailstorm and years of work go down the drain.'

'What about the warmer winters? Do they help you?'

'It's hard to tell; we had a good rainfall this year. Now if we combine that with enough sunshine, then we'll have some nice juicy grapes. It's too early to tell now. Some insects may have survived the mild winter and that makes controlling pests a bit of a challenge. Did I mention that we're certified organic?'

Nina went back a few pages in her notebook. 'Yes, you mentioned that right at the beginning.'

'Excellent. We're really trying to make a difference here.'

'It sounds like a labour of love.'

'It has to be. We have to survive. If I took all my investments into account, I should sell each bottle for double the price, but I can't. Customers won't pay more for a bottle of sparkling wine than they would for a mid-range bottle of supermarket champagne. There's an emotional barrier.'

'Well, hopefully I can break down some of these barriers.'

Several ominous clouds gathered on the horizon and cast a long shadow over the vineyard. It started to drizzle not long afterwards, when they were at the top of the slope. The slight breeze suddenly felt a lot chillier. Nina turned up the collar of her jacket and lifted her shoulders, shivering. She was underdressed for this time of year. The rain got heavier, and within minutes the soil was oversaturated. Small streams formed and gained momentum as they ran down the hill.

'Let's walk back to the main house and the cellars. I'll let you taste some of my wines so you can judge for yourself. It's the best way to warm up on a day like this.'

Nina was glad that she'd packed her wellies. Her feet sank into the mud, halfway past her ankles. Walking between the vines took effort. She was careful not to slip.

'I enjoy these walks,' said Jonathan. 'Every day I walk between these vines. I feel I know them all personally. I'm like a hawk. I see every new leaf, every misshapen branch. I dream about each twig I've pruned to perfection – it's a work in progress. And of course, it's beautiful out here. It's a true privilege. Smell the air and compare it to London air, day and night. I'd never want to go back to that rat race again. Look in the distance. Do you see how the fields follow the old glacial riverbed?'

Nina was shielding her eyes from the rain. She wasn't sure what Jonathan was talking about. It looked all the same to her.

'Yes, interesting.'

'In a way, because of what happened during the last ice age, we now have the perfect conditions to produce excellent wine. But that's nothing new; even the Romans knew about it. It's a little known fact that the English produced wine even in Roman times.'

'So it has nothing to do with global warming or climate change?'

'I'm no expert on it, but I don't understand these global warming alarmists. People say that our climate was a bit warmer two thousand years ago. Then we had a cold snap during the Middle Ages and wine production disappeared completely. And now we're back on track,' Jonathan said proudly. 'Instinctively, we know we're doomed. Think about how a billion cars and thousands of coal-fuelled power stations bellow out clouds of pollution day in, day out. At some point, we'll have to pay the price for that, a hefty price. But we can worry about that later. Right now, I'm more concerned about what cheese to serve you with your wine.'

Jonathan had an old-world charm about him. He looked the part of the perfect English gentleman, lord of the manor.

She admired his perseverance in what seemed a hard outdoor life.

'Well, all this fresh air and walking around your vines has made me feel peckish,' Nina said.

'I'm sure that my wife Annabelle's prepared something nice for us.'

Slowly Jonathan and Nina walked back towards the old Edwardian mansion. Compared to its French counterparts, it was rather modest in size, but very cosy. Jonathan guided Nina down an old granite staircase at the side of the mansion leading into a large cavernous cellar with a musty scent where hundreds of bottles of wine were stored at a perfect eleven degrees Celsius. In the far left corner of the cellar was a small bar and tasting area, illuminated by a dozen wax candles. Annabelle had arranged a selection of hard cheeses on a wooden board.

'Welcome to our wine cellar, Nina. Let me introduce myself, I am Annabelle Appleton, Creative Marketing Executive.'

'I am sorry, I thought you were Jonathan's wife.'

'That's correct, I am his wife and his business partner,' Annabelle was quick to explain. 'I am sure that all that talk about wine has whetted your appetite. Please help yourself to some cheese. We've got six different types of organic Cheddar and Stilton to complement our exquisite wine.'

'Allow me to offer you a glass of our vintage sparkling wine,' Jonathan said. He had just opened a bottle with a delicate plop. The glass he poured was overflowing with overexcited bubbles.

'I am so sorry, clumsy me. I'll pour you another one

straight away.'

Nina felt slightly uncomfortable to be all on her own drinking in the early afternoon. 'Are you not having any? Please join me.'

'Oh no. We prefer to keep our heads clear, don't we, Jonathan?'

'It's too early for us to start drinking. If we start now, we may never stop.'

'That's a challenge in our profession. We have to run a business and resist the temptation to spend all our time down here in the cellar sampling one bottle after the other,' Annabelle giggled whilst busying herself buttering some oatmeal crackers.

Nina enjoyed her wine and placed her empty glass next to the cheeseboard.

'How was that?' Jonathan asked.

'Very nice.'

'Very nice? What about the fruity bouquet? Did you notice how the taste melts away like frost in the early morning sun and how it leaves a refreshing aftertaste?'

'I guess so.'

Jonathan looked disappointed. She was clearly not a connoisseur.

'Now, you must compare this with our white wine, deliciously crisp and perfectly chilled. You have to try it. I can't let you leave us without having experienced our latest wine which we only bottled recently.'

Annabelle produced a new glass. 'Drinking from the right glass is equally important. This is Irish crystal, Waterford.'

Nina nodded, she felt a bit dizzy.

Jonathan opened a bottle of white wine and poured it into a new glass.

Nina hesitated; she waited for Jonathan to continue with his wine tasting master class.

'Now, swivel the wine a tiny bit, let it waltz around your glass.'

Nina followed Jonathan's instructions.

'It releases its aroma slowly when you do that. Now you have to inhale through the nose. You know why?'

Nina shook her head; she still hadn't swallowed her first swig yet.

'You can detect many more flavours with your nose than with your tongue. The nuance of a complex aroma really only gets deciphered in the back of your nose. Can you smell the fresh apples, a hint of citrus?'

'Well, I certainly learned something new today.'

'Let me give you a top-up, Nina.'

'No thanks, Jonathan, that's very kind of you but I really must be on my way. It's getting late.'

'Oh dear, let me get you a large glass of water before you hit the road, it will clear your head,' Annabelle said.

Nina felt trapped in a pushy marketing exercise and started making a move to leave.

'When do you think you'll post your blog?' Annabelle asked.

'Perhaps as early as tonight.'

'Would you mind sending a draft to me first?' she said, smiling a bit too forcefully.

'Indeed,' Jonathan added. 'You can't be too careful these days. One wrong blog can ruin our reputation with the click of a mouse.'

'That's not how journalism works, really. I appreciate your hospitality. You've given me a good impression of your work and all, but you have to trust me to write an article our readers are interested in.'

Jonathan swallowed. He looked flushed. 'Of course, my wife didn't want to insinuate anything at all. We trust you. What she meant was, if you need any further information or if you want to double-check some facts, feel free to contact us.'

'Here's my business card. It has a link to the Yellow Sparkle website. You can see for yourself when my blog's been posted.'

Annabelle accepted the card and turned it around several times.

'I like the design.'

'Thanks.'

'You see, these days, design is everything. Did Jonathan tell you that we work with a local artist who designs our labels? She's really gifted, we're so fortunate to work with her.'

'I'd noticed the nice labels. Thank you very much for reminding me. I'll mention them in my blog.'

'Well, we can't let you leave without a gift,' Jonathan said. 'Three bottles of white wine and three bottles of sparkling wine. I'm sure you'll enjoy it.'

'Our customers can order these from our website,' Annabelle continued. 'It's really popular.' She played with her hair. 'Last Christmas alone we sold over three-hundred gift boxes. They're very competitively priced at just under two hundred pounds.'

'I see,' Nina replied with a deadpan expression.

'That's part of our branding. We can't sell our products too cheaply.'

'Exactly. It's a premium product aimed at connoisseurs, the real wine lovers.'

'What about the tourists? Can't you set up a little shop on your property?'

'Good heavens, no!' Annabelle recoiled. 'We're not interested in hordes of day-trippers coming over buying a bottle here and a bottle there, trampling around our vineyard.' She then quickly put her hand over her mouth. 'Sorry, I didn't mean it like that. I don't think we can accommodate an influx of tourists at this stage. Perhaps in a couple of years' time, we can host tours on the estate and open a shop.'

'Well, thanks for your hospitality,' Nina said. 'I really must be going on my way. I haven't even found a place to spend the night yet.'

'Oh, darling,' Annabelle exclaimed. 'You should have told us. I know exactly the right place for you. Leave it to me!'

Annabelle rushed upstairs to make a phone call.

'We had some bad experiences in the past. Lots of people write to us asking for free bottles of wine and then they write bad reviews.'

'It's a bit like an Internet troll,' Nina said. 'But you can't let them ruin what you believe in. Relax, I like your wine and I do hope it'll become a big success and that you'll sell even more gift sets next Christmas.'

Nina could hear Annabelle stumbling down the wooden stairs again.

'Darling, I've got it all arranged for you. There's a room for you at the Chestnut Hill Inn. You'll absolutely love it. It's nostalgia galore. We know the owners, a most charming elderly couple. They'll look after you. And if you have any further questions, please come by and we'll help you out.'

'Got it, thank you.'

Jonathan accompanied Nina to her car. He was insistent on carrying the gift box. He laughed when she opened the boot of her Mini.

'Oh dear, the box only just fits.'

'Just move the suitcase along a little bit. There's a lot more space than you think.'

Nina got into the car and rolled down the window. Jonathan leaned through the window and repeated the directions to the hotel.

'At the T-junction, bear to your right and then right again by the old phone box. Keep going until you hit a small hamlet, a Co-op shop, a primary school and a village green with two majestic looking chestnut trees. It's on the road to the old airport. You'll see signs to the local flying club. You can't miss it.'

'I'll use my satnav.'

'That won't work around here, I'm afraid. Cheerio!' Jonathan added cheerfully and gently rapped the roof of the Mini.

22

Claudia had a cramp in her right arm from picking up stacks of papers and holding them in front of her. It was the same repetitive movement, changing speed only according to the number of passers-by. The last fifteen minutes had been the worst of the rush-hour, and her hands were getting cold. She'd enjoyed her job for over two months but the novelty had worn off. Today was her last day and she was desperate to start her new job on Monday. In that respect her friend Virginia had been right. Handing out papers and meeting the odd customer had proven to be a good jumping board to get to the next level in life. The lights turned green, and there was a sudden lull in the relentless stream of commuters. She took off her gloves and breathed into her hands. It was freezing!

Claudia looked at the clock near the station. It was almost half past six, another hour to go. She hoped that Jimmy wouldn't show up too late for another batch of the latest edition. Claudia craned her neck several times standing on tiptoe, holding on to her trolley. She skimmed over the thousands of heads, thousands of hurried people, eager to get home. Was that the van in the distance, stuck in traffic? Claudia squinted her eyes and moved her fringe sideways. She reckoned it would take Jimmy another couple of minutes. The traffic light was turning red. Claudia put her gloves on again – time to get back to work.

Handing out papers had become automatic. She no longer looked customers in the eye, having learned quickly that eye contact was seen as weird, too confrontational, evoking feelings of guilt in people. She had to try as much as possible to be invisible. Customers, commuters – they were just anonymous faces in the crowd. The quicker she could get through her pile of papers, the quicker she could have a break, until Jimmy brought the next batch.

Claudia wasn't paying attention when she heard her name. In all those months in London, nobody ever called her name, apart from Peter. She'd recognise his clipped unemotional voice immediately. The man calling her name sounded different from the voices she heard in London. This one didn't sound British at all. It sounded American. It had a certain drawl, the kind she'd heard a million times in Hollywood movies and television shows. 'Miss Valenti,' the voice said, 'can I have a word with you?' It made her shiver.

She turned towards the man. He was probably in his late-thirties or even early forties. It was hard to tell in the darkness of the evening. The orange neon light had a flattering effect. He was tall with slim shoulders and accompanied by a much shorter man who was massively obese. They were both wearing thin trench coats and seemed underdressed for the time of year. Together they interrupted the commuter flow. With no papers left, this wasn't a problem. At least not until a new supply was delivered.

'You're Claudia Valenti, aren't you, miss?' The tall man was angling for an affirmation.

'Yes,' Claudia said, trying to sound matter-of-fact.

'I was wondering if you could help us with our investigation,' he continued.

'Would you mind taking a walk with us to our car?' the large man said in a menacing voice.

'I'm in the middle of my shift,' she said. 'Can't this wait till later?'

Claudia looked in the direction of the oncoming traffic but couldn't see the car they mentioned. The last thing any sane woman in São Paulo, or anywhere else in the world would do, was get into a car with strangers.

'I'm definitely not coming to your car!'

Both men inched forward, the tall one folding his arms. The large man opened his coat and took out a brown envelope, A4 size.

'Let me show you some pictures, miss. This might convince you to talk to us in private.'

Claudia nodded apprehensively. She looked over her shoulder; there were no customers and Jimmy's van was still stuck in traffic.

'This, Miss Valenti, is the headquarters of a company called Amazorico at eleven o'clock on Saturday morning, January 19th. Do you recognise this building?'

Claudia didn't reply. She turned pale.

The large man took the lead. He was impatient.

'Well, to refresh your memory, Miss Valenti, this is the

building where you worked as a cleaning lady. Can you confirm that?'

'Yes, I used to work as a cleaning lady in that building, so what?'

Claudia bent down to pick up a few discarded papers and put them on the bottom of her trolley. A pavement littered with paper didn't look good. She tried to spot Jimmy's van. Relief came when she noticed the green and white van creeping towards her. She had to keep talking, if only to buy time.

'Here's a picture of the same building taken thirty minutes later.' All Claudia could see was a cloud of dust.

'It's no longer there!' she said.

'Exactly. That's a good observation. None of the employees managed to escape.'

'I am sorry to hear that.'

'Is that all you have to say?'

'Of course I feel bad, I knew most of the people who worked in that building.'

'I feel that we are on the right track, Miss Valenti,' the large man said.

'I agree. We're here to solve a few problems and get some answers. The more you can tell us, the quicker we get out of your life,' the tall man added.

'Who else was working with you? Your boyfriend?' the large man continued.

'He doesn't know about anything!'

'That's what he said until the very end.'

'What do you mean?'

'Our investigators in Brazil had him under surveillance

after the attack. They had reason to believe he was involved.'

'Mario? All he knows is how to make cocktails and talk to women,' Claudia sneered.

'Maybe it's a different kind of cocktail he was making. You agree with that?'

'No, no, no! He's innocent. He has nothing to do with this. We hooked up once in a while and that's it.'

'That's what he said in the end.'

'You keep saying "in the end". What do you mean by that?'

'According to our report, it says that his last words were: "I have no idea what that stupid bitch was up to. She was just one of the many girls I fucked. So what? I have nothing to do with her any more".'

Claudia swallowed. She felt a lump in her throat and tears welling up in her eyes.

'Is that why he's no longer coming to London?'

'He's not going anywhere!'

'Your boyfriend's dead, Miss Valenti,' the fat man said. 'And before he died, he confessed. Now all we need to know is who else is involved.'

'I don't believe you. Mario has nothing to do with this! You're bluffing.'

'Show her the pictures.'

'The tall one took off his black leather glove and reached into the inside pocket of his overcoat. He opened the large envelope and took out several photographs.

Claudia's heart stopped for a moment as she held her breath. She was shocked. She wiped away her tears. The net was closing around her rapidly. She felt like a deer caught in the headlights of a fast approaching car.

'Is this the same Mario we're talking about?' asked the fat guy.

Claudia nodded, barely recognizing his beaten up and naked body. Seeing his bloodied face was too much to bear. You could tell he had been beaten up savagely, repeatedly, for a long period of time; even his scrotum was swollen and bruised. His hair was matted. His anguished look, his haunted eyes, wide-open and in despair: she would never forget his beautiful eyes. Claudia leaned to the side and vomited.

She straightened up slowly and wiped her mouth on her sleeve.

'You bastards!' Claudia shouted. She now realised she was in danger, in a foreign city with seemingly nowhere to run.

Some of the passers-by stopped.

'Are you alright, miss?' a man in a dark padded coat asked, looking concerned.

'No, I'm not,' Claudia said, bursting into tears.

'Maybe you chaps should leave her alone or I'll call the police!' the man said.

'That isn't necessary. She's coming with us.'

Mike flashed his badge. It was impressive from a distance, like a CIA badge.

'Sorry, I didn't mean to interrupt.' The man shook his head and left.

Claudia's knees trembled. She wanted to escape, but her boots seemed glued to the pavement. Time crept by. She had to think fast. She heard a familiar engine, the sound of an old rattling engine and a hole in the exhaust. She smelled strong diesel fumes before suddenly seeing it leap over the edge of the pavement.

Jimmy's van came to a screeching halt. The two special agents jumped out of the way.

'Quick, Claudia! Help me off-load. I'm in a rush to get to Whitechapel.' Jimmy stayed behind the wheel, revving his engine.

Claudia did as Jimmy asked. She off-loaded as many piles of newspaper as she could, creating a barrier between her and the agents. It caused some commotion among the commuters.

'Hey!' Jimmy shouted. 'Are you mad? Put those back in the van. I need them for the other distributors.'

Then Claudia jumped into the back of the van.

The two agents watched patiently, not wanting to use any force, especially within sight of so many commuters.

'Hold back, Mike,' said Dave. 'We've got no jurisdiction in this country. We're not even here, remember? Low profile.'

'Yeah, but this might be our only chance.'

Mike ran to the van and grabbed Claudia's gloved hand. She panicked as Mike pulled harder, but held on to a metal rail with her free hand.

'Step on it, Jimmy! Get the hell out of here! I'll explain later.'

Jimmy didn't hesitate. Mike ran alongside the van and yanked Claudia's hand, and she fell forward on the cargo floor, gliding towards the edge of the van. The sliding door was wide open.

'Hold on tight!'

Jimmy stopped abruptly. Claudia hit her head on the metal edge of the partition bar. Mike was still holding her hand. As Jimmy reversed rapidly, the wheels emitted a waft of burning rubber, which filled the back of the van and made Claudia's eyes water. Jimmy stopped again and changed gears. Claudia felt her hand slip out of her glove. She was free! She got up and managed to hold on to the front seats while the van sped across the bus lane towards the next traffic lights. With her left hand, she closed the sliding door, eliminating all the street noise. She sat down with her back against Jimmy's seat. She felt safe for now.

'Are you in some kind of trouble? Did those blokes try to kidnap you?'

'I'm in a lot of trouble.'

'Heh! You don't have to tell me. Let's get you out of here first.'

Claudia nodded. She leaned forward, resting her head on her knees and thinking where to go next.

Jimmy slalomed his way through traffic. Claudia couldn't look out the window. She had no idea where he was going.

'Were those guys American?'

'They sounded like Americans.'

'Well, Claudia, that explains why a large American car is following us. You don't see many of those in London. That's no coincidence.'

'Fuck!' Claudia slammed the floor with her fist.

'Don't worry! They'll never overtake us, trust me. This van may be slow but I know all the backstreets and short cuts. Next stop is Whitechapel station. Jump out and get on the Tube. Just disappear in the crowd, that's your best bet.'

'Thanks, Jimmy. I'm in deep shit. If I survive, I'll tell you all about it.'

'You need a place to stay?'

'Not sure. I'll figure something out. I think I need to get out of London, as far away as possible. If they can find me here, they can probably find me anywhere.'

'Anytime, no pressure, love…'

Claudia got her phone out and texted Peter. 'I'm in danger. Am being followed. This is SERIOUS!! You've got to help me. I'm at Whitechapel.'

A minute later a reply came: 'Take the Tube to Bromley-by-Bow. There's a bus stop. Wait there. I'll pick you up. Look for a red Volvo estate.'

'OK,' Claudia replied.

'What does a red Volvo look like?' she asked Jimmy.

'Red and square.'

Jimmy accelerated then turned into a tiny street. Someone was trying to park and was holding up traffic.

'Damn, they're right behind us! Hope those cars start moving.'

Another car got in between Jimmy's van and the black sedan.

'Sharp right turn coming up! You better get in the passenger seat and strap yourself in.'

'Are you mad? They might shoot me.'

Jimmy looked in his side mirrors. The black car wasn't far behind.

'Hold on, let me just overtake these buses. That'll slow them down.'

The van's rear skidded as Jimmy abruptly changed lanes.

Claudia was thrown around the back of the van, making her sick. She checked the back pocket of her Levi's for her Oyster card.

'Sharp turn coming up!' Then the van came to an abrupt stop. Jimmy opened his window and called to some bystanders. 'Hey! Help this lass to the station, would ya, lads?' Jimmy knew the local vendors. He often bought fruit and vegetables from them when while delivering papers.

'This way, miss, this way,' he heard people shouting. Two middle-aged women dressed in black abayas held Claudia between them, shielding her until they reached the station entrance.

When Jimmy looked up, he saw her striped hat disappearing past the check-in gate, then down the stairs. She got away.

The black car stopped behind the van. Mike raced towards Jimmy.

'Do you know who you just helped escape? We're not finished with you!'

'Sorry, mate. Got no idea what you're talking about. I'm just delivering my papers.'

Dave shrugged. It was a lost cause.

'Should we go after her?'

'There's no point. There's a train every few minutes, and there are three different lines, six different directions. She's gone, we've lost her.'

'Damn, we were so close.'

'At least our suspicions are confirmed. She's the one we're looking for.'

'And we've got her glove.'

'Let's send it to DC for DNA processing. It should get there by tomorrow. And if Terrence can pull some strings, it'll get fast-tracked.'

'Then he can match this sample with the DNA from the underwear tested earlier.'

'Yeah, and also with the DNA taken from the stains on that filthy mattress she shared with her guy. Last I heard, a team of researchers from Public Health was analysing it. They called it "chlamydia paradise".'

'Honestly, I don't want to think about it. It might put me off sex forever,' Dave said.

'Good you're single, then!'

'Shut up. Where should we head next?'

'Back to Suffolk and our country inn.'

Dave played with his car keys and flicked them in the air several times. He was keen to move on.

'But it's a good three-hour journey from here. We won't get there before ten. The kitchen closes at nine; can you believe that?'

'No, I can't get used to that – stupid limited opening hours,' Dave said.

'I'm starving. Let's eat something before we hit the road.'

Mike walked over to two young men standing near a butcher's.

'Hey, buddy, can you recommend a good place to eat?'

'Are you for real? You're in the culinary heart of London. Left, right, anywhere! You can't go wrong. But my uncle owns the best curry house this side of Bangladesh,' the young man said.

'Sounds great, buddy. The spicier the better,' Dave said.

'You're adapting quick,' Mike teased Dave.

'When in Rome… Anyway, I hear curry's the best food in England.'

'You see those traffic lights? Cross the street, first left, then turn right. My cousin owns the off licence where you can by some beer. Then cross the street again and join the queue.'

Dave looked at his watch. 'It's a three-hour drive back to the hotel.'

'Don't worry,' the young man said. The queue's long, but it moves quickly. Don't trust any restaurant without one.'

'I'll take your word for it.'

'You have to bring your own drinks, though.'

'Got it!'

'You see,' Mike said. 'That's what I like about London; one minute you're in the financial centre, all shiny high-rise office blocks and fancy restaurants; the next you're in a different world. Look around you, this could be Mumbai or Dhaka!'

'Shame about the weather… Feels like a never-ending winter in England.'

'Give it a few more decades and London will be as hot as Asia.'

'By then, Dhaka will be underwater, given the relentless rise of sea levels. More and more of those low-lying lands are going under, not just Florida and New Orleans.'

'Then again, their culture and cuisine will have gained a strong foothold over here, so it's guaranteed to survive.'

'You've gotta admit, that's forward planning and adapting to the extreme!'

23

Nina was pleased with the hotel Annabelle had recommended. It was a quintessential Tudor-style inn with small windows, black timber beams, white plaster and impressive brick chimneys. It was right on the village green next to the local Co-op and post office.

She knew she'd never have found a more idyllic setting than this one without Annabelle's help. It put her in the right mood to write about the booming wine-industry. No doubt that was Annabelle's intention. Best not to bite the hand that feeds you, thought Nina.

A young receptionist named Tess, wearing a large name badge, gave her a warm smile when she walked through the door with a case of wine in one hand and her carry-on and iPad in the other. The wooden door was heavy, and Nina was struggling to keep it open long enough.

'Let me give you a hand, Miss Simmons,' Tess said. 'Most of our customers struggle with this door. It's solid oak and weighs a ton.'

'It's alright, I'll manage.'

'I've prepared all your paperwork. We've been expecting you.'

Nina opened her jacket and balanced the case of wine on top of her carry-on.

'The room we reserved for you has the best views. I'm sure you'll like it. Fields, trees and marshland as far as the eye can see. I hope you don't find it too quiet,' the receptionist continued without looking up.

'It'll be a welcome relief from London, I'm sure of it.'

'I can well imagine that. I wouldn't fancy living in London.'

'Just one question; do you have Wi-Fi?'

'Of course we do, miss. We also have hot running water, soft towels and three-layered toilet paper!'

'I didn't mean it that way!'

'Don't worry. I get asked that question a few times a day.'

'It doesn't seem that busy a place.'

'We do get our regulars all year round, and most weekends are booked months in advance. It's a perfect escape. Sometimes we get the odd overseas visitor who comes via TripAdvisor recommendations. We even have some Americans staying with us.'

'Well, who would have thought?' Nina replied deadpan.

'You'll find your Wi-Fi code in the information pack on your desk.'

Nina was very content with her room. It was small and cosy with a double-size bed, dark wood panelling and exposed oak ceiling beams, a large antique wardrobe and a small desk near the window. To her further satisfaction, the vibrant dark red floral wallpaper complemented the cream-white flower patterned curtains, making it more quirky than designer chic. The bathroom design was a triumph of minimalism – sleek and modern. The shower had so many dials, knobs and built in LED lights that it looked like a time machine.

Nina walked over to the small window. She opened it briefly to have a better understanding of where she was staying exactly. Her room looked out over fields and woodland. Leaning a bit further out she could see to her left the small village church and its old graveyard among majestic oak trees. It made death look almost appealing. She closed the window quickly when a sudden gush of wind stirred up the papers on the desk.

Nina unpacked her carry-on. She was planning to write her first blog after dinner. A shelf next to the coffee maker had a small selection of crystal glasses of different sizes; some were chipped. It seemed like a random collection bought at a flea market over the years to give the room a personal touch. She looked forward to writing her blog about vineyards in Suffolk with a glass of wine within reach, her iPad at her fingertips and her feet next to the warm radiator. It was a perfect escape from reality.

She hadn't felt this happy since she'd met Ravi during her first blogging venture. She remembered it whilst staring out of the window. What followed their meeting was a whirlwind romance cut short by a lucrative job-offer in Australia. 'We'll stay in touch,' were his famous last words. A few emails and text messages at lengthening intervals followed before he took up a research post in the bush without Wi-Fi and went radio silent. Nina was sure that he'd long forgotten her. Her career dipped quickly after her rise to blog stardom. Should she have gone to Australia with Ravi, after all? It would have been so much more exciting to report on the impact of climate change-bushfires, extensive draughts or the bleaching of the Great Barrier Reef, compared to writing about wine-tastings in Suffolk. If any continent were to pay the price of global warming in the next decade it was Australia. Perhaps she should get in touch with him again, make the first move?

Nina stowed her empty carry-on underneath her bed. She didn't want to spend much longer in her hotel room. As a journalist she had to explore the area, make new contacts and get more stories for her blog. It had started to drizzle. It was getting dark, too. With the outside temperature close to eight degrees and a strong westerly wind blowing across the Suffolk fields, a walk in the countryside wasn't an option. It was a perfect excuse to sit downstairs near the fire with a pint of ale and read a book.

The bar was busier than Nina had expected. The owner and his wife stood behind the bar, the wife speaking enthusiastically with some of the regulars, while the owner pulled pints with patience and dedication. He nodded once in a while when his wife included him in the conversation. The locals who were nursing their pints didn't look up when Nina walked in. They seemed absorbed in local gossip.

Nina overheard only snippets of their conversation, their dialect hard to understand. She walked over to the bar to order a drink.

'George, don't let the young lady wait forever!' the owner's wife said.

'Of course, Marjory.'

'What'll it be, miss?'

'It's Nina. I'm staying for a couple of nights. A pint of ale would be nice, a locally brewed one if possible. What do you recommend?'

'Good to have you with us, Nina. You've come to the right place. All our ales on draught are locally brewed. They've got centuries of experience between them,' he said.

George started pulling a pint slowly. 'This one's the most popular, the Golden Avocet. It's a bit lighter with a hint of honey.'

Nina nodded approvingly. She looked over her shoulder and saw an invitingly vacant sofa near the fire. She hoped nobody would take it before George had served her pint.

'I'll be back in a second,' Nina said.

'Take your time!'

Nina walked over to the sofa, rearranged a few cushions and placed her book on the seat near the fire.

George smiled. At this time of night, nobody would have taken that seat. Most ramblers had gone home some time ago after tea.

When Nina walked back, she overheard George talking to an older man he called Phil.

'Those two fellows who are staying here. I think they've left for London earlier today. They asked for directions.'

'It's unusual for those Yanks to stray from their military base. It all sounds very suspicious to me. Doesn't add up. Strange things are happening here right under our noses.' He continued in a solemn voice with a slight slur, pausing to take another swig of his pint and gauge George's reaction.

'They're just some tourists.'

'Two blokes travelling together in a place like this? It's way off the beaten track.'

'Who knows, maybe they're ex-Air Force, comin' back to where they were stationed,' Marjory chipped in. 'Just old buddies reminiscing. Back in the day, we had loads of those lads coming in. It was packed every weekend. They were lovely lads – very loud, though. Meetin' their girlfriends, havin' a dance, a bit of romance.'

'Those lads from back then must be in their seventies now. These men were in their early to mid-forties. One was tall, the other fat, not your average pilot's physique. They'd both have trouble squeezing into a cockpit.'

'Did you see that fat bloke? His plane'd have no chance of becoming airborne,' another local laughed.

Phil looked dismayed.

'Let me tell you something else. You know I keep my combine harvester at Doreen's barn. Today, I went there to make a few adjustments and I noticed a lot of muddy footsteps on my machine. After a closer look, I saw lots of fingermarks on the window. Somebody had been messing around. I suspected sabotage. I went through the harvester with a fine-toothed comb; turned on the engine to check if it was running smooth. At first I thought I heard something funny, but that soon got smoothed out. I always keep my machines clean. I got so annoyed seeing the harvester covered in mud. I went looking for my bucket in the usual place. Gone!'

'Interesting story, Phil,' George teased, as he started cleaning some glasses.

'No, listen. That's not it. Somebody must have used my

bucket, which I don't mind. That's the kind of guy I am, easy-going – as long as they bring it back. I spent over an hour looking for it. In the end, I found it in the other barn.'

'You must be a happy lad now, reunited with your bucket,' George joked.

Phil didn't pay any attention.

'When I found the bucket, I had a look around. I know it's not my business, but what I saw was quite something. It was the size of a camper, but it had a couple of engines attached to it. It was dark, so I couldn't make out any details. It was either an alien spaceship or they're building a secret rocket.'

George started laughing. 'How many beers have you had tonight? One more than your usual and now you come up with stories.' Others in the pub started laughing too. 'Phil, they didn't abduct you, did they?'

Phil got angry that nobody was taking him seriously. 'First of all, they've got no right to mess with my machines. Second, you can't trust these people. Every weekend they race through our village; next we've got the Americans coming in. Before you know it, we'll have a space odyssey in our own back yard.'

'But you know it's only Peter and his family,' George replied. 'Ask Barry. Peter's helping him with some kind of project.'

Nina looked at George, who'd nearly finished pulling her pint. Her journalism instincts kicked in. Perhaps the old man had a story.

'Hi, Phil, the name's Nina. Sorry, I just happened to overhear your story. An alien spaceship, you say?'

'Aye, miss. I may be old, but I still got all me marbles.

When I say that something ain't right, something ain't right.'

Nina nodded, trying to encourage Phil to continue.

'Peter and Barry were always playing together when they were young, during the holidays. Then he stopped coming when he grew older and bingo! Thirty-odd years later he's back, wife and kids in tow. Barry, in the meantime, built up this huge airplane-salvage recycling business and now they're best buddies again.'

'But why build a spaceship in the middle of the country? Seems a bit far-fetched.'

'Not at all, it's the perfect location, completely isolated – we all keep to ourselves. Barry's got access to all sorts of engines, even some classified ones. And that's where these Americans come in. I bet they're working on some kind of mass-produced escape pods in case things start heating up around here.'

'I don't follow you,' Nina giggled as though she was talking to her granddad who suffered from mild dementia and would come up with the most bizarre conspiracy theories.

'Don't you see it? We've lost our way, we're doomed.'

'Crikey, that sounds a bit gloomy. I just interviewed some wine-growers and they were pretty upbeat about the future.'

'They're just a bunch of opportunists. It won't be long before it'll be too hot to grow wine, grain, anything. It'll be a parched earth. Trying to feed hundreds of millions of refugees from all around the world, all of 'em heading towards the Isles, will be impossible. That's why we have to leave Europe. We have to cut ties, draw up the footbridge, close the seaports and airports, fill up the Eurotunnel with concrete…'

'Or fly away!'

'Exactly, miss! I'm glad you understand me.'

Nina took another sip of her ale, having forgotten all about her book.

'I've made some lovely pies, Nina. Care to have one for supper?' Marjory asked.

'I'd love that, something to warm me up.'

'Welcome to the Chestnut Hill Inn, your sanctuary in this mad world,' George said. Phil stumbled off his bar stool and went to the toilet.

'Sorry about him, he's a bit of a local character. But if you ask me, he's a bit bonkers. In a nice way, though! We go back a long ways, almost sixty-five years. Don't believe everything he says.'

'It sounds rather interesting, though. Where can I find this farm?'

'It's half a mile down the road… Peter's aunt's a bit of a recluse. She hates cold-callers though; I wouldn't drive over and knock on her door without having an invitation,' George said. 'I'll tell you something else funny.' George looked over his shoulder to make sure that Phil was still out of earshot. 'Phil told the same story to those Americans and they totally fell for it.'

'I hope they won't be planning a full-scale invasion based on the ramblings of a bloke they met in a pub.'

'I wouldn't be surprised. Those so-called weapons of mass destruction in Iraq were never found, but it triggered the implosion of the entire Middle East.'

'That's the scary part of modern politics.'

'It must have been like that throughout history.'

'I guess this is where robust investigative journalism comes in!'

'I couldn't have said it better,' Marjory said. 'You've got your work carved out.'

Nina walked over to the sofa near the fireplace. Marjory brought over the homemade pie with a fresh salad and a dollop of mash on the side.

'It's a good old-fashioned beef and Guinness pie, an old-time favourite!'

'Thanks, just what I need.'

'Enjoy. Just let me know what you'd like to eat tomorrow. We don't expect many guests, so you can choose.'

'I'll have a think about it. Something hearty – I might go for a walk in the country.'

'All right, then… shepherd's pie it is. It'll warm you up in no time.'

Sitting by the fire, Nina felt a thousand miles away from her busy Shoreditch office. She loved the rustic setting, the delicious food and the entertaining stories. This could turn out to be a journalist's dream come true.

Shortly after Nina finished up, she went upstairs, having declined an offer of pudding. She opened one of the complementary bottles of Suffolk white wine, poured a glass and had a few sips to boost inspiration. The first sentence flowed easily and set the scene for her food blog, and when her eyes started to feel heavy, she sent it to her editor, along with images she'd taken earlier in the day, with a quick 'thank you' email to Jonathan. He really had pulled some strings for her; she'd repay him with a glowing review of the wine she'd thoroughly enjoyed. After another swig from her glass she felt dizzy; the alcohol was going straight to her head. She was happy and relaxed for the first time in months and riding on the crest of a wave she posted a short second blog about the sighting of a spaceship in rural Suffolk. Just for fun, to add some spice to her blogging life.

Getting ready for bed, Nina undressed and threw the clothes onto a chair in the bedroom. While brushing her teeth, she suddenly had an idea. She smiled.

She stepped into the fancy shower cubicle and switched the ambient bathroom colour to an electric blue, which gave the cubicle a futuristic appearance. She stretched out her right arm, holding her iPhone. With her left index finger, she hovered above an illuminated digital temperature gauge and directed her gaze towards the phone. She tried several different smiles and settled for a mischievous expression, then took the picture. She wrote a message: 'Been working on a space-time-compressor prototype. Ready for a trial run. Give me your GPS coordinates and I'll be over in a flash.' Nina sent the message to Ravi in the hope he'd reply.

24

Peter had just finished packing the family car when he received the message from Claudia. He dropped a large bag with clothes and boots when he read her alarming message.

'Guys, we have to move quickly, let's go!'

Peter sent a reply, hoping that she'd read it in time.

'What's the rush, Peter?' Joanne asked. 'Come on, kids. Daddy's ready to go.'

Peter was already sitting behind the wheel revving the engine. Tom and Lilly jumped in and rearranged pillows and duvets. Joanne slammed the door shut.

'What's the rush?' Joanne asked a second time.

'Read this!' Peter handed his phone to Joanne while he reversed out of the driveway.

'Who the hell is Claudia, and why is she turning to you for help?' Joanne demanded.

'I met her a couple of months ago.'

'And this is the first time you mention her to me?'

Peter smiled sheepishly. He knew he should have told his wife weeks ago about Claudia. Whatever he'd come up with, as an explanation, would only make him look more suspicious.

'And what's this message all about? It doesn't make any sense to me.'

'Darling, it doesn't make any sense to me either.'

'Don't "darling" me. I find this most peculiar. Are you having some kind of an affair? Living a double life? How do you expect me to react?'

'Right now, all I want you to be is supportive. Who knows what this woman has been through. Let's hear her story first.'

'What did you get yourself into? I hope you told her you're married with kids.'

'I'll explain in a minute. First let's find the quickest way to the Blackwall Tunnel.'

'You're mad! That's the daftest idea I've heard in a long time. Only an idiot would go through the Blackwall Tunnel at this time of the evening. It's bloody gridlocked. But then again, perhaps you're desperate, after all.'

'Cut it out, it's not what you think.'

'I'm not thinking anything. I'm just waiting for the next surprise.'

'Are you having a fight?' Lilly asked.

'No, we're having a difference of opinion, that's all. Now go and read your book.'

'So you are having a fight' Lilly said. 'You always tell me to read my book when you're telling Daddy off.'

The drizzling rain turned into a downpour. The windscreen wipers squeaked, struggling to keep up with the torrent. The car started fogging up. With the back of his hand, Peter cleared a large section of the window before turning up the heat.

'Watch out!' Joanne screamed as the brake lights of the car in front of them flashed brightly. 'Slow down! The weather's just awful. I have no idea why you put your family at risk for this Claudia woman.'

'I'm not driving fast at all. We're not even doing ten miles an hour. At this rate, it'll be another hour until we're through.'

'And guess what? Look at the sign: "Lane one closed for maintenance". Why can't they do this any other time of year?'

'Beats me. I tell you, I'll be glad to be out of here.'

'You're right, I'll never drive through the Blackwall Tunnel again.'

'What were you thinking?'

'I had to think fast. I didn't know where else to pick her up.'

'From Whitechapel? She could've taken the Overground to Crystal Palace. It would have taken her twenty minutes. And if she really was that desperate, she could have offered some housesitting for us and watered our plants.'

'If she's in danger, she'll be better off staying with my aunt.'

'Whatever. I'm sure your aunt'll be thrilled to have another guest staying with her.'

'We're almost there. Let's see who can see her first,' Peter said to cheer everybody up.

'What does she look like, your girlfriend?' Lilly asked.

'She's not my girlfriend! She's in her early twenties, blonde, wears her hair in a plait. Wears boots, jeans and a bobble hat, blue and white striped.'

'I'm glad you didn't go for a younger version of me.'

'Honey, she's nothing like you. You're the mother of my children, damn it. I'd never leave you for anyone else.'

'We'll talk about this later. I want to see what she has to say.'

'All right.'

Joanne turned around to face Lilly and Tom. They were both watching something on the iPad.

'Lilly, move to the middle. We have to pick up a friend of Daddy's.'

Lilly did as she was told.

'It's too bumpy in the middle.'

'It's only for a short while. Why don't you try to catch some sleep?'

'It's too early.'

Joanne turned around again and checked her phone.

'I'm just looking at Google maps. The traffic's pretty bad everywhere. We can follow the A12 towards Colchester and then go up towards Norwich.'

'Sounds good to me. I like a bit of variety.'

Joanne looked cross, she couldn't believe how her husband could act so casual.

'Estimated time of arrival 22:35. Will your aunt be up by then?'

'She'll leave the back door open.'

'You'd better tell her that you're bringing a guest.'

'Could you ask her? It might be better if it comes from you.'

'She's your aunt and you are bringing a guest. You know what she can be like with unexpected visitors. It ought to come from you!'

'I'm driving!'

'In that case, I'll use your phone.'

'Thanks.'

While Joanne wrote a message, Peter moved back into the left-hand lane.

'Darling, can you see the bus stop?'

'I'm not sure.'

The drizzling rain made it hard to see.

'There should be a bus stop for the 108 and the 488 not far from here.'

'There's a bus right behind us; we don't have much time. I hope that this Claudia of yours will be there waiting for us.'

'Oh, there it is. That bus stop looks pretty empty.'

'I hate these kinds of scenarios. Hope I won't get a ticket. I can't just pull over and wait.'

Peter slowed down. Several cars had slipped in between their Volvo and the bus, which was now more than six cars away. As Peter pulled into the slip road, he saw a young woman with a bobble hat leap out from behind one of the billboards.

'Yes, that's her!'

Peter signalled with his headlights that he'd seen her and stopped the car. Claudia leaned forward to peek through the open window.

'Peter! Thanks a million!'

'Jump in, Claudia, it's pouring! Take a seat in the back. I can't stop for long.' Claudia opened the rear door and sat down. She said a cheery hello to the kids, who replied enthusiastically. Joanne turned around.

'You must be this lady of mystery Peter's been talking about. I'm Joanne.'

Claudia nodded. 'Yes, I am indeed. Nice to meet you. Peter's told me so much about you.'

'Did he?'

Peter looked relieved. Claudia leaned forward and put her right hand on Peter's shoulder. Joanne frowned.

'Peter, you have no idea how grateful I am.'

'You did surprise me. This afternoon you were talking about your potential new boyfriend and now you're in my car with my family.'

'It's been a horrible day. I'm so sorry,' Claudia said, beginning to sob. Lilly and Tom looked shocked. Tom put his arm around his sister.

'The bastards, they killed Mario! They just killed him. He was beaten up so badly, I hardly recognized him. There was blood coming out of his ears and his mouth. It was horrible. They just killed him, just like that, for no reason. He had nothing to do with this at all. He was innocent; they didn't have to do this. I hate them, I tell you! Whoever did this is going to regret it. He was beaten and tortured without any proof. They made him confess to something he didn't do or even know about,' Claudia cried.

Joanne looked at Peter, who gave her a blank look.

'It's so unfair, the whole world is unfair. It's corrupt, and innocent people die all the time. I bet you the governor will escape without punishment. Well, let me tell you: it's impossible to escape from me. I'll set the record straight. That bastard will have to rot in jail for the rest of his fucking life.'

Lilly and Tom were scared, especially by the way Claudia

talked about blood coming out of somebody's ears.

'Have my blanket,' Lilly said after a while.

Claudia wiped her eyes. 'That's very kind of you, sweetheart. Sorry I just gate-crashed your family outing.'

'That's all right,' Joanne said. 'Why don't you close your eyes, you must have had a stressful day.'

Peter sped up the windscreen wiper, which made big sweeping movements to fight off the rain. It was slow going. They'd only just passed the M25.

At ten to nine, Peter pulled over at a petrol station, hoping to get some coffee from the Jolly Bean Cafe and stretch his legs. He bought a bottle of water for Joanne and some chocolate bars to share. He wiped the rear window clear and peaked into the car. The kids and Claudia were fast asleep. He didn't want to wake them up.

Before driving off, Peter scanned his surroundings. He looked over the roof of his Volvo and saw a large black car parked at a distance, near the air compressor. Did it look familiar? Was it an American model? He wasn't sure.

'That's odd,' Peter said to Joanne when he got inside. 'There's a large black car parked at the edge of the forecourt. It looks like two chaps just sitting there and waiting.'

'Perhaps they're waiting for the rain to stop.'

'Why would they do that? Rain like this will go on for days.'

'Maybe they just got tired and needed a rest.'

'I suppose you're right.' Peter looked in the rear-view mirror once again. 'I swear to you that I've seen that car before.'

Joanna was still feeling miffed with Peter. She had this

nagging feeling that he was hiding something from her. 'We'd better get going. It's later than you think.'

Peter started the engine. The wipers swung back into life, providing a comforting ambient sound.

25

After breakfast, George the innkeeper walked over to the table where the two Americans, Dave Johnson and Mike Dimito, were sitting, having started the day early. Nina, the only other guest, was still in her room.

'If you gentlemen would like to follow me after breakfast, I can show you our gun-room. You'll be suitably impressed. It's very well stocked, and even the most demanding huntsman will be spoilt for choice. As our brochure says, we can organize a shooting party for up to twenty people.'

'That'll be plenty,' Dave said.

'Our clients prefer the more intimate experience,' Mike said.

'In a more civilised environment.'

'Lion and rhino hunting has received a lot of bad press lately. Our clients like to keep a low profile.'

'Nowadays, posting a picture on Facebook with a dead endangered species is commercial and social suicide.'

'Yes, totally bad publicity.'

'Some old fashioned hunting in the English countryside is

much more social media friendly.'

'Exactly! In the end it's about networking and friendship. England has so much to offer when it comes to hospitality,' George added.

The wood panelled gun-room was next to the library and had the rustic smell of oak. One wall was lined with floor-to-ceiling glass display cabinets, each containing a large selection of rifles.

George opened the door closest to the entrance. Mike paid close attention. The doors didn't seem to be locked at all.

'Look at this beauty, gentlemen. A Ruger 77. We've got twelve of these for our guests. Are you familiar with this rifle?'

'It's a good one. I prefer a Rigby.275 myself.'

'I understand. That's an excellent choice, but perhaps more useful for game hunting in the Scottish highlands – deer hunting especially. What you'll find here are grouse, pheasants, waterfowl and moorhens. Whatever you shoot, Marjory will prepare for you and your friends for dinner. It'll be a feast, I can guarantee you that. You provide the game, we'll provide the wine.'

George handed the rifle to David, who looked impressed. He passed it on to Mike. Mike inspected it and held it in various positions. He nodded and returned it to George, who closed the cabinet and opened the next one.

'And here we've got the Sako 85, with a strong three-lug bolt. Of course, we've got some Remington 700s, too.'

'That would make most of our friends happy,' Dave remarked.

'I thought you'd be impressed. Hold it, it's nice and light, with a sturdy grip.'

Dave gave the rifle back to George.

'And gentlemen, over here, I've got two fine copies of a Holland & Holland .375 rifle, the scope is made by Swarovski. I don't think there's more to add to that.'

'Certainly not, George. You've got an impressive collection here.'

'We'd love to try out some of your rifles but the weather has been a bit of a let down the last few days. It's kind of unpredictable. That may be an issue with our customers,' Dave said.

'Exactly. It's a long way to go, if you know what I mean,' Mike added.

'Of course, I understand, but we've got clothing for all weather; nothing can keep us indoors. I find that a minor inclement in the weather might actually enhance the team-building spirit, a fight against the elements, a warm wood fire in the evening, a nice well-deserved meal in the evening after a day in the rain and all that kind of thing.'

'I guess you are right George. I never saw it that way. You're right. Bring it on!' Dave enthused.

George looked very pleased. 'Well, why don't you grab a few rifles tomorrow, shoot some rabbits and we'll take it from there. But mind you, nothing else or I'll get in trouble. This hunting side business is keeping our hotel afloat. I can't afford to lose our firearms licence.'

'Understood, George. No worries.'

'Or you can try it today, but the weather's not that great. It rained all day yesterday and the fields are soaked. Too muddy for my taste.'

Dave looked at Mike. 'We've got plans for today. Got to get back to London for some business.'

'Of course, I understand. As I said, help yourself to any of these rifles. Try them out and you can create your own menu. Afterwards, perhaps we can arrange a trip to the UK for your hunting association in the States.'

'All right, buddy, sounds good. Rabbit with a nice red wine and cream sauce will do for me!'

'I'll have a word with Marjory. Now, if you'll excuse me, I'd better help my wife clear the breakfast room.'

'Thanks, George. See you tomorrow.'

Dave and Mike retreated to the small library. It was a private reading room where they could talk without being disturbed.

'I like this place. It has this gentleman's country club atmosphere. Seems like life hasn't changed much over the last few hundred years.'

'I like the rhythm of it all, the gentle pace of life. And the food, oh man. This trip beats our stint in Paris, hands down.'

'Glad to hear you're happy!'

'Mind you, we have to report back to Terrence. I think we've won George's trust. He fell for our story. It's a great cover.'

'Just scouting the region to plan holidays for others. Maybe that should be our next career.'

'You took the words right out of my mouth!'

Dave showed Mike his iPad.

'Look, this is the place where we picked up Claudia's signal after she disappeared at Whitechapel station. She must have travelled on the District line to somewhere in East London, Bromley-by-Bow to be precise, to meet her accomplice in a getaway car. She had half an hour's head start, but we'd caught up with her.'

'I'm glad we didn't line up outside that restaurant those guys recommended.'

'Not in our job. We can't take our eyes off the ball.'

'That take-away kebab was just what I needed.'

'It was spot on. Filled me right up.'

'You think the driver spotted us at the gas station?'

'If he did, he didn't show it.'

'Peter Miller... We meet again.'

'Nice family outing, eh?'

'The plot is thickening.'

'So what the hell was he doing in a VW camper in the middle of nowhere?'

'Beats me.'

'And where's Claudia now?'

'Less than a mile away from here. The tracker hasn't moved since last night.'

'It must be their secret base.'

'Speaking of a secret base, do you remember that local from last night? Phil?'

'The crazy one who saw a spaceship?'

'What if it's not a spaceship but a weapon? A missile?'

'Let's talk to Terrence. He can fill in the missing pieces. And let's find out more about Miller. If he's still here, we can pay his family home a little visit.'

'Let's go to London. I want to close this case before the end of the weekend. I miss my kids and I'm ready to go home.'

'Nothing beats being home, buddy. I'm with you there.'

Dave and Mike walked to the car park at the back of the inn.

'Have you seen that small car before?' Mike asked.

'It's a Mini.'

'I wonder who it belongs to?'

'Maybe the receptionist?'

'Lots of mud on the side panels.'

'Somebody likes to go off-roading.'

'Let's take a picture of the licence plate and send it to Terrence. He can run a background check.'

'Good work, buddy. I can't believe how close we are to Claudia after she managed to escape from us.'

'If only she knew.'

'She'd freak out for sure.'

'I knew she'd hold on to those pictures of her Mario.'

'I felt sorry for her. She must be heartbroken. I don't agree with those tactics.'

'That's what happens when Terrence hires a Brazilian firm. They're not familiar with our refined psychological interrogation methods, so they panic when they don't get any answers and resort to violence and torture. In the end, you get some half-baked confession and nobody knows if it's true or not.'

'And a dead body.'

'And another investigation and a trial that could drag on for years.'

'So why did you give her the photos?'

'Remember I put a tracking device in the envelope. It's tiny but extremely accurate. And right now, that envelope's not far from this village.'

'Of course.'

'One thing, buddy, don't let looks deceive you. Heartbroken or not, remorseful or not, this Claudia is a ruthless and calculated killer. What she did with that office building is an act of terrorism, she is a mass murderer. She can't get away with it; she has to be stopped before she strikes again.'

'I'm with you. I've seen worse than her but she's just getting started. Let's take her out, but first we have to go back to London and tie up a few lose ends.'

'Terrence is convinced that Zoblovski is the mastermind behind it all.'

'Time to do some leg work, buddy.'

26

Nina was a late riser. Marjory had left her a small plate with some fruit. After finishing her cup of tea, she asked George for directions to Barry's famous scrapyard. Though the innkeeper said it was easy to find, it involved country lanes obscured by hedges along a winding road, and a final two-mile stretch along a dirt track. Locals knew exactly which large oak tree to turn left at, but to Nina every oak tree looked the same. 'Look for the one with the crooked lower branch,' George had told her.

The scrapyard wasn't as easy to find as George had said. The elusive oak tree with the crooked branch was impossible to find even after passing it three times; maybe the branch had snapped off in a recent storm. Nina reversed several times, before asking a cyclist in blue Lycra for directions; he said he'd never seen a scrapyard in the area. A farmer on a tractor became cross with Nina when she blocked the road while making a three-point turn. But he turned out to be helpful, and pointed Nina into the right direction.

Finally, a group of ramblers with an old-fashioned

Ordnance Survey map showed her the entrance to the scrapyard along the perimeter of a small airport. It was well hidden. After two more turns along the country lane, Nina was relieved to see the hull of a giant airplane hovering above the hedge. She stopped the car to take some pictures. It was a surreal experience to see this giant blue and orange airplane in the country; it would be a great picture for her blog. After a few more twists and turns on an unpaved road, she saw a small wooden sign with paint chipping off it: Barry's Metal Recycling Works. She stopped her Mini and got out, taking a few more pictures. The old airplane looked even more impressive looming large over Barry's desolate junkyard: a giant mechanical carcass of a proud airplane, washed up on a field in Suffolk, as if picked bare by vultures. The wing flaps were missing. The nose cone, which housed the radar, had been removed, disfiguring its once handsome profile.

Nina knew she needed a pretext for her visit. Rule number one in journalism: get people on your side so they'll open up. Nobody likes a barrage of questions fired at them by complete strangers. Too many journalists take but never give, always moving on to the next story. Since this wasn't part of her assignment, she decided to include it in her own blog. She had a cunning title: Space Gate Suffolk.

After only one day in the country, the car was caked in mud. There was no damage to the bumpers or side-panels, and the exhaust looked pretty good too. On closer inspection, the exhaust resembled the bottom of a beer can. In the distance, she could hear a dog barking. Nina took a step back and with a quick karate kick, smashed the left-side mirror. Shards of glass fell into a water-clogged pothole. Nina had no desire to try and retrieve them.

Back in the car, she drove on for a short distance. Stopping near a shed she switched off the engine. She remembered George warning her that Barry could be rough and ill-mannered at first. A dog ran to the car barking, then circled it. Nina hesitated to open the door. Suddenly, the shed door opened wide. A large figure with an untidy beard and wearing a brown parka, combat trousers and army boots stepped out; he looked menacing, just like his dog.

'Get off, come here! Now!' he barked.

The heavy-set man walked to the car. 'Hey, miss, it's safe to get out. Don't worry about him; it's all noise, no teeth. He's just excited. We don't get many visitors around here.' He sounded gruff. He cleared his throat and spat sideways. A large piece of phlegm landed in a puddle a metre away.

Nina carefully opened the door of the Mini.

The Rottweiler calmed down and sat on its hind legs a few inches from her, carefully watching her.

Nina leaned forward and patted its nape.

'I think he likes you!'

'You've got a beautiful dog, nice and lean.'

'Welcome to Barry's scrapyard, miss. What can I do for you?'

'So stupid. I broke my mirror while parking. Got too close to a wall, I suppose. It was just a scrape, really. I'm staying at the Chestnut Hill Inn and George the landlord told me I should come and see if you've got a spare.'

'You've come to the right place indeed, my dear. But you shouldn't have bothered coming all the way out here. George could have phoned me and I would have delivered your mirror this afternoon. I'm at the post office shop nearly every day, followed by a nice pint at his inn, of course.'

'Well, I'm here now,' Nina said cheerily. 'Look, it's this mirror.'

Barry scratched the back of his head. 'It's a 2007 model, right?'

'Not sure, I only borrowed it from our office.'

'Cars are my world, miss. It's a 2007 model. Follow me.'

Nina followed Barry and his dog to the storage shed through a maze of old cars that were stacked high.

'What do you do with all those cars?'

'Well, first of all I remove the oil and petrol and then I take out all the recyclables – plastics, chairs, you name it. I record them and then store them in my warehouse. Some parts have more value than others. Side wings and bonnets I can always use. You see, we have a lot of narrow roads in these parts. Lots of collisions. Some cars are a total write-off, as you can see; others can be patched up easily. Supermarket car parks are a good, steady source of minor but expensive-to-repair accidents. I make good money on those.'

'Interesting. I never thought of recycling this way.'

'I may not look it, miss, but I care about the future of our planet. I hate to see it being destroyed as it is right now.'

'And all the metal you can't use, where does it go?'

'Right now it's not going anywhere. The commodity market's flat…'

Barry drew a horizontal line in the air. 'Flat as a pancake! I can't get rid of the stuff. Years ago, the Chinese would buy the whole lot. Each month truckloads were carted off to Harwich and then loaded onto big ships sailing to China. But that's no longer the case. It's a matter of waiting. The good times'll come back again.'

Barry opened the door of a rickety looking warehouse. Nina was impressed. From the outside it looked worn out, but inside it was immaculate. Every item had been cleaned, itemized and stored in clear boxes.

'So tidy.'

'I learned that from the airplane recycling regulators; I just followed it through. It gives a good impression, and customers have no problem paying a little extra for this.' Barry winked. 'They wouldn't like me to pick up a mirror from a large bucket and ask a tenner for it. But if it's wrapped in a clear box, they're happy to pay forty pounds. A layer of bubble wrap will add another fiver to the price. Bingo! I'm giving away all my secrets, aren't I?'

Barry logged into his computer and started typing. 'Let's have a look: a 2007 Mini, left wing mirror unit. There we go. Row eleven, shelf thirty-seven, next to the Vauxhall Astra wing mirrors.'

Nina strolled off and was amazed by the sheer amount of spare parts; exhaust pipes hung from the ceiling like legs of ham in a butcher's shop, rows and rows of bonnets in all colours and shapes. Thousands of boxes with all sorts of items, ranging from petrol tank caps to window wipers, speakers, stereo sets and mirrors.

'I love your place, I really do!' Nina shouted from a distance at Barry. 'Can I take some pictures?'

'Be my guest,' he hollered.

After a few minutes, Barry climbed down a stepladder with a box in his hand.

'I've found what I was looking for. I think you only need the mirror glass; the casing of your mirror unit seems to be undamaged. Remind me, what kind of accident was this again?'

'Not sure, I think I scraped it along a wall, perhaps when I was reversing,' Nina said, sounding vague.

Barry grumbled. 'I see.'

'I don't want to take up much more of your time, Barry, you've been very kind.'

Barry and Nina walked back to the car. The dog ran ahead of them.

'Were you planning on fixing it yourself?'

'If you could help me with that, that'd be great!' Nina played with a strand of her hair, her gaze on the ground, turning her foot in the dirt.

'Well, let's get on with that then before it's time for lunch.'

Barry went into his office and came back with a small toolkit. He leaned over the left mirror and inspected it from several angles. Then he stood up to his full height. He cleared his throat and squinted his eyes when he looked at Nina.

'Miss, why are you really here?'

'What do you mean? I need a new mirror.'

'I've been in this business since I was sixteen – that's almost thirty years! I've seen thousands of car wrecks, ten thousand damaged mirrors and hundreds of young women like you, making up some kind of excuse so their husbands or boyfriends don't find out about their precious car being scratched or damaged. Sometimes, when I think about all those relationships I saved by patching up those lovely cars before anybody found out, I see myself as a counsellor.'

Nina laughed.

'I guess so,' Nina replied, feigning ignorance.

'This mirror, I can assure you, wasn't damaged by a scrape against a wall, or hitting a lamppost while reversing. Someone deliberately damaged this mirror. It was either with a stick, a baseball bat or a kick, but I doubt anybody can kick this high. I hope you're not in danger, miss. This could have been a warning!'

'Now you're scaring me.'

'Anyway, it's fixed now.'

'How much do I owe you?'

'Give me a tenner and we won't talk about it! Your secret's safe with Barry.'

'Thanks, I'm glad to hear it.'

Barry put his tools in his pocket and waited for Nina to get into her car and drive off. Nina hesitated for a minute. She opened the door, but before getting in, she turned around. 'Can I ask you a question?'

'Be my guest, as long as you don't ask me to marry you. I'm a happy bachelor,' Barry chuckled, then cleared his throat and spat out another large lump of phlegm.

Nina laughed.

'Last night in the bar of the Chestnut Hill Inn, I overheard a conversation about a friend of yours named Peter. He's building some kind of a spaceship.'

Barry started laughing, his whole belly shaking. He bent double. 'That's a good one. Let me guess? You were talking to Phil!'

'Yep, he was going on and on about it.'

'That doesn't surprise me. And he'd had several pints

already?'

'He seemed pretty pickled to me.'

'He's an old alcoholic, don't take any note of him. Peter building a spaceship? You know that he works as an accountant? He's a typical City boy. He washes his wellies every time before he puts them back into the boot of his car. Peter's an old friend of mine. We go back many years; his aunt lives not far from here. In fact, you can see her farm right over there, in the distance, beyond the little stream and fields. He and his son Tom are building a mock spacecraft for me. I'm planning to put it near the main road so people can find my scrapyard without driving around in circles. It's a gimmick, nothing else.'

Nina started laughing too. 'That explains it all!'

'Look, he got some kind of promotion at work, plus a bonus. He came to see me a couple weeks ago after reading my ad for one of those old VW campers you young people go wild about. I've rented it out in years past to students going to the Latitude festival, down the coast. One weekend, Peter tried camping in a field nearby, and that was enough for him to realise he didn't want to buy the camper after all.'

Nina nodded. It made more sense than the story she'd heard. She leaned forward to stroke the dog again. As long as the dog was happy, Barry kept on talking.

'I know that some of those campers sell for lots of money, but they're not worth it. They're ancient! From the Flower Power era,' Barry chuckled. 'Happy times they were, but to be honest Nina, those campers are plain dangerous. They're death traps. They were built in a time before cars were fitted with airbags, ABS and crumple zones to absorb the kinetic energy when you collide. You hit a modern car with an antique van like that and you're gone. No hope of survival. The brakes are ancient and slow, the gearbox is rubbish and the engine's not suitable for modern traffic. Overtaking a lorry or a tractor on roads like these needs serious advance planning.'

'That's a shame, really. They look cute. Surely you could keep renting out your camper a bit longer?'

'Of course, I could keep renting it out for lots of money to young hipsters like yourself, but you see, it doesn't sit well with me. I simply couldn't live with myself if anything went wrong. I don't want to have an accident on my conscience. So I suggested to Peter he turn it into a spaceship, hoist a few jet engines on top of it, paint it a funky colour and bingo! I've got the best marketing gimmick in the east of England. Think of all the publicity. I may open a burger bar next to it for the weekend crowd.'

'That's one hell of an enterprising spirit. Do you mind if I use it for a blog?'

'Not at all. As long as you mention ol' Barry can post all spare parts anywhere around the world.'

27

Back at the inn for lunch, Nina caught up with Marjory who was preparing the tables for lunch while humming to a melody on the radio.

'I don't remember that tune,' Nina said.

'Oh, it's from way before your time, love,' Marjory sighed.

'It seems catchy enough.'

'The seventies were bliss,' Marjory said with a melancholic expression. 'Right over there in the corner, darling, we had a big jukebox and all the lads would come over every night of the week. Fridays and Saturdays were busiest. That's when they'd take out the local girls. Dancing, drinking, those were happy days. Young pilots, charming lads, real gentlemen: Americans, Canadians, always nice, always polite. Generous with tips, if you know what I mean. Those were the best years of my life.'

'What happened?'

'Well, didn't Barry tell you? They closed down the airport. It was considered too small for those new fighter jets. They opened up another one, not far from here, but that's more like a fortress. We never see anybody from there. It's not the same. And now what do we get? Some weekenders, some tourists and ramblers; mind you, they never tip. They walk all around the inn and the upstairs corridor in their muddy boots. On the whole they're not a jolly bunch, no party spirit. All they do is talk about birds. How exiting is that?'

'I guess not very.'

'Those ramblers, they want to experience life on the cheap. Some of them even bring their own sandwiches inside and hide them under the table when I walk by. They sit inside here all afternoon sharing a pot of tea between them. Every so often I look up when the door opens and hope those young lads walk in again, throw a coin into the jukebox and let the whole place light up with music, laughter and dancing.'

Nina didn't know what to say. Marjory drifted away with her nostalgia and reminiscing.

'Can I ask you a question?'

'Of course, my dear.'

'I spoke to Barry this morning, and he mentioned Doreen, his friend Peter's aunt. I'd really like to meet her. Can you introduce me to her?'

'I tell you what, Nina. She usually comes out to the Co-op early-afternoon, driving an old Ford Fiesta, you can't miss it. She brings her home-made jam. It sells quite well. Most weekends it sells out.'

'Those ramblers, perhaps?'

'Exactly. They buy a jar of jam and a loaf and share it between them. They'll eat it on the village green, before moving on with their rambling. Some weekends we get hundreds of 'em.'

'That's a lot of jam.'

'They could come and have scones and tea in my inn instead!'

'Maybe you should serve her jam with your scones. Might be a winning combination. I could write about that.'

Marjory shook her head dismissively.

'You know what, Nina? Why don't I go over to the shop with you later on and introduce you to Doreen. You can ask her about her jam-making operation and perhaps she'll open up. But I can't promise it. She may get the hump, and then you'd better stay out of her way.'

'It's worth trying.'

'I'll find you when I see her car. She often stays for twenty minutes or so.'

Nina went up to her room. She sat on her bed against a pile of pillows. The room was warm and cosy. The view over the fields had a calming effect on her. Her latest blog had done well overnight. Lots of Americans had posted comments about spacecraft building. It wasn't just something loonies in Suffolk were occupying their time with. There were posts from South Dakota to Iowa and Missouri. Nina giggled; perhaps she was on to something. Some uploaded images of their space-projects and others posted practical advice on what rocket-fuel to use to reach escape velocity on the cheap. She decided to string it along for a couple more days. All she needed was a snapshot of Peter's spaceship.

28

After a three-hour journey, Dave and Mike arrived in Crystal Palace. Mike found a parking space around the corner from the Millers' house.

'Let's walk the rest and see if their car's back.'

Dave scanned the street thoroughly from behind a bus shelter.

'No sign of any red Volvo. It's gone. I bet you it's still in Suffolk.'

'It's a nice quiet neighbourhood, nice houses and neatly maintained front gardens.'

'And that's the scary part of our work,' Dave said.

'What do you mean?'

'It's scary that such an unassuming family's involved in such a grand scheme. You don't know who to trust or who to suspect. Look at Peter, your average Mr Nice Guy, a family man. Suddenly, from one day to the next, he becomes a threat to mankind. All that stuff we learned in the first week with the agency, psychological profiling and all of that. It's all a load of mumbo jumbo.'

'Maybe when we dig deeper into his case we'll find things from his past that explain why he's involved.'

'I doubt it, buddy.'

'We've got Claudia the eco-terrorist and Zoblovski, who wants to control the Russian Space Programme. Somehow it's all linked to this family house on a hill in south London.'

'At least he won't get his feet wet once the sea starts rising.'

'They've always risen; there's nothing new in that. During the last Ice Age, the sea levels were so low you could walk from Russia to Alaska and from England to France.'

'Yeah, but the rate it rises at has increased.'

'In that case, we have to adapt! Don't retire in Miami! Buy a condo in Denver instead.'

'Thanks for the tip, pal.'

'Anyway, we'd better get down to business. It's Saturday morning, eleven o'clock, and for the last ten minutes I haven't seen a single soul walking up and down this street.'

'Because it's cold and damp.'

'I mean, the coast is clear. Let's go inside. Let's look for some more clues.'

Dave and Mike walked up to the house and opened the front garden gate. It squeaked.

Mike looked over his shoulder. 'Are you ready? Pass me a small card, bit of plastic.' He opened the front door with a quick swipe. 'Easy-peasy… They didn't even set the alarm.'

'There you go. They must have left in a hurry and forgot,' Dave said.

'In that case, let's sweep the place and get the hell out of here.'

'You do upstairs. I'll check down. Any laptops, iPhones, just take them. We'll get them analysed later.'

Dave looked at the fridge. It looked like a typical family fridge. Several magnets, tacky souvenirs from holidays in the Canary Islands and France, held an array of papers in place, list of errands, an invite to a school play, the local church fair and a shopping list for random stuff like limescale remover and fabric softener.

'Apart from an old TV in the corner of the living room,' Dave shouted in the hallway, 'there are no other electronic devices. All the toys are neatly stacked in the corner. The kitchen counter's clean, the tap's dripping and the dishwasher's been emptied. All in all, looks like a nice, clean house – nobody left here in a hurry.' After a few seconds, Mike hollered from upstairs.

'Hey, Dave, come and have a look!' Mike sounded pleased rather than panicked, his typical response when confronted with a dead body, as if it'd sprung to life all of a sudden. In the master bedroom, four costumes hung off an ironing board. Bright yellow suits and four helmets with a glass visor. 'What do you make of that, pal?'

'Not sure. Take some photographs.'

'It seems a bit elaborate for a school play.'

'Yeah, but too amateur for a serious trip to outer space.'

'That's for Terrence to decide. Let's take some pictures, get the hell out of this place and pay Zoblovski a visit.'

29

Nina stopped writing her blog when she heard footsteps on the corridor followed by a gentle rap on her door.

'Nina, I'm going over to the shop, would you like to come along, dear?'

Nina closed her MacBook and tucked it into her daypack, slung it over her shoulder and put on her black Doc Martens.

The Co-op was nothing more than a small village shop, but there was a good selection of newspapers and magazines, some fresh produce and a post office counter with a digital scale to weigh parcels and letters.

Nina rummaged through the shop and picked up a Kit Kat and a small bottle of water in case she ventured out later in the day. The weather had cleared; it was still cold and grey but no longer raining, and there were more vineyards to visit.

There was only one other customer, an elderly lady with a frayed winter coat and a floppy hat. She stooped and looked older than she was, her voice a croak. She laughed and giggled with the saleswoman, who seemed roughly the same age.

'They've known each other since primary school,' Marjory whispered. 'Once they start talking, it goes on forever.'

Sally, the saleswoman, asked Marjory, 'Are you in a rush, my dear?'

'If you don't mind,' Marjory said. 'Sorry, Doreen, how are you?'

'I'm fine, thank you very much,' Doreen said curtly. 'Always rushing about,' she mumbled under her breath. 'Well, young lady, why don't you go ahead too!' she continued.

'Contactless?' Sally asked.

'Wow, you surprise me,' Nina said.

'We move along with the times, don't we, Doreen?'

'Time never stands still. No time for nostalgia.'

Nina looked at Marjory's deadpan expression. No doubt she had heard these sneering remarks before. When Nina had paid, she turned to Doreen and said, 'I've heard so much about your jam, would I be able to buy a jar?'

'Too late, my dear, they've all sold out. I have to make a new batch.'

'Shame, really. I would have loved some to take home.'

'Are you in the area long, my dear?' Doreen asked.

'A couple more days. I'm doing some research on vineyards and local produce.'

'This is Nina,' Marjory explained. 'She's a journalist. She's staying with us for a couple of days, courtesy of Jonathan Appleton.'

'Of course, that posh wine-farmer.'

'A journalist, you say? You should come over. I can show you an old-fashioned working farm before the last one disappears and gets turned into a weekend retreat for city folk.'

'That would be great. I could come over now if you'd like me to.'

'That's the problem with you young people – always in a rush. Anyway, I must be going.'

'I can follow you in my car.'

'Very well, young lady, since you're so persistent! Let's have a spin through the countryside, see if you can keep up with me,' Doreen chuckled mischievously.

Marjory smiled. Doreen was unpredictable at times.

Nina looked in her rear-view mirror. She was parked close to a large tree and next to a refuse container. There was little room to manoeuvre. She hoped that Doreen would wait for her. As soon as she left the car park and got on the main road, she saw Doreen sitting in her car. White smoke was billowing out of the exhaust of her old Fiesta. She was revving her engine nervously. It seemed out of character. As soon as Nina pulled up behind her, Doreen shot off and disappeared around the corner. A tractor approached in the distance. Nina accelerated, and the front tyres spat up some gravel. She turned around the same corner, but there was no trace of Doreen's car.

Nina wasn't accustomed to driving at high speed on these winding country lanes; she had to slow down. Now the tractor was catching up on her. After half a mile, she saw the grey Fiesta waiting for her at a small junction. It was in a bend of the road, obscured by a large hawthorn tree – she was glad that Doreen had waited for her; she would surely have missed the turn. As soon as Nina was close by, the Fiesta accelerated again like a bullet, as if Doreen was an eighteen-year old who had just learned a new handbrake trick. Nina was left in a cloud of dust and had to wait for it to settle. The tractor trundled past her and honked. Not sure if this was a warning or a greeting, Nina waved before closing the window.

The farmhouse was at the end of a poorly maintained track. The Fiesta's suspension must have been worn out the way Doreen drove it. Knowing her Mini was designed for urban conditions, Nina didn't want to scrape the exhaust or damage the bodywork by driving at top speed. She had no intention of visiting Barry and his scrapyard again.

'It used to be the young ones racing along these country lanes,' Doreen cackled. 'I was worried that you lost me.'

'Well, it takes nerve to drive like that.'

'I've got nothing to lose. I'd rather die in a car crash, adrenaline rushing through my veins, than petering away in an old folks home sitting in a corner with a bunch of drooling geriatrics for company.'

'Yeah, well, I've got some years ahead of me and I'd rather not spend them in a rehabilitation clinic.'

Doreen giggled. 'You're quite right, my dear.'

'Give me a few more days and I'll catch up with you.'

'Only kidding. You're still faster than my nephew. He drives that Volvo of his at snail's pace as though he might kill a loose chicken.'

'Or a child, a cyclist, or a cow.'

'Come on, I'll make you some tea before I show you how to make jam.'

'Do you mind if I take some pictures for my blog?' Doreen

didn't reply. Nina assumed it would be OK. Doreen disappeared and Nina stayed behind in the dark wooden panelled reception room.

The farm was in desperate need of repair and Nina contemplated the possibilities. A house makeover show could transform it into a designer's dream. She'd scrape the paint off the barn doors and paint them bright red to match the brick walls. She'd install double-glazing for better insulation. The large barn could host weekend club nights. The main farmhouse could be turned into a luxury B & B with an outdoor Jacuzzi overlooking fields and wetland. And at the bottom of the orchard, she'd install a small Swedish sauna, with guests having the possibility of taking a refreshing dip in the stream. She imagined steam from the sauna rising up through the canopy of the majestic trees on a cold autumn night. It was within reach of London, a perfect weekend escape and close enough to Stansted airport to woo European travellers. The quaint village nearby ticked all the right boxes. She'd buy a few old telephone booths and line them up next to the barn. They could host an interactive art-project connecting strangers. Nina was letting her dreams go wild.

'Your tea, darling,' Doreen said, waking Nina from her reverie. 'You were miles away!'

'I often get like this when I'm out in the country. It's so tranquil and beautiful.'

'And that's how I like to keep it. Hope you won't give away the address. I'm not particularly keen on visitors.'

'I'm sure Marjory would welcome more visitors to keep her inn going.'

'Marjory? She should speak for herself. She never shuts

up, always chatting to everybody; no secret is safe with her. She broadcasts everything she hears and sees without a second thought. I wonder how her husband copes with her, the poor soul. He's a nice chap really, but she must drive him mad, all that talk about those American pilots. She was in love with all of them; I'm sure she must have told you.'

'Yes, she did. But they work in an inn; they need to socialize. I think she's helpful and entertaining.'

'I call it verbal diarrhoea!'

Nina blew on her tea before sipping it.

'Why don't you join me in my kitchen, my retreat from the modern world.'

'It's more like a retreat within a retreat.'

'I don't follow you, my dear.'

'Never mind.' Nina took a few more pictures with her iPhone.

'But first we need to get some fruit. Come with me, my dear, to the back of the farm. Doreen opened the door to an outbuilding directly adjacent to the main house. It was in the same state of repair as the shabby farmhouse. The air smelled mouldy. A large freezer stood in the corner, a gentle hum filling the silence.

'This freezer, my dear, is full of raspberries, blueberries and strawberries. Enough to last me until the new harvest. I grow them myself. Mind you, it's all organic of course. I'm not using any pesticides. Sally sells my organic jam at a premium to all those ramblers visiting our village. Some weeks, I can't keep up with the demand.'

'I'm impressed. You've got quite an operation here.'

Doreen didn't react. Nina wasn't quite sure if she was

hard of hearing or if she deliberately ignored her comments.

'You want to see how I make jam? It only takes an hour.'

'I'd love that.'

Doreen walked back into the kitchen and emptied one of the boxes with frozen raspberries into an oversized cooking pan. She added lemon juice and turned up the heat. In the meantime she rinsed empty jam jars and lined them up on the kitchen worktop. Then she shuffled to the larder and came back with a large bag of jam sugar.

'Be a darling, can you tip half of the sugar in with the raspberries?'

Nina nodded.

'Now all we have to do is keep on stirring. Perhaps you can do that. It's quite hard at times but you've got young and strong arms.'

Doreen handed a large wooden spoon to Nina.

'Make sure you scrape the spoon along the bottom of the pan, it shouldn't get burned.'

Nina made sure she followed Doreen's instructions. She felt like she was winning her trust.

'You mentioned Peter earlier on,' Nina recollected. 'You said he drives very slowly. What's he like?'

'My Peter? Health and safety is his middle name. He's always fixing things, forever worrying that one day I'll fall and break my hip.'

'I see. In the inn last night, I heard someone talk about Peter being involved in building some kind of spaceship.'

Doreen gave a suspicious look. She folded a tea towel slowly and walked over to the window.

'Is that why you're here? To ask me about Peter?' She

sounded miffed.

'No, no, no,' Nina was quick to reassure her. 'On the contrary, I just thought that they were having me on – you know, naïve girl from the city.'

'You know what the trouble is with these villagers? They have nothing better to do than to gossip. They talk all day long, and the more they drink the more farfetched their stories become. I have no idea what they say about Peter, but he's a good man. He's a lovely father, works hard and is the only one who comes to see me.'

'I hear that he's coming more often these days.'

'Well, his kids are getting older and it's good for them to get out of that dirty city, get their eyes off their iPads. I tell you: young people these days, all they do is stare at tiny screens. It's not good for their eyes, it's not good for their imagination and it's not good for their posture. Kids have to run around, spend time outdoors, climb trees, get wet, chase animals.'

Nina just nodded.

'Like we used to do. And Peter, too, when he was a little boy. All he wants to do is to give his kids the best of both worlds. Those villagers are just jealous.'

'I agree. Your farm is the perfect antidote to stressful city life.'

'Why don't you have a look around? The jam needs to simmer for a good while. I'll stir and you can help me fill some jars later on.'

'Sure. I'll be back in half an hour or so.'

Nina handed over the big wooden spoon to Doreen. She rinsed her hands in the sink and went outside.

She walked over to a small wooded area, lured there by a cheerful blanket of bluebells: the perfect photo. She took several shots from different angles. A gap in the clouds allowed the sun to break through and brighten up the flowers' blue hue. Nina flicked through the images she'd taken and was very pleased with the results. She could hear the stream in the distance; it was peaceful and alluring, with a bird chirping in the distance and insects hovering above. Tourists would love to visit this place and kids could build a little dam in the stream. She was imagining them spending hours playing in the stream and getting soaking wet. What fun!

She sat down on a tree stump and leaned back and took a deep breath. It was true: the air was so fresh it almost made her dizzy.

What could she possibly write about? The great outdoors? Making organic jam? Perhaps she could partner with a shop in London and sell luxury food online. She wasn't sure if Doreen was up for it. Nina's mind flowed freely. Her imagination conjured up a global organic food distribution network.

She was suddenly startled out of this daydream when she heard banging. Nina looked up; it didn't seem to be coming from the kitchen where Doreen was making her jam. It came from the opposite direction.

The banging continued. It was a shrill and hollow sound, like metalworking. Out of sheer curiosity, Nina rushed to the large barn nearest her. The windows were covered in cobwebs and were too high for a good peek anyway. Then the banging stopped. Nina opened the large barn door, the hinges creaking, light streaming in and illuminating the interior. Nina stopped. Apart from her own heartbeat, she didn't hear a sound. She looked around to see if there was anyone inside. A slight breeze made the door sway. Dust particles hurled into the turbid air scattered the beam of light in random directions. All Nina could see was an enormous combine harvester. She bent her knees to look underneath the machine. Footprints were on the dusty floor but nothing else. She was sure that she was alone. Taking a closer look at the footprints, she noticed how small they were, smaller than hers, they seemed fresh. They could belong only to a child, which reassured her. She straightened up and walked back. As she closed the barn door, she heard banging again. There was only one other barn left, twenty metres or so further down the yard. She began walking in that direction. There was no mistaking it; someone was working with metal.

'Nina!' Doreen hollered. 'I need your help.'

She closed the barn door and ran towards the farmhouse.

'You took your time! You've been away for more than half an hour. Anyway, I'm ready to fill some jars.'

Nina followed her. Doreen walked more carefully than she drove. At the door, she held on to avoid tripping.

The kitchen smelled like cooked raspberries. Doreen stirred the new batch one final time, then lifted the large wooden spoon and let the dark red emulsion run down. 'Look! Just perfect. You see the consistency? That's the tricky part, that takes years of practise.'

'I'm impressed.'

'You should be, darling, you should be!'

Nina smiled politely.

'Now if you'll just lift the pan ever so slightly and tilt it at a steady angle so I can fill each jar.'

Nina strained at the weight of the pan. She was concentrating, worried that she'd slip and all the jam would stream down onto the floor. When more than half of the jars were filled, the pan got lighter and she held it more evenly. She thought it was the right time to ask some questions.

'Is Peter around?'

'No dear, he isn't, I am sorry. He won't be back for a while, they all went shopping in Norwich.'

'I heard some banging,' Nina said. 'Quite loud. Is there perhaps somebody else on the farm?'

'I didn't hear anything.'

Nina looked at Doreen and paused for a few seconds. She was sure that her hearing wasn't as good as her own.

'Listen, you can hear it right now.'

'That must be Phil. He owns the combine harvester and sometimes comes in to do some minor repairs.'

'I had a look; there was nobody in the barn with the harvester. It came from the second barn.'

'Oh, that's the one Peter uses for his project, but he isn't here right now. You'll have to come back another time.'

'I'm pretty sure that I heard somebody.'

'Nonsense. I think you're imagining it. Or perhaps it's his old mate, Barry. He often shows his face around here. Anyway, I think we're done. I don't want to hold you up any longer, you must be on your way. Marjory doesn't like it when guests are late for tea.'

Probing Doreen would only make her more suspicious. A good journalist knows when not to cross the thin line of trust.

'I'll be off then. Thanks for the lesson. I'll upload the pictures tonight.'

'Goodnight, my dear, and drive carefully,' Doreen giggled. 'The locals drive like lunatics.'

Doreen started washing the big pan and utensils. Having estimated that she'd be busy for another twenty minutes, Nina rushed back to the second barn. One of the windows on the side had been wiped clean, but it was still too high up. Even on tiptoe, Nina couldn't look in. Then she heard it again, more banging followed by the distinctive sound of an electric drill. Someone was working. Perhaps the villagers were right after all.

Nina looked around, spotting a couple of tractor tyres near the barn. But they were too heavy to carry over to the window. A couple of empty crates seemed easier to move. She placed them on top of each other and climbed to the top, but it still wasn't high enough. She looked over her shoulder; she was out of the main farmhouse's view. She took out her iPhone, jumped as high as she could and snapped a photo through the window. She took a few more from different angles. She was sure she'd find something. Then she heard a door slam. Nina jumped off the stack of crates, stuffed her phone in the pocket of her jeans and headed towards her car. Doreen saw her and tried to get her attention. She was panting.

'I'm glad I caught you. I couldn't let you leave without a jar of the jam you helped making.'

'Thanks, that's really kind of you.' Nina felt the need to come up with an excuse for her detour. 'Sorry, I had to pee, so I went behind the barn.'

Doreen shook her head. 'You should have told me. You could have used the toilet in my house. Anyway, it's good to see a city girl improvising.'

'I sure was!'

'Come by any time. I don't mind having some company once in a while.'

Nina shook Doreen's hand. 'See you soon, I promise.'

She got into the car and drove off. Before turning into the main road towards the village, she looked at the pictures she'd taken on her phone. There were a dozen shots of window frames and dark ceilings. Six were more fruitful. She noticed a young woman with a blonde plait drilling holes into the side of an old Volkswagen camper, two engines were strapped to either side and a larger one was placed on top of the van. It was painted in bright colours, orange, purple and yellow. Nina laughed, this was just what she was looking for. She composed a short blog: 'What the hell is this? A spaceship? A prop? A hoax?' Her followers would have lots to comment on.

30

On Saturday mornings the City of London is a ghost town. A few empty buses trundled up and down Bishopsgate. A small queue of people was waiting outside the Heron Tower to be ferried up to a top-floor restaurant for brunch and the best views in London.

'Turn left at the next street,' Mike said, his eyes peering at a Google map. 'It's one way. Park along one of the single yellow lines.'

Dave drove carefully, he was still not used to driving on the left of the road.

'Zoblovski's office is right here,' Mike said after a few minutes.

'I am glad to get a break. This place is like a maze. It drives me mad, there doesn't seem to be any logic in the layout of this city.'

'Yep, Manhattan it ain't.'

Dave looked over his shoulder and shifted his body to get a better rear view. Parallel parking was a challenge. There wasn't much room either way. The black Buick touched the bumpers of the cars on both sides.

'Don't smash the other cars, we don't want any alarms going off and drawing attention to our car.'

'Take it easy, buddy. You wanna drive next? Be my guest.'

'I'd rather be your navigator. Look, I've got a set of maps emailed to me, extremely detailed. Stay right here. Better kill the engine, we may be here for a while.'

'Are you kidding me? You expect me to switch off the engine and freeze to death?'

'What's your problem? It's very mild out there. You can be so dramatic.'

Dave switched off the ignition and sighed. He was getting tired of Mike's sneering remarks.

Mike scrolled through several documents and attachments sent to his phone.

'OK, Zoblovski drives a Rolls-Royce, and it's parked inside the garage, the entrance to the car elevator is just around the corner from here, it's a tight corner.'

'I'm impressed with Terrence's research. Is the engine hot or cold?'

'According to Terrence's report, the car hasn't moved since yesterday morning.'

'How do we know if Zoblovski's inside?'

'The report says he stays in a penthouse apartment on the top floor during his visits to London. He often works on Saturday mornings before flying home to Moscow from City Airport.'

Mike opened another attachment; images of a small jet at City Airport and a detailed flight schedule. 'Without fail… Every Saturday for the last two months he's left the office at half past twelve. Arrives at City Airport at one and is airborne twenty minutes later.'

'In that case, we better do what we do best.'

'Sit in a car and wait.'

'Exactly. You take the first shift while I have a little snooze,' Mike said.

An hour went by. Only three cars had entered and left the car park. The entrance was hidden behind a classical facade and a large metal gate. Cars had to wait near the gate for the car elevator to be called, one by one. During rush hour a long queue of cars would quickly build up and block most of the narrow street. Leaving the car park on Saturday mornings could be quick. David couldn't risk missing Zoblovski's car when it came out of the lift.

After his rest, Mike put his chair in an upright position. 'Time for your power nap, buddy.'

'Wait, I hear something,' Dave said. 'The gate's opening. I'd better start the engine.'

'Is that his car?'

'Could be; it's big and blue.'

'Hot pursuit mode now!'

A sapphire blue Rolls-Royce Phantom was slowly turning onto the main street, twenty metres in front of their car. Dave had the car still in neutral.

'Quick, back out and let's get moving!'

'Relax, what's the rush? Let's not scare him right away. He'll spend at least three minutes waiting at the lights.'

'How do you know?'

'I've timed it. Nothing better to do.'

'You're a sad man,' Mike said.

'No, I simply observe and pay attention. It's all about the details.'

'Just drive. You make me nervous. Before you know it, another car will cut in. If I'd known it would take such a long time…'

Dave slowly manoeuvred the car from its tight spot and drove up to the traffic lights. It stopped a few metres behind the Rolls-Royce, leaving enough space not to intimidate the driver.

'What time is it?'

'Nearly twelve twenty-five.'

Mikhail Zoblovski relaxed in the back of his car. He enjoyed being driven; it was one of life's simple luxuries. Zoblovski had known his driver, Rudolph Murphy, since moving to London, and he felt comfortable with the way Rudolph slowly navigated his way through traffic. He found a CD in the console of the car next to his seat and put it into the overhead CD-player. The rich and robust sound of Rachmaninoff's 'Piano Concerto Number 2 in C minor' filled the rear compartment of the car. Mikhail sat back and enjoyed the ride. Within a few minutes he was completely absorbed in the music, forgetting all of his daily concerns about his company. Rachmaninoff was one of his favourite composers, a compatriot who had managed to capture the Russian spirit so well.

Completely absorbed in the beautiful piano playing, Mikhail hadn't noticed that Rudolph was speeding up. Only when he felt the car leaning more than he was used to whilst making a sharp turn, and he had to hold tight to avoid knocking his head against the window, did he realise that something was wrong. He paused the recording and knocked on the partition window.

'Rudolph, why the hell are you driving so fast?'

'I think we're being tailed, sir.'

'Don't be silly, what do you mean?'

'Look behind you. The same black car has been following us since we left the parking garage, and now it's behind us. Before we left, as I was waiting for you, I looked at some of the more recent CCTV footage. That black car was parked there for at least an hour.'

'Why didn't you say anything?'

'I wanted to be sure, sir. I've driven the same circle three times in the last fifteen minutes. They keep following us. Their car is glued to our bumper.'

'Speed up, Rudolph. Try to get rid of them, shake them off!'

'I've tried, sir. There's too much traffic and too many lights.'

'Do they have guns?'

'I don't know. They haven't made any attempts to shoot. That would be pointless, anyway. This car is bulletproof; the windows are seventy millimetres thick. You're well protected.'

'I rather call it bullet resistant glass. If these guys are professionals, we don't stand a chance.'

'If they wanted to kill you, they would have done it when we came out of the garage. I think they want to know where you're going.'

'We'll have to confuse them. What kind of car are they

driving?'

'Don't know. Something American, sir.'

'That's peculiar. All these years, I've been trying to protect myself from my fellow Russians. I always thought that if I ever took a bullet to the head, it would be fired from a trusty Makarov pistol.'

Mikhail Zoblovski looked over his shoulder. The black American car was stuck behind another car. He couldn't make out the face of the driver or the passenger.

'The problem is that whoever's looking for me knows how to find me. No place on earth will be safe to hide. Damn the bastards; they've condemned me to a life of paranoia.' Mikhail slammed his hand against the window. 'You can try to shake them off this time but they'll come back for sure. Once in a while, they check up on you to remind you they're still after you. And all that time you know your number's up. So many of my friends from the old days have disappeared or got involved in car accidents which were never investigated.'

'That's awful, sir.'

Zoblovski tried to stay calm, but he noticed that his palms were getting sweatier by the minute. Rudolph was an excellent driver, but in London he stood no chance of shaking off his pursuers. Mikhail looked out of the window to see which way they were heading. On the left-hand side was the entrance to Moorgate station; Rudolph turned left at the traffic lights and looked in his mirrors.

'They're still following us, sir. What shall I do?'

Zoblovski considered getting out and running for the Tube but he was sure that one of these guys would run after him, and despite his head-start, he'd be no match for well-trained assassins who spent most of their working life in the gym. They'd catch up with him in mere seconds.

'Listen to me,' he said. 'Take a right on Old Broad Street. When we reach Tower 42, stop the car and open the boot. Then drive the car back to the office and I'll contact you on Monday. Take the rest of the weekend off.'

'Very well, sir.'

At the traffic lights on London Wall, a bus glided between the Rolls-Royce and the Buick, conveniently obscuring the pursuers' view.

'Excellent,' Mikhail said. 'I was hoping for something like this. It's the first time I'm pleased with the bus service in London.'

Rudolph stopped the Rolls-Royce just outside Tower 42. He deliberately blocked the road so the bus wouldn't be able to overtake him. He gave a hand signal to the bus driver indicating he would only need a minute. The bus was almost empty and the driver didn't seem to mind stopping a bit longer. He yawned and stretched his arms.

Zoblovski got out of the car and walked to the boot. It was already open. He took out a small backpack, a personalised bug-out-bag containing more than just a few essentials for unexpected overnight stays. He slung the backpack on and gave the straps a firm pull. The bus driver was now getting impatient and hooted twice. Mikhail gave him a thumbs-up, indicating it wouldn't be much longer. All this time, the black Buick lingered behind the double-decker bus. He couldn't have wished for a better diversion. Mikhail leaned forward a bit more and took out a small foldable bike. With the skill of a seasoned commuter at London Bridge station, he unfolded his red Brompton bike in less than eight seconds – he had practised this so many times. He knew that one day this bike would save his life. That moment seemed to be now. Mikhail knew this area very well.

Right next to Tower 42 was a small pedestrian passage, which led back to Bishopsgate, a popular shortcut. No car would be able to get though. Mikhail jumped on his bike, and just when Dave and Mike grasped what was happening, Mikhail cycled past the Japanese restaurant and rode through Bishopsgate into Great St Helen's past a large building site leading to Undershaft. He continued along another pedestrian path passing the iconic Gherkin. He kept on cycling on the pavement, narrowly avoiding pedestrians. He raced as fast as he could towards Aldgate East station.

Mike and Dave were furious.

'Damn it!' exclaimed Dave.

'Stuck behind this stupid bus.'

'Try getting past it.'

'I don't think it's possible.'

'Try going over the pavement.'

Dave reversed the car and then steered it onto the pavement overtaking the bus. Shocked and angry pedestrians jumped out of the way and one stern looking woman bashed on the driver-side window with her handbag, berating Dave for endangering her life. He took no notice of her.

'Look. There's the Rolls-Royce. I think our man's disappeared.'

'What do you mean?'

'I can't see him any more. So that's why the bus was stalled. I thought it was weird that the bus stopped; I couldn't see a bus stop.'

'Great. That's all we need. What now?'

'I suggest we go and eat something. I'm starving and my mood isn't getting any better.'

'Let's find a restaurant.'

'That's easier said than done. You know any restaurants in London where you can show up and park outside?'

'I do miss home. Everything's just so much more convenient. You can go to a drive-through, order your meal. Drive around to collect it two minutes later. Piping hot. Park your car and eat your meal in peace and listen to your own music in your own car.'

'Well, that says it all,' Mike sneered.

'What do you mean?'

'Nothing, nothing at all. Different countries have different customs. Let's go grab lunch and a beer.'

'A warm beer, you mean.'

'Stop complaining. It's really getting on my nerves. You'll be home soon enough.'

'I am allowed to have an opinion,' Dave said. 'I don't need your permission to say what I want to say, pal. I think London's a great city and it'd be even better with few drive-through restaurants strategically placed across the centre.'

'There was a restaurant along the highway that I spotted on the way, probably no more than a half hour from here. The Little Chef if I remember rightly. Looked real classy too.'

'Sounds good to me!'

31

Foggy Bottom, Washington DC

Terrence was reviewing the file, which his assistant Rosa had left, on his desk. The images spoke for themselves and the DNA evidence was robust. He had just gotten off the phone with Secretary of State John McClark. Damage control was the best they could hope for; taking out the stinger would be his only option. Having to operate abroad was never easy; the potential political fallout could be embarrassing for those directly involved. 'Discretion is our motto,' McClark had reminded him.

He stared at the grey concrete wall – four storeys down in an anonymous office block. No window, no connection with the real world. His sleep cycle was off. Was it day or night? There was a lot at stake, and with five years to go before his retirement from the service, losing his reputation would be too a steep a price to pay.

'Rosa, please get Mike and Dave on the phone. I need updates.'

Terrence loosened his tie and leaned back in his chair, putting both feet on the desk as he waited for the connection.

He had his phone on speaker mode.

'I need an update, guys,' he said into the speakerphone. 'How's England?'

'Freakin' freezing.'

'I bet it's not as bad as over here. I can't wait for the weather to warm up. I've been stuck in this damn basement for the last few days.'

'You should get out more, Terrence.'

'Not before you guys are on a plane back home. I'm your backup during this mission. A lot's at stake.'

'Some bad news first. We lost Mikhail Zoblovski,' Dave said.

'When did this happen?'

'A couple of hours ago. He gave us the slip,' Mike added.

'How?'

'Some bystanders saw him getting a small bike out of his trunk and he pedalled away like a circus clown,' Dave said.

'Did you follow him?'

'We couldn't – a car like ours is useless in a city like London,' Dave said.

'Do you have any idea where he could be?'

'We've got a hunch.'

'We can't act on hunches. We need to have a good visual. Work on it.'

'Sure thing.'

'And where's our eco-terrorist?'

'She's still hiding on a farm in Suffolk.'

'Yeah, we've got the coordinates of that farm and some satellite footage. I'm working with the authorities to get a drone fixed above our target area so we can get a live feed.

That may take a couple of hours. Until then, you're our eyes in the field.'

'Right,' Mike said.

'And something else... We examined that glove you sent for DNA analysis to our lab in London. We compared it with the DNA from Valenti's underwear, which was analysed in São Paulo.'

'And?'

'It's a hundred per cent match.'

'We had no doubt about that,' Dave said.

'Neither did we. She struck once, she may strike again, and soon.'

'What do you mean?'

'The web around Claudia Valenti is closing. In the eyes of the organization, she's a terrorist. Don't be fooled by her appearance. It'll only be a matter of time before she surprises us again.'

'She doesn't match the profile of a terrorist, with her blonde hair and innocent fresh looking face,' Mike said.

'Underneath her wholesome appearance she's a tough one, I can tell you that. You let her escape and that's created some tension over here. Some are doubting your abilities. Let me be frank: your futures are at risk. I hope you can pull this off.'

'No problem boss. We're the best team you've got!'

'Before I let you go, there's something else. Our team did some target profiling in Suffolk. Some folks in the organisation are extremely concerned. This is strictly confidential. If anybody finds out, it could incite a mass panic.'

'That goes without saying.'

'If you log into the system, I can show you where we are and what we're looking at. Less than fifteen miles from the farm where Claudia's hiding, there's a nuclear power station. Environmentalists have been protesting against it ever since it was built in the 1960s. Now it's like a fortress. There's no way anybody could get near the main plant without going through several checkpoints. It's heavily guarded.'

'Unless you fly over those checkpoints.'

'The core of an atomic power station is surrounded by thick layers of concrete several metres thick. Nothing will penetrate it.'

'Unless you've got some serious explosives.'

'Or fly a rocket into the main block.'

'So those rumours by the villagers in the inn weren't that far-fetched.'

'They may have been right all along. She's taken us by surprise.'

'Still, these nuggets of information build a strong case against Miss Valenti.'

'We hear you, Terrence.'

'You've got backup. If it ever comes to a launch, our boys at the Suffolk airbase are on stand-by. They can get scrambled and airborne within seven minutes and intercept that rocket in seconds.'

'Seven minutes is a long time.'

'It's the best we've got. Again, we can't make any mistakes. We might get only one chance. We have to show that we've learned from previous foreign operations. If we pull it off and save London from a nuclear disaster, we'll be the world's heroes once again. If we mess it up, we're just arrogant imperialists. Given the various European trade deals in the pipeline, we have to be seen in the most positive light ever.'

'One more question, boss. How do Peter Miller, his family and Mikhail Zoblovski fit into it all?'

'Peter Miller's a bit of a wild card. Apart from the fact that he works for an insurance company owned by Zoblovski, who's heavily involved with the Russian Space Agency, I don't see any other connection. Then again, as a desperate middle-aged guy, he might just want to leave his mark, maybe a paragraph in a history book. Can't be satisfied being just a face in the crowd. The guy wants to impress his family...'

'Your average nut?'

'Something along those lines. Dangerous, nevertheless.'

'You want us to take Zoblovski out too?'

'Zoblovski is well connected. He may be of use to us in the future. Taking him out may be too risky. Let him run.'

'Understood, boss.'

'One more thing. You'll have to operate undercover. You guys have to be smooth and slick, leave no traces. It'll be an in-and-out job. No wild car chases; they will only leave expensive insurance claims and attract unwanted attention. Just take the girl and deliver her to the US Air Force base. They'll take over from there. I want you guys back within twenty-four hours. That means your one and only plane out of there leaves at 11:45 tonight. You miss that flight and you'll be on your own.'

'Roger that.'

Dave tilted his head back and closed his eyes. 'I can't wait to get home.'

32

Mikhail took great pride in his knowledge of the London Underground system. Though some of the stations weren't as elaborately decorated as the Moscow Metro, the size of the system was impressive. Whenever he gave his driver a day off, he enjoyed travelling incognito – it beat going to an exhibition or a gallery. The sheer cultural diversity on show in any given carriage was a feast for the eye.

He felt he had a deeper understanding of people's similar needs, desires, and values, whoever they were, wherever they came from. The Tube was a melting pot, he thought, proof that we're all the same. Unfortunately, those underground travellers were disconnected from those above ground making decisions about the future of the planet. In that respect, democracy was being eroded by big businesses and oil companies with lobbying powers that the public grossly underestimated. With their short-term vision, politicians were oblivious to the environmental damage they abetted, rubber stamped and perpetuated. Mikhail had long given up hope of another global uprising, another revolution, a world where the environment was at the heart of political concerns. With the clock ticking, his bones aching and death surely approaching, he was certain that the only way to save mankind was to escape it all and resettle somewhere else temporarily. Mars was the most obvious and practical choice. Create a base on the red planet, select a number of people with diverse genetic make-up, procreate and wait for climate change to do what's necessary and return to Earth once the deserts were green again. Admittedly, this would take millennia.

When Zoblovski arrived at Aldgate East station, he figured that at the most he'd have a head start of ten minutes. Waiting too long for the train could cost him this advantage. He went up to the ticket office and asked for a zone 1–6 travel card. He probably wouldn't need it, but he didn't want to run the risk of getting caught in the wrong zone with the wrong ticket and unable to escape. Not knowing who was following him, he knew he couldn't risk anything. His business rivals would think nothing of hiring contract killers to shoot him dead in a train carriage full of bystanders. They'd kill in cold blood and flee without a trace. Before the police could cordon off the station and launch an investigation, they would have left the country on a private jet out of City Airport.

Mikhail quickly folded his bike and carried it through the gates. Just in time. He took the staircase down as quickly as he could without bumping into hurrying pedestrians making their way up the same stairs. At the last steps, he could just hear a train slowing down and a voice calling out: 'Mind the gap! Mind the gap!' Without giving it much thought, he ran towards the train and jumped on board as the doors were closing. He glanced at the platform to see if anybody was following him. On the overhead display unit in the front of the carriage, he read the name Barking in bright red LED. At least it was far out east, an unlikely hiding place for a fugitive.

33

The brochure stand next to the reception desk had a small selection of leaflets, maps and flyers for local attractions and day trips. Nina picked a two-page guide outlining a local footpath – a two-hour round trip through splendid Suffolk, she'd be able to complete this before supper. She skimmed the guide and then tried to get Marjory's attention, who was idling at the bar. It was quiet, the calm before a storm, as the regulars wouldn't start coming in for an after work drink before five.

'I'm going for stroll in the country.'

'Good for you, a nice stroll will boost your appetite. I'll prepare tea later on. You'll be back by then?'

'I guess so.'

'Did Tess already tell you that we've got two delightful American gentlemen staying with us? Typical DC,' Marjory whispered, fancying herself an expert on placing American accents. 'They seem like government officials out on a jolly. I hope they're doing their research on top-notch R & R options for their senior staff. I've given them a generous helping of bacon with their fried eggs. It may go a long way, if you know what I mean.'

'Uh-huh...So what would bring two Americans to Suffolk in the winter?'

'You should ask George about them. He showed them our rifles yesterday. They're into hunting, small game mainly. They said they're organizing trips for small groups of Americans – team-building and networking, that kind of thing.'

'Ah, that kind of trip,' Nina replied.

'Could be good for business. We've got too many rabbits and hares running wild anyway, might as well shoot and eat them.'

'Did they say anything else?'

'No, but George was very impressed with them; they sounded very knowledgeable about rifles.'

'Interesting.'

'Isn't it? We love to have those kinds of guests.'

'Did they leave behind any ID?'

Marjory looked at the receptionist. 'Tess, did they?'

'No they didn't, but I scanned their IDs when they checked in, you know George, he is a stickler for regulations.'

'Could I perhaps have a look at those scans?' Nina asked.

'Oh, for heaven's sake, of course not,' Tess replied. 'That's confidential information, we've got a relationship of trust with our guests.'

'Of course, I understand. As a journalist I respect your integrity. But if you hear of anything, please let me know.'

'Is there anything else I can do for you?' Tess asked.

'No thanks. I'd better be on my way. The weather's

cleared up.' Nina folded the leaflet and tucked it into her back pocket.

'I'm sure it'll stay dry,' Tess said. 'The ramblers have been out in full force all day.'

Nina walked over to her car and changed into her wellies, which she kept in a large shopping bag. The entrance to the footpath was easy to find, just across the village green from the Co-op and next to the school. A group of six elderly but spritely men and women in brightly coloured jackets were getting ready, waiting for some of their friends who were buying provisions for the walk. Nina didn't want to get too close to the ramblers; their constant chatter could draw attention to her and the group. She planned to inspect the farm for a second time and find out what that young woman was working on. She was determined to put rumours and rural legends to rest by unearthing and exposing the truth.

Being in the countryside cleared her mind. Her discussion with Alistair Mohair was now a distant memory. Compared to Suffolk, Shoreditch was like another world, a surreal world where a blog could either be launched into the stratosphere of fame or crash to earth, scattering the blogger's reputation for good. The stakes were high and fame was short-lived, like a fast-burning comet.

Nina walked fast and at a steady pace, halfway between jogging and running with the occasional leap over puddles and muddy patches. She climbed nimbly over fences, sure that she had an advantage over the group of hikers; they looked impressive with their Nordic walking sticks, but these were often just for show. Soon they would catch up. Nina looked over her shoulder and could make out the village church tower in flat Norman style. From that distance, it looked like the watchtower of a castle.

Nina had made steady progress. The path was well maintained and had ample signposts. She passed through a field with sheep and some newborn lambs, and continued along a hedge of thick hawthorn and blackthorn until she reached a stream. In the distance, she could make out the wooden footbridge marking the border of Doreen's farm. She checked her watch. Thirty-five minutes! Not bad for a city girl. She was walking briskly and had hardly broken a sweat.

Before Nina would reach the footbridge, she looked for a vantage point from which to observe the farm. She steadied herself against a tree and raised her binoculars. To the right she could see several cars, including a red Volvo estate, a typical family car, probably belonging to the Millers. There was little activity. Nina paused for a few minutes before taking up her position again. She reckoned she could climb up the tree and sit there for half an hour and just observe the farm from a safe distance. The doors to the barn where the combine harvester stood were open. She could see two children, a boy and a girl, emerging, but they didn't close the doors. The girl was taller than the boy, and was perhaps ten or eleven. They were chasing each other and laughing. It was the picture of innocence. There was another car near the barn, closest to the footbridge. The door was open, too, and Nina saw a young woman talking to a man. He was fat, wearing a brown parka and a cap. He was leaning against an old car, a black Ford Mondeo estate. It looked well worn, splashed with mud. There was no doubt in her mind that it was Barry. The woman was gesticulating. Her body language seemed more Latino than North-European, but she was tall and blonde, her hair in a plait. Perhaps she was Polish or Ukrainian, working as a farmhand. Nina leaned against the trunk and dozed a little. There was no rush. She had all day to find out what was going on.

'I'm sure that was a blue tit.'

'Pass me the binoculars.'

'It's gone now!'

'What a shame, pass me the binoculars anyway.'

Nina was startled awake. She wasn't sure how long she'd been asleep. Luckily she was perched in the fork of the tree and there was no danger of falling out. She was horrified to see that the group of chattering pensioners had caught up with her. They were likely not only to scare away all the birds and wildlife, but would also draw attention to her.

'Excuse me, miss, have you been here long? Have you seen any interesting birds?'

Nina shuffled to get to her rear pocket and took out the hotel brochure. Inside the leaflet there were illustrations of all the birds one could find along the path. Nina tried to look convincing posing as an avid bird watcher. She glanced at the guide to refresh her memory, as bird names weren't her forte.

'You're right, there was a blue tit, but at this time of day, they go towards the stream, so you better head to the bridge if you want to see them. I also saw some tree sparrows and a blue-headed wagtail. If you're really quiet, you can hear a green woodpecker.'

That got everybody excited.

'You hear that? A woodpecker! We'll leave you in peace,' they said. 'Thanks for your help. Come on, let's move on.'

It took a while before the last person disappeared around the bend and peace was restored. She was slightly annoyed with herself for having missed half an hour of crucial observation. She raised her binoculars again. The blonde woman was no longer in her line of vision. Two men were carrying what looked like an airplane seat inside the barn. So far her theory about a spacecraft was holding.

The front door of the main house opened and Doreen stood in the doorway, seemingly hollering at the two men. Nina was disappointed; this didn't look very exciting at all. It certainly didn't look like a state-of-the-art spacecraft assembly line. More and more she felt like she was wasting her time and had nothing to write in her blog. Even the birds had gone. She couldn't gain any more information from where she was sitting. She needed to talk to someone, needed to unleash her inner journalist. She looked to her left. The group with the brightly coloured waterproofs had set up camp at the footbridge. They looked comfortable and settled for the time being. Hang on, she thought. One of the women was opening a backpack and took out a large blanket. This was serious – they were in it for the long haul. They had reached the end of their walk and would sit there, until it would get dark or start raining again.

Nina considered her options. In the near distance, she heard another group of hikers coming towards her. She climbed down the tree and stretched her legs, stuffed her binoculars into her backpack, ate her Kit Kat and took a big swig of water. She decided to take a few pictures of the idyllic scenery and return to the same spot after dark when the ramblers had gone.

34

The journey to Barking would take twenty minutes. Mikhail peered into the long corridor of the carriage. Nobody was paying any attention to him. He was just another Londoner with a Brompton bike. He had to admit that he was slightly out of breath. Several scenarios were running through his head. Going back to the office or his penthouse flat wasn't a viable option. Going to City Airport and boarding his private jet could be tricky. The plane might be under surveillance and international airports are not an easy place to avoid CCTV and security. There was a big chance that they'd be waiting for him near the airport. He'd walk straight into an ambush. First of all, he needed something to eat and a place to sit down, clear his mind, reflect on past events and make a plan.

After walking through the automatic gate at Barking station, he turned right and made a beeline for one of the best Indian restaurants he knew in this part of London.

The restaurant hadn't changed much over the years. A waiter welcomed him but didn't show any signs of recognition. Why would he? The last time he'd visited this place was to meet up with his personal assistant Sylvia several months ago.

'A table for two, please,' Zoblovski said.

'Very well, sir, please follow me.'

Mikhail took his mobile phone out of his jacket and called Sylvia. Time was of the essence. Someone could be tracking his phone and he needed a quick escape. Triangulation of his call would bring his followers to a busy high street in Barking, near the station. That would be pretty useless as a clue. He'd be their needle in a haystack for some time. Much to his delight, Sylvia answered straight away.

'It's Mikhail here.'

'Mr Zoblovski, is there a problem in the office?'

'Not at all, not at all. I was just wondering if you could join me for lunch? Same place where we met a few weeks ago.'

'Sure, I remember. The food was excellent.'

'And so was your company!' Mikhail said.

'Stop flattering me. I can be there in ten minutes.'

'Shall I order for you? I'm in a bit of a hurry.'

'Sure, same as last time. But what is this all about?'

Mikhail hung up, reached for his bug-out bag and stored his iPhone safely away in a signal blocking pouch. This was guaranteed to prevent any further tracking. He swiped the beads of sweat from his face. A waiter approached.

'Are you ready to order sir?'

'Yes I am, my friend will join me soon. We are in a bit of a rush.'

'No problem sir, why don't you order now and we can

serve it as soon as your friend has joined you,' the waiter suggested.

'Excellent. Poppadoms for two please, a Tiger beer and a bottle of sparkling mineral water, plus a chicken korma, rice and dal makhani and a chicken tikka masala, and please don't wait to bring my beer.'

Zoblovski looked around. The restaurant was filling up quickly with the lunch crowd and tired shoppers, which created a welcoming buzz and a protective human shield.

Sylvia looked radiant when she walked in. She was dressed in a comfortable velour tracksuit, light grey with an orange stripe at the side to accentuate her slim figure.

'You know how to surprise a woman. I was just on my way out for my yoga class.'

'In that case, I'm glad that I caught you in time.'

The waiter approached the table with a trolley. After clearing the empty poppadom basket, he laid out several dishes. It was a colourful display.

'So what's the hurry? And are you taking me somewhere? What's with the bike? What happened to your driver?'

Mikhail leaned forward. 'I'm in a spot of bother, I'm afraid,' he whispered.

He paused to make sure the waiter was out of earshot.

'I've been followed by two Americans. I managed to escape. I have no idea why they're after me.'

'That's odd. Could it have to do with Peter Miller's investigation into fraud at the New York branch?'

'Mmm… Perhaps you're right… yes, that must be it. Perhaps he's onto something. Maybe he's in danger too? Can you contact him?'

'Not sure but I can try. He's usually in the country at his aunt's house at weekends.'

'It's worth trying. Could he have uncovered some dodgy American businessman or politician?'

'He would have told me, I'm sure.'

'Yes, but you remember the case we had in Hong Kong?'

'I do remember, but you never told me anything about it. All you said was that you'd sort it out. And to be honest, that often only means one thing.'

'Sorry, Sylvia, but that's how I protect myself. In any case, that trial collapsed because the three employees implicated in the process committed suicide before they even entered the courtroom.'

'I didn't hear about that.'

'It happened behind closed doors.'

'It sounds terrible. Those guys must have been under a lot of pressure to protect someone else.'

'That usually means that the stakes are high, we are only scratching the surface.'

'First of all, we must get you to a safe place now they are after you. Let me do some research.'

'But above all, let's not let our food get cold,' Mikhail said. 'We'd better get a move on.'

'I'll get the bill in the meantime to speed things up.'

Mikhail was a silent eater. He wanted to enjoy his food and saturate his taste buds in the different flavours without any distraction.

Sylvia left her plate untouched. She had her eyes glued to her mobile phone. Once in a while, she'd comment on some messages.

'I found Peter. He's expecting us… my God, it's a long drive. More than three hours!'

'We better stay the night somewhere.'

'Good, brilliant. Yep… that's all confirmed – the Chestnut Hill Inn. Excellent TripAdvisor reviews. Breakfast seems to get the most points and there's a well-stocked whisky bar. They also arrange game hunts for small groups.'

'I'm not interested in that,' Mikhail said with his mouth full, shaking his head.

'OK, I'm booking two single rooms.'

Mikhail nodded absent-mindedly.

'My car is parked around the corner. I could pick up some stuff from my flat on the way.'

'That may take ages!'

'Oi… I know how to travel light,' Sylvia corrected Mikhail.

Mikhail declined the offer of pudding and settled the bill. They left the restaurant and Mikhail managed to squeeze his bike into Sylvia's small white BMW 1 series.

'That leaves barely enough space for a toothbrush,' she said.

'They may have one at the hotel.'

'In that case, let's go right away, before those Americans track you down.'

'I doubt they will, I paid cash.'

'CCTV facial recognition is pretty accurate.'

Mikhail winced at the thought of it.

Traffic out of Barking towards the M25 was slow. It took Sylvia more than half an hour to join the motorway. From there it would be a smooth journey through Essex and Suffolk.

'What do you know about Peter?'

'He's reliable, punctual, a family man and has a strange passion for building a spaceship.'

Mikhail started to laugh.

'What's so funny about that?' Sylvia asked.

'I like that naïve optimism in people. Does he know what's involved?'

'I guess so. A friend of his is supplying him with jet engines.'

'You can't be serious?'

'Everybody in the office thought it was a joke at first but now they even help him with some background research. It's keeping the spirits up.'

'That's what I mean. It sounds like the guy has no idea at all. Does he know that he's embarking on a bloody suicide mission?'

'You can ask him that yourself. We won't be staying far from him.'

'Perhaps we can pay him a visit later today.'

'I'll suggest that to him.'

'Something else, Sylvia. Is there any airport near the place we'll be staying?'

'I checked that, there is but it's tiny.'

'That doesn't matter too much, I'll ask my pilot to divert there from City Airport, I prefer to keep my plane on stand-by and not too far away from where I am. It's a little luxury in life that I permit myself at my age.'

Mikhail fired off a few text messages to his pilot before reclining his chair. Soon he was nodding off. Sylvia laughed to herself when he started snoring. She turned on the sound system and chose 'Fast Car' by Jonas Blue and Dakota from her playlist. It seemed appropriate – nothing but Ibiza-like sunshine and an empty road in front of her. She pressed the accelerator, sending the car blazing through the bleak Essex hinterland.

The journey to Barking would take twenty minutes. Mikhail peered into the long corridor of the carriage. Nobody was paying any attention to him. He was just another Londoner with a Brompton bike. He had to admit that he was slightly out of breath. Several scenarios were running through his head. Going back to the office or his penthouse flat wasn't a viable option. Going to City Airport and boarding his private jet could be tricky. The plane might be under surveillance and international airports are not an easy place to avoid CCTV and security. There was a big chance that they'd be waiting for him near the airport. He'd walk straight into an ambush. First of all, he needed something to eat and a place to sit down, clear his mind, reflect on past events and make a plan.

After walking through the automatic gate at Barking station, he turned right and made a beeline for one of the best Indian restaurants he knew in this part of London.

The restaurant hadn't changed much over the years. A waiter welcomed him but didn't show any signs of recognition. Why would he? The last time he'd visited this place was to meet up with his personal assistant Sylvia several months ago.

'A table for two, please,' Zoblovski said.

'Very well, sir, please follow me.'

Mikhail took his mobile phone out of his jacket and called Sylvia. Time was of the essence. Someone could be tracking his phone and he needed a quick escape. Triangulation of his call would bring his followers to a busy high street in Barking, near the station. That would be pretty useless as a clue. He'd be their needle in a haystack for some time. Much to his delight, Sylvia answered straight away.

'It's Mikhail here.'

'Mr Zoblovski, is there a problem in the office?'

'Not at all, not at all. I was just wondering if you could join me for lunch? Same place where we met a few weeks ago.'

'Sure, I remember. The food was excellent.'

'And so was your company!' Mikhail said.

'Stop flattering me. I can be there in ten minutes.'

'Shall I order for you? I'm in a bit of a hurry.'

'Sure, same as last time. But what is this all about?'

Mikhail hung up, reached for his bug-out bag and stored his iPhone safely away in a signal blocking pouch. This was guaranteed to prevent any further tracking. He swiped the beads of sweat from his face. A waiter approached.

'Are you ready to order sir?'

'Yes I am, my friend will join me soon. We are in a bit of a rush.'

'No problem sir, why don't you order now and we can serve it as soon as your friend has joined you,' the waiter suggested.

'Excellent. Poppadoms for two please, a Tiger beer and a bottle of sparkling mineral water, plus a chicken korma, rice and dal makhani and a chicken tikka masala, and please don't wait to bring my beer.'

Zoblovski looked around. The restaurant was filling up quickly with the lunch crowd and tired shoppers, which created a welcoming buzz and a protective human shield.

Sylvia looked radiant when she walked in. She was dressed in a comfortable velour tracksuit, light grey with an orange stripe at the side to accentuate her slim figure.

'You know how to surprise a woman. I was just on my way out for my yoga class.'

'In that case, I'm glad that I caught you in time.'

The waiter approached the table with a trolley. After clearing the empty poppadom basket, he laid out several dishes. It was a colourful display.

'So what's the hurry? And are you taking me somewhere? What's with the bike? What happened to your driver?'

Mikhail leaned forward. 'I'm in a spot of bother, I'm afraid,' he whispered.

He paused to make sure the waiter was out of earshot.

'I've been followed by two Americans. I managed to escape. I have no idea why they're after me.'

'That's odd. Could it have to do with Peter Miller's investigation into fraud at the New York branch?'

'Mmm... Perhaps you're right... yes, that must be it. Perhaps he's onto something. Maybe he's in danger too? Can you contact him?'

'Not sure but I can try. He's usually in the country at his aunt's house at weekends.'

'It's worth trying. Could he have uncovered some dodgy

American businessman or politician?'

'He would have told me, I'm sure.'

'Yes, but you remember the case we had in Hong Kong?'

'I do remember, but you never told me anything about it. All you said was that you'd sort it out. And to be honest, that often only means one thing.'

'Sorry, Sylvia, but that's how I protect myself. In any case, that trial collapsed because the three employees implicated in the process committed suicide before they even entered the courtroom.'

'I didn't hear about that.'

'It happened behind closed doors.'

'It sounds terrible. Those guys must have been under a lot of pressure to protect someone else.'

'That usually means that the stakes are high, we are only scratching the surface.'

'First of all, we must get you to a safe place now they are after you. Let me do some research.'

'But above all, let's not let our food get cold,' Mikhail said.

'We'd better get a move on.'

'I'll get the bill in the meantime to speed things up.'

Mikhail was a silent eater. He wanted to enjoy his food and saturate his taste buds in the different flavours without any distraction.

Sylvia left her plate untouched. She had her eyes glued to her mobile phone. Once in a while, she'd comment on some messages.

'I found Peter. He's expecting us… my God, it's a long drive. More than three hours!'

'We better stay the night somewhere.'

'Good, brilliant. Yep… that's all confirmed – the Chestnut Hill Inn. Excellent TripAdvisor reviews. Breakfast seems to get the most points and there's a well-stocked whisky bar. They also arrange game hunts for small groups.'

'I'm not interested in that,' Mikhail said with his mouth full, shaking his head.

'OK, I'm booking two single rooms.'

Mikhail nodded absent-mindedly.

'My car is parked around the corner. I could pick up some stuff from my flat on the way.'

'That may take ages!'

'Oy… I know how to travel light,' Sylvia corrected Mikhail.

Mikhail declined the offer of pudding and settled the bill. They left the restaurant and Mikhail managed to squeeze his bike into Sylvia's small white BMW 1 series.

'That leaves barely enough space for a toothbrush,' she said.

'They may have one at the hotel.'

'In that case, let's go right away, before those Americans track you down.'

'I doubt they will, I paid cash.'

'CCTV facial recognition is pretty accurate.'

Mikhail winced at the thought of it.

Traffic out of Barking towards the M25 was slow. It took Sylvia more than half an hour to join the motorway. From there it would be a smooth journey through Essex and Suffolk.

'What do you know about Peter?'

'He's reliable, punctual, a family man and has a strange

passion for building a spaceship.'

Mikhail started to laugh.

'What's so funny about that?' Sylvia asked.

'I like that naïve optimism in people. Does he know what's involved?'

'I guess so. A friend of his is supplying him with jet engines.'

'You can't be serious?'

'Everybody in the office thought it was a joke at first but now they even help him with some background research. It's keeping the spirits up.'

'That's what I mean. It sounds like the guy has no idea at all. Does he know that he's embarking on a bloody suicide mission?'

'You can ask him that yourself. We won't be staying far from him.'

'Perhaps we can pay him a visit later today.'

'I'll suggest that to him.'

'Something else, Sylvia. Is there any airport near the place we'll be staying?'

'I checked that, there is but it's tiny.'

'That doesn't matter too much, I'll ask my pilot to divert there from City Airport, I prefer to keep my plane on stand-by and not too far away from where I am. It's a little luxury in life that I permit myself at my age.'

Mikhail fired off a few text messages to his pilot before reclining his chair. Soon he was nodding off. Sylvia laughed to herself when he started snoring. She turned on the sound system and chose 'Fast Car' by Jonas Blue and Dakota from her playlist. It seemed appropriate – nothing but Ibiza-like sunshine and an empty road in front of her. She pressed the accelerator, sending the car blazing through the bleak Essex hinterland.

35

'Please take a seat in our lounge while Tess prepares your rooms,' Marjory purred. Never before had her hotel been fully booked this time of year. 'You've got the last two rooms. They both have en suite bathrooms, naturally.'

Mikhail felt rested despite the long journey. Sylvia went ahead to the bar.

'Welcome to the Chestnut Hill Inn,' George said. 'What will it be?'

'What can you recommend?'

'We've got quite a good selection of whiskies.'

'I read that on TripAdvisor,' Sylvia said.

'It's a bit of a hobby of mine. Once a year I spend a week in Scotland visiting distilleries and discovering new labels.'

Mikhail looked at the impressive row of bottles displayed on a shelf behind the bar. George stepped aside to give Mikhail a better look. He turned around, rinsed some glasses in the sink and set them out to dry.

Mikhail scanned the shelf teeming with different whisky bottles.

'A glass of Jura Superstition for me, please.'

'Russian?' George enquired.

'Indeed, but I've been here since 1990.'

'Doing business?'

'Correct,' Mikhail said sharply to prevent the chatty barman asking more questions.

'And for you, miss?'

'A gin and tonic, please.'

'You're not Russian, obviously!'

'East London, born and bred,' Sylvia replied politely but firmly.

George nodded his head. He knew when to stop asking questions. Were they father and daughter or businessman and lover? It was a sensitive topic. His wife was better at finding out the gossip.

'Let's move over to the fire,' Sylvia said.

Mikhail followed her. He carried both glasses.

'What a day. I still don't know why I was involved in this car chase.'

'Are you worried about it?'

'Of course I am. Why else do I have security staff?'

'Let's relax for now. We're safe here.'

'I love this place; it's like stepping back in time.'

On a couch opposite Sylvia and Mikhail, Nina was reading the comments on her blog. There were a lot about artisan jam making. It seemed like she had tapped into a new vein of followers. She wasn't sure how to keep her fans entertained: more jam stories, more champagne stories or more spaceship stories? Nina took off her shoes, stretched her legs out on the couch and propped her feet close to the fire. She felt relaxed, until she overheard Sylvia and Mikhail's conversation.

All she could tell was that a large man with a strong Russian accent and a loud laugh was telling a story about how he'd got on a bike and managed to shake off his pursuers in the middle of London.

'Can you imagine the look on their faces, seeing me, this big Russian bear on a tiny red bike? It was like being in a circus act. But it turned out to be the perfect getaway vehicle. Everyone should have one in their car boot. Also great in case you're running late for an appointment.'

'I'm glad to hear about your cunning escape plan.'

'Mind you, it was well rehearsed.'

Mikhail emptied his whisky glass in one gulp.

'I'm feeling better already.'

'Shall we visit Peter and his family before or after dinner? I'm worried we won't have enough energy to go over after we eat.'

'Wait, let me get another round of drinks first. We've got plenty of time.'

'Which means we'll go and visit Peter tomorrow.'

'Relax, it's early, not even five o'clock. This is just a pre-dinner drink.'

Mikhail turned around and raised his empty glass, signalling to George that he needed a refill. George nodded, looking content. He knew that this kind of customer would rack up a nice bill, once seated near the fire. He had every intention of keeping the whisky flowing.

'Za zdaróvye, Sylvia! Thanks for coming to the rescue. I can't wait to meet Peter and his rocket.'

Nina was all ears. Was this a coincidence or was the plot thickening? She opened her blog editor – it was time for an update. The pictures she'd taken yesterday had an air of conspiracy around them. Her followers would love them. She added a few lines to the blog: 'Is this a hoax, a prop, a space capsule or a rocket? Nina's investigation is in full swing with a live feed from seven p.m. tonight'. She knew she had to go back and interview the woman with the blonde hair. She could be her main informant.

'A few things are bugging me,' Mikhail said. 'Something doesn't add up. I've been involved with the Russian Space Programme for more than twenty years. To build a spacecraft and leave our planet, you need serious funding. Nobody who works in an office has access to that kind of money, unless he or she's involved in some serious money laundering.' Mikhail paused. 'And Peter's the guy investigating our finances. He has access to all our accounts. Don't tell me that he's been diverting money into this private venture. I'm begging you, Sylvia. You can't do this to me, not after today. Tell me it's not true.'

'That thought had occurred to me. According to the finance department, this isn't the case, so relax.'

'How can I relax? This is just unbelievable. I want to meet this Peter! Now!'

Nina was wondering if she should take a risk and interrupt the conversation. She weighed the pros and cons. In the worst case, they would dismiss her and ask her to respect their privacy… No, that was the best case scenario. In the worst case scenario, she would realise too late that she had missed an excellent opportunity. Nina smiled and turned around.

'Excuse me, I'm sorry to interrupt.'

'Not at all, young lady,' Mikhail said. 'I was getting worried about your feet getting burned. You're holding them too close to the fire.'

'My feet are perfectly all right, thank you for your concern.'

'May I offer you a drop of whisky?'

Mikhail turned around. 'George,' he called, 'we need another glass.' Nina felt immediately at ease. Mikhail seemed to be the epitome of Russian hospitality. He wouldn't take no for an answer.

'Let me introduce myself. I'm Mikhail Zoblovski and this is my PA, Sylvia Taylor.'

'How do you do, I'm Nina, Nina Simmons, journalist and blogger.'

'Nice to meet you.'

'It may seem a bit impertinent but I couldn't help overhearing your conversation about a spacecraft.'

Sylvia raised her eyebrows. She wasn't too impressed by Nina's interruption.

'I am sorry, we'd really like to continue our conversation in private without anyone eavesdropping.' She sounded frosty.

Mikhail frowned trying to calm down Sylvia. He nodded gently and encouraged Nina to continue. 'Let me show you a few pictures I took yesterday,' Nina said turning around her phone so Mikhail could flick through her images.

'Wow, that's quite something. I don't know what to make of that,' Mikhail replied.

'Me neither,' Nina said.

'I've put them on my blog and will check in a few hours to see what people think. Sometimes good old fashioned crowdsourcing may provide the answer.'

'Are you mad?' Sylvia interjected. 'It won't be long before hordes of people come and have a look.'

'I didn't reveal my source or my location. It'll be like looking for a needle in a haystack.'

'I wouldn't bet on that,' Sylvia said curtly.

Mikhail leaned back; the soft couch was comfortable. He could sit here by the fire for hours.

'OK, launching a rocket is not impossible,' he said. 'It's an old technology and the principles of a launch haven't changed that much. Engine technology has improved a great deal since the 1960s. Modern rockets are more powerful and efficient. To reach enough speed to exceed escape velocity isn't too hard either. But what bugs me is where will he get the fuel from to propel his rocket into space?'

'I don't know. Perhaps he uses nuclear power? After all, we're not far from a nuclear power station,' Nina said.

'It gets more and more bizarre – this is plain stupid. We all know what happened in Chernobyl. This guy has to be stopped, he's a danger to mankind,' Sylvia said.

'Look, I've worked it all out. He's either bluffing or he's involved with something much bigger. In any case, we have to stop him,' Mikhail slurred his words.

'That's the bottle talking, I'm afraid,' Sylvia said.

'Not at all, I'm used to drinking vodka straight when I was a young man; it kept me warm on those long journeys across Siberia in my old Lada with the heating kaput.'

'Well, I'll be doing the driving tonight,' Sylvia said.

'Young lady... Nina, I mean. Listen, do you think that with modern technology a middle-aged man, on his own, is capable of designing and building a spacecraft?'

'Sir, can pigs fly?'

'Ha ha ha, I like that expression. Clever answer. Of course they can't fly, but then again, not all pigs are equal.'

'George Orwell!' Nina exclaimed.

'He was right after all. That was the problem with communism. Our leaders gave it a bad name.'

'I'm not an economist, but in my opinion at present we're on a destructive path. We consume way too much and destroying what is left of our forests and jungles in the process. Soon we'll need several planets to feed us all,' Nina said.

'It'll all end in tears,' Mikhail added.

They looked at each other. Sylvia started to laugh. 'You're all getting too serious. In the grand scheme of things there's nothing we can do.'

'There is, there's always hope. And that's why I want to meet this Peter Miller guy.'

The door to the bar opened.

'Welcome back, gentlemen,' George said. 'What can I do for you? A pint?'

'Thanks, that'd be great.'

Mike and David sat on the bar stools nearest the door, their backs turned to the fireplace. Mike looked over his shoulder once but didn't seem to recognise Mikhail Zoblovski.

'Americans,' Nina whispered.

'That is too much of a coincidence,' Sylvia said. 'Are those the same men who tailed you?'

Mikhail lowered his body, he sunk deeper into the soft couch but his head was still sticking out. He looked puzzled. 'What are the chances that those are the same characters who chased me earlier today? A million to one! England must be teeming with Americans.' He gave a dismissive shrug and sat up straight again.

'Do you recognize them?' Nina probed him.

'Not sure. I tried to get a look when they were chasing me, but I didn't have a chance. They just look like a pair of nondescript guys in black suits.'

'With the amount of whisky you've had, I wouldn't trust your judgment anyway,' Sylvia said.

'Nonsense!' Mikhail barked before emptying his glass. 'Nobody is going to intimidate me. If those guys are professionals they would have killed me a long time ago. These are just a bunch of clowns, amateurs. I've got nothing to be afraid of.'

Mike leaned over trying to have a quiet word with George.

'George, would you mind if we helped ourselves to a couple of those rifles in a minute? It's a beautiful evening out there and this is the best time for hunting.'

'Be my guest. The door to the rifle storage room is locked but I'll give you a key. Make sure to lock it again. You'll find several boxes with bullets in the top drawer. I'll add those to your bill.'

'Steady on, buddy. What's the rush? Let's wait another

few minutes, I haven't finished my pint yet.'

Nina was telling Sylvia about her work as a journalist and how difficult it was to make a living with blogging. Sylvia had warmed up to Nina. She was impressed how much information she had gathered already. She seemed quite resourceful, a very useful attribute.

'Why don't you drop me an email on Monday? We can always use a copy writer or a social media advisor; at least that will pay your bills and you can do your blogging in the evenings or weekends.'

'Thanks for your offer but I am on an assignment right now and I want to finish that first, I have no idea where it is leading.'

'You can tag along with us; we are going to visit a colleague of mine,' Sylvia said.

'Thanks for the offer, maybe another time. I've got some writing to finish first,' Nina said. She preferred to do some further investigation on her own.

'Excuse me, ladies,' Mikhail said, standing up. 'I need to go to the bathroom.' He stumbled past the couch.

'I think what you need is some fresh air.'

'I'll be just fine,' Mikhail slurred.

'Meet me in the car park, we'll go for a drive,' Sylvia said.

'A pre-dinner drive through the country, that's the ticket!' Mikhail slurred his words. He couldn't walk straight. He narrowly missed the oak pillar holding up an old ceiling beam in the middle of the bar, and instead crashed into the large American who was blocking the narrow passage between the bar and hallway.

'I'm so sorry.' Mikhail padded the protruding abdomen of the man he walked into. 'I'm really sorry.'

'That's alright, buddy.'

'My friend is shockproof,' Mike said. 'He's got plenty of padding.'

'Let me offer you a drink as a token of goodwill.'

'We won't say no to that,' Mike replied.

'George, another round for these fine gentlemen and put it on my bill.'

'Of course, Mr Zoblovski!'

Mikhail continued his search for the toilet.

'Mike, did you hear that?'

'I'm perplexed. This is too easy. Let's play dumb. We'll offer him a drink in return when he comes back and ask him some questions.'

'With the state he's in, he'll be an open book.'

'Do you think he recognised us?'

'I doubt it, he walked straight into me,' Dave said.

'I'd better let Terrence know. Man, this really is private investigation for dummies.'

'Home tomorrow morning!'

'I can't wait to see my kids.'

'I can't wait to have a decent burger.'

'Funny you mentioning that, I thought you'd already forgotten about your beautiful waitress.'

'Of course not! I am not that fickle.'

'Cheers, buddy!' Mike lifted his pint glass and took a large swig.

'I must say that this English craft beer is growing on me,'

Dave said.

Nina excused herself. 'Please thank Mikhail for the drink. Much appreciated. I'm going back to my room.'

'Good luck with your blog, Nina,' Sylvia said. 'I'd better go after Mikhail and check that he didn't collapse in the bathroom.'

'Are you sure you can handle him by yourself?'

'I've seen him far worse!'

As soon as Nina got back to her room she changed into her old jeans, a warm sweater and knee highs. She had to go back tonight and see for herself what was going on at the farm. It was already dark outside, pitch dark. The moon was obscured by heavy clouds. Her eyes would take a while to adapt. She packed a small torch and hoped it would stay dry outside.

36

Nina sprinted along the path. It had taken her less than twenty minutes. She checked the time: twenty past six. She stopped near the bridge across the stream. There was a small footpath leading up to the main farm, past the barn. One of them was silhouetted against the night sky, but the lights were on inside the other. The same two cars she'd seen earlier in the day were still parked outside. She went up and touched their bonnets – both were cold. Nina stopped for a moment and held her breath. She couldn't hear anything. She decided it was worth the risk of knocking on the half-opened barn door.

Claudia looked up.

'Who are you?' she said, looking harassed.

Nina made a V-sign with her right hand. With her casual look and purple streaked hair she looked unthreatening enough to get Claudia on her side.

'I heard you earlier today when I was visiting Doreen and watching her making jam. I heard some banging noises in the distance and guessed there was someone working in here.'

'You should have come in then, why didn't you?'

'Don't know. Not sure if Doreen would have let me.'

'Come on, she's not that bad!' Claudia smiled.

Nina nodded.

'She helped me with an article. I'm writing about life on a farm in modern England.'

'That sounds interesting.'

Claudia wiped her hands on a cloth and walked over to Nina.

'I'm Claudia.'

'Nice to meet you, I'm Nina.'

'Sorry, I haven't got anything to offer you.'

'Don't worry, I don't want to disturb you. What are you working on? It looks cool.'

'A lot of things. Tom, the little boy, thinks it's a spaceship. Barry, the owner of a nearby scrapyard, thinks it'll be a boutique hotel, and Peter sees it as therapy for his midlife crisis.'

'And you?'

'An escape vehicle,' Claudia laughed. 'That was a joke of course. Nothing really. I'm just killing time, and I quite like building projects, so yeah… I'm just helping out. If it could be used as an Airbnb, that would be cool.'

'So how did you get involved in this project?'

'That's a long story. I'm sure you don't want to hear it.'

'Depends. I've got time.'

'I don't even know you. Why are you here?'

Nina smiled. 'OK. I'm a journalist and a blogger, and I'm in the area to write a story about the relationship between climate change and shifting agricultural practices. I interviewed some wine growers yesterday. They recommended a local hotel, here in the village, so that I could spend some time writing and researching. Well, last night, I was having a drink in the hotel bar and overheard some locals talking about someone building a spaceship. They were pretty serious about it so I just had to find out. I've got a curious streak; I'm a journalist after all!'

'You say you're a blogger? How many followers have you got?'

'It fluctuates. Last year, close to half a million, then it dropped to fifty, including my mum. The last time I checked I'm back on track, with almost ten thousand followers. I had no idea there were so many people interested in food, space-travel and global warming.'

Claudia looked away and then walked over to the building project.

'Come inside, it's quieter. Nobody can overhear us.'

Nina followed Claudia up a small metal ladder. Once they were inside, Claudia closed the sliding door. It looked very cosy, and bigger than expected.

'Nice chairs!'

'That's the latest addition. This is what inspired Barry to turn it into an Airbnb. You can fold them all the way back to create a giant bed. Enough space for two!'

Claudia demonstrated for her, even showing how the footrest moved up. It took a couple of minutes, and the process was noisy and clunky, but in the end there was a giant bed. She spread herself out like a snow angel.

'There's even a small fridge,' Nina said.

'Yep, salvaged from an old Learjet. You can keep a bottle

of champagne in there.'

'I'm really impressed. Personally, I think taking this pod into space is completely bonkers, but as an Airbnb it would be great. I really like the curtains and the paintwork.'

'I did that. Only took me a couple of hours.'

'And what's that? A game console?'

Claudia positioned her on the edge of the bed next to Nina. 'Yep, and there's surround sound too.'

'Wicked.'

Claudia wiggled closer to Nina and grabbed her hands. She held them firmly and gazed deeply into her eyes. She waited for Nina to respond. Claudia squeezed Nina's hands tighter. Nina felt uncomfortable, she shifted, but didn't want to move too close lest she encourage Claudia. At the same time, she didn't want to be dismissive; she felt that Claudia had a story to tell. So she just swallowed and waited. Tears welled up in Claudia's eyes. She sniffled and let go of Nina's hands.

'I need your help,' Claudia said, wiping away tears on her sleeve. 'I want the whole world to know.'

Nina didn't respond straight away. She observed the details of Claudia's artwork. Was she onto something here? Perhaps she'd better rig up a small camera in the corner of the camper to video Claudia's story. She balanced her iPhone on a shelf and started recording. Claudia looked straight into the camera.

'I want everybody to know that they murdered my boyfriend!'

Nina jerked her head and stared intensely at Claudia. 'Hang on. I didn't get that. Who murdered whom?'

'It's a long story. I hope you've got some time.'

Nina nodded, encouraging Claudia to continue.

'Ever since I was a schoolgirl, I've heard stories about the Amazon, how it's getting smaller and smaller all the time. Illegal logging, soil erosion, tribesmen being killed, rare species disappearing. And what for? Just to have cows grazing on some parched land? And you know what? It's all because of greed – making a quick buck. Politicians are the worst.'

'That's a universal problem.'

'Trust me, in Brazil it's a lot worse than in England. Corruption fuels society, but in the end, it destroys civilisation and the rainforest.'

'At one time,' Nina said, 'all of England was covered in a dense forest. And look for yourself: there's nothing left.'

'That's different. That happened a thousand years ago, before we had any notion of global warming, climate change and rising CO2 levels. The Amazon rainforest is a lot bigger than England, so there's a lot more at stake.'

'So what has your boyfriend got to do with this? Was he involved?'

'No, not at all. He was a bartender for God's sake! He wasn't interested in politics. He just wanted to have a good time.'

'So why was he murdered?'

'Many of my friends are determined to save the environment, but all they do is ask people to sign petitions online. That's just hopeless. You might as well sit on your butt all day long and pick your nose.'

'Armchair activists!'

'Exactly. And I wanted to do something.'

Nina didn't say anything, a natural pause encouraged Claudia to continue with her story.

'So I blew up this building, the head office of one of the largest logging companies in Brazil. The owner was a real jerk. His cousin was a state governor and he made sure that all the contracts went to him, in exchange for money and "favours".'

'You mean drugs?'

'Probably, but I heard rumours about parties, yachts, women, foreign trips to Uruguay, you name it. Those guys were living the high life at the expense of the Amazon.'

Nina reflected on what she was hearing.

'Hang on... Did you just say that you blew up a building?'

Claudia nodded.

'Did anybody die?'

Claudia looked down, avoiding Nina's gaze. She was shaking. Tears were rolling down her cheeks.

'That's the worst part of it all.' Claudia couldn't hold back her tears. 'It's so bad, so bad. Five people including the owner were trapped inside the building when it exploded.'

'Oh my God, that's awful! Do you realise what you've done? This changes everything.'

Nina moved away from Claudia. 'That's mass murder.'

Claudia began to weep. 'I'm so sorry. I didn't plan it like that. The building was supposed to be empty. It always is during the weekend. I feel awful about it. I don't know what came over me. One day I'm part of a movement protesting against the destruction of the rainforest, the next day I see myself as the saviour of the rainforest. Oh God. What have I done? What damage I've caused! But I'm not a bad person, honestly I'm not. You can ask my friends, my family – I couldn't even hurt a fly. But whenever I read about the decimation of the jungle, it made me so angry, so furious that nobody was doing anything to stop it. People just talk and talk, and in the meantime the chainsaws keep on cutting down tree after tree, millions of acres. I just couldn't take it any longer. I had to do something.'

'There's a fine line between eco-activism and eco-terrorism,' Nina said. 'You crossed that line.'

Claudia wiped her tears on her sleeve. She was silent for a moment.

'Blowing up a building is nothing compared to what they're doing to the rainforest, I honestly didn't know there were people inside.'

'Yes, but taking the law into your own hands, that's extreme! What's next?'

Claudia shrugged. 'Nothing, I guess. My boyfriend was supposed to come over and start a cocktail bar, have a new beginning.'

'But you said he had nothing to do with all this.'

'That's right!'

'And why was he murdered?'

'I guess they thought he had information about me.'

'Christ, that sounds grim.'

'That's why I'm here, in the countryside.'

'Escaping from the law?'

'No, escaping from those American thugs who want revenge.'

Claudia cried. Nina hesitated and then moved closer

again. She had no idea what to make of her story or how to tell it. She had to talk to her editor. Reporting the truth was one thing but condoning terrorism was way beyond her mission.

'Two Americans approached me in London. They showed me pictures of Mario, after he was tortured. His face was a mess, just awful. I've had nightmares ever since I saw those pictures.' Claudia wiped her tears on Nina's jacket.

'Your story keeps getting more and more sinister.'

'I am telling you, I'm scared for my life. Peter helped me. He discovered that lots of money was being transferred from the company's account to the state governor. Millions of dollars, all stashed away in the Cayman Islands. And even some American congressmen are involved in this; Peter's got a list of them.'

'Who is Peter?'

'A friend of mine, a very good friend in fact.'

Nina waited hoping Claudia would elaborate. 'Who else knows about this?' She asked after a short silence.

'Nobody!'

Nina straightened her back. Something told her that she was on to something. This was just the kind of story she wanted to tell. Organised destruction of the Brazilian rainforest, corrupt government officials bankrolled by some wealthy American congressmen. It couldn't get any juicier than this!

'Well, they do now. My editor will make it go viral. My blog'll be enough to get the ball rolling. I'll write the rest later. Damn, there's no reception in here!'

'Sometimes there is and sometimes there isn't.'

Nina stretched her arm out so it was almost touching the ceiling, and pointed her phone towards the barn door, but it made no difference.

'You'll get more luck in the reception room in the farmhouse.'

'Cheers!' Nina stuffed her phone in the inside pocket of her jacket. She looked at Claudia. She couldn't see a way out for her.

'If I were you I'd hand myself in to the police. You have to stop this before more people get killed.'

'No way! I thought long and hard about it, I'd rather die fighting till the end, a martyr for the rainforest. All I ask from you is to expose those congressmen who are behind the destruction of our beautiful rainforest. You have to help me.'

'That's up to my editor really. This is way over my head. At least you are safe here. You can stay under the radar for the time being and help Aunt Doreen making jam.'

'There is no point. It will be impossible to escape these guys. It may take weeks or months, but in the end they'll get me. And take my word for it, they won't show any mercy.'

Claudia was trembling. Despite abhorring Claudia's act of terrorism Nina felt sorry for her.

'Where's Peter now?'

'He's inside with his family and Barry. Aunt Doreen is preparing dinner. I just wanted to be out of the way. I need some time to think. Please don't tell him what I've told you.'

'I am sure he'll find out sooner or later.'

Claudia couldn't stop her tears. She lay curled up on one of the beds with her head resting in Nina's lap. 'Will you stay with me for a while? I'd feel more comfortable with you being here too.'

Nina nodded.

'If only this bloody tin can could fly to Mars for real, I'd be off in a flash.' Claudia banged her hand against the sliding door out of frustration.

'You're not serious?'

'I'd do anything to get out of here – as far away as possible. A one-way trip to Mars would be perfect.'

'A one-way suicide mission.'

'Who cares? My number is up anyway, I might as well do something radical.'

'I think you've done enough radical things in your life already.'

'At least I'll be remembered as the first woman going to Mars.'

37

A car arrived at the farm; its headlights shone through the kitchen window before it came to a screeching halt on the gravel yard.

'Are you expecting any more visitors?' Aunt Doreen asked, sounding irritated. 'Nothing surprises me any more. Did somebody organise a party, an open house? I'm busy cooking. Peter, have a look and see if you can shoo them away.'

Peter opened the front door and looked at the small car as it came to an abrupt standstill. He heard a heavy bass throbbing through the windows and recognized Sylvia. She was leaning over an older man, trying to wake him up. Giving up, she opened the door. Thumping music got blasted all over the yard. Who was that man? Her dad? Zoblovksi, their boss? Why would she bring him?

'Sylvia, what a surprise,' Peter said. 'I didn't expect you until tomorrow. How can you drive with that racket?'

'Trying to keep Mikhail awake. I'm afraid he had a bit too much to drink. He zonked out as soon as we set off.'

'All right, all right. I can get out myself, I don't need any help.' Peter heard the man groan.

With great effort, he managed to hoist himself out of the car.

'Peter, let me introduce you Mikhail Zoblovski, owner of the company we both work for.'

'Nice to meet you.' Peter said.

'The pleasure is all mine, I heard so much about you. I am dying to see your rocket,' Mikhail slurred.

Peter smiled. He felt chuffed. 'Why don't you walk over to the barn? I'll show you my pet project. I have to fetch Claudia anyway.'

'Ah, the mystery lady you met in the coffee shop. She's here now? I hope she's getting on with your wife,' Sylvia teased him.

Mikhail followed a few paces behind Sylvia and Peter. At the same time, Claudia and Nina were leaving the barn.

Sylvia's mouth dropped. 'What a coincidence!'

'Small world indeed!' Nina exclaimed.

'Do you know each other?' Peter asked.

'No, not really, we just met in the hotel. We shared some drinks,' Sylvia said.

'Let's all head back to the farmhouse. I think we should compare our stories,' Peter suggested.

Mikhail stopped, took a deep breath and yawned. Then he turned around and followed the others into the farmhouse.

'We've got some more guests,' Peter said jovially.

'A full house, indeed,' Doreen muttered.

'I hope you don't mind?' Peter replied.

'I only wish somebody had told me. I would have made

more food.'

'Don't worry about me,' Sylvia was quick to say. 'I'm not a big eater.'

Mikhail opened his coat and took out a bottle of whisky. 'I didn't come empty handed. Let's have some drinks first and make a toast. To our wonderful host and to Peter and his space machine! I want to hear all about it. And, of course, to Sylvia who came to my rescue when I was running away from two Americans.'

'Two Americans?' Claudia asked, looking panicked.

'I don't know for a fact, but they were driving an American car.'

'A black 2009 Buick by any chance?' Barry asked. 'It's been parked behind the Chestnut Hill Inn for the last two days.'

Claudia looked alarmed. She felt her pulse racing.

'Those guys at the bar,' Nina said.

'What did they look like?'

'One was tall and the other one fat. I only saw a glimpse of them,' Sylvia added.

'They know you're here?' Claudia asked.

'Why would they?'

'Wait a minute, guys,' Nina said. 'What links all of you, Peter, Claudia and Mikhail Zoblovski, to these men?'

'Beats me,' Mikhail replied. 'I've never seen Peter or Claudia before in my entire life.'

'If they came after the two of you specifically, you must have a common enemy.'

Peter was quiet. He looked at Claudia. She looked defeated. Why was she so afraid, why were they after her? After a minute, he cleared his voice. 'Perhaps I can shed some light on this.'

'I've been waiting for an explanation too,' Joanne said, looking frosty.

'I met Claudia three months ago; she asked me to look into some financial transactions between a Brazilian company called Amazorico and the state governor,' Peter continued.

'I never had any dealings with Brazil,' Mikhail said quickly. He poured himself a generous measure of whisky. 'Help yourselves, my friends. Cheers.'

'No, but there's a link in the third degree,' Peter continued.

Mikhail looked upset. 'Don't do this to me!'

'The state governor received money directly from various US mining conglomerates. Some of these companies had US congressmen on their payroll.'

'How come nobody knew about this?'

'They used a legal loophole involving various law firms and banks in the Turks and Caicos Islands,' Peter said.

Nina took notes. 'This is very interesting,' she said. 'I have to post this on my blog.'

'Some of your financial advisors, Mikhail, have close ties to these law firms.'

'The world of crooks is a small world indeed,' Sylvia remarked.

'Damn fine work, Peter!' Mikhail cried. 'But we need to get to the bottom of this.'

'If I understand correctly,' Nina summarized, 'some American congressmen have been bribing the state governor in Brazil to guarantee exclusive exploitation and mining rights for US companies.'

'Yes, that's correct.'

'Have you got any names?'

'Actually, I do… I can email you the list on Monday.'

'And some of these congressmen are non-executive board members of said mining companies?'

'In a nutshell.'

'You've made my day, Peter. And, I've got a 3G connection! I'm sending a few tweets now.' Nina was typing whilst talking.

'And why are those Americans after both of us? I've got nothing to do with this whole saga,' Mikhail protested.

'That part of the story remains a mystery.'

Claudia looked pale. She kept her head down. Should she tell them now?

The atmosphere was tense.

'Perhaps with Amazorico out of action, part of their money laundering operation's been jeopardized and these congressmen are getting nervous,' Peter postulated.

'What do you mean?' Mikhail asked.

'Well, according to some news clips I found, Amazorico's head office got blown up,' Peter explained.

'The bastards!'

'This is nasty stuff.'

'Peter, I hope that our family is not in any danger.'

'Of course not, darling. We are in the middle of nowhere on a farm and in twenty minutes we're all going to enjoy a lovely meal.'

Aunt Doreen walked over from the kitchen. She'd missed most of the conversation. 'Joanne, my dear, can you get the kids to set the table? I lost count of how many guests Peter has brought along.'

Barry stood up. 'Let's forget those grim theories for now and have a close look at the real reason we are all here tonight.' He cleared his throat and emptied his glass. 'Why don't we all go to the barn and have a look at our project. Next week there'll be an air show at the airport and our spacecraft will the showstopper, for sure.'

Everybody raised their glass.

'Cheers to Barry,' Peter said.

'I can't wait any longer, let's go now,' Mikhail slurred.

'Can we stay with Auntie Doreen?' Lilly asked. 'It's too dark outside.'

'After you've set the table you can help me prepare the largest apple crumble I've made in a very long time,' Doreen said. Joanne laughed. She couldn't tell if Doreen was still cross with Peter for bringing all these extra guests or if deep inside she enjoyed having a full house. Tom started peeling a large pile of apples and Lilly folded the napkins.

Outside, Mikhail walked ahead. The fresh air had cleared his mind. He was as excited as a child the night before Christmas. He opened the heavy door. Sylvia craned her neck to peek in through the opening.

'Is it a pimped up hippy van, a flying Batmobile or a state of the art spaceship?' Sylvia teased him. 'Peter, help me understand.'

'First of all, I went along with Barry's idea of strapping a few engines to the back of a VW van, and then we decorated it a little bit.'

'And I added a splash of colour,' Claudia added.

'It all started as a joke really,' Barry chuckled.

'A joke? This looks pretty serious to me,' Mikhail said.

'You've shown improvisation and vision. That will get you far.' In the state he was in Peter and Barry weren't sure if he was being cynical or serious.

'Tom, my son, got really excited about it and it took off from there. We've been spending many weekends working on it,' Peter added.

'I'm really impressed. Good work, guys,' Mikhail slurred.

Sylvia shook her head.

'It's thanks to Barry really, this is all his recycled stuff,' Peter said.

'The best part is the fridge and the pop-up TV screen. People will love it,' Barry said. 'Have a look inside. See how big it is. Enough space for two.'

'Can you imagine a trip to Mars, seven long months?' Nina asked.

'Well, if the future of mankind depends on it, why not?' Claudia said.

Mikhail had a closer look inside.

'Speaking of going to Mars,' he said, 'it seems farfetched, but did I ever mention that I'm involved in revitalizing the Russian Space Programme? Once we were the envy of the West. The first man in space was a Russian, Yuri Gagarin, in 1961. My mission is to push mankind even further than our wildest dreams. But time is running out, I'm getting older, and I don't have any children.'

'I'm so ready to go to Mars,' Claudia interjected. 'I can't wait to escape this mess.'

Mikhail jerked his head sideways, looked over this shoulder and crawled backwards, exiting the camper. He recognised an opportunity when he saw one.

'You know what, miss? I may take you up on that offer. We need to have a private discussion one day about setting up a space colony.'

'How about talking about it right now? I'm ready to go. My bags are packed!'

'I don't see why not,' Mikhail said, sounding genuinely interested.

'Enough of this science fiction,' Joanne said. 'Let's get back to the farmhouse and have some dinner.'

'If you are serious, Claudia, come with me to Russia. I should have been there already but my plans got scuppered. I've got my plane waiting at a nearby airport. We could leave tonight or tomorrow morning.'

'I am serious. I can prove how serious I am.'

'Come on, come on, let's get back inside, sober up and stop making all those empty promises,' Sylvia said.

'I think that Claudia and I understand each other very well,' Mikhail said. He straightened his back and took a deep breath. 'For the record, I am as sober as a judge and I am a gentleman. I intend to keep my promises.'

Claudia smiled.

Whilst walking back, Claudia and Mikhail trailed behind the rest to discuss the possibilities of joining his project in Russia and being part of the crew.

'Your age is definitely an advantage, but you'll have to join a rigorous training programme and that is not for the faint hearted.'

'I think I can bring something far more interesting to the project,' Claudia replied.

Mikhail turned his head toward Claudia and squinted

his eyes a little. He wondered what she had in mind. 'I'm intrigued, tell me more.'

Claudia stopped, grabbed Mikhail by his elbow and whispered something in his ear. He had to stoop and started laughing.

'That would be one hell of a promotional stunt. Everybody would love that.'

Claudia smiled. Her escape plan had just been hatched.

Doreen's mood had improved a great deal. She had roasted another bag of potatoes and there was plenty of roast pork for everyone. Mikhail was in an entertaining mood, charming Doreen with his stories about meeting famous musicians backstage at the Wigmore Hall. She was thrilled. She wanted to know all sorts of details, from the dresses they wore to the encores they played. She listened to Radio 3 all day long. She loved opera more than anything else. Her initial irritation with all the unannounced visitors quickly dissipated.

'Puccini is my favourite composer,' she said. 'I listen to all the live broadcasts.'

'Why don't you come along next season?' Mikhail said. 'I'm a patron of the Royal Opera House. I always keep a box reserved in case I want to bring some friends along. The view is magnificent. Unfortunately, the food isn't as good as yours,' he chuckled.

Doreen beamed. She hadn't been to London since her husband's death. A night at the opera would be beyond her wildest dreams.

After dinner, Peter helped clear the dishes. Tom and Lilly

loaded the dishwasher. Joanne and Mikhail moved to the living room.

'Do you mind if I browse through your CD collection?' Mikhail asked Doreen.

'Of course not, my dear.'

'It's quite an eclectic mix,' Joanne remarked.

'Let's liven things up a little bit, the atmosphere is way too dour for a Saturday night like this.' Doreen said. 'I am hearing too many stories about Americans chasing you and Claudia. You're here to escape it all.'

'I couldn't agree more. We need to get some feet moving!'

'I've got a couple of Iron Maiden CDs in my car, I can get them,' Barry suggested.

'Perhaps another time, pal!' Peter laughed. 'They may not be ready for your sophisticated taste yet.'

'The Scorpions perhaps?' Barry asked hopeful.

'Let's have a look … Here we are, Saturday Night Fever. How apt, I remember this one very well. One of the first CDs I imported from Germany. It was very popular in Russia at the time. I think we sold over a million copies. It kick-started my business. We spent hundreds of hours copying these disks and printing covers on an old dot matrix printer.'

Mikhail got on his knees and rolled back the carpet exposing a polished wooden floor.

'Joanne,' he said, standing up, 'finally meeting your husband made my day. What vision, what perseverance and what determination! I'd like to invite you and your family to move to Moscow. We've got very good international schools. Peter can get involved in the space project. We always need a good accountant. So far my project has been one big money drain.'

'You could easily offset those costs against some profits elsewhere. I thought that was the reason you bought the insurance company in the first place.'

Mikhail slammed his hand on Peter's back. 'Let's toast to that!'

Joanne laughed. She felt proud of her husband and would certainly support his career change to help put the first man on Mars.

'If Peter will be the accountant, I will definitely come along,' Claudia said a tad too enthusiastically.

Joanna frowned. She still had no idea what was really going on between her husband and Claudia.

'Doreen, can I have the first dance with you?' Mikhail asked. She agreed instantly. Mikhail turned out to be a lively dancer. He waved his hands above his head enthusiastically and twisted his hips to the rhythm of 'Staying Alive'. He looked like an excited rabbit with a brand new Duracell battery. Joanne mixed another whisky with Coke. When the song 'Night Fever' started, she persuaded the others to join her on the dancefloor.

Claudia walked over to Peter. 'They're having fun,' she said.

'I wonder what Mikhail and Aunt Doreen have been talking about. I've never seen her so merry.'

'It might be the whisky. Come on, let's join them.' Claudia touched Peter's hand with the back of hers. Peter turned towards her.

'I'm not much of dancer, I'm afraid,' he said.

Everybody seemed to be having a good time. 'Night

Fever' got most people on the makeshift dance floor. Even Barry was dancing. He held Nina's hand and whirled her around him like Princess Odette.

Claudia scanned the scene before her. Joanne was now dancing with Mikhail, he winked his left eye when he caught Claudia's gaze. She nodded and smiled. They had an agreement. Aunt Doreen had gone back to the kitchen. She guessed that Mikhail wouldn't stop until the entire CD was played and the bottle of whisky was finished – it was still half-full. She smiled at Peter, grabbed him by his lower arm and pulled him to the door. 'Let's go back to the barn,' she said. 'I need to show you something.'

38

'So much for buying Mikhail another drink; I think he's given us the slip again.'

'Excuse me, George?'

'Another pint, gentlemen?'

'That couple who came in, the Russian fellow and his mistress, did you see them come back?'

'They went for a pre-dinner drive,' Marjory said, overhearing their conversation.

'Thanks, Marge.'

'Come on,' Mike said. 'I've got a strong suspicion he's not all that far away. I bet you twenty bucks that he joined Miller and his eco-terrorist at that nearby farm.'

'I've got the same hunch, pal. I am not wasting my twenty bucks on such a lousy bet.'

Dave and Mike got into the Buick and drove slowly through the village towards the turn-off to the farm. Dave glanced at the mirror a few times.

'Anybody following us?'

'Not sure. Some guy's been behind us since we left the village.'

'Do you recognise the car?'

'Nope, it's one of those small European hatchbacks. They all look the same.'

'Let him overtake us. I want to see his face.'

Mike lowered his window and lodged his rifle between the mirror and window frame.

'It's freaking cold, close that window!'

'Is he overtaking us?'

'Looks like it.'

'Watch out, there's another car heading towards us. They drive like lunatics around here.'

'No wonder. I haven't seen a police patrol for days.'

'There he comes.'

The car behind them veered to the right and accelerated ferociously. The small engine revved like a shrieking fox.

'It's more noise than speed.'

'Typical immature teenager driving; uncontrolled hormones, trying to impress his girlfriend with a heavy foot.'

Mike leaned forward to peer through the visor.

'Don't!'

'It'll teach him a lesson.'

'Let him go. He's just a loser.'

'He's giving us the finger, the jerk!'

'Forget about it. We've got bigger fish to fry, and close that fucking window. I'll have a stiff neck tomorrow.'

'Sharp turn to the left coming up,' Mike said.

Dave slowed down and stopped the car a hundred meters after entering the gravel road leading to the farm.

'We can walk the rest.'

'Let's touch base with Terrence first. He may have an update on the situation.'

Dave opened the door. Taking a deep breath he said, 'I love this crisp air. There's a hint of spring.'

'Cows roaming in the distance, us lounging under this ancient oak tree, a rifle in my hand ... This is as good as it gets,' Mike chimed in.

'Be quiet. Listen, I hear music... "Saturday Night Fever"?'

'Is that some kind of joke? Is this how New Age eco-terrorists operate?'

'It's a disguise, no doubt.'

'Let's move closer and get a visual.'

39

Claudia closed the front door, but Peter could still hear the disco beat through the window. 'Who could have imagined Mikhail getting Aunt Doreen onto the dance floor?' he said.

'We forget sometimes that old people used to be young once and the right music can transport them back to their youth. Music is the best time machine.'

'Time travel's all in the mind!'

'Come on, philosopher, come up into the spacecraft. There's something I want to show you.'

The door to the barn was still open. Claudia took Peter by the hand and dragged him towards the sliding door. Peter felt fuzzy – the whisky had gone straight to his head and he found it hard to think clearly. He hesitated for a minute. He knew the spacecraft inside out. He'd spent the entire day crawling underneath it and discussing with Barry how to improve it. What could he have overlooked which Claudia needed to show him?

'What's taking you so long, space cadet?' Claudia was already in the capsule and looked down at Peter through the window in the open awning. She seemed exuberant.

Peter finished his drink and put the empty glass on the workbench. He walked over to the capsule and climbed on board. It was quiet. He could see a lit candle in the corner. A pair of jeans lay next to the entrance and a bra not far from there. What was she playing at?

'Shhh.' Claudia held her finger to her lips. She took his hand and pulled him towards the centre of the capsule. Two first class chairs were assembled together and put in a reclining position – it looked like a giant bed. She closed the sliding door and started to pull Peter's sweatshirt and T-shirt over his head. 'Quick,' she said in a sultry voice, 'we've only got a few minutes before your wife or one of your kids comes looking for you.'

'What are you trying to do?'

'What does it look like? You better give me a hand.'

'I'm married. My wife is less than fifty metres away from here. My kids are right there. They may be playing hide-and-seek in this very barn. If they find us, all hell will break loose.'

'Don't worry, it's all part of a plan. Mikhail's dancing with your wife and your kids are being entertained by your aunt, relax!'

'What do you mean? I don't get it.'

'I just want to make sure that whenever you go on your space mission, you have more than one reason to take me with you.'

'I don't get you at all,' Peter protested.

'I'm on the run and I want to get the hell out of this place, as far away as possible and if Mikhail is serious about having me on your team, then that's the only chance I've got, you get it?'

'The guy is as drunk as a skunk. I never met him before, you never met him before, so what is this all about?'

'You have to understand my situation. If those American guys can find me in London, it'll only be a matter of time before they find me here.'

'Can't you get plastic surgery and live somewhere else with a new identity?'

'I quite like my appearance and I have no intention of changing it. Too many lunatics in Brazil already do that.'

Peter was finding it hard to think logically with Claudia lying right beside him stark naked. She was stunning. She caressed his chest and moved her hand towards his groin and began stroking his pubic hair. Peter was getting aroused.

'I didn't pack any condoms.'

'You don't need one.'

'I see,' Peter said sheepishly, like an inexperienced teenager on a first date. At the same time, he was disappointed in himself for failing to resist Claudia's advances.

'Admit it, you wanted to have sex with me the minute you saw me handing out those newspapers.'

Peter didn't say anything. He was silent for a minute, closing his eyes.

'Judging by your reaction, I take that as a yes.' She moved closer and started kissing him. Peter felt a throbbing sensation in his groin. He had passed the point of no return. He wouldn't let his conscience spoil a moment of bliss, a moment he would remember fondly in his twilight years. When was the last time anyone but his wife had shown any sexual interest in him? Having sex with a gorgeous young woman in a spaceship he had designed himself – how much better could life get in middle age? This was his masterpiece, and an intimate moment with Claudia would be the jewel in the crown. Only a fool would walk away now.

His mind was racing. He had a vision of flying through space towards Mars, half a year of endless sex with Claudia in their love-cocoon. He was floating. This was his spaceship and this was his escape from his boring life as an accountant for an insurance company in London. He had transformed his life, followed his passion, and was lying next to Claudia, smiling. The faint candlelight had an orange glow. Claudia's body was warm, her head rested on his chest. Peter put his arm around her, his initial surprise and trepidation had transcended into lust and passion. He parted Claudia's legs and moved on top of her. She kissed him and held him even tighter. She closed her eyes. This would be her best chance of escape. This would be her ticket to Mars. She tried to synchronise her hip movements with Peter's. For a moment she imagined being with Mario, she felt a warm glow in her groin. Then she felt Peter entering her. Claudia's mind was brought back from a sweltering cocktail bar to a cold and damp camper in a barn. She opened her eyes. It was Peter, definitely. In the dim light of the candle he looked like an English poet, a wayward gentleman. She gyrated her pelvis a couple of times, gently, and then he came, silently.

Peter closed his eyes trying to make his moment of bliss linger a little longer. In a galaxy far away, he could hear music, very faint music. He couldn't make out the words. It didn't matter. This was his defining moment. A new Peter had been born.

Claudia held him close whilst he was lying on top of her. 'I just want to lie down a little longer,' she said.

Not long afterwards Peter felt guilty. He was no longer able to supress this feeling, it became more overwhelming with every passing minute. He was no longer able to enjoy the closeness of Claudia's body. He had to leave now before he got caught out. He moved away from Claudia and scrambled across the capsule collecting his clothes.

'Why don't you go ahead, it will make it less obvious,' Claudia said.

Peter leaned forward and kissed her. 'It's a strange situation, I usually don't let myself go just like that.'

'Shhh. Just go ahead, there is no need to explain yourself, space cowboy. It just happened. Forget about it.'

Claudia felt relieved that Peter had left so quickly. She smiled. It was a gamble she'd taken. The chance of success was perhaps less than one in twenty but it was the only chance she had. This could be the trump card she needed to persuade Mikhail to let her take part in his space programme, if he'd still remember it when sober. Being pregnant during the journey and delivering the first baby on Mars would certainly add to her bargaining power. She had to admit, it sounded ridiculously surreal. Over the next few months newspapers, TV stations and Internet sites would be tracking her journey through space, and with each passing month, her belly would be getting bigger and bigger. Only then would Peter start to realise that his offspring was part of the next generation in space. She couldn't help laughing. Life was looking up.

Peter opened the heavy barn door. He ruffled his hair a bit before flattening it with both hands. Before closing the door he sniffed his sweatshirt. It smelled of Claudia's sweet perfume, a smell that could linger for days. He flapped his arms several times in the hope that the fresh evening air would disperse the scent. He could hear music coming through one of the windows; it sounded like 'If I Can't Have You'. Looking through the window he saw Doreen putting a bottle of Famous Grouse next to the CD player. He saw Mikhail dancing with his wife and Barry dancing with Sylvia. They all seemed merry. For sure nobody was missing him. He looked over his shoulder hoping to see Claudia emerging from the barn. She wasn't. He slowed down. He could go back to Claudia. He turned around and headed towards the barn. After ten steps he stopped in his tracks. Did he hear something? He saw a bat flying low, and a tree was rustling in the wind, the breeze had picked up. He listened a bit longer. The music was overpowering. He wasn't sure. Did he see a shadow move along the path, along the shrubs leading to the main road? Peter waited a little longer but didn't see any movement. Perhaps he wasn't thinking clearly. It was a sign to get back to his family.

Just as he was about to open the door to the farmhouse he looked over his shoulder once more, he saw Claudia walking towards him. She didn't rush, she didn't linger, she walked in a casual manner as if nothing had happened. Perhaps it had meant less for her than for him. How could he ever forget? Should he tell Joanne and elope with Claudia, starting a new life? He had less than ten seconds to make up his mind. He looked at the house. He saw Nina sitting on the windowsill, apparently texting someone. It was the only place in the house with mobile phone reception. Had she witnessed them going into the barn together, Claudia taking him by the hand? Could she read Claudia's body language, like only a woman could? How would Claudia behave for the rest of the evening, in front of his family? Perhaps he'd better get back in the barn and work on the final touches. She was now less than twenty metres away from him. Should he open the door of the farmhouse and join his family or run towards Claudia, embrace her and declare his eternal love? Risk it all? He hesitated, he dithered, he pondered over possible fall-out, the irreparable damage he would cause to his family. Peter stepped forward and reached for the door handle, it was the only sensible option. He was sure. Then he heard a shot. It seemed only a few metres away. It was deafening. He heard a scream. He turned around and saw Claudia falling to the ground, then curling up and gripping her leg. Peter froze. He couldn't comprehend what had happened.

Nina saw it too. 'Claudia's been shot, we have to help her!' Nina yelled at Mikhail. The music stopped after a short delay. She took a few pictures with her phone before jumping into action. Peter saw shadows moving past the barn. Would they shoot again? He had to help Claudia, he had to be with her, even if his own life was at risk. He rushed towards her, though it seemed an eternity before he reached her and kneeled next to her in the dirt. In the distance he heard a ping, a mobile phone, receiving a message. He glanced at the spot where he'd seen shadows. A light was hovering near the fence. Was it a phone display?

Mikhail arrived on the scene at the same moment.

'Quick,' Peter hollered, 'bring Claudia inside, she's bleeding.'

'What about you, Peter? Come back inside. You don't stand a chance against those bastards.'

Peter lifted Claudia by her feet whilst Mikhail carried her by the shoulders.

Sylvia bolted the door. 'What the hell is going on?'

'I'm going to phone the police,' Doreen said.

'Is there a back entrance?' Mikhail asked.

'Through the kitchen, next to the larder.'

'Wait!' Mikhail exclaimed. 'I need to organise our escape, those guys will strike again.' He got onto his knees and crawled towards the window in the reception room. He needed to send an urgent message to his pilot. Whilst lying on the floor he lifted his arm a few centimetres above the windowsill clenching his mobile in his fist. He waited. Nobody was shooting at him. He looked at his phone. The display read 3G. He typed quickly and sent the message: 'Prepare for take-off.' It remained silent for another three minutes. Mikhail didn't trust this. It could mean anything. For all he knew another attack was being prepared. It was not safe in the house. They had to get out. His head felt heavy, too much whisky. He rolled onto his front and crawled back to the join the others.

'I think they're gone,' Peter said, trying to reassure the others.

'Let's give it another five minutes, then we'll take Claudia to the nearest hospital,' Joanna suggested.

'That's a long journey. I better call our local doctor. He lives in the village,' Aunt Doreen said.

Claudia looked pale; she had lost a lot of blood. Peter leaned forward and kissed her forehead.

'I'm sorry.'

'It's not your fault, I shouldn't have involved you and your family in all this.'

'Move away, Peter,' Doreen said briskly. 'Let me apply a bandage to Claudia's leg. It'll need some pressure; otherwise you'll bleed to death, my dear. Trust me, I'm an old hand at this. Did I ever mention to you that I was a nurse during the war?'

'You weren't even born then, Auntie!'

'Shut up and show some gratitude, I meant the Falklands War. Be a gentleman and help carry this young lady to the back of the house. I've got my car parked near the kitchen door.'

40

'You missed, you idiot.'

'It was my damn phone,' Dave said. 'It vibrated just as I was pulling the trigger. I must have moved a millimetre.'

'A millimetre makes all the difference. You should have switched off your phone. Who was sending you that bloody message?'

'Terrence. He's sending one message after the other, it's driving me crazy!'

'Well, he better have a good reason for contacting us.'

Dave looked at his phone.

'Fuck, six more messages. What the hell! Is he a control freak or what?'

'Let me read them. "Abort mission. Do NOT kill the woman. Do NOT kill the woman!".'

'Why did he change his mind?'

'Not sure... Wait, there's a link to a blog.'

'When did we start listening to bloggers?'

'Hang on, let me check it out... There's a blog by a journalist named Nina. It reads: "Brazilian link to US state senator exposed". It's breaking news on all the main networks.'

'Since when does Terrence start taking advice from bloggers instead of us? It's an insult. We're his eyes on the ground.'

'Reading her blog, she appears to be right here, right here in the heat of the action. She claims to have interviewed Claudia.'

'You know what? We came this far, I'm going to ignore that message.'

'I'm totally with you. If this is the future of intelligence and fighting organized crime, then there really is no hope.'

'So plan A has failed. We're going over to plan B.'

'It was a moonless night and the final act is about to begin.'

'Shut up with your amateur drama talk.'

'Put your phone on silent. No more distractions. We've got less than two hours to get to the airport. A lot needs to get cleaned up before we can say our mission is complete.'

'Man, I'm so looking forward to that bourbon on ice the minute our jet is airborne.'

'Follow me. They'll expect us to come through the front door. Let's go through the meadow and circle around towards the barn. There's enough shrubbery to provide cover. Stay near the edge and close to the ground.'

They moved towards the barn and paused for a few seconds.

'I don't see anyone.'

'They must have moved away from the windows.'

'Stay here. I'll deflate their tyres so they can't escape.'

'I'll cover you.'

Mike could hear hissing. It took Dave less than a minute to immobilise all the cars. Nobody reacted. He was sure that Peter and his gang of eco-terrorists were unarmed; they were trapped. There was only one way to get them out of the farmhouse.

'Let's destroy that spaceship or missile, whatever it is, before it's too late. At least we can avert nuclear fallout. The UK'll be grateful to us for years to come,' Mike whispered.

'I'm sure Terrence'll remind the US government that the British owe us big time,' Dave said.

'That's always a good bargaining chip.'

'We've got bags full of bargaining chips.'

'Time to raise hell. Let's stay with the same theme, "Disco Inferno".'

'I'll come back. You stay here.'

Mike walked over to their car, opened the boot and returned with two medium-size jerry cans filled with petrol.

'I'll torch the barn and their missile; you make your way over to the farmhouse. It's mostly made of wood; it'll go up in flames in no time. We'll move to the rear entrance and wait till Claudia comes out, coughing like a miner, walking straight into our arms. We'll bundle her up and drive her to the airbase. They can sort out the details later.'

Dave opened the barn door wide open. He stopped in his tracks, scanned the barn and moved inside.

'What the fuck is that?' he said to Mike who was right behind him. 'Some kind of joke?'

'It looks like an art installation for the Burning Man festival back home.'

'This is just too bizarre, a camper painted in psychedelic

hippy colours with some jet engines attached to it. I can't see any fuel tanks though, how will it ever take off? We can't show this to anyone. Nobody'll take us seriously any more.'

'Let's destroy the evidence and get the hell out of here. I'm so ready to go home. What a joke this mission is.'

'We better make sure no one witnesses this incompetence.'

'We'll be the laughing stock back home.'

'Torch this place and make sure that Claudia Valenti can't testify.'

'Roger that. I'll take her out the next chance I get.'

Mike acted swiftly. He splashed petrol all around the barn. With all the hay left over from last autumn, the barn would light up at the drop of a burning cigarette. 'This place is a fire hazard; I am sure the insurance company will agree. They won't waste any time on an in-depth investigation,' Mike gloated when he heard the fire crackling. The barn was soon ablaze. He could see his shadow cast across the farmyard. In twenty minutes, there would be nothing left but a few smouldering embers and a molten metal frame.

'Follow me, the farmhouse next. Let's keep the momentum up.'

Mike poured petrol in front of the door. It seeped underneath into the hallway. He kept pouring, and the faster he poured, the faster the petrol flowed beneath the wooden door. Soon the stream of petrol would rush through the main building.

Dave threw his lighter down upon the threshold. He turned around to shield his eyes. Then there was a big whoosh. The doormat was alight within a split second.

The word 'Welcome' was instantly consumed by flames. Windows cracked. He heard screams.

Dave sniggered. 'By the time the fire brigade gets here, there'll be nothing left but a glowing heap of ash.'

The two walked around the house towards the back entrance.

'Let's wait over there,' Mike said, 'behind the large tree. Once they're all out, we'll grab Claudia and take her away, then make her confess.'

'Let me go and get the car,' Dave said. 'It's too far to carry her all that way.'

'Be quick. They won't last long inside that oven.'

Mike felt good. He was glad that the mission was almost over. He missed his kids. That was the major downside of his job. It was a young man's game, a game for the unattached.

41

Peter felt tears welling up in his eyes as the flames destroyed Aunt Doreen's beautiful farmhouse. Joanne put her arm around him trying to console him. He felt guilty. His dalliance with Claudia had cost him dearly. He had been a fool to take her to Suffolk and put his family in danger, too naïve to assume they were safe on the farm in the middle of nowhere. It was so isolated; nobody would find their bodies for days. And now Joanne was holding him in her arms, and his kids were hugging him. It was too much. Peter's tears started flowing. He cried out, 'It's all my bloody fault! It's all my bloody fault!'

'It's not, Daddy, it's not,' Tom said. 'It's those Americans.'

'Peter, come on. Let's get the hell out of here before those gunmen come after us. There's no time left,' Joanne shouted.

'Lilly, follow me. I know where to go,' Tom said as he broke loose from his parents. He took his sister's hand and raced to the kitchen door.

The smoke was obscuring Peter's vision. He started to cough. 'Everybody on all-fours and stay close to the floor.

Don't inhale the smoke. Let's move.'

Claudia was trembling with fear and pain. She was losing a lot of blood. Barry and Mikhail carried her away from the farmhouse.

'Everybody to the other barn. It's the only shelter left,' Peter shouted at the top of his voice.

'We have to get out of here. We must get back to the village,' Joanne screamed.

'I can run and get help,' Sylvia said.

'That'll take too long.'

'I've just added some video footage to my blog,' Nina said. 'Hopefully someone will respond.'

'You're wasting your time, love,' Barry grumbled. 'It's too fucking late.'

'It's the best hope we've got, at least they can use the video footage in court.'

'That's no bloody use for us then,' Barry said.

Peter began to panic. 'Where are the kids? Oh my God, where are they?'

'I saw them leaving through the back door. They were the first ones out. They just shot off.'

'They've been exploring the farm for years. Let's hope they've found a safe place,' Joanna said, her voice almost breaking.

'And Aunt Doreen?' Peter shouted. 'Where is she? We need to get her out.'

Nina looked pale. 'She said she was going upstairs to fetch a picture of her husband.'

'Have you seen her since?'

'No, she just said not to worry about her. "As long as I'm

with my husband" she said, "I'll be alright".'

'Those bastards!' Peter cursed.

He looked at the staircase, which was engulfed in flames. Going up to get Aunt Doreen would be a suicide mission. Peter hesitated.

'Don't,' Joanne said.

'Is there any other way to get her out?' Nina asked.

'It's too late, Nina; it's too late,' Peter wailed. 'What a waste of a life. What a fucking nightmare. She was a good woman. She was like a mother to me, a grandmother to Tom and Lilly.'

Joanne put her arm around Peter. 'Let's all stay together, I don't want to lose you too.'

Peter shook his head in despair. He looked at the staircase once again. The middle part had collapsed and a thick carpet of smoke obscured the top end. He knew that his aunt had stood no chance. Then he got up and held Joanne by her hand. 'Run, we need to find Tom and Lilly, we can't lose them.'

The kitchen door was wide open and Peter saw Nina running towards the second barn. The air was thick with smoke and ash, stirred up by a strong breeze. He could barely make out the contour of the large structure. They joined the others. Mikhail and Barry had carried Claudia and placed her on a couple of bales of straw near the door.

Claudia was drifting in and out of consciousness.

'They stop at nothing,' she said in a daze. 'They're ruthless killers, I told you.'

Nina managed to put another bale of straw underneath a small window. She stood on top of it and scanned the surroundings with her binoculars. The fires had turned night into day.

'Wait, do I hear a siren in the distance?'

'Noise travels far at night. That can be a good sign or a bad sign.'

'Rescue is on its way,' Joanne said to soothe Claudia.

'No, it's not,' Peter said. 'It's just speeding things up. It's a catalyst. Those thugs will hear the sirens too and realise their time is up. They'll have nothing to lose, so they won't think twice about eliminating witnesses.'

'We're so fucked,' Barry said.

Suddenly there was a loud thundering noise behind them. The barn filled with smoke and diesel fumes. Peter started to cough. He looked up expecting the roof to collapse.

'I told you, they're on to us. We're trapped.'

They heard tyres screeching on the concrete floor. Nina looked around and saw a giant combine harvester moving towards her. She jumped from the bale of straw and took a picture with her phone. Its giant silhouette was impressive, like a dragon trailing a raging fire in the background.

'Quick, open the barn door!' Lilly shouted.

Peter looked up with a smile of relief. He saw his Tom behind the controls like a proud prince on a throne too big for him.

'Climb on board through the opening at the back, quick!' Lilly yelled.

'I'll tell you what,' Peter shouted over the engine noise, 'this thing may be slow, but its grain tank is bullet proof!'

'Not only that,' Tom said, beaming, 'it's the perfect off-roader.'

'So true,' Barry chuckled. 'That big American car of theirs

will get stuck mid-field in minutes, I bet you!'

'I also bet they're coming after us.'

Tom moved the harvester towards the burning farm. He could see the surprise on the Americans' faces. They loaded their rifles and fired several shots at it. All they could hear was clanging as the bullets bounced off the metal rear.

'This makes top-reading!' Nina screamed. 'This'll make you instant celebrities! Your friends at school will be so jealous.'

'I can't wait to tell them all about it,' Lilly said.

'Watch out, Tom, there's a ditch right in front of you! Where do we go now? There are just acres and acres of fields ahead of us.'

'Peter,' Barry asked, 'what was always the quickest way from your aunt's house to my scrapyard?'

'Right through the field.'

'Exactly, and that's where we're heading.'

At fifteen miles an hour, they moved towards the scrapyard, leaving a burning farm in the distance.

'They're not even trying to come after us. They're reversing their car and heading towards the main road,' Mikhail said.

'If those thugs can read our minds and take the long way, they'll catch up with us in ten minutes.'

'Ten minutes is a long time.'

'I've got a plan,' Mikhail said. 'I worked it all out while you and Claudia were in the barn.'

Peter flinched.

Mikhail put his hand on Peter's knee. Joanne was sitting in the front cabin next to Tom and Lilly. The noise of the engine was deafening. 'Thanks, Peter, you've served mankind well.

I'm sure it wasn't too much of a sacrifice?' Then Mikhail roared with laughter.

'What do you mean, was it all a set up?' Peter looked frightened.

'No, not really. I just know when to make the best out of a bad situation. That's what brings success!'

Claudia winced, a sharp pain shot up from her wound when she tried to get more comfortable. Mikhail leaned forward and stroked her head. 'We're nearly there,' he said. 'From now on, you'll get the royal treatment. You'll be regarded as the saviour of our species.'

'Whatever that means,' Claudia said, closing her eyes and drifting back into unconsciousness.

'Keep on going, Tom. You're doing great.'

Nina was recording Tom driving and Lilly leaning out of the cabin giving directions.

'More to the left!'

Tom jerked the combine harvester back into the middle of the field, avoiding the softer parts of the meadow. Getting stuck now would be a disaster.

Nina uploaded the short clip to her blog. There were hundreds of messages. Some people said they were coming to help the fight. Nina smiled. She was back on track! She was in her element.

The last message she received was from Alistair.

'Congratulations! You've received cult status! Advertising revenue is going through the roof!'

But this wasn't the message she was hoping for. Nina stared at the screen. Her battery was low, fifteen per cent remaining. For a roving journalist in the field, this was bad news.

42

Terrence was tapping his fingertips on his wooden desk. He was waiting for a call from his team. He felt uneasy. Dave and Mike were supposed to be his eyes in the field. Instead he was reading a blog by a journalist called Nina Simmons. He had crosschecked her credentials. She was the real thing. She was reporting live from the scene. She had recorded a shooting and she had unravelled the truth, all in the space of half an hour. It was unbelievable. If only he could get hold of his team in England, this whole saga, this complete misunderstanding, could be resolved swiftly before it all descended into a big farce with him as the laughing stock of the organisation. How could they've been so wrong? 'Come on,' he shouted at nobody in particular. His secretary had left the office hours ago and the clock didn't show any sympathy either. Its arms were moving at a snail's pace. He was counting the seconds. He'd give Dave another ten seconds before he'd phone John McClark, US Secretary of State.

John had the habit of talking on the phone whilst looking at a row of computer screens, which would not be out of place at a stockbroker's desk. He'd absorb information like a sponge but he also left you with the feeling that he hadn't listened to a word you'd said. Sometimes the answers he provided bore little relevance to the question he had been asked. But as he had the final word, Terrence had no other choice but to obey his orders. Only John had the power to release jets and drones from their hangars on foreign soil. Terrence had to make a strong case and make sure that John McClark trusted him in his judgement, even when the evidence was gossamer-thin and the most reliable information came from a twenty-odd-year-old blogger specialising in wine tasting, jam making and spaceships.

Terrence took a deep breath and dialled McClark.

'What took you so long, buddy? I've got a few bad case scenarios on the go, one in Yemen, a couple in Syria and an even worse one in the South China Sea. Tell me you've got some good news from your men in England. I want your guys out of there by midnight. You understand?'

Terrence tried to interject his flow. 'There have been some new developments.'

'Excellent work, Terrence, but make sure that whatever that damn missile hidden in that barn is, it gets destroyed. We Western powers have to pick our battles. The main source of future conflicts will come from rising sea levels, changing weather patterns and the resulting chaos. Hurricane Katrina and the subsequent flood in New Orleans were grim reminders from the recent past. Hurricane Sandy in New York was another example demonstrating how ill prepared we were. This is the new reality. We are under attack by nature. No army in the world will be able to offer protection.

Countries building dykes and extensive canal systems will be better equipped to combat climate change than countries like us investing in more and more sophisticated arms, nuclear missiles and aircraft carriers. Unfortunately, Terrence, we are not only fighting the wrong battle, we are fuelling it. We are only moments away from an uprising. A revolution is long overdue. Mind my words. Our future is hanging on a thin line. Get your men to complete their job and get their asses on a jet, we've got more pressing cases to work on,' John McClark said.

'They are completing their mission as we speak,' Terrence said trying to put McClark's mind at rest.

'Call me when it's all over, I've got to go.'

'Wait, John. The situation is more delicate than we ever imagined.'

'I know, I know. It's frightening. It will be a stampede soon. We're running out of time, Terrence, and you won't be able to stop it. The true progressives are already lining up to a buy one-way ticket to Mars or beyond. Over the next decade, more and more wealthy billionaires will pack up and leave.'

'And we can't let this happen.'

'Exactly.'

'John, now listen carefully. This is not about escaping to Mars or anywhere. This is about our own US congressmen bribing Brazilian government officials to grant them logging and mining rights. The Amazon is being destroyed, a fragile eco-system gets unbalanced and we get more hurricanes as a result. That's how simple it is. Our own congressmen are instigating this all and for what? Personal gain, more power in the short-term? It's self-destruction in the extreme. Yes it is true that Claudia Valenti blew up an office building in Sao Paulo but she didn't intend to kill anyone, that's why she chose to blow that building to smithereens on a Saturday morning. The building was supposed to be empty.'

'This seems small-fry to me, pal.'

'Exactly. Claudia is not the one we have to go after, we have to expose those congressmen who are behind the wholesale destruction of our planet.'

'Hang on, Terrence. I need some time to concentrate on this. Let me walk over to a quiet place.'

'The problem is I can't get hold of my team. This journalist called Nina seems to have the right access to the right people at this moment in time.'

'I am with you. We will defend our democracy, that's our duty. Corrupt politicians hell-bent on destroying our planet for the sole purpose of lining their own pockets, can't drag this nation down. We have to draw a line. It's a matter of principles and values.' McClark didn't mince his words. 'I'll have a quiet word with the president but you've got my support to abort this mission with immediate effect. I'll go after those damned congressmen myself, they are a flea in the pelt of our nation, the cancer of our democracy. This needs radical surgery. Leave it to me, pal. Well done for getting your facts straight.'

'Who would have guessed that the intelligence service right now is dependent on a young blogger with a purple streak in her hair?'

'I'd say the future is in save hands. We need free spirits like her.'

'Thanks, John. I'll get my men home.'

'Let's do lunch on Friday, I'll be in your neck of the woods anyway.'

Terrence felt relieved after his conversation with McClark. The long arm of the clock had suddenly skipped a quarter of an hour illustrating the fluidity of the concept of time. What would he do if he couldn't get hold of Dave? What if they ran their own operation without consulting him? It was nearly ten p.m. in the UK. He'd been home only once in the last four days, and that was only to take a shower and change his clothes. As soon as Dave and Mike were safely aboard their plane, he'd take his wife out for dinner and have a well-deserved rest.

He shook his head. He was frustrated at the lack of communication with his two agents in the field. If they'd only answer their phones, total disaster might still be avoided. All he could do right now was to pour himself another coffee and hope for the best. Perhaps he should contact Nina directly. It was a risk but she was the best-informed person on the ground. He was impressed with the way Nina had singlehandedly managed to expose the complexity of the situation in Brazil and England that he was dealing with. Claudia was no longer his priority; there were bigger fish to catch. He was glad to have McClark on his side. Claudia would be extradited to the Brazilian authorities and they could continue their own investigation; as a murderer she'd spend the rest of her life in jail. Terrence had set his eyes on exposing these corrupt congressmen now the truth was out. Nina's blog had gone viral and the cat was out of the bag. He rested his head in his hands for a while and sighed. If only he could get through to his team on the ground and tell them to call off the mission and come back, he could return home and debrief the Chief of Staff early in the morning.

Terrence checked Nina's latest blog again. He was shocked to see video footage of the carnage caused by his agents. The bloody fools. How could he get them to listen to him? Terrence scratched the back of his head. Contacting bloggers was seen as a last resort. He heard kids screaming in the video. It had to be stopped. Terrence typed a short message to Nina. 'This is Terrence Jackson, US New Dawn Counter Intelligence Organisation. Please make contact. It's urgent. You are our main source of information.'

Terrence leaned back in his chair. Those bloody idiots. Why were they ignoring his messages? What else could he do? Speak to the Air Force commander in England and get him to scramble a few jets and take them out? Activate the drone? He was weighing his options, thinking how he might convince John McClark that this was the only option left, that it was a painful but necessary decision. It was ten p.m. exactly and time was not on his side.

43

'Damn, they're getting away! We need to get Claudia.'

'I hear sirens. The police are on the way!'

'Let's get the hell out of here.'

'I've got an idea. Drive it back, halfway down the path. We'll park it behind some shrubs and wait till the cops drive past us, then we go back to the main road and catch up with that bloody harvester.'

'Any idea where they're heading?'

'Claudia's tracker is still active. She's kept the envelope with that picture in her jacket all this time.'

'Must have been love!'

'The girl played with fire. She was in way over her head. She shouldn't be surprised that the world's crushing down on her.'

'She'll spend the rest of her life wearing an orange coverall.'

'Not sure she'll last that long. It's safer to just make her disappear.'

'Step on it!'

The Buick's rear wheels were spinning. The tyres lost their grip on the gravel, and the car spun out of control. Dave quickly lifted his foot off the pedal and let the car correct itself. As soon as the car had some traction, he gunned it down the path.

'Stop!' Mike called. 'There it is! Sharp turn to the left, handbrake spin.'

Dave's pulse was racing. He loved these situations. Years ago, he had been in many high-speed chases tailing crack dealers in supercharged cars. This was once part of his daily routine, his bread and butter. Those amateur gangsters had had a habit of leading the police into deserted warehouses and dark alleyways where they waited in ambush with their friends.

As soon as he'd backed the car behind a tree, a small police car raced past them.

'Is that all they've got?'

'In this part of the world, I guess so.'

'One tiny car, two officers.'

'They couldn't have seen us. Wait another ten seconds and drive away slowly. Turn off your lights.'

'I've already done that, what do you take me for?'

The Buick glided down the path until they reached the main road. Dave switched on the headlights and turned right into the village. The car accelerated.

'Stay on the left side, buddy. This is England, they drive on the wrong side.'

'I prefer to stay in the middle of the road. Damn potholes everywhere. Just hold on.'

A second later, Dave jerked the car to the left and almost

scraped it against a brick wall beside the road.

'What did I tell you! Watch out. What was that?'

'It was big and red, and driving fast.'

'A fire engine?'

'Affirmative.'

'Where's your tracker now?'

'It's heading at six miles per hour towards a junkyard, which is next to an old airport.'

'A commercial airport?'

'Doesn't look like it. More like a sports club. There are loads of abandoned World War II airstrips in this part of England.'

'You got a satellite image on your iPad?'

'Follow the road through the village. Before the inn, turn right, past the school and head straight north. It's eight miles to the airport entrance and another mile along a dirt road towards that scrapyard. It's less than two miles from the farm.'

'They've got a head start.'

'But not for much longer.'

The Buick raced along the road. Mike was a perfect navigator.

'Prepare to slow down. There's a sharp turn on the right coming up in twenty seconds.'

Dave slammed on the brakes at the last minute and made an elegant turn to the right. The road got bumpy. They could either go very slowly or extremely fast. Dave chose the latter. Mike held on to the headrest with one arm and the dashboard with the other.

'There, I can see it – a big dark mass trundling towards

the scrapyard.'

'Once they're there, they can hide anywhere.'

'If scrapyards here are like the ones in the US, there must be a secret stash of weapons in a car trunk somewhere. We don't stand a chance with our rifles.'

'Damn, it looks like they're winning.'

'Park the car here; we'll do the rest on foot. We'll surprise them.'

'And if all else fails, shoot the girl. Aim for the chest this time!'

44

Tom struggled to keep the heavy combine harvester in the middle of the narrow path. His feet barely reached the pedals. The brakes were heavy and required all his strength. The harvester slowed down and Tom steered the machine into the scrapyard.

'The end of my dreams,' Barry said with a sense of understatement when they passed a clearing.

Sylvia gave him a quizzical look.

'My Spaceship Airbnb. Near this very entrance.'

'Seriously?' Sylvia laughed. 'Who in his right mind would choose a B & B next to a scrapyard?'

'There are some serious petrolheads out there, and they often bring along their girlfriends. In fact, some of my best clients are women. I'm sure they'd like to stay with me. I can cook a mean fry-up, none of that muesli and fruit nonsense.'

'I guess so,' Sylvia said, holding on to a strap in the back of the cabin.

'Mind my office, young lad,' Barry called to Tom, who had put the combine harvester on a collision course with the wooden structure.

Tom turned around and smiled. 'Don't worry Uncle Barry, I've had a lot of practice!'

'Nobody has ever called me Uncle Barry before,' he said, looking chuffed. 'It has a nice ring to it.' Then he leaped forward and jerked the large steering wheel. 'That was close,' Barry chuckled. 'I told you not to drive into my office.'

'I didn't know that was an office. It just looked like a pile of rubbish.'

'Now don't you get cheeky with me, young man!'

Nina opened the small hatch in the side of the grain tank, which usually connects to the unloader. She held on to her phone and stretched out her hand as far as she could. She felt her iPhone vibrating – more than a dozen emails and messages came through.

'Yes, yes, yes!' she shouted enthusiastically. 'I've got a connection!'

'Welcome to Barry's world! Of course I've got Wi-Fi. I couldn't survive without it!'

Nina didn't react. She sat in a corner of the grain tank skimming through her messages.

'What now?' Peter asked. 'I saw their car a couple of hundred yards from here. They made a U-turn and then parked it near the main road.'

'They're preparing for a quick getaway,' Barry suggested.

'One thing's for sure,' Mikhail said, 'they haven't given up. They're determined, and with the police busy at the farm, we can't rely on any backup. It's us against them!'

Peter cushioned Claudia's head in his lap. Her eyes were closed as he stroked her clammy forehead.

'She's lost a lot of blood.'

'We need to move fast,' Mikhail said. 'I've got a little surprise in store.' He leaned over to Barry and whispered something in his ear.

'Sure,' he replied. 'Tom, just follow me, but first I need to get something, go as slow as you can but keep moving.'

Barry climbed down the harvester's side-ladder, jumped from the third step and landed with a thud on the ground and then waddled over to his office. He switched on the lights. Joanne saw him rummaging through a drawer.

'How long will it take? What on earth is he doing?' Joanne asked.

After a mere five seconds the lights went off again and Barry emerged holding a gun in his hand. He waved at Tom in the harvester and started walking towards the middle of the scrapyard. Tom followed slowly. He didn't want to collide with a stack of rusty old cars.

'Peter, do something. I don't like the look of this gun at all. You're putting your family in danger.'

'It's the only chance we've got. I have no idea why those guys are so determined to get to us.'

'It's all my fault,' Claudia groaned. 'I..., I....' She didn't finish her sentence.

'Save your energy, we'll get the answers later,' Joanne soothed her.

Barry kept looking over his shoulder. He could make out two shadows in the distance. They weren't far behind. Two avenues lined with metallic carcasses made a perfect bullet-proof cover. As long as Tom kept the harvester on course they had a chance of reaching the fence and making their escape.

Peter leaned forward. He was sitting on the straw walker in the pitch-black grain tank and it was getting uncomfortable. His right hand, which he used to press on Claudia's wound, was sticky. The wound was still oozing. 'Nina, can you shine your phone onto Claudia's leg?' Nina directed the light on her phone towards Claudia and took several shots at the same time. She winced at the gruesome sight of the deep and seeping gash in her thigh. 'Hang in there, Claudia,' Nina said. 'I've put every word you said out on Twitter and on my blog. It's for the world to read.'

Claudia grimaced. 'Thank you!' And then she sank back into unconsciousness.

Mikhail turned around. 'Just a couple more minutes and you'll have the best medical care at your disposal.'

'Is that some kind of sick joke?' Peter said. 'Don't give her false hope.'

'I'm not joking.'

'Tom, can't we stop this bloody harvester? Forget about this mad escapade, and get Claudia to the nearest hospital. She'll die out here!' Joanne shouted.

'The nearest hospital is miles away.'

Tom yanked the wheel and made a sharp turn to the left.

Then they heard a high-pitched clang. A bullet had been fired at the harvester. The hollow grain tank amplified the sound like a steel band. A second clang followed within seconds.

'Duck, Tom, they're right behind us!' Lilly screamed. 'They are aiming at the cabin.'

'I know, that's why I'm following a zigzag course.'

'Hold on tight everyone, another sharp turn coming up,'

Lilly yelled.

Suddenly they heard several shots, followed by silence. Mikhail took his phone out of his pocket and sent another text message. 'Taxi to the runway.' He knocked on the partition window between the cab and the grain tank.

'Tom, how about reversing this beast?' Mikhail suggested.

Without looking in his wing mirror, Tom shifted gears in reverse and crashed into an eight-metre high pile of scrapped cars. Shortly afterwards he heard someone swearing.

'Damn it, Dave! Run! Run!'

'Shoot the bastards!'

'Run before it's too late!'

Then they heard a crashing noise. A stack of car wrecks tumbled down, dragging another pile of cars with them like dominos.

Then there was another roaring noise, even more deafening, more menacing than the harvester. Tom looked up. He could see a group of bright lights speeding towards them, three strobe lights and several beacons, green, red and white. They blinded him. 'It's a plane, it's heading towards us,' he shouted excitedly, holding his hands in front of his eyes. He had lost sight of where the harvester was going. Then there was another loud roar; it was coming from behind the harvester. When Tom opened his eyes again he could see Barry laughing. Lilly leaned out of the cabin. 'Tom, you idiot!' she shouted. 'You reversed into hundreds of cars. They've all fallen down!'

'Good lad, Tom,' Barry hollered. 'Now turn the wheel and head towards the fence as fast as you can!' Tom couldn't hear what Barry was trying to say.

Barry was now running in front of the harvester. He held his gun outstretched in front of him. He was scanning the row of cars to his right.

Then there was another clang. A side window broke.

'Watch out, Tom!' Lilly said. 'Hide underneath the dashboard!'

Tom ducked, barely holding on to the controls.

'Faster, Tom! Go faster!' his sister urged him.

'This machine will never get through the fence!'

'We don't have to go through it, just damage it!' Mikhail said.

Tom had difficulty focusing on the fence. The lights in the distance were still moving towards him and had become even brighter, blinding him. He had to cover his eyes and regained control over the combine harvester whilst peering through a narrow gap between his fingers.

When Mikhail realised this he fired off another text message. Three seconds later, all lights got switched off.

'Wicked!' Tom exclaimed. 'That's much better, how did you do that?'

Mikhail didn't reply.

Tom hit the fence with a thud. It gave way a little but wasn't ripped apart. He tried to pull some levers to make the cutter head grind up the bottom part of the fence, but it didn't work – the reel just mangled a narrow strip of metal fencing before grinding to a halt. 'That's too bad.'

'At least there's a narrow gap underneath the fence now, almost big enough to crawl through,' Barry said after inspecting the fence. 'But definitely not big enough for me!' he chuckled.

Peter held on to Claudia. It was an awkward situation. Claudia hadn't responded since he last checked her wound. Less than an hour ago she had seduced him, they'd made love, passionate love, and now she was hovering in the twilight zone between life and death, carrying his sperm, perhaps even his baby. Joanne looked at him. Peter couldn't tell if she knew or not. She stroked his hair. 'We've been through a lot in the last twenty-four hours.'

'We have indeed,' Peter said, placing his hand on Claudia's forehead.

'Friends, stay inside your harvester,' Barry shouted through the rear opening. His voice echoed through the entire body of the machine. 'I can keep those guys at a distance. When the coast is clear, slide underneath the fence and run away from here as fast as you can. I'll distract those bastards and keep them entertained.'

'Wait Barry, I'll come with you,' Nina said. 'So far I'm the only one reporting from the scene. I'm getting the exclusive on this one.' Nina got up and moved towards the rear of the harvester, climbing over Claudia and up the straw-walker. She hesitated when she placed herself in the chute. It was difficult to estimate the length and height; she prepared herself mentally for a significant drop at the end of it.

'I guess I won't be able to stop you,' Peter said.

'No you won't.' She looked over her shoulder. 'You better look after Claudia.'

'In that case, stay close to me,' Barry hollered. He used the harvester as a shield.

Nina rushed down the chute and rolled over to her side cushioning the impact of the hard landing.

'Run as fast as you can towards the enormous heap of car wrecks once the harvester moves back again. It will provide some cover but not for long.'

'Tom, try to make this hole in the fence a bit bigger. We all need to get to the other side, to the runway. You see that plane? It's waiting for us, but we have to move quickly. It's our escape plan!' Mikhail announced with pride.

'Just in time! Let's climb onto the roof of this thing and jump over the fence instead. It'll be a hard landing, but it's the only option we've got,' Peter said.

'What about Claudia?'

'I'll jump first and then you'll slide her under the fence. There's just enough space now. I'll pull her through from the other side.'

'That's madness. She'll die; she'll bloody die,' Joanne panicked.

'Your husband is right; there's no other choice,' Mikhail said before ducking to escape a bullet headed for him.

'Hurry up Tom, there's no time left!' Joanne said.

'I can't get any further,' he yelled.

'Just do it. Reverse and try again. Ram the fence, full speed.'

Mikhail was busy texting. In the distance, they could hear some shots; one of them ricocheted off the harvester's grain tank. Barry took aim and fired back.

'Where did you get that gun from?' Nina asked.

'Found it in the boot of an old Jaguar, underneath the spare tyre. I suppose the owner forgot about it.'

'He never came back for it?'

'The car and the owner were dragged up from a canal

years ago. I kept it just in case.'

Barry's dog came running and barking towards them.

'Where were you when I needed you?' Barry leaned forward to give the dog a good rub. His stubby tail wagged furiously. 'What's the matter, old boy?'

Nina was busy capturing more footage for her blog. She felt the adrenaline rushing through her veins, she felt alive, in the heat of the action. This, for her, was what being a journalist was all about. Her heart was beating fast. Her phone was vibrating in her hand; several messages were coming through in quick succession. She paused for a minute to scan through them. Then she received two more messages, one from her editor. He seemed impressed. Nina smiled, she had no time to read his lengthy analysis of her situation. Just as she was going to put her phone in her pocket and move in between two rows of cars, she got an email from someone called Terrence. It was an odd message: 'Dear Nina, you're the only one who can save Claudia. Tell those snipers to abort their mission. Terrence at New Dawn Counter Intelligence Operation.' This caught her attention. Her moves were being watched; she could use this to her advantage. She would be able to call on her witnesses if needed.

'Hurry up, Nina, you're the last one,' Mikhail shouted from a distance.

'Barry's still here and so is Sylvia.'

'Yep, I'm not going anywhere. This is my scrapyard, and if there's one place I know like the back of my hand, it's here,' Barry replied. He was annoyed with Mikhail. He wished he would keep quiet.

Nina took shelter in between two cars. She wasn't sure what to do. Was this message from the so-called 'Terrence' genuine? She had no time to verify it or to discuss her next steps with Alistair. It was a risk she had to take. Was it madness to just walk up to them, armed men, trained to kill? She wouldn't stand a chance. She guessed that from a distance she looked vaguely similar to Claudia – same build, same height, jeans and boots. Her hair colour was different, but in the dark no one would notice.

'Miss Valenti,' she heard one of the Americans shouting. Soon they would find Claudia and take another shot. Nina looked at Terrence's message once more. There was nothing for it – she would have to talk to the two men and try to convince them to leave Claudia alone. There was no alternative.

'Miss Valenti.' The voice was getting closer now and it sounded more threatening too. It was a gamble, a massive one. Would she get shot on the spot or would she be able to talk sense into the two men? Nina got out from between the cars, scanned her surrounding, took a deep breath and started walking towards the end of the row of cars. Barry nodded at her. He pointed his gun at the chest of the large American. The two men were on the other side of the row of cars. Barry had her covered. Nina held her arms above her head and made big gestures, using her mobile phone as a torch to guide her way, looking like a political prisoner about to be exchanged on the Glienicke bridge.

Two men were now standing in front of her, about thirty metres away. Nina moved forward slowly. She was filming the scene and streaming this to her blog as a live feed. Nina moved forward, step by step.

With each step, Nina moved closer to the two men. They held their rifles in front of them, peering at Nina through their sights, watching her steadily. Nina held her head high and started walking more briskly. Now she was standing in front of them, in full view, with nowhere to run to. This was no longer a gamble; it was an act of self-destruction. Nina realised that her number was up. Dying during the call of duty at her tender age was not what she had intended, no story was worth this much. She had grossly underestimated her vulnerable position and grossly overestimated her own fame as a blogger. She was out here on her own. She started trembling.

'Claudia Valenti?' Dave hollered.

'I'm aiming at her chest,' Mike said.

Nina shook her head.

'Miss Valenti, is that you?'

'No.'

The two men lowered their rifles and walked towards Nina.

'So who are you?' Dave shouted.

'My name is Nina, journalist for Yellow Sparkle News.'

'Damn it!' Mike said.

'Wait… I've got a message from Terrence.'

'Terrence? How the hell did you get his number? It's classified. Only we have direct access to him.'

'You're bluffing,' Dave said.

'That's no longer your exclusive right. The truth is, Claudia's not the one your organisation's interested in, at least not for now. Let her go!'

'I don't believe a word of what you're saying, show me some proof.'

Nina handed over her phone.

'Turn that damn camera off! I don't want to be all over the Internet. You're endangering our families. We're operating undercover.'

Nina showed the conversation she'd had with Terrence.

'Dave, can you check all the messages you've received?'

Dave spent the next minute reading through some of them. Mike kept his rifle aimed at Nina's chest. He held his finger on the trigger. 'And, is she bluffing?'

'Dave, I think she is telling the truth. I've got a dozen missed calls from Terrence and even more text messages. He advised us to abort our mission a while ago. I think we better head back to the military airport.'

'Copy that. Nina, you're one hell of a brave journalist. I almost killed you.'

'Let's go. Just under an hour left before our jet leaves.'

Nina snatched her phone from Dave's hand and sprinted away.

'What about her, this journalist? She got valuable footage and this can be used against us in court.' Mike whispered when they were out of earshot.

'We left no evidence behind on the farm. We can't just leave this scene like this, we've gotta clean it up. You know what I mean?'

'Yeah. It has to be done. You take the gruff guy out, I'll take the girl.'

'And there is a third one.' He pointed towards Sylvia who was standing next to the combine harvester.

'Three is a crowd.'

'Buddy, we've got two guns, a hundred bullets and there are enough car trunks in this place to make sure that their bodies won't get discovered for a very long time.'

Dave and Mike turned around to reload their gun. Nina was looking at her phone whilst making her way back to the others.

'Nina.' Barry shouted. 'Move behind me – I've got you covered.'

Barry stepped sideways shielding her behind his large frame whilst aiming his gun at the tall American.

'Drop your weapons.'

Dave looked at Mike. 'Game's over!'

Dave threw his rifle on the ground in front of him. Mike followed suit.

'Now turn around slowly and walk back to your car. I'll return those rifles to George. He won't be very pleased knowing that you violated his licence.'

'We gave him a handsome tip to cover it. He's got nothing to complain about.'

'So long, Nina,' Mike said.

'It wasn't personal,' Dave added. They walked over to their car.

Nina sprinted back to the fence. Only Peter was still waiting. He lifted it as high as possible to let everyone slip underneath. Claudia had been the first to go through. She was lying on the ground at a safe distance; Joanne was comforting her. Peter walked up to Nina.

'That was very brave of you. I have no idea what you said to those gangsters, but it seemed to do the trick,' Peter said.

'It turned out that Claudia was the least of their worries. Their target had moved. You managed to expose some prominent American politicians; it's all over the Internet. Heads will roll,' Nina replied.

'Well, who would have thought,' Peter said. 'But still, it's a shame about our spaceship.'

'That's peanuts, mate, we rekindled our friendship and that's worth a whole lot more,' Barry said. 'Besides, I've got some new ideas for an even bigger one. I've got ample space here. When the summer comes, I'll start building on-site.'

'Count us in, Barry,' Peter replied.

'As you can see, there's plenty of metal at your disposal. Shame about the fridge, though; that was vintage, you won't find one them again easily.'

'Nina, are you coming along?' Mikhail asked.

Nina could make out the contour of a private jet and smiled.

'We could use a good journalist…'

'Live podcast from Mars?'

'Something along those lines.'

Nina got down on the ground in front of the fence and rolled underneath. She took her phone out of her pocket. It was vibrating. She read the most recent message: '27.8233S, 153.4143 E. I miss you! Ravi xxx.' Nina's heart started racing; she sat up and looked around her. It was freezing, the jet-engine blew her hair into her face. She huddled to cover herself. The message brought back many happy memories of lying in a skip with Ravi in circumstances not very different from these. Perhaps it was destiny, perhaps she was meant to be with him after all. She looked sideways. Barry was still standing near the fence. He had his gun at eye-level and was scanning the yard like a fox just in case the Americans changed their minds.

'Hey Barry, have you got a phone charger?'

'There's one in my office. I can make you a nice cuppa while you wait.'

Nina gave the thumbs up. As the jet moved closer, the noise became overwhelming.

'Well done Nina, you must feel proud of yourself. How did you string all those pieces of information together? You're one hell of an investigative journalist,' Barry said as they were heading back towards his shed.

'Thanks to you, Barry. You were the one who pointed me in the right direction.'

'Don't mention it, I am just an old geezer trying to survive in a mad world.'

'Don't underestimate yourself; you were crucial to my story. I've quoted you several times.'

'Fame at last!' Barry laughed. 'What's next for you?' He asked when they arrived at the shed.

'For me?' Nina's eyes sparkled. 'Next stop will be Australia!'

'You'll have to go without me,' Barry chuckled. 'Way too hot for me!'

Nina smiled; underneath his rough appearance there was a real gem. In the distance she saw a large car disappearing at high speed, throwing up a cloud of dust. She looked relieved and closed the door behind her.

'Guys, let's all move towards the runway,' Mikhail said.

'Peter and I'll carry Claudia. Kids, you go first. How about a trip to Moscow? No school on Monday.'

'Wicked!' Tom replied and immediately started running. Mikhail sent another message; the doors of the jet opened and a small staircase came out.

'Are you coming or not?' Mikhail shouted at Sylvia, who was still hovering near the fence.

'No thanks. I've seen enough of your mad adventures. I'd rather go back to my own flat. Besides, I've got your company to run!'

Mikhail knew that Sylvia wouldn't change her mind. There was no point trying to convince her. Time was running out.

Tom and Lilly were the first to get into the jet. A steward carried Claudia to the back of the plane into a small private bedroom. Peter looked worried. He hoped Claudia would make it, but how on earth would he explain it all to Joanne?

By the time the plane was airborne, the steward had rigged up an intravenous drip to replace the fluid Claudia had lost and hooked her up to a blood pressure monitor. He'd keep her stable and pain-free until she could be transferred to an emergency department in Moscow.

'A penny for your thoughts, Peter,' Mikhail said as he put his arm around Peter's shoulder. 'Relax, this is all part of a plan, a big plan. You and Joanne will be staying in a nice river-view apartment in Moscow. Your kids will enrol in the international school and in the coming months you'll be helping out with Project Mars.'

'As the senior accountant, right? I don't fancy going to Mars myself.'

'Not quite, I've got a different role for you in mind. We

need someone with your naïve enthusiasm. Once in a while you can attend team meetings and motivate us.'

'You mean I'll be the court jester.' Peter feigned a slight disappointment.

Mikhail laughed. 'That's exactly what I mean. We could do with someone like you. All those aerospace engineers; they're so bloody serious the whole time. No imagination, no vision, it's all about efficiency and technical perfection. We need a dreamer like you.'

'In that case, I'll be on the first plane out of Moscow.' Peter sounded miffed.

'It was a joke, Peter, it's all a joke, life is a joke. You and your family can stay in Moscow. Yana, my girlfriend, will show your wife around and you'll do the accounts. And then when you've got enough of my generous hospitality, you can go back to London. Or you may decide that there are more opportunities in Russia after all. And I bet you that you'll stay.'

'Twenty pounds that I'll be gone within two months.'

'You'll lose that bet, Peter, guaranteed.'

'And what about Claudia?'

'Claudia... Claudia... She'll get the best treatment. Sasha, our steward, is an ex-ITU nurse. Of course I pay him double what he would get at his local hospital. We'll look after her. She's volunteered to lead the first trip to Mars, and if all goes well, she'll deliver Mars' first child. That would be truly legendary and a great legacy for you!'

Peter almost choked. 'What do you mean?'

Mikhail winked. 'Peter, what happens in space, stays in space!'